GW00726708

Little Devil

Little Devil

Charles West

Charles West

ROBERT HALE · LONDON

First published in Great Britain 2005

ISBN-10: 0-7090-8010-7
ISBN-13: 978-0-7090-8010-7

Robert Hale Limited
Clerkenwell House
Clerkenwell Green
London EC1R 0HT

2 4 6 8 10 9 7 5 3 1

Typeset in 10/11½pt Janson
Printed in Great Britain by St Edmundsbury Press
Bury St Edmunds, Suffolk.
Bound by Woolnough Bookbinding Ltd

I'm being evil
So very evil!
'Cause that's my only claim to fame

(*Pantomime song*)

'Make your children lerne
Good in their youth, or they
Falle to malice.'

Earl Rivers (1477)

CHAPTER 1

Kicking that door down changed things. It changed her life. It wasn't the only thing that changed her life that day, but it was the first.

It happened after the lunch break. She was in a bad mood anyway, because she'd had to sacrifice her one free period that morning to fill in for a colleague who was off sick, which meant she was behind with her paper work, which meant that she would have to take it home, which meant she would have even less leisure time than usual. Grr.

It didn't help that the afternoon classes were in the Annie – the school's name for the tatty old building officially known as the Annexe. Joanna loathed the place. It dated from the 1950s, and stood some distance away from the main school, a sad, squat, ugly shed, in stark contrast to the spanking new gymnasium that was being built next to it. No one knew why it was called the Annexe. It consisted merely of two scruffy classrooms separated by an inexplicably wide, dingy corridor. It had been under threat of demolition for at least seven years, but it still survived; and while it survived, the headmaster would find a use for it.

She guessed what the problem was as soon as she entered the place; but in case she was in any doubt, the cheerful louts of Form 10M were keen to enlighten her.

'The door's stuck, miss!' twenty-odd voices yelled. 'Again!'

'All right, all right!' Joanna shouted tetchily. 'Keep the noise down, will you? And get out of my way.' They quietened down a little as she pushed her way through, but there was no mistaking the carnival atmosphere. This was a hell of a lot better than lessons.

'It really is stuck this time, miss,' one of the boys assured her. 'I mean, you know – stuck solid.'

He wasn't joking. The door was open a couple of inches, but its bottom edge was wedged firmly against the floor. Joanna gave it a tentative shove, but it was big and heavy, and felt as unyielding as a brick wall. Further along the corridor the other classroom door opened and Dick Berry, one of the English teachers, poked his head round to see what the commotion was about. He saw immediately that Joanna was about to ask for help, and he disappeared like a lizard behind a rock.

'OK,' Joanna said wearily. She opened her briefcase and hunted for a scrap of writing paper. 'One of you take a note to the caretaker, and—'

There was a general whoop of triumph. 'Mr Vail isn't here today!' they chorused. 'He's got the flu!'

Joanna, her temper rising, glared at them tight-lipped. 'Then fetch his assistant. Fetch somebody. They can't all be off sick.'

'Yes they can, miss!' She had never seen them look so happy. 'There's nobody in the office. They've all got the flu!'

'Yeah, well,' one young cynic added, 'it *is* Friday, you know. I mean, they often skive off on Fridays, innit?'

The last time Mrs Howard had looked as mad as this, she had actually uttered the word 'fuck' under her breath, and the class waited eagerly for a repeat performance; but she controlled herself just in time and offloaded some of her frustration by aiming a feeble kick at the door.

'That's not the way to shift it, miss.' Joe Greenaway, the burliest and most amiable boy in the class was quick to offer advice. 'You'll break your toe that way. What you have to do is to lean back and kind of stamp at it with the flat of your foot.' He leaned back, and demonstrated the technique to general applause, by kicking at the air.

Joanna was impressed. 'How do you know that, Joe?'

Joe shrugged. 'I seen Bruce Willis do it in one of the Die Hards. Shall I have a go, miss?'

'Certainly not. If you injure yourself I'll get the sack.'

She looked down at her feet. If she had been wearing her weekend shoes, she would never have contemplated it. But these were the good, sturdy, wedge-heeled brogues she kept for school wear. Against her better judgement she leaned back and stamped at the door.

All she achieved was to jar her knee and evoke a moan of sympathy from the crowd. The door didn't budge. 'Pesky thing!' Joanna snarled.

Someone at the back said derisively: 'Well, that's it, then. Might as well go home, like the maintenance blokes.'

'Shut up, Daniel,' Joanna snapped. 'If you're going to be insolent, I'll put you in Mr Atherton's book.'

There was no such thing as Atherton's book, but the kids didn't know that, and the very vagueness of the threat, coupled with the mention of the headmaster's name was enough to make them uneasy. For a few moments there was comparative silence, the boys impressed at Joanna's unfailing ability to recognize a guy just by the sound of his voice, without even looking in his direction.

But Daniel's scorn had touched a nerve. Joanna was damned if she'd be thwarted by a rotten piece of wood that ought to have been on the scrap heap years ago. 'Frigging door!' she muttered under her breath.

'Have another go, miss,' Joe Greenaway urged. 'Give it all you've got.'

It was terrible advice, and she knew it, but her temper was up. She leaned back, her energy fuelled by anger and frustration, and gave it all she'd got.

The result was spectacular. The door ripped off its rotten hinges and crashed into the classroom, taking down a table and a pile of books with it; while Joanna shrieked something unrefined and fell flat on her back.

This time there was complete silence as Form 10M surveyed the wreckage. Then someone – even in her dazed state, Joanna recognized the voice as Wayne Otley's – said 'Wow!' in an awed whisper, and the whole class began to cheer.

To their credit the boys were genuinely worried that Joanna might have hurt herself. Joe Greenaway and another boy helped her to her feet, dusted her down and propped her against the ruined doorpost, and she found that she needed to reassure each child individually that she was all right, as they filed past. It was only when the last boy had wandered to his seat and she started to move to her own desk that the agony struck. The spasm was like a knife thrust in her back, and her right leg felt as if it was threaded with red-hot wire. She gasped and stood stock-still, afraid to move. The boys gaped at her, fascinated. No need to ask now if miss was all right: she looked, as one boy murmured throatily, 'right knackered.'

Cautiously, Joanna pulled herself upright. 'I seem,' she said, with a half-hearted attempt at nonchalance, 'to have winded myself. It'll pass in a minute.'

She realized, as she made her painful way to her desk, that there was no point in trying to combat their holiday mood, and she didn't attempt it. 'We'll scrub today's lesson,' she told them, and held up a warning hand to silence their reaction. 'I don't care what you do right now, as long as you're quiet. But the first guy that kicks up a racket gets a Wednesday-night detention, along with the three people sitting nearest to him. Risk it if you dare.'

It was a shrewd thrust. There was a local football match on TV next Wednesday night, and the kids would rather be flayed alive than miss a minute of it. So they obeyed her meekly enough, and kept the din down to a subdued babble. Some of them simply sat and stared, awe-struck at the splintered door, which Greenaway had thoughtfully propped by the blackboard.

There was some animated discussion about what exactly Mrs Howard had shouted when she fell over. The general consensus was that it was "Oh, shit!" which, they agreed, was fair enough in the circumstances.

'She didn't say "fuck" this time,' someone said, disappointed. 'But she did say "frigging".'

'It means the same thing,' his neighbour said.

'Nah. Frigging ent the same as fucking. They're quite different.'

Joanna, whose hearing was exceptionally acute, had followed the debate closely, and was disappointed when neither boy explained what he thought the difference was. She swallowed another codeine and got on with catching up on her paper work.

As the afternoon wore on she realized that the pain in her back was getting worse. Sitting still was not too bad; but the slightest movement was agony. The discomfort began to make her very depressed and, without wanting to, she found herself taking dismal stock of her life. Here she was, pushing thirty, with a failed marriage and two disastrous relationships behind her – the latest of which was still giving her grief – and stuck in a job she didn't enjoy. She had read somewhere that true happiness lay in finding what you wanted to do, and then doing it with all your heart. Whoever wrote that hadn't thought of the corollary: to find what you want to do, and then not be able to do it, would break your heart.

She was OK at her job – in fact, she was better than most – but she wasn't born to teach. She did it because she needed the money.

She eased herself out of the chair, and headed painfully towards the staff room. It was Friday afternoon, and the Wine Club would be in session. Joanna had paid her subscription, and she needed a drink. She expected a certain amount of raillery over the door incident, but she could cope with that. She had a reputation for style and panache; her colleagues would expect her to tough it out like a good little sport. She gritted her teeth, squared her shoulders, and did her best not to hobble.

On her way she met Cynthia Bell, scurrying as usual to get home before her beloved husband.

'You're limping!' Cynthia cried. 'What's happened?'

'Nothing. I fell over and ricked my back. Long story,' Joanna said. 'You'll hear all about it on Monday. Go home and pamper that lucky sod of a husband.' And of course, Cynthia went.

The staff room, always a relaxed and rowdy place after work on Fridays, erupted into noisy applause the moment she opened the door. The arts teacher, who was already half-drunk, cheered and stamped his feet, while Marian Flint screamed and pretended to hide behind a cupboard. There was a lot of laughter, not all of it sympathetic. As a reception it was grossly overdone in Joanna's opinion. She had often noticed that teachers off duty were just as obstreperous as the kids they taught.

The Wine Club table was crowded, so she eased herself carefully into a chair by the window. It emerged that Dick Berry had already given them a colourful account of the door incident, and they were disappointed by her more prosaic version.

Simon Rose, head of the English department, was in charge of the bottles, and poured a glass of wine for her.

'No blood?' he asked, with an exaggerated pout of dismay. 'What a pity. On the whole, I think I preferred Berry's account. He waved his arms about a lot, and made himself look ridiculous.' He pushed the glass across the table to Tom Short, who rose and carried the glass over to her.

'Thank you, Tom.' Joanna smiled up at him, but Tom turned away, avoiding her eye. He had remained ostentatiously silent and stony-faced since she entered the room. Still sulking, she supposed. Well, that was his problem. His sulks were not going to make her feel guilty. Not any more.

For a little while the banter continued: some of it quite barbed. A couple of the younger women in particular seemed determined to take her down a peg or two. It was a consequence, Joanna realized, of her recent status as a celebrity, which she had certainly not sought. Ever since her so-called triumph at the *Elijah* concert and the subsequent press coverage, these two were convinced that she had grown too big for her boots. Now, they were hinting, in jocular fashion, that her exploit that afternoon was a ruse to get her picture in the paper again.

On the other hand, most of the teachers were proud of her: Maurice Banks and dear Cynthia Bell, for instance, were as happy for her as if her achievements were their own.

Inevitably the conversation turned to the disgusting state of the Annexe. Most of the women were indignant, and said the Annie ought to be pulled down and replaced with something decent, while most of the men preferred cynicism. It wouldn't happen, they said, not in their lifetime. 'No money,' they said.

'That's bollocks!' Marian Flint turned quite pink with disapproval. 'They're building a socking great new gymnasium, aren't they?'

'It's called a sports complex,' someone offered.

'Whatever the hell it's called, it'll cost millions. How come they can afford that?'

'Because,' Simon Rose explained wearily, 'they sold the bloody playing-field. That's how they raised the money.'

Maurice Banks, the head of the maths department, came into the room in time to hear the last remark, but made no attempt to comment. He had heard this particular grievance aired many times before.

It was a standing joke in the staff room that Maurice lusted after Joanna with a hopeless yearning. At any rate he never missed an opportunity to make himself agreeable to her, and today was to be no exception.

'Cynthia tells me you've had an accident,' he said anxiously. 'Are you all right?'

'I had a bit of a fall.' In spite of herself she was pleased by his concern. 'I tweaked my back, and it's playing up a bit, that's all.'

'Are you sure that's all? You look a bit peaky, to be honest.'

'I'll be fine. I'm going home soon, anyway.'

'Look,' Maurice was careful not to sound too eager, 'maybe you ought not to drive if your back's bad. I could take you home if you like.'

If only he were a bit more fanciable and a lot less boring I'd take him up on that, Joanna thought. She sweetened her refusal with a smile.

'That's really kind of you Maurice, but I'm sure I can manage. It's only a few minutes' drive. And anyway, I don't want to leave my car here over the weekend.'

'Well, I could …' He broke off, embarrassed. 'Yes, well, it was only a thought.'

'And a kind one, Maurice. Thank you.' He was a pathetic soul, but she was quite fond of him.

He hovered, debating something in his mind. 'Well at any rate,' he said eventually, 'the least I can do is to carry your case to your car.'

'Maurice, you're a prince!' Joanna didn't need to feign her gratitude. 'I would really appreciate that.'

Out of the corner of her eye she saw Tom Short's head come up, and caught the anguished glance he threw in her direction. Oh God, she thought, now I've given his jealousy another bone to chew on. Why can't he realize that mooching about looking moody and reproachful isn't romantic, it's just bloody irritating? Why can't he grow up? That was an unfortunate phrase. Tom was sensitive about his stature, and was never allowed to forget that his surname was only too appropriate. He regularly endured the kind of cruel witticisms that only a boys' school is capable of.

Part of her exasperation was simple guilt. Although she hadn't actively led him on, she hadn't actively discouraged him either. The bargain had always been explicit, at least on her part. She had made it clear from the beginning that their affair was never going to develop into anything permanent; so why couldn't he accept the inevitable break-up with a little dignity?

One irony of the situation was not lost on her. All through their affair he had insisted on keeping their relationship a deadly secret; but now that it was over he was sulking publicly like a love-sick adolescent.

Mrs Milner, the school secretary, ducked into the room, smiling and nodding apprehensively. She was afraid of the teaching staff, and convinced that they all disliked her.

'Oh good, Joanna. I was afraid you might have gone home already.'

'From the look in your eye, Mrs M, I guess I should have done,' Joanna said drily.

'Yes, well, I'm really sorry to trouble you, but the headmaster says, would you be so good as to pop in and see him?'

'Now?'

'Yes. I'm sorry, but he did say it was rather urgent.'

'Is it about that wretched door?'

'Door?' Mrs Milner contrived to look bewildered and inexplicably shifty at the same time. 'I'm afraid I don't know what it's about. But the headmaster did say it was urgent.'

'OK, I'll be along presently.' Joanna scowled at the secretary's retreating back. 'Rotten end to a rotten week,' she muttered, riffling through her handbag. 'Maurice, I've no idea how long this is going to take, so don't wait for me. But I'd be really grateful if you'd deal with my case. Here's the key to my car. Just leave it in the boot with the case, will you? I've got a spare set.'

'I really don't mind waiting, if it would help,' he said wanly.

'No, honestly, I'll be OK. I'd rather you didn't go to any more trouble.'

'Yes, all right.' He bore his disappointment bravely. 'Well, have a restful weekend, anyway. And take care of that back.'

On the way to the headmaster's room, Joanna hastily finger-combed her hair, smoothed her skirt, and ran a quick check on her blouse-buttons. Automatic gestures merely: she was consistently the best-dressed woman in the place, and she knew it. Still, the head would expect her to look coolly stylish and well-groomed, even at the fag-end of a fraught Friday afternoon.

He had better not try to push me around, she thought grimly; I'm not in the mood for it. She had been tempered in the fire: she was tough enough to face anything.

She ought to have known better than to tempt Fate. For once, she had forgotten her father's favourite saying: 'Nothing is ever so bad that it can't get worse.'

CHAPTER 2

Piers Atherton, head teacher of the Jas Priestley School for Boys, Dovebridge, was no rough diamond. He was a smooth man, from his pink rounded chin to his shiny black Oxfords. If he had any imperfections or human frailties, they were carefully hidden from his staff. His hair was never tousled, nor his Old Warburtian tie even slightly askew, while his wrinkle-free collar might have been chiselled from the purest marble. He cultivated the demeanour, as he thought, of an old-fashioned diplomat: firm, courteous and unflappable. Joanna respected his abilities, but couldn't bring herself to like him. She knew only too well that underneath that suave exterior was a cold and ruthlessly ambitious bully.

He rose from behind his desk at her entrance and crossed the room to shake her hand. Even by his exaggerated standards of civility this was unusual and Joanna was immediately suspicious. The sly bastard was after some favour. He was probably planning to lumber her with some boring – and unpaid – extra work. Well, he was going to be disappointed: the mood she was in, all that slippery charm was going to be wasted.

Another strange thing: although he shook her hand warmly enough, he wasn't wearing his Teflon smile. His face had a curiously indeterminate expression, half-friendly, half-sombre, like a priest at a funeral.

'Joanna! It's good of you to come at such short notice. I was rather afraid you had gone home,' Atherton said. 'Please sit down, won't you?'

He backed away, and Joanna saw that there was another person in the room: a gaunt, elderly woman sitting in one of the armchairs facing Atherton's desk. She had a yellow document-holder open on her lap and a sheaf of papers in her hand. The bright colour somehow emphasized her drabness, made her look even greyer than she was.

Atherton cleared his throat: a dry double-cough. It was his customary way of signalling that he had something important to say.

He had circled back to his own place behind his desk, and now stood looking from one woman to another, his manner affable but wary.

'I believe you two know each other.'

'Do we?' Joanna was startled. She could have sworn that she had never set eyes on the old biddy before in her life.

The grey-haired woman smiled thinly. 'I have obviously changed much more than you have, Mrs Howard. I'm Philippa Crouch.'

'Philippa!' Joanna sat up, wincing as her back gave her a sharp reminder. 'From the Social Services! Of course! You have to forgive me – I'm one of those peculiar people who are better at names than faces. Never forget a name – hardly ever remember a face. It's a social handicap, believe me.' She was prattling: trying to cover up not just embarrassment but shock. Philippa Crouch! This thin, grey, *old* woman was Philippa Crouch! She must be ill, Joanna thought; she's about the same age as me, but she looks positively ancient. Uncomfortably aware that she was sounding over-hearty, she smiled glassily at Atherton. 'Philippa and I were social workers together – on the same team, I mean. Years ago. Would you believe, I took up teaching because I couldn't take the stress of social work?'

The irony was wasted on the headmaster. 'Ms Crouch is still with Social Services,' he said stiffly. 'She mentioned that you and she had once been professional colleagues.'

Joanna pulled herself together. 'Excuse me, headmaster. I realize that you didn't invite me here to indulge in idle reminiscence. Is this a pastoral matter? Should I fetch my files?' God, she hoped not: the trip would be agonizing.

Philippa Crouch eyed Joanna coolly. 'You are involved in pastoral care? In this school?'

'I'm a head of year,' Joanna said slowly, surprised by the question. Why hadn't Atherton briefed the woman properly?

The headmaster looked uncharacteristically abashed. 'I'm sorry, I should have apprised you of Mrs Howard's status,' he said hurriedly. 'She took on her pastoral responsibilities only a short time ago – in January, to be exact.' He made the point heavily, as if to stress its importance.

'I see.' Ms Crouch was solemn, too, as if she fully accepted the significance of the head's remark.

Joanna was beginning to feel uneasy. There was a strange, strained atmosphere in the room: an atmosphere that seemed to be signalling bad news. Her conscience was clear – apart from that stupid incident with the door – but all the same, she couldn't fight off an irrational twinge of apprehension.

Ms Crouch came to a decision, and spoke weightily, like a chairman in charge of a meeting: 'No, it won't be necessary to examine your files at this time, Mrs Howard. But I am indeed here on a pastoral matter. It concerns a boy called Nick Tanner.'

'I can't help you there, I'm afraid. He wasn't one of mine, thank God.'

'What do you mean?'

'I mean, I didn't teach him. He wasn't in any of my classes.'

'But you did know him?'

Joanna shook her head decisively. 'No, Philippa. I know *of* him, of course, because of all the fuss. He was the kid who got expelled for punching a teacher.'

'I see. That's why you said "Thank God"?'

'Yes.'

The headmaster interrupted, prefacing his comment with his nervous double-cough. 'Tanner was not actually expelled, in point of fact. At the time of the incident his parents had already given notice that they were removing him from the school. The family was moving out of Dovebridge—'

'They moved to a council flat on the Wickerbrook estate in Aldersgrove,' Ms Crouch said. 'My department was involved in the decision to rehouse them.'

'So you see, the question of expulsion didn't actually arise.' Atherton sounded defensive, as if he anticipated criticism. 'I did, of course send a detailed report of Tanner's conduct to the head of his new school.'

Joanna frowned. 'I'm sorry, headmaster, but I don't quite see the relevance of all this. To me, I mean. You said this matter was urgent, yet it concerns a boy I know absolutely nothing about. What on earth has this child done?'

'Ah.' Atherton looked magisterial. 'I think Ms Crouch should answer that.'

But Ms Crouch was in no hurry to answer. She fiddled with the papers in her yellow folder.

'Did you know that Nick Tanner was on the "At Risk" register?'

'No. But it doesn't surprise me.'

'Why not?'

'Because most of the over-aggressive kids – the ones who turn to violence at least – are themselves the victims of violence. Usually at home.'

Philippa pursed her lips. 'That sort of broad-brush generalization is considered a little old-fashioned nowadays. However, it is true that the stepfather – Fred Steen – is prone to acts of violence. Particularly when he is under the influence of alcohol.'

'You're saying that when he gets drunk he beats up his wife and son?'

'His stepson. Yes.'

'Chalk one up for old-fashioned, broad-brush generalizations, I'd say,' Joanna murmured, straight-faced.

Ms Crouch ignored that. She bent her head over her notes as if reading from a prepared script. 'The situation improved dramatically after the family moved into better accommodation, and particularly after Fred Steen found regular employment. Mrs Steen – Nick's mother – assures us that the violence has stopped, and that Nick and his stepfather are on friendly terms.'

'That sounds suspiciously like a happy ending.' Joanna commented. 'But it can't be, can it? Otherwise you wouldn't be here. So there's still a problem.'

'Indeed.' Ms Crouch lifted her head and looked directly at Joanna, her face sombre. 'In spite of the improvements at home, Nick's behaviour at school is if anything worse than ever. He is uncooperative, insolent, aggressive – and his attendance record is appalling. What would you infer from that, Mrs Howard?'

'What would I infer? Look, I know I have a reputation for being able to handle difficult children, but I'm no expert. You surely didn't come over here just to ask my opinion about a kid I've never even spoken to?'

'Indeed I have.' An edge of hostility crept into Philippa Crouch's voice. 'I would be grateful for *anything* you care to tell me about this boy.'

'Well,' Joanna didn't try to conceal her irritation, 'this is pure conjecture, of course, but an old-fashioned view might be that since the treatment hasn't worked, the diagnosis wasn't accurate. Just moving house hasn't resolved the kid's problems.'

'What sort of problems would you think we should be looking for?'

'How should I know? I haven't got any of the facts. Look – do you want me to talk to the boy? Is that what this is all about?'

'No. Would it surprise you to learn that the boy now claims to have been sexually assaulted?'

'Surprise me?' It seemed an odd question, and Joanna hesitated, unsure how to tackle it. 'I'm not qualified to give an opinion on the causes of aberrant behaviour. When a child is difficult in class, I do what most teachers do: I deal with the problem the best way I can. I told you, I'm no expert. I really don't understand why you're consulting me about this boy, particularly since I don't know him.'

'But he claims to know you, Mrs Howard. Intimately. According to his account, you seduced him about eight months ago, and have been having regular sexual intercourse with him ever since.'

CHAPTER 3

Joanna gaped, speechless with shock and anger. She could feel the sudden heat in her cheeks, and the thought that her blushing might be taken as a sign of guilt made her even more angry. After a few futile attempts, she eventually found her voice, though it was little more than a croak. 'Me?' Her lips trembled, and despite herself she began to stammer. 'W – with Nick Tanner?' With an effort she got her breathing under control. 'That is the most disgusting and offensive thing I've ever heard!' She stood and advanced on Philippa Crouch hardly aware of the knifelike pains in her back. 'How dare you! You—'

'Now steady on, Joanna!' Abandoning his magisterial dignity, Atherton scuttled round his desk, ready to interpose his bulk between the warring factions.

'Headmaster!' Joanna turned the full force of her fury on Atherton. 'You have known me for over four years. Are you telling me that you really believe I could be capable of – of anything so disgusting?'

'No, no.' Atherton tried to push the idea away with his hands. 'Of course not, Joanna.'

'I've told you, I don't even know the kid. I wouldn't recognize him if he walked into the room right now!' Joanna's voice was still shaking.

'Nevertheless,' Philippa Crouch calmly slid her papers into the yellow folder, and the folder into her briefcase, 'now that the child has made this allegation, we have no alternative but to take it seriously. We are bound by strict procedures.' There was the ghost of a smile on her thin lips as she added the last comment.

Apparently assured that the threat of violence had passed Atherton retreated to his place behind his desk.

'May I ask whether the – ah – police are involved at this stage?'

'Child abuse is a crime, Mr Atherton,' Ms Crouch said severely. 'We are obliged by law to notify the police whenever there is the slightest suspicion that abuse has taken place. I understand that a senior officer of the Child Protection Unit will interview the Tanner boy as soon as it can be arranged.'

Atherton pursed his lips and stared gloomily at his uncluttered desk top. 'You understand, Joanna, that I too am constrained by procedure,' he muttered, avoiding her eye. 'Naturally I believe that this accusation is malicious and without foundation; but in the circumstances I have no choice but to suspend your employment here with immediate effect.'

'Are you saying I've been found guilty before this stupid charge has even been investigated?' Joanna's voice rose to a shout, trying to bring some sense into the argument by sheer force. 'That's not just unfair: it's madness!'

Atherton flapped his hands in the air, as if he was beating an imaginary pillow into shape.

'Please calm down, Joanna. This ghastly situation is not of our making. Once that revolting boy had made his allegation, machinery was set in motion over which we have no control. You will be vindicated in due course – I have no doubt of that – and things will return to normal. In the meantime, we simply have to do things by the book.'

'In the meantime, my reputation will be torn to shreds,' Joanna said bitterly. 'Can't you see the message that putting me on suspension sends out? You know what people will say – "No smoke without fire!"'

'Please understand, my dear, my hands are tied.' Atherton pressed his wrists together to illustrate the point. 'God knows, this couldn't have happened at a worse time. I really can't afford to lose you. We're short-staffed; the supply teacher in geography is costing a fortune, and Richard Berry rang up half an hour ago to say that his wife and daughter have the 'flu, and he thinks he is developing the symptoms himself.'

'There's a lot of it about,' Philippa Crouch observed, unsympathetically. 'And it seems even worse this year than last. Now, Mr Atherton, unless there are any points you wish to raise, I must be away and about my business.'

'I think,' Atherton said heavily, 'that we have covered everything of immediate significance, thank you, Ms Crouch. Do you think you can find your own way out, or shall I ring for assistance?'

'I can manage, thank you. Goodbye to you, sir.' She made a point of ignoring Joanna as she hurried from the room.

Joanna made to follow her, but Atherton waved his arms wildly at her from his chair. 'Wait!' he whispered. He stared at the ceiling and nodded his head as if counting or beating time. 'That woman ...' he began, but then checked himself. He got to his feet, plodded to the door and flung it open. Satisfied that there was no one outside, he crossed the room, produced a key and opened a small cabinet. 'That woman is a chronic pain in the bum,' he said, in a voice quite unlike his usual weighty tones. 'I need a drink, and I suspect you could do with one, too. May I offer you a glass of sherry?'

'Just a small one, Piers.' In spite of her distress, Joanna automatically observed protocol: Atherton insisted that his staff use his first name unless what he called "outsiders" were present. 'I've already had a glass of wine in the staff Room.'

'Ah yes, the Friday night Happy Hour. A splendid institution. Most civilized.' The sherry seemed to cheer Atherton up immensely. 'Right,' he said, leaning back and holding up his glass. 'Battle plan.'

'Battle plan, Piers?'

'Yes. The first thing you do is contact your Union rep. If the police know you've got a legal representative on your side, they're going to tread very carefully. Also, there's a society, an association – I don't know what it's called – anyway, it's a group of teachers who've been falsely accused of abuse by malicious pupils. Get them alongside. Don't,' he wagged his head, '*don't* assume the police will get it right without lots of assistance.'

'Thank you.' Joanna was bewildered. This was a side of Piers Atherton she had never encountered before: a side she never knew existed.

'Now,' Atherton finished his drink and poured himself another, 'I couldn't help noticing that you are experiencing some difficulty in walking. You have a pronounced limp.'

'Yes.' Joanna wondered exactly how much Atherton knew about that afternoon's fiasco. 'I've strained my back.'

'Ah.' The answer seemed to afford him considerable satisfaction. 'In that case, I think we can put off any public announcement of your suspension for a few days. Officially, the decision to suspend you has to be ratified by the governors; and I happen to know that the chairperson is spending the weekend with her married daughter in Wiltshire. So, if you will be so good as to provide us with a medical certificate stating that your back is in a truly deplorable condition, we can in the first instance, ascribe your absence to sick leave.' He paused and cleared his throat with his customary double-cough. 'We must do our utmost to quash this wretched calumny before it is made public.' He waved aside her murmured thanks. 'I've seen this kind of thing happen to other schools. If it's allowed to fester it could seriously affect our position in the league tables.'

It was hardly the most tactful endorsement in the world, but Joanna expressed herself grateful for it.

'That's very thoughtful of you. I'll see my doctor as soon as possible.'

'It might be as well to take home your personal things, too; particularly from the little office you use for pastoral work. I'll get Vail to help you, if you like.'

'That won't be necessary, Piers: I can manage. But I would prefer to do it tomorrow, if you don't mind. I have some of the boys' exercise books at home, and I would like to bring my class notes up to date for whoever fills in for me.'

'Good thinking,' Atherton said warmly. 'Mrs Milner will be here for a couple of hours in the afternoon. Liaise with her about it, will you?' He sipped his wine appreciatively, taking much longer over his second glass than his first. 'I can't tell you how distressed I am about this development, Joanna. You must know that I have long considered you a real ornament to the school.'

For one panicky moment Joanna thought that Atherton was trying to flirt with her; then she realized that he was referring to the *Elijah* concert. The old fraud had about as much musical discernment as a deaf monkey; but he wasn't above exploiting the publicity from her unexpected success for the benefit of the school.

'You flatter me, Piers,' was all she could think of to say.

'Not at all. I only wish I could have been present to witness your triumph.'

Joanna cast her eyes down shyly in appreciation of the great man's praise. She knew there was never the remotest chance of Atherton attending a classical concert: his taste in music had been set in stone by the time he bought his first ABBA recording.

'You did us proud that night, I must say.' Atherton emptied his glass, and eyed the bottle speculatively. Apparently deciding that he had relaxed enough in front of a colleague, he terminated the interview. 'We must fight this malicious attack tooth and nail, Joanna,' he said. 'Those tight-arsed buggers in Social Services see paedophiles behind every blasted bush. We must bring them to their senses.'

'Thank you, Piers.' Joanna prepared to go. 'I can't tell you how much I value your support.' There was nothing else she could say, although she knew only too well that Atherton, that master of *realpolitik*, would desert her the moment it seemed expedient for him to do so.

Atherton nodded graciously. His hand made only the slightest move towards the sherry bottle as she took her leave.

The pain in her back had grown worse and the emotion of the last half-hour had left her dizzy with exhaustion. She negotiated the stairs to the ground floor slowly and with great caution, moving like a sleep-walker, and occasionally gripping the wooden handrail with both hands as if to reassure herself of its solidity.

Once she was outside the fresh air cleared her mind a little, and by the time she had limped painfully around the new gymnasium to the staff parking-lot the tiredness had given way to boiling rage. It was insufferable of Philippa Crouch to bring such a charge, and intolerable that the headmaster hadn't dismissed it out of hand.

As for that lying toad Nick Tanner, she would happily twist his beastly head off his disgusting shoulders. For a few minutes she allowed herself the luxury of imagining the tortures she would like to inflict on that repulsive little monster. It helped, though not much; but after a while she began to breathe a little more easily. Maybe she was reacting too violently to the situation. It was all so totally absurd that it was bound to be cleared up in no time. Wasn't it?

'Miss! Miss?' A stocky, thin-faced youth darted along the path after her. He had obviously been loitering near the car park, waiting for her to appear.

Joanna groaned inwardly. As usual, young Darren Palmer was demonstrating his talent for lousy timing. She knew what was on his mind – he had ambushed her six times in the last three weeks – and she shrank from having to give him the bad news yet again.

'Sorry, Darren,' she said briskly. 'Can't stop now: I'm on my way home, and I'm already late.'

The boy padded along at her side, looking up anxiously at her profile.

'Well … I only wanted to ask about the Windgate camp, miss? Whether you've made up the list and that?'

'Not yet, Darren. I haven't yet had replies from all the sponsors.' Getting sponsorship – begging – was the only way that projects like the summer camp could be funded.

'But the trip's still on, is it, miss?'

'I hope so, Darren. Provided we can get the money together. But—'

'I really do want to go, miss. It was great, last year.'

The pain in Joanna's back was making her breathless. 'I know you want to go, Darren. But you do understand, don't you, that you can't go for free this year? It has to be someone else's turn. That's only fair, isn't it?'

'Yes, miss.' But it was clear from Darren's expression that he hadn't given up the fight yet.

'Look,' Joanna tried to sound optimistic, 'as soon as I know what the cost will be, I'll write to your parents, OK? If they can contribute something—'

'I've already asked them, miss,' the boy said bleakly, his face dark with the shame of having parents who were poor and unemployed. 'They say they can't afford it. But miss, last year …' He broke off, distracted by the expression on her face. 'Are you all right, miss? You look ...' He couldn't think of a tactful way to put it. Mrs Howard was looking terrible.

Joanna forced a smile, touched by the boy's concern. 'I'm OK, Darren: just a bit tired. It *is* the end of the week, after all.'

'Yes miss.' Darren was embarrassed. He shouldn't have mentioned the way she looked. Miss was probably going through one of those mid-life crisis things they kept banging on about on the telly. Doggedly, he returned to his own agenda: 'Miss, I know I can't go to Wingate camp again for free, like I did last year. But I heard ...' He hesitated, struggling to put his case as diplomatically as possible. 'I heard that, well, on top of the two free places, there were some places that were ... sort of ... only *partly* paid for.'

'That's true, Darren. We try to spread the sponsorship money as widely as possible. But we ask parents to pay the full amount if they possibly can.' In fact, most parents, even those on income support, were pathetically keen to pay something towards their kid's holiday.

Darren pushed on, eager to make his point: 'Well, miss, what I wanted to ask was – how much would be enough? I mean, I've been doing a paper round, and I've saved up a bit. And my uncle Mick always gives me a couple of quid for my birthday. And—' he had saved up the best for the last – 'I got this. I won it in a competition.' He took a square of paper out of his breast pocket. 'It's a book-token, miss, for five pounds. That could go towards the cost, couldn't it?'

'What competition, Darren?'

He blushed. 'I wrote an essay, miss. It came out top.'

Joanna forgot her aching back in a fierce rush of pity and rage. It simply wasn't fair that a fourteen-year-old kid should have to grovel like this, just because his parents were poor. And it wasn't fair that she should have to be the one to dish out disappointment to the kid. For a moment, anger made her speechless.

'We'll have to see what we can do,' she said eventually, ashamed of her own cowardice. She knew she ought to tell him the brutal truth: that last year's dollop of charity was his lot for the foreseeable future. Cravenly, she tried to spread the blame: 'I'll mention it to the educational social worker.'

'You won't forget, miss?'

'Darren,' Joanna made a feeble attempt to lighten the atmosphere, 'you know and I know there's no way you're going to let me forget, right?'

Darren nodded and looked thoughtfully up at her face. She suspected that he was mentally decoding the sub-text of her words: *go away and stop bothering me*. Even stupid kids could understand *that* familiar message, and Darren was far from stupid. Unsmiling, he nodded again and turned away, the slump of his shoulders as eloquent as any spoken protest.

She had left her car at the far side of the parking-lot, where a line of plane-trees and a few overgrown bushes marked the boundary between the school and the street. As she gloomily calculated the distance she still had to walk, her eyes were caught by a movement under the trees. Someone was walking rapidly towards the main gate, keeping to the shadows. At first she thought it was one of the senior boys, wearing one of the fashionable curved-peak baseball-caps; then, as he passed under a streetlight, she saw that it was in fact Tom Short.

Impulsively Joanna called out to him, but it seemed he was too far away to hear her. Before she could call again he had passed beyond the furthest clump of shrubbery and out of sight.

Joanna's shoulders slumped with disappointment. Until she had caught that glimpse of Tom she hadn't acknowledged to herself how great was her need to talk to someone, to pour out her troubles into a sympathetic ear. Another vexation. Nothing was going right. Life was a bitch.

Common sense returned with a jolt. What the hell was she thinking of? Whatever made her imagine that Tom, of all people, would lend her a sympathetic ear? They had had an affair, and she had dumped him. Although she had brought the affair to an end in what she believed was a civilized and considerate way, she had no doubts about how hurt and offended he was. His was definitely not a shoulder she could cry on.

In fact she couldn't think of a single living soul she could turn to. Her parents were dead; her ex-husband had remarried and was being spoilt and pampered by a very rich older woman; Gerald, her next partner, had turned out to be a merciless cheat, and Tom was having a fit of the sulks because she had dropped him.

Her female friends were no use, either. Most of them were members of the choral society; and they had grown distinctly cool towards her after the *Elijah* concert. There were mutterings that the whole thing had been rigged; that she had been warned in good time that the soprano soloist was unwell and likely to cancel. Otherwise, why was Joanna so well prepared? Favouritism, that's what it was. She was probably having an affair with the musical director, was the opinion of the older women, apparently unaware that the fellow was as gay as a lark.

Anyway, even if she had been on better terms with any of her female friends, she would never dream of confiding her latest troubles to them. Not even the staunchest of them could be trusted with gossip as juicy as this. There was simply no-one she could turn to. As she fumbled in her purse for her car keys, she was engulfed by a wave of self-pity.

The moment passed; she told herself that she was behaving like a stupid, neurotic ninny. 'A stupid, neurotic ninny,' she said aloud, finding the sound of her own voice strangely comforting. There was something pleasing, too, about the word 'ninny'. It seemed solid, old-fashioned, reliable: the kind of word her father might have used. 'Ninny, ninny, ninny,' she said, several times; but was disappointed that the repetition robbed the word of any meaning. Still, it was a distraction: better than whimpering like a sick baby.

All the same, she didn't underestimate the mess she was in. Even when this wretched accusation had been disproved and discredited, the scars would remain. Well, she would have to deal with that when the time came.

She had come through bad times before and survived. She was pretty resilient. She wasn't just going to curl up and die. She would tough it out.

She eased herself painfully into the driver's seat and arched her back to try to ease the tension out of her spine. A glance at the dashboard clock told her that less than an hour had passed since she had been swapping banter in the staff room. It was hardly credible: her familiar workaday life seemed to be light-years in the past.

The agony in her back abated a little and she sat still, breathing deeply, savouring the relief. She was much calmer now, but she wished she could shake off her sense of shame over her outburst in the head's office. How on earth had she allowed herself to lose control like that? Shrieking like a passionate harpy at that bloody Crouch woman. Until that moment she had thought of herself – and had convinced most of her acquaintance – that she was the epitome of sang-froid. Even the kids admitted that she was "pretty cool". Now, her self-image had definitely taken a knock. She felt older and somehow diminished.

She shivered. All at once she felt deathly cold; her hands and cheeks were like ice. She started the engine and pushed the heating control to maximum. Her whole body began to shake uncontrollably. Delayed shock, she supposed. She was certainly in no fit state to drive. How the hell was she to get home?

Gradually the warmth began to seep through, and her body responded to it gratefully. Maybe she would be able to cope after all, if she drove with extra care. The trembling became sporadic, then stopped completely. She switched on the lights and put the car into gear.

Her heart lightened the moment she passed through the school gates. In a few minutes she would be home!

In the end, it took longer than she expected. It wasn't simply that she was driving slowly – unnaturally slowly, by her standards – but the conviction grew on her by the time she reached the main road that she was being followed. She told herself that it was nonsense, that she was being paranoid; but every time she looked in her rear mirror, she saw the same set of headlights behind her, mile after mile. She felt sure they were the same lights, because one of them, on the near side, had a strange blue tinge, which didn't quite match the other. Following cars, irritated with their funereal progress, whizzed angrily past them both; but blue-light stayed sedately on her tail. Unnerved, she slowed even further and moved over to let the car overtake. It moved over too, and matched her speed, apparently content to crawl along behind.

She was doing her best not to panic, but she had to do something to resolve the situation. Either she was being followed, or she wasn't. There had to be a way to find out. With a little thrill of satisfaction, she thought of one.

She accelerated up to something like her normal speed. To hell with caution, she thought. Ahead of her was the big roundabout at Stampers Gill, where five roads met. She normally left it at the second exit, which was the main road to Aldersgrove, but this time she had other ideas.

Her plan was simple. She would just go round the roundabout – twice, if necessary – and then turn off quickly into the Canal Road exit. It was a very minor road, not much more than a country lane; and there was no heavy traffic on it because of the restriction on the old bridge. Still, it would get her to Aldersgrove, albeit at the wrong end of the one-way system. Anyway, if blue-light was still on her tail after all that manoeuvring she would know he was up to no good.

The plan worked like a charm. She had Canal Road entirely to herself. No oncoming traffic, and definitely no sinister headlights behind. False alarm. Unnecessary panic.

All the same, after a minute or two, she began to suspect that there was something distinctly odd about Canal Road. She remembered it as being quiet, but not as quiet as this. There was usually *some* traffic about, particularly this early in the evening.

She soon discovered why the road was so deserted. As the street-lamps of Aldersgrove came into view she saw the signs by the roadside. The first one said; NO THROUGH ROAD. The second offered the explanation: UNSAFE BRIDGE.

Joanna stopped the car and swore vigorously, with a breadth of vocabulary that surprised even her. One more sodding awful event in a sodding awful day. She wrenched the car round and raced back the way she had come, working out her frustration by driving like a maniac for a few miles, until a couple of narrow escapes on the sharp bends brought her to her senses.

She noticed grimly that the warning signs near the road junction had been upended on the grass verge; that was why she had missed them. Some idiot's idea of a joke, she supposed. Probably one of the kids from her school.

It occurred to her as she approached the Stampers Gill roundabout again, that the car that had been following her could be waiting ahead, in a lay-by off the main road. She tried to dismiss the idea as ridiculous, but it lingered stubbornly in her mind.

She needn't have worried: the rest of the drive home was as uneventful as on any normal day. She could have kicked herself for letting her hyperactive imagination run away with her.

Given the run of things, it was no surprise that some yahoo had parked in her space on the street. Her house was in a narrow cul-de-sac in the oldest part of Aldersgrove: there was a reserved parking-bay at the far end of the street, but she, like most of her neighbours, preferred to park immediately outside her house. Cursing under her breath, she drove down to the parking-bay and backed into her slot. It didn't improve her mood to see how carelessly aligned some of the other cars were. Her own parking was scrupulously neat; and for people to dump their cars any old how seemed to her sloppy and antisocial. She growled in disapproval. She couldn't remember when she had been in such a thoroughly bad temper.

When she moved to get out of her car her back pain struck with such force that she yelped aloud. She sat back in her seat and tried to summon enough courage to move again. She longed to be in her own home, but she dreaded the agony of getting there. Getting her briefcase out of the boot and carrying it would be sheer hell; dare she just leave it where it was for the weekend? Problems, problems.

Then she was appalled by the worst problem of all. It was Friday. There were no supplies in the house. None at all, not even the basics. She would have to shop for the weekend. At Buchanan's. She bowed her head and allowed herself – for the first time that day – to weep like a lost soul.

CHAPTER 4

Ignoring the warning cough from his junior partner, Jack Dabdoub spoke his mind.

'It 'ud be a waste,' he said flatly. 'A waste of my time and your money.' He just wanted the chippy little man to go away. It was late on Friday afternoon and Dabdoub had better things to do than listen to bloody nonsense from a bloody loud-mouthed Antipodean midget. He himself was a big, broad-chested man, with a beer-belly and a massive, hairless head that looked as if it had been clumsily carved out of a chunk of knotted pine. His client, Mr Guest, was sharp-featured, thin, small and wiry, his close-cropped hair grey, his skin burnt brown and wrinkled as a walnut.

'It's my money,' Mr Guest said stubbornly. 'I can be the judge of whether it's wasted or not.' His Australian accent twanged resonantly around the little office.

Tony, the junior partner, nodded vigorously. 'Absolutely right, Mr G. Jack, you're being downright negative. Who's Mr Guest going to turn to if we refuse to help?' Tony, who was twenty-five, was one of those men who are fated always to look years younger than their true age. His face was round and smooth, and his eyes as wide and innocent-looking as a baby's. His habitual expression was one of worried concern, as if he was afraid that disaster might strike at any moment. His nickname at school had been Charlie Brown; but Dabdoub, who had employed him because he was the smartest kid he had ever met, said it should have been Charlie Brain.

Dabdoub scowled at his young partner and shifted clumsily from one side of his chair to the other.

'Eh! Now, you shut up, you greedy bugger.' He shrugged and waved a hand at Mr Guest. 'Pay no mind: the mention of money makes him go soft in the head.' All the same, he was uncomfortably aware that Tony had probably clocked something that he himself had missed. 'All right,' he mumbled ungraciously. 'So what did the police say?'

'Much the same as you. It all happened over seven years ago. They caught the guy who killed my mother – a no-hoper called Melvin Tares – and he went to gaol. End of story.'

'Yeah. Exactly. End of story. What makes you think it ain't?' Dabdoub was getting more crabby by the minute. This little guy was obviously a crank; and if you worked for a crank they made your life hell. If they weren't on your back they were up your nose. He really did not want this job. Unfortunately, it looked as if Tony was hooked, and once that little mongrel got his teeth into a problem, it was the devil's own job to shake him loose.

As if on cue, Tony spoke gently to the client. 'It was that newspaper article, wasn't it?'

'Yes.'

Dabdoub ground his teeth. 'What newspaper article?'

'You must have read it,' Tony said. 'It was by that Anita Mons.'

Dabdoub muttered something libellously offensive about Anita Mons under his breath.

'Don't tell me, let me guess,' he said heavily. 'She's gone and uncovered yet another miscarriage of justice.'

'Well, yeah.' Tony was unabashed. 'That's what she does, right? She printed an interview she had with an ex-con who'd shared a cell with Melvin Tares. This guy told her that Melvin had sworn to him that he was innocent of the killing of Carole Guest. He had been paid to take the rap for it, and threatened with death if he refused.'

Dabdoub was unimpressed. 'Journalistic crap. Did this ex-con tell Ms Mons who had made these death threats?'

'No. He said that Melvin wouldn't tell him.'

'OK.' Dabdoub had the look of a man whose patience was being sorely tried. 'So what did Tares say at his trial?'

'Well, first he said he hadn't been near the apartment; then he said he *had* been there, noticed the door open, found the body and run off in a panic; then he said it was an accident: Mrs Guest had invited him in, they quarrelled, he pushed her and she fell. Every time they caught him out in a lie, he made up another one.'

'But he never tried to implicate anybody else?'

'No. According to Anita Mons's informant, he was too scared to.'

'He thought that if he grassed up his accomplices they might kill him, too?'

'Something like that.'

'It makes sense,' Mr Guest put in eagerly.

It didn't make sense to Dabdoub, but he let it ride. He could see that Tony wanted this case, and Tony could be a right pain if he was thwarted. He temporized. 'If I know Ms Mons's methods, she won't have left it there. She'd have got an interview with Tares himself, right?'

'She tried,' Tony said.

'And failed? That's hard to believe. That woman's got a will that would vaporize concrete. How did they keep her out?'

Tony wasn't above needling the big man. 'She had a cold,' he said. 'A bad one.' He had planned to tease out the joke a bit longer, but Dabdoub's baleful expression changed his mind. 'Tares is in an isolation ward,' he said hurriedly. 'He has full-blown Aids, and he's very weak. A cold virus could finish him off.'

Dabdoub fell silent. He knew he had been ambushed, but it was his own fault for not boning up on the brief. So Melvin Tares had Aids, eh? That certainly made a difference.

Mr Guest couldn't resist pressing the point home. 'Tares knows he's dying. Death threats don't frighten him any more. He's telling the truth. He didn't kill my mother by himself. Other people were involved. I want them caught and brought to justice.'

Dabdoub didn't give up the argument without a struggle. 'Just because the guy's dying doesn't mean he's telling the truth. He's a crook: he could just be making mischief.'

'True,' Tony conceded. 'But Mr Guest is entitled to his doubts. And he's entitled to the truth, if we can dig it up for him. He's been to the police, and they've refused to help. Where else can he turn?'

It was a rhetorical question, and Dabdoub ignored it. 'We can try,' he agreed reluctantly. 'But we can't give any guarantees. Face it, Mr Guest: the odds are it'll all be a waste of time and money.'

'But you will give it a go, yeah?' Mr Guest was pathetically eager. 'I've been told you're the best in town.'

Not at this kind of work, Dabdoub thought irritably, but Tony interposed smoothly before he could say anything.

'We would need you to sign a contract, Mr G. Just the usual thing – client confidentiality, acting on your behalf, etc, etc. And the financial arrangements of course.'

'Sure.' Mr Guest seemed anxious to get it settled before Dabdoub changed his mind. 'What'll it cost me?'

'Our basic charge is five hundred a day,' Tony said without blinking. 'Plus expenses, of course. We would report progress on a regular basis, but it would be unrealistic to expect any positive results in less than four days.'

'I guess what that means,' Mr Guest said calmly, 'is that you want two thousand quid up front, right?'

Tony beamed. 'It's a pleasure to do business with you.'

'OK.' Guest wrote out a cheque and scribbled his name on a virtually illegible boilerplate contract. 'Understand one thing: I'm not looking for courtroom proof. I'm the only guy you have to convince. I just want to know who killed my mother.'

Dabdoub was alarmed. 'Wait a minute – you're not planning to do anything stupid, are you? We can't be any part of some kind of crazy revenge scenario.'

Guest smiled without humour. 'Perish the thought, mate. Perish the thought.'

When he had gone Dabdoub gazed at his junior partner in awe.

'Five hundred quid a day? Plus expenses?'

Tony grinned. 'You never do your research, do you? That was Mr Bauxite.'

'Who?'

'The guy has made his money in aluminium. He's got more millions than you've had hot dinners. He probably spends five hundred quid getting his eyebrows plucked.'

Dabdoub scowled. 'Which means he's got the money to sue us.'

'What for?'

'For fraud. For breach of contract. For taking money under false pretences. How are we going to solve a seven-year mystery that's already been solved? How the fuck did I let you get us into this mess?'

'We've got an edge,' Tony assured him. 'Like the man said, we're the best.'

'We're good at what we do. We track down debtors, insurance fraudsters, moonlighters, adulterers; we negotiate deals with thieves and blackmailers; we supply information to people who are too lazy or ignorant to look it up for themselves; often, we do pointless things for silly people. What we *don't* do is solve murders. In particular, we don't try to second-guess a seven-year-old case that the police have already wrapped up.'

'Well, but,' Tony's young face for once was shining with optimism, 'you were a cop yourself at the time. In the CID.'

'Not in the Murder Squad, I wasn't. Didn't want to be, neither.'

'But you must know some of the guys who were? I know you've still got contacts in the force. Surely one of them worked on the Guest murder?'

'So what? That team got a great result. What makes you think that they're going to turn round and say, "Oh golly gosh! We made a mistake! We put the wrong guy behind bars! Aren't we the silly-billies?" Get real, for God's sake!'

Tony was an expert at smoothing his employer's ruffled feathers.

'You're underestimating your powers of persuasion. I'm willing to bet you could get one of your old chums to let us have a look at the files on the Guest case.'

'Whaddyer mean? You think I'm gonna try to bribe one of Manchester's finest?' Dabdoub tried to look shocked.

Tony smiled. 'Wouldn't be the first time, would it? Anyway, it's worth a try. We've got a virtually unlimited expense account. We can afford it.'

'You sneaky little bugger.' Dabdoub's eyes sparkled. As Tony had anticipated, his boss was enthralled by the idea of corrupting his old colleagues. 'OK, so we get the files. What are we looking for?'

Tony oiled the wheels with a little flattery. 'Jack, you know better than I do how these things work. Like, in some cases I've read about, important evidence got overlooked because nobody realized its significance at the time. Maybe there's something in those files that points to the existence of an accomplice. Something that got pushed to one side, because the cops were convinced Tares was acting alone.'

Dabdoub groaned. 'Kid, you're just guessing.'

'Sure,' Tony agreed. 'But I'm guessing on somebody else's time, don't forget. Even if I'm wrong, we'll be five hundred quid a day better off.'

'Mind your language, you greedy little sod.' Dabdoub was appalled to discover that his assistant was even more mercenary than he was himself. 'If we do this job, we'll do it right. The guy is entitled to value for his money.'

'So, you'll contact one of your old mates in the CID?'

'Or I'll tear up Guest's cheque, which is the option I prefer. Look, Melvin Tares left fingerprints at the murder scene, and he had some of the old lady's knick-knacks in his pocket when he was picked up. The cops got him bang to rights. At his trial nobody even brought up the possibility of his having an accomplice. Now, seven years later, some low-life bandit spins a yarn to a gullible journalist about an alleged secret confession Tares made in gaol. It's got all the imprints of a con trick. And not a very subtle one.'

'Yeah, but while there's an element of doubt, our client's suffering mental anguish, right? Whether the cops got it right or got it wrong, we ought to try to prove it one way or the other. That way, the guy can achieve closure.' Tony was in deadly earnest, but his smooth round face only revealed an expression of comical anxiety.

Dabdoub winced, as he always did when the word 'closure' cropped up.

'You really do want to do this job, don't you? And it's not just for the money, is it?'

Tony ignored both questions. 'There's something else. While I was poking around, I found out something about the Carole Guest murder that didn't come up at the trial. I don't know how significant it is, but I want to follow it up.'

'Oh?' Dabdoub tried to sound bored. 'So what did you find out?'

'Well,' Tony wanted to draw this out, 'I found out what Carole Guest's job was. What she did for a living.'

'Which was?'

Tony paused for effect. 'She was one of us.'

'One of us?'

'Yeah. In a manner of speaking.'

CHAPTER 5

Buchanan's was Aldersgrove's local supermarket. It was smaller and more expensive than Tesco's or Sainsbury's, but those stores were miles away on the outskirts of town. Buchanan's was plumb in the middle, overlooking the old market place. It was popular, not just because it was convenient, but also because it was a local institution. The Buchanan family had run a grocery store in the town for as long as anyone could remember. The citizens of Aldersgrove were proud of the place. It had style, they said.

Right now, Joanna thought bitterly, I'd swap all the style in the world for a delivery service. With gritted teeth, she pushed her trolley along the narrow aisles and tried not to groan when she had to reach down to a bottom shelf. The only consolation she could offer herself was that the ordeal would soon be over. Things could only get better. Fate had done its worst, for that day at least.

As usual, she had underestimated Fate and forgotten her father's warnings. Nothing is ever so bad that it can't get worse. If she hadn't been so weary and bad-tempered, she might even have seen some perverse humour in the situation. It was infuriating. It was ludicrous. That some randy, over-dressed tomcat should choose this day of all days to try to pick her up was just about the final straw.

'Hi,' he said, grinning at her as if he had known her all her life. 'God, is this place always like this?'

She fixed him with a basilisk stare, so overwhelmed with rage and frustration that she could think of nothing appropriate to say. 'Piss off!' was the only thing that came readily to mind, and that was not the kind of thing a respectable citizen would utter in a place like Buchanan's.

If he noticed her look he was not disconcerted by it. 'This system's got me baffled,' he said cheerily. 'Found the green olives by the strawberry jam; but it's the black olives I need. Any ideas?'

Wordlessly, she jerked a thumb over her left shoulder. It was the nearest equivalent to 'Piss off!' that she could manage.

'Of course!' He shrugged his shoulders in mock-Gallic fashion.

'Next to the cornflakes. I should have guessed.' He strode off, swinging his basket jauntily.

Joanna disliked everything about him. She particularly hated his suit. It was so perfect, so obviously grossly expensive. It was the kind of suit that Gerald would have drooled over. Gerald was always banging on about cut and hand-sewn lapels and how many buttons cuffs ought to have. Boring. Even if she had been in her sunniest mood, a guy wearing a Gerald-type suit would have been a turn-off.

The Friday-evening scrum in Buchanan's seemed even worse than usual. There was some sort of row going on at one of the check-outs, but Joanna couldn't hear what it was about. Voices were raised, and there was a lot of grumbling and shuffling of feet.

'Excuse me?' It was the Suit again. 'But are you OK? You look a bit ...' This time he did register her expression. His face fell comically and he stepped backward, bumping clumsily into the pet-food shelves.

'I am perfectly all right, thank you,' Joanna said icily. 'Not that it's any business of yours.'

'No.' For a moment, the man looked thoroughly bemused. 'No, of course not. Sorry. My mistake. So sorry.' He made for the exit, shaking his head slightly. She was pleased to see that she had knocked some of the bounce out of him. It wasn't much of a triumph, but considering the general grottiness of her day she found the Suit's discomposure quite gratifying.

At the check-out she discovered the cause of the earlier commotion. One of the aisles had been closed, making the queues even more congested than usual. Most of the shoppers stood by their trolleys with an air of patient resignation; but one woman was giving shrill vent to her feelings.

'I dunno if it's the same one, but if it is, I reckon she's doin' it a purpose. It was the same last week and the week before. Right in the middle of the busiest time of the week, one of the gels throws a wobbly and they close the till while she goes and has a lie down. Reg'lar as clockwork. I mean, you'd think they'd of sussed the routine by now. Why haven't they got somebody standing by?'

She had a point, Joanna thought. Now that the woman mentioned it, there was nearly always a problem at the check-out on Friday evenings. Still, there was no real point in complaining about it. Buchanan's dealt with complaints with ruthless efficiency: they ignored them completely. For all her strident fury, the shrill woman couldn't actually expect anything to change. Joanna resigned herself to the fact that there was really nothing she could do but wait in line with what patience she could muster.

She noticed that the Suit was well ahead of her, in another queue.

He would be long gone before she even got to the till. Good riddance.

She was already dreading the prospect of having to carry her groceries home. She lived only about a quarter of a mile away, but she knew that every step would be agony. Buchanan's scorned to offer a delivery service. Such pampering might be all right for the soft-bellied South, but Northerners were made of sterner stuff. Everybody carried their own bags home in Aldersgrove: it was no place for weaklings. Joanna braced herself for one final, agonizing effort. Then, thank God, she could kick her shoes off and rest.

Lifting the bags off the counter was the worst part. Once she had got them more or less balanced, the pain lessened from the unbearable to the merely excruciating. She gritted her teeth and began walking. Things can only get better, she reminded herself again.

It was as if the very thought invited disaster. When she got out of the store. The Suit was waiting for her, sheltering from the drizzle in a shop doorway.

'May I help you?' he asked, looking theatrically concerned. 'Honestly, you look all in.'

'For God's sake!' Joanna was almost stuttering with rage. 'Why can't you mind your own business? Why the hell can't you leave me alone?'

'Well, I—'

'Look,' She was determined to lay it on the line, so that even this idiot could understand, 'even if I was in the mood to be picked up – which I'm not – I certainly would not be picked up by some bloody smug bloody tailor's dummy!' She wanted to add that, in spite of his expensive clothes, he had the most ordinary-looking face that she had ever seen; but she couldn't think of a sufficiently cutting way to say it.

'Picked up?' Oddly, he sounded quite indignant. Then, in a gentler tone, he said: 'Is it the suit?'

'Oh!' She was not a violent person, but at that moment she could have kicked him, if only she had the energy. 'Just – get lost!'

'OK.' He stepped back in the doorway and watched her hobble away.

Two minutes later, she turned round, wincing. 'Are you following me?'

'No.'

'Yes, you are!'

'No.'

'Then why are you walking behind me?'

The man sighed gustily. 'Because I'm going the same way you are, Mrs Howard.'

'What!' She almost dropped her bags in alarm. 'How do you know my name?'

'Because I live next door to you, Mrs Howard. You live at number 7, on the Causeway,' he pronounced it 'corzey', in the local way, 'and I live at number 8.'

'Number 8? That's where Mr Gelson lives.'

'Mr Gelson is in America, visiting his son. I'm renting the place while he's away. I've been living there for about four weeks. I'm Matthew Clements, by the way.'

'Oh.' Joanna could feel the heat rising in her cheeks. 'Have we ...?'

'*Please* let me take those bags, Mrs Howard. Watching you struggle is making me feel quite breathless.'

'All right.' Joanna relinquished her load with a sense of relief. Then, realizing that her response had been less than gracious, she added 'I mean – thank you. Thank you very much. Look, I'm sorry about—'

'That's OK. Natural misunderstanding.'

'I mean – we have met, then?'

'Sort of. We've said "good morning" a few times. Over the fence. In the front garden.'

'Oh, Lord.'

He said, as if it were the most natural misapprehension in the world, 'I expect it was the suit.'

'No, no, it's just ... well, I'm not very good on faces.' Joanna regretted the remark as soon as she had uttered it. 'I mean, I had never ...'

He finished her sentence for her. 'You had never seen me in a suit before.'

'Yes ... I mean, no.' She wasn't quite sure what she meant.

'You've only seen me in my working togs. Today, I've had to entertain a client. In Manchester. Hence the posh gear.'

'Oh.' Joanna was floundering, trying to remember whom it was she had greeted in the next-door garden. She had a mental picture of an ordinary, tweedy person, she had assumed he was a local handyman, tidying up Mr Gelson's garden. She attempted some sort of apology: 'You see, my ex-partner used to wear suits like that. Expensive, I mean.' Now that she had made it, the explanation seemed absurd. Embarrassed, she elaborated further; 'I suppose I had built up a prejudice about smart suits. Ridiculous, really.'

'Not at all, your attitude seems eminently reasonable. I was once jilted by a girl in a floppy hat, and I've been wary of girls in floppy hats ever since.'

She glanced up at him suspiciously. His face was perfectly straight, but his mouth seemed to be twitching a little. It was hard to tell in the uncertain light from the streetlamps.

'Are you making fun of me?'

'Absolutely not, Mrs Howard. I have too much respect for you. I'm a fan.'

'A what?'

'I heard you sing, last week. You were marvellous.'

'Oh, that.' She pretended indifference, but her heart leapt with pleasure.

'I've been telling people ever since that I'm your next-door neighbour. They're very impressed.'

'I think you're very unkind,' she said warmly. 'I've had a pig of a day, and now I'm lumbered with a bloody comedian.'

'I'm truly sorry.' Laden as he was with her groceries as well as his own, he did a little apologetic shuffle, which made her smile in spite of herself. 'I've had a pig of a day, too. Tell me about yours.'

'No.' In case her tone had not been emphatic enough, she added, 'Not bloody likely.'

'Ah.' He let a minute go by, then changed the subject. 'You said that you weren't very good on faces. Isn't that a handicap, in your job? I mean, all those kids. How do you tell them apart?'

She felt a touch of resentment at his cheerful questioning. 'How did you know I was a teacher?'

'One of the neighbours told me. The one with the wig and no teeth.'

'Mrs Whalley.' Joanna acknowledged the description with a reluctant smile. 'Look, I didn't say that I was completely hopeless at recognizing people. What I meant was that I have problems recognizing faces out of context. But to compensate, I am very good at recognizing voices. I never forget a voice, or the name that goes with it.'

He nodded gravely. 'I suppose that's a by-product of your musical training. So I take it that my voice is now safely filed in your memory bank?'

She shrugged. 'If that's what you want.'

'Yes,' he said emphatically. 'Yes, that would be very nice.' Before she had time to decide whether he was being serious or sardonic, he changed tack once again. 'Just as a matter of interest, did you fall out with your ex-husband because you don't like suits, or did you come to hate suits because of your ex-husband?'

'The latter, I suppose. Only I didn't say "husband", I said "partner". My ex-husband's suits were OK.'

'What was so special about your ex-husbands suits?'

'Nothing: that's the point. Look, I don't dislike suits in general, only flashy ones. Like yours.'

'Flashy?' He sounded genuinely hurt. 'The tailor said it was rather, um, discreet.'

'Oh, come on! A cut like that, with those hand-finished whatsits, costs a fortune. Believe me, I know. Gerald used to bang on and on about hand-finished whatsits.'

'Did he? How very off-putting. You're clearly better off without him.'

'Yes, I know that. What I don't know, is why we're having this utterly silly conversation.'

'Silly? I was rather enjoying it. At any rate, it has brought us to your home.' He put a couple of the bags on the ground and opened her front gate. 'You know, I really love these long front gardens. They make this little street look quite classy.'

She found herself warming to him for the first time. She loved to hear her house praised.

'This street is called "The Causeway", you know, because it was originally the raised bank of a canal,' she said. 'That ditch over there used to be an important spur off the Macclesfield Canal. There was a big warehouse just here, and a huge mill to the east, where the spur ended. After the war, a private developer bought up this whole area, demolished the warehouse, extended the gardens, tarted up the houses, and sold them separately. Made a fortune.'

'Interesting,' he said politely, but his thoughts seemed to have wandered. 'Did you know you had left your house lights on?'

'What! No, I'm sure I …' She hesitated, trying to remember what she had done that morning, it seemed a lifetime ago. 'I mean, I don't usually …' She stopped, aware that her voice was shaking. It was ridiculous to feel so apprehensive. She had forgotten to turn a light off, that was all. There was nothing sinister about it. It had been such a rotten day, she had just lost her bottle completely.

The man picked up the bags and stood for a moment, staring doubtfully at the house.

'I think …' he said vaguely, then lapsed into silence. He seemed to have forgotten what he wanted to say. Then, briskly: 'If you don't mind, I'll carry your things indoors for you and help you unpack.'

'Well …'

'I insist. I'm a little concerned about that back of yours.'

'Thank you.' It was embarrassing to feel so relieved by his offer. She was acting like an hysterical schoolgirl, starting at shadows. 'I'm sorry I was so churlish, back there. I'm really grateful, honestly.' She unlocked the door, and held it open for him. 'The kitchen is through here. I'll just—' She stopped abruptly.

'Something wrong?'

'Yes,' she said tensely. 'The kitchen light's on. As well as the one in the living-room. I might have forgotten one, but there's no way I would forget both. Anyway, it's not all that dark in the mornings.'

He carefully lowered the bags to the floor. 'Are you saying that someone's been in here?'

'Yes.'

'Wait here.' He pushed open the living-room door and looked inside. 'No one here. You say the kitchen's through there?' He moved quickly, light on his feet for such a big man. 'Nobody in here, either. It doesn't look as if the place has been ransacked. You'd better come and see.' He stood aside to let her enter, and then carried the groceries in from the hall. 'What do you think?'

'It all seems OK.' She lowered herself wearily into a chair. 'I must have been mistaken.'

He looked unconvinced. 'Does anyone have a key, besides yourself?'

Before she could answer there was a noise from upstairs: the unmistakable sound of a lavatory being flushed. Then, footsteps on the stairs. And a voice:

'Hon? Don't be alarmed: it's only me!'

It was Tom Short, not morose, as when she had last seen him, but grinning with embarrassment. He was still wearing his baseball cap. 'Sorry, sorry! I came round to see how you were – you looked so completely knackered in the staff room, I thought … Anyway, you weren't in, and I waited a bit, and suddenly I was – pardon the pun – took short. I mean, really – no time to lose. I just had to use your bathroom. God, I hope I didn't frighten you?' He had been waving his arms about comically while he was talking, but now he suddenly became aware of the stranger in the room. His face fell. 'Oh, sorry, Jay,' he mumbled sulkily. 'I didn't know you had company.'

With an effort, Joanna kept a check on her temper. 'Mr Clements, this is Tom Short, a colleague of mine,' she said coldly.

'Matthew,' the man said, stooping a little to shake hands. 'Most people call me Matt.' He seemed suddenly uncomfortable, and glanced ostentatiously at his watch.' I'd better be getting along, Mrs Howard. If you need any help – on account of your back, I mean – remember I'm just next door.'

'Thank you, but I'm sure I'll be fine.'

'OK.' He nodded to Tom and strode off towards the front door. Then he turned back. 'Excuse me – that back problem of yours – have you had it for some time?'

'No.' She grimaced. 'I injured it this afternoon. A stupid accident.'

'Ah. Well I've just had an idea.' He was talking rapidly, seeming curiously ill at ease. 'Look, I'll give you a call in the morning. Not too early. We'll talk about it when you're rested.' He was gone before she could protest.

Tom threw himself into a chair. 'So that's it?' he said bitterly. 'I ought to have guessed. And he lives just next door, eh? How convenient.'

Joanna shook with rage. 'How dare you! Of all the incredible bloody cheek! How dare you? To waltz into my house and use it as a public lavatory—'

'I couldn't help it. I told you, it was an emergency. I only came here because I was worried about you. Anyway, how was I to know you were going to bring your latest fancy man home?'

'Tom, you're being ridiculous. I only met the fellow five minutes ago.' Her indignation was on the wane; she was just too exhausted to maintain it.

He made a ghastly pretence of laughing. 'Pull the other one,' he sneered. 'Ever since Gerald dumped you, you've been on the look-out for another public-school type. Christ, this guy even wears the same bloody Savile Row suits.'

She felt a stab of guilt and pity. His whining jealousy made him such a pathetic little figure.

'Tom,' she said gently, 'I'm not having an affair with him, or with anyone else. It's just that – well, you and I had our fling, and now it's run its course. I'll always be grateful for your support after Gerald "dumped" me, as you call it; I admit your courtship was balm to my wounds. But if I used you, then, by the same token, you used me.'

He took a moment to work it out. 'Sex, you mean?'

'Yes.'

'You're telling me it wasn't any good?' He was starting to get angry.

'No. I'm not saying that. I'm saying that I needed more than sex.'

'Yeah. Like Savile Row suits and poncy accents.'

She was feeling less sorry for him by the minute. 'Tom, I swear to you I'm not involved with anyone else. I like you, and I'm grateful to you, but the bottom line is that I don't love you. Anyway, you've always been so secretive about our affair; I never dreamed you were getting serious about it.'

'Oh, yeah.' He hunched his shoulders and stared at the floor. 'I should have known you would make it all my fault. Well – if we don't love each other, and never have – and if, as you say, there's nobody else in the picture – why don't we just go on as before?'

Now she knew her sympathy had been wasted. 'Go on as before? What exactly do you mean?'

He shrugged. 'You know.'

'No, spell it out. You mean, you wouldn't mind popping round for the occasional fuck?'

'Why not? At least, until posh Mr Right comes along. If he ever does.'

It was time to finish it. 'Tom,' she said quietly, looking up into his face. 'I always knew you were pathetic. What I didn't realize until now, was that you're also a disgusting little shit.'

'Jay—'

'Just go.' She was already ashamed of her cruelty. She had never called him 'little' before. She knew that would probe the rawest nerve in his body.

He turned pale, and his lip trembled; but she thought she detected a calculating gleam in his eye, as if he was working out whether it would be worth his while to burst into tears. However, he turned away without a word, and walked slowly to the door, shoulders slumped and head bent, like a dog expecting a whipping. With a sad gesture, he closed the door quietly behind him.

Too late, Joanna remembered something. 'Bloody hell!' she mumbled. 'I meant to ask for my key back. Tom!' But he had gone.

She leaned back in her chair and closed her eyes, utterly drained. The Suit – she had to make an effort to remember his name – Matthew, that was it – had been going to help her unload her groceries, but he'd bolted like a startled rabbit when Tom made his appearance. Probably thought he was being discreet. Jumping to the obvious conclusions. Joanna Howard's 'colleague' has the key to her front door. Just good friends, ho, ho.

She sighed and opened her eyes. A bit late to start worrying about your reputation, my girl, she thought. Anyway, it was probably all for the best. If that Matthew bloke was on the make, that little episode ought to have put him off for good. He'd probably avoid her like the plague from now on. Which suited her just fine; he was definitely not her type. In fact there was something about him – she couldn't figure out exactly what it was – that made her feel uncomfortably self-conscious. His magnanimous offer to help her to unload her groceries turned out to be a load of bunkum, too. Men! The only thing about them you could really rely on was that they would let you down. She stared balefully at the heap of bags on the table.

'To hell with it,' she said aloud. 'They'll just have to keep till the morning.'

She heaved herself out of her chair, and noticed, for the first time, that the light on her answering machine was blinking. She shook her head at the machine and addressed it severely. 'I warn you, I don't think I could take any more bad news today. I'm just going to ignore you, and pamper myself with strong drink.'

But once she had the drink in her hand, curiosity overcame her resolution. She pressed the Play button and collapsed back into her chair.

It was a voice she didn't recognize, high and strained and breathless.

'Hi! miss, it's me, Nicky. I really wanted to talk to you tonight. Please ring me soon, please. I need you. I want you so bad, it hurts. Oh, miss, it's been such a long time. If I don't fuck you soon, I'll go crazy. Look, I'm sorry if they're making trouble for you. It's all my mum's fault. I'll explain when I … I've got to go now. I love you, I really, really do. I love you. 'Bye!'

For the second time that day, Joanna found herself frozen with shock. She tried to tell herself that some kid had dialled the wrong number; but she couldn't make herself believe it. It was a joke, a sick joke; somebody was winding her up. But why?'

'Jesus Christ!'

The new voice startled her so much that her glass slipped from her hand and shattered on the floor.

'Tom!' She was shaking uncontrollably with bewilderment and fear. 'What are you …?'

'I brought your key back,' he said thickly. 'My God, you're something, eh?'

'How long have you been …?'

'Long enough. Christ, I can't believe it! And you had the nerve to call *me* disgusting!'

'It's a mistake!' She was shouting in her anxiety to convince him. 'A wrong number! Can't you see?'

He wasn't listening. 'I may be a shit,' he said haughtily, 'but I've never stooped to messing with kids.' He threw her door-key on the floor among the glass fragments. 'You know what gets up my nose? You, pretending that sex wasn't enough, you, raving on about true love and all that bullshit. And all the time you're shagging some poor benighted kid whose voice has hardly broken. I suppose you know it's against the law? Or was that part of the thrill?'

Joanna knew that her arguments wouldn't reach him. But she had to try.

'Tom, you're jumping to conclusions. You're making a big mistake.'

He sneered. 'No. My only big mistake was ever getting involved with you.'

This time, he left with his head held high.

And this time he did bang the door.

CHAPTER 6

'Sorry, did I wake you?' The voice sounded unrepentant. 'I thought you'd be glugging your morning tea by now. It's nearly ten o'clock, you lazy cow.'

'Is it?' Joanna made a half-hearted attempt to sit up, but tiredness defeated her. 'I'm sorry, I took a pill last night, to help me sleep. I'm still pretty woozy.' She had also taken a generous dose of pain-killers, and their combined effect seemed to have slowed her brain down to a crawl. She half-recognized the voice, but she couldn't immediately put a name to it. 'Am I meant to be somewhere? Have I missed an appointment or something?'

'Not as far as I know, my pet. Relax. Shake off that sad, drug-induced lethargy, for I have some news for you.'

'Patrick?' Stupid question, she thought. The voice and the manner were unmistakeable, and could only belong to Patrick Pringle, the musical director of the Aldersgrove Choral Society.

'Patrick? Patrick?' He was trying to sound offended, but his voice was shrill with excitement. 'Of course it's Patrick, you silly tart. Who did you think it was? Julian Clary?'

Joanna groaned. 'Patrick, for pity's sake, ease up on the camp dialogue, would you? It's giving me a headache.'

'Camp, *moi*? Look, If you're going to be ugly and plebeian, I shan't tell you my ravishing news.'

'Don't be silly, Patrick. If it's so ravishing, you couldn't bear not to tell me.'

'Well all right, then. Rejoice, rejoice, sweetie, our revered choral society is saved!'

'Saved? What do you mean saved? Saved from what?'

'Saved from bloody bankruptcy, that's what. We were really up against it, old dear. Flat broke and running into debt. The committee was seriously talking about packing it all in.'

'Scrapping the choir? But the society is over a hundred years old! It's an institution!'

'I know, I know. But things were really that bad. But just in the nick of time, a white knight has galloped to our rescue!'

'A sponsor? I know you've been appealing for one for ages. But don't we get grants from the Arts Council, and stuff like that?'

'We get some grants, lovey. The trouble is, they're so bloody unreliable. We never know from year to year whether Lady Bountiful or Lord Catchpenny will be holding the purse-strings. Anyhow, it's never enough. We had to borrow against the promise of next year's grants to put the Mendelssohn concert on at all. Now, thank God, we can stop worrying about money and concentrate on just making music.'

'That's really great, Patrick! Who is this knight in shining armour?'

'Well it's not one of your zonking big companies, it's a priceless band of little angels. Some local businessmen have formed a consortium to chip in enough cash to keep the society going for the foreseeable future.'

Joanna responded to the animation in his voice. 'Local companies? Patrick, that's marvellous! I'm so pleased for you.'

'Ah, but I haven't told you the really tasty bit.'

'Which is?'

'Why, we owe it all to you, sweetie! This is all a direct result of all the lovely publicity we got over the *Elijah* concert. Did you know that the *Guardian* critic wrote a follow-up piece to his review?'

'No. Actually, I was amazed that the *Guardian* reviewed us at all.'

'Just an incredible piece of luck, darling. He came along because he'd heard good things about that young Scottish baritone we booked.'

Joanna chuckled. 'I bet he was one of those who groaned when you announced that I was going to sing in place of de Courcy.'

'Listen, ducky, I was bloody apprehensive myself. We'd slaved for months over that work, and I could see all that effort going for nothing because our sop soloist got the dreaded lurgi at the last moment. I only picked you because I couldn't trust any of the other sops to sight-read and stay in tune.'

'That isn't what you said at the time, Patrick. You said "I know you can do it, girl. Glory beckons." Or something like that.'

Patrick sighed theatrically. 'Yes, well, it's the kind of thing you say when you're shitting yourself with terror. Anyway, you made it a fairy-tale occasion, dearie. Understudy triumphs. Cinderella turns into a princess. I still don't know how you managed it. You sang it as if you'd known the piece all your life.'

'I have, Patrick. Known it most of my life, anyway. It was part of my grandmother's repertoire. Along with the *Messiah*, *St Matthew* and *St John's Passions*, Stainer's *Crucifixion*, Mozart's *Requiem*, and all those old war-horses. I listened to her practising them, hour after hour. I spent most of my childhood with my grandparents. My father was drafted overseas for much of his working life.'

'Oh.' Patrick sounded vaguely disappointed. 'Your grandmother was a professional singer?'

'Not a famous one, but she made a living.'

'Oh,' Patrick said again. The information seemed to have thrown him off his stride for a moment. 'You never told me that.'

'I'm surprised it never came up. I'm very proud of my gran.'

'Well, anyhow,' Patrick still sounded vaguely put out, 'perhaps you ought to feel proud of yourself. It was the *Guardian* articles about the society – and you – that prompted our new sponsors to step forward. We owe you a vote of thanks.'

Joanna felt a sudden rush of affection for the man. 'No, the thanks are due to you, Patrick, for all your patience and hard work. As for me – well, that concert was the biggest thrill of my life. I'll never forget it.'

'Nor will I, little one, nor will I. Only ...'

'Yes?'

'Well, some of the girls – particularly the older ones – are a bit miffed about all the attention you've been getting. They've threatened to resign if you get any solos in next season's programme.'

'Oh, Patrick!' Joanna was genuinely amused. 'I don't mind. I've had my moment of glory. I'm happy to serve in the trenches again. All I want is to sing. It keeps me sane.'

'Good girl.' Patrick didn't try to hide his relief. 'All the same, I've always thought you were special. I want you to know that.'

'Thank you.'

'Hey!' Now that the serious business was over, Patrick could relax. 'What's this I hear about you shagging one of your pupils?'

'What!' Joanna reacted so sharply that a bolt of agony shot through her back. 'What are you talking about? What have you heard?'

'Only that you've been having naughties with one of your larger lads. What larks, eh?'

'Patrick, it's a disgusting lie! Who told you that?'

'Oh, I can't remember offhand. Somebody.' Patrick back-tracked rapidly in the face of her violent reaction. 'So it's just idle gossip, is it?'

'It's a filthy, offensive and malicious lie, that's what it is. I want to know who's putting it about.'

'Sorry, old thing. I honestly can't remember.' That was so blatantly untrue that Patrick tried to cover it by being waggish. 'Not that it would be any big deal, surely? Lucky kid, that's what most people would say.'

'Patrick! I—'

'Hang on, sweetie, there's someone at the door. I'll have to go. Talk to you later.' He rang off in some confusion.

As soon as she put the phone down, it rang again.

'Hello? I hope I'm not disturbing you? This is your neighbour – the one with the suit.'

She was still trembling with anger, and it took her a moment to compose herself.

'I recognize your voice,' she said eventually. 'Good morning, Mr Clements.' She tried to sound polite but cool. If the fellow was entertaining any romantic notions she wanted to discourage him as soon as possible.

'How is your back this morning?'

'It still hurts. I haven't got up yet.'

'Well, I've had an idea. I think you should see a friend of mine – a physiotherapist called Janice Pounder. She and her partner specialize in treating that kind of injury.'

'That's kind of you. I'll contact her as soon as I can. Do you have her number?'

'No, I didn't mean that.' He was speaking hurriedly, and sounding uncharacteristically flustered. 'I mean you should see her right now. This morning. As soon as possible. She has what she's pleased to call "a window of opportunity".'

She was indignant. 'Do you mean you've arranged an appointment for me? Don't you think—'

'No, no, it's not like that. Look, it's complicated. I'll explain on the way there. Just get ready as soon as you can. Don't waste time tarting yourself up. Put on a track suit, or something comfortable. I'll have the car waiting outside.'

She still felt irritated, but she was finding it difficult to express herself forcefully enough. 'I don't—' she began, but he interrupted her again.

'Please don't waste time arguing, Mrs Howard. Just say yes. Go with the flow.'

'OK,' she said weakly. She tried to tell herself that it was ungracious of her to be so vexed with the man. He was only trying to help, and he was right that she needed treatment for her back. All the same she wasn't at all keen on meeting Matthew Clements again. It was pretty obvious that the man fancied her; and the last thing she wanted right now was another emotional involvement. Groaning, she got out of bed and made herself ready. It was all very well for him to tell her just to chuck on any old track suit, but life wasn't that simple. Even a track suit needed to be chosen with care; and to expect her to step outside uncombed and without make-up was sheer lunacy. Still, one of the skills she had learned during her unhappy time with Gerald was to make herself presentable at a minute's notice; so in fact she didn't keep Matt waiting long.

'You're very pushy, you are, Mr Clements,' she said as she eased herself painfully into his car. 'This had better be worthwhile.'

'Oh, I'm sure it will be.' He too had apparently taken some care over his appearance, and had discarded his suit for slacks and a smart polo shirt. He looked younger in casual clothes than in a suit, she thought: younger, and somehow less confident. His face wasn't perhaps quite as ordinary as she had first thought, but it certainly wasn't handsome by her standards. Actually, she would have found it more attractive if it had been uglier. A broken nose, perhaps, or a duelling-scar would certainly make it more interesting. But even with the best of intentions it wasn't the kind of makeover one could actually propose.

'You promised me an explanation,' she said, as soon as they were on their way.

'Yes, of course. I think I told you that Janice and her partner Alec specialize in treating sports and industrial injuries. Janice has agreed to make time to see you.'

'On a Saturday morning?'

'We're lucky. Any other morning it would be out of the question.'

She noticed that he was driving very carefully, trying to make the ride as smooth as possible. She had assumed they were going into Manchester; but then he turned off into an unfamiliar road.

'Where are we going?'

'Bottersley.'

She had seen the name on signposts, but she had never been there. 'Is that where Janice and Alec live?'

'No. It's where they're working today.' He could see that the explanation could be put off no longer. 'On Saturdays, and one afternoon in mid-week, they work for the Bottersley Rugby Club.'

She didn't know whether to laugh or cry. 'You're taking me to a Rugby club?'

'Yes.' He hastened to reassure her. 'They've got three treatment rooms – cubicles, really – so you'll be quite private.'

'Not sharing a space with great hulking football hooligans, you mean?'

He looked hurt. 'Rugby players aren't hooligans. Not really.' He sought for a convincing argument. 'I used to play Rugby.'

'But not any more?'

'I don't get picked.' There was a note of genuine regret in his voice. 'Time was, I could show the whole pack a clean pair of heels. Now there are at least three kids in the squad who could give me a two-metre start and pick me off before I'd carried the ball twenty paces.'

Joanna didn't even try to make sense of this. 'So Janice whatsername is going to take time off from looking after her Rugby roughnecks to see me?'

'Yes.'

'Why?'

Matt was reluctant to answer. 'Because – well, let's just say that Janice and Alec are friends of mine.'

'I know you,' Janice Pounder said. 'You're that singer. I saw your picture in the paper.'

'Yes,' Joanna said awkwardly. She found it difficult to respond gracefully to the compliment while she was stripped down to her knickers.

'I know absolutely nothing about music.' Ms Pounder made it sound like a boast. 'Matt tells me you injured your back at work.'

'Yes.'

'OK. Stand over there and turn round. Let's have a look at your back. Now, lean over a little. Ouch!' She groaned on behalf of her patient. 'Big spasm. That hurt, I can tell. OK. Lie on the bench, face down.'

Joanna obeyed, meekly enough. She had pictured Ms Pounder as a beefy, muscular individual, and was a little awed by this slim, confident young creature who looked as if she belonged in the Royal Ballet.

Janice sounded crisp and efficient. 'Alec's had a look at your X-ray, and there's nothing drastically wrong. It's a muscular problem. Did you play hockey at school?'

'Er – yes.'

'Get knocked about?'

'I suppose so, a bit. We all did.'

'The little 'uns got clobbered rather more than the big 'uns, in my experience,' Janice said, philosophically. 'I guess you were a little 'un.'

'Yes.'

'Well, whatever the cause, I reckon you suffered a minor injury in your youth. You got over it, but it weakened a few of these muscles,' she ran a cool finger along Joanna's back, 'and that weakness, aggravated by the passing years, has been waiting for a chance to tickle you up a bit. What did you do to bring this on? Spot of furniture removal?'

Joanna was distinctly miffed at the implication that she was old and feeble. 'I kicked a door down,' she said tersely.

'And you suffered this injury at work?' Ms Pounder sounded impressed.

'Yes.'

'I'd better not ask what kind of work you do. Anyway, your spine's out of kilter, and it's nipping the sciatic nerve. It's probably the commonest form of injury that we have to deal with.'

Oh good, Joanna thought, so now I'm boring as well as senile. 'It's a slipped disc, then?' she asked crossly.

'That's what the vulgar call it. The fact that it's not a disc and hasn't slipped is immaterial. Now, as to treatment. Well, the bad news is that on the whole, you're going to have to cure yourself. The good news is that it's not difficult. Right now, I'm going to give you a bit of heat and ultra-sound, followed by gentle massage, to ease the pressure. Then – and this is the important bit – I'm going to show you a short exercise routine, which will gradually strengthen your back; and I'm going to make you promise to do it every morning for the rest of your life. Any questions?'

'Yes.' In spite of the discomfort, Joanna twisted round to look directly into Janice Pounder's face. 'As you may have noticed, I'm not a Rugby player. Why are you doing this?'

'Matt asked me to,' Ms Pounder said.

'And you do anything he says?'

The physiotherapist looked amused. 'Matt's company is our principal sponsor. Matt is a director of the club. You want I should cut my throat?'

Joanna digested this in some disquiet. 'I really don't think I should be here. I believe in the National Health Service. I don't approve of private medicine.'

'Bollocks.' Janice busied herself setting up an infra-red lamp, and gently pushed Joanna into position on the bench. 'Any friend of Matt is a friend of mine. Anyway, this is saving the NHS money, which they can spend on more deserving cases.'

Joanna didn't have a ready answer to this. 'What company does Mr Clements work for?'

'He works for himself. He owns Clements and Figgis, the engineering firm. They've got the contract for the canal work.' She finished making adjustments. 'There – that's all set. Tell me if it feels too hot.'

'Right now it feels rather good,' Joanna said gratefully. 'What's all this about the canal? I haven't heard anything about it. What's going on?'

'It's all going to be cleaned up and repaired, and linked up again with the Macclesfield Canal. The council is hoping to make it a tourist attraction.'

'Oh. Is that why the Canal Road bridge is being repaired?'

'Actually, it's being rebuilt. The old bridge has been repaired so often that the arch is too narrow for any boat to get through. Matt's firm designed the new bridge.' There was no disguising the note of pride that crept into her voice with this last comment. Janice obviously had a soft spot for Matthew Clements. She went away and busied herself elsewhere for a few minutes. When she came back she had something on her mind. 'I take it you don't know Matt all that well?'

'No. He's my next-door neighbour, but we hadn't really spoken until last night.'

'Ah!' Janice said, as if Joanna had confirmed her suspicions. 'You were in some distress, I bet.'

'You could say that. I was struggling to carry my groceries home. He came to my rescue. Why? Does he make a habit of rescuing damsels in distress?'

'I wouldn't be surprised. He's a compulsive tidy-upperer.'

'Tidy-upperer?' Joanna wasn't familiar with the phrase, but she saw at once that no vocabulary was complete without it.

'Be warned. He'd be hell to live with, I reckon. If he sees a mess, he can't rest until he's tidied it up. If there's a problem, he's got to solve it. No wonder his wife left him.'

Joanna didn't know how to respond to the last remark. 'Well I guess I ought to be grateful that he saw me as a mess to be tidied up.'

'Yeah, well, just watch your step. He's a lonely man, and you're a beautiful woman. One of you could get hurt.'

After that, Ms Pounder made it abundantly clear that idle chatter was no longer on the agenda. She set about her business with a cool efficiency that was both reassuring and infinitely soothing. Her very self-confidence alone made one feel better. Joanna knew that she ought to feel guilty about what was obviously privileged treatment, not to mention shameless pampering, but on the other hand, having come this far, it would be churlish not to continue. And – there was no denying it – the pampering was very enjoyable.

Even better, after all the pummelling and tweaking and exercising, her back felt considerably easier. It was still sore, but the pain was nothing like the agony of the night before. Ms Pounder patted her shoulder as she left, and muttered something that Joanna didn't quite catch. It sounded very much as if she was congratulating herself.

The room where Matthew was waiting for her had been empty when they arrived, but was now packed to overflowing with large, beefy men shouting cheerful insults at each other. When she entered, the noise-level went down abruptly, and she made her way through a sea of grinning faces to the accompaniment of low, lascivious moans and muted wolf-whistles.

Matthew was standing by the street door, chatting to a huge, overweight, bald man who looked like every casting-director's image of Falstaff or Friar Tuck.

'Yeah,' the bald man was saying. 'It's been over a month now. You want my guy down there to check out the situation again? Maybe I should brace him to do it on a regular basis? Say every four, five weeks?'

Matthew shrugged. 'Yes please, Jack. I guess that would be best.' He didn't sound happy about it. He turned, sensing Joanna's presence, and his mood changed on the instant. His face positively lit up with pleasure, as if he were greeting an old friend he hadn't seen for ages. 'Hi!' He beamed. 'How was it?' Then, as if responding to some subtle nuance in her expression, he looked gratifyingly anxious. 'I mean, how do you feel?'

'Better,' Joanna said crisply. 'Why didn't you tell me that you owned this bloody club?'

'He doesn't,' the fat man said. 'He was just trying to impress you. I'm Jack Dabdoub, by the way. I don't own the club either, but I do play in the team, which is more than you can say for Mister Softie here.'

'Jack, this is Mrs Howard,' Matt said hurriedly. 'She injured her back, and Janice said she'd have a look at it.'

'Janice!' Dabdoub shuddered theatrically. 'That woman's a sadist. You're lucky to escape her clutches in one piece. And a very dainty piece too, if you don't mind my saying so.'

'I'd better take you home, Joanna, ' Matt said, scowling at the fat man, 'before this slobbering beast has a heart attack. What you need now is rest.' He escorted her to the car as attentively as if he expected her to faint clean away at any moment.

Dabdoub looked thoughtfully after them. That certainly was one gorgeous lady. He felt he was beginning to understand why he had just been instructed to go down to Devon and check on Matt's wife.

Matt drove her home as carefully as he had brought her out. His driving was typical of the man, Joanna thought: careful and unostentatious, and – well, pretty boring, actually. On the other hand, if he had tried to impress her with a macho display of skill, she would have found that even more boring. She suspected that her attitude was not entirely reasonable, but she couldn't help it. She felt an urge to nag. She was tetchy and irritable, and although she couldn't figure out why, she felt sure it was Matthew Clements's fault.

'Why didn't you tell me you were working on the canal?' she demanded suddenly. 'You let me rabbit on about the Causeway like an idiot.'

'I'm sorry.' He looked really contrite. 'But anything I said then would have sounded like a real squelch.'

Which was true, she thought.

They didn't speak again until he turned into the Causeway and pulled up outside her house. He got out of the car and bustled round to open her door.

'Can you manage, do you think? Is there anything I can do?'

'No, you've been wonderful. I feel fine. And thank you – I can't tell you how grateful I am.' She was laying it on a bit thick, trying to pretend she wasn't relieved to be escaping from his company. She debated with herself whether to shake hands, and decided against it. 'Well, *au revoir*, then. And thank you again.'

But before she had even opened her gate there was a commotion.

'Jo-hanna! Jo-hanna!' A thin, bony, almost hairless old woman came out of a door further along the street, and began to hobble down the garden path. The fag end of a lighted cigarette bobbed between her lips, and every few steps she paused and gasped for breath. She was obviously very excited. 'Jo-ho-hanna!'

Joanna moaned. 'Oh, God!'

'It's Mrs Whalley,' Matthew said, wide-eyed. 'Without her wig!'

'She's our resident Jeremiah,' Joanna said, wincing. 'If there's bad news, she wants to be the first to announce it.'

Mrs Whalley waved a clawlike hand at them. 'Have you,' she wheezed, 'have you …' She succumbed to a prolonged fit of coughing, making a wet, gravelly sound deep in her throat. 'Oh, bugger it!' she croaked. 'Wait a minute.' She took a deep drag on her cigarette and panted heavily, puffing smoke like an ancient locomotive.

'What is it, Mrs Whalley?' Joanna asked apprehensively. 'Is something wrong?'

Mrs Whalley nodded vigorously, still breathing hard. 'You haven't—' She looked up and caught Matthew staring at her. 'Hey up, you!' she said distracted. 'You're the new lodger at number eight, aintcher?'

'Yes.'

'Ay. I seen you doin' the weedin'. How d'ye get on wi' the old man?'

Matthew shrugged. 'He's in America.'

'Yes, well.' Mrs Whalley tapped her nose. 'You want to watch yourself, son. He's a funny old bugger.'

'Thank you for the warning,' Matthew said, straight-faced.

'Yes, well. You can't be too careful. So,' she switched her attention back to Joanna, 'you haven't seen your car, then?'

'My car? What about my car?'

'It's been whatsernamed,' Mrs Whalley said with relish. 'It's them bloody kids again, most like.'

'Whatsernamed?' Joanna already feared the worst.

'Yeah, you know – not vindaloo-ed; that other word.'

'Vandalized, you mean?' Matthew said.

'Thassit. I knew you hadn't seen it, Jo-hanna. As soon as Jake told me, I said I bet Jo-hanna don't even know it's happened yet.'

'No indeed. Thank you for telling me about it,' Joanna said grimly.

Matthew reacted swiftly. 'Get in the car. I'll drive you down; it'll be quicker.'

Joanna slumped in the seat. 'Oh, shit!' She was close to tears. 'As if things weren't bad enough already!'

'I gather you've had problems down here before?'

'Yes. As Mrs W says, it's probably kids from the council estate. They pinch hubcaps, break side-mirrors, deface logos – petty vandalism, but it's bloody annoying, all the same.'

But the reality was worse than annoying. Her car was a mess. Both headlights had been smashed, all the tyres were flat, and the side mirrors had been ripped off.

But for her the most shocking thing of all was the graffito sprayed on the windscreen. In blood red, gruesomely misshapen letters was the one word:

SLAG

CHAPTER 7

'Vandalism?' The officer at the desk sucked her teeth discouragingly, like a plumber examining a leaky cistern. 'Well, I dunno. We can't send anybody out at the moment: we're a bit short-handed, see, on account of there's a big match on in Manchester. London yobbos, know what I mean? And the one officer we've got left here is out on something important.'

'Well, I just wanted to report it,' Joanna said wearily.

'Yes, OK. I've got all your details written down here, see? And the description of the incident: "Vandalism on victim's car in parking area at west end of Causeway." I've marked it as a motor crime, so you won't have any trouble with the insurance. Any other cars involved?'

'No.'

'Ah. Do you think it's personal, then? Has somebody got a grudge against you?'

'I don't know. I don't see why anyone should have.' Joanna wondered briefly whether she should mention her quarrel with Tom Short the night before, but decided against it. That subject was extremely embarrassing. Anyway, it was unthinkable that Tom would stoop to anything so crude.

All the same, she couldn't stop herself wondering about it. Someone was responsible for the vandalism. If not Tom Short, then who?

'Right,' the officer said dismissively. 'Well, somebody will be in touch, I expect.' She scribbled on a notepad. 'Here's the crime report number. You'll need it for your insurance claim.'

Joanna looked round for Matthew. He had driven her to the police station, but had slipped away when she began talking to the officer at the desk. She found him outside in the street, muttering into his mobile phone. As soon as she appeared, he signed off, folded the phone and put it in his pocket. He smiled encouragingly at her.

'All done?'

'I suppose so.' Joanna didn't return the smile. 'That policewoman didn't seem terribly interested. She told me that all the local officers were out doing something important.'

'I don't suppose she meant to be tactless. They're overworked and understaffed. From their point of view, vandalism doesn't have a high priority.'

She was not going to be comforted. 'You can afford to be philosophical. It's not your car.'

'True. Come on, let me drive you home.' He escorted her to his car, saw her safely seated in the passenger seat, and settled himself behind the wheel. 'You're absolutely right: philosophy isn't much comfort when life is giving you the rubber-truncheon treatment. We'd do better to be practical.'

'Excuse me?' The desire to vent her frustration on someone fuelled her indignation. 'What's with this "we"? I don't remember asking for your help. In fact,' she warmed to her subject, 'not once in our short acquaintance have I asked for your help. You volunteered. At the supermarket, the physio, the police-station – you *offered* your help. I didn't ask for it. Now, all of a sudden, it's "we", as if we're a couple, or something. Now, don't get me wrong: I'm grateful for everything you've done. But if you hadn't been around, I would have managed. On my own.'

'A couple?' He sounded genuinely bewildered. 'No, no, how clumsy of me. I was making a generalization. I meant to say, *people* would do better to be practical. Believe me, Mrs Howard, I am no threat to your independence.'

Joanna was not as pleased as she ought to have been at this intelligence. She remembered Janice Pounder's assessment of Matt's character: a 'tidy-upperer'. She didn't like to think of herself a mess he was determined to put in order.

'I'm sorry,' she said gracelessly. 'I'm a bit overwrought.'

'I understand. Anyway, here we are.' He parked outside her house. 'Now, at the risk of incurring your displeasure, I'm about to suggest something.' He made quieting gestures with his hands. 'No, hear me out. Let me make something clear. You may think – and it would be a perfectly reasonable assumption – that because you're an attractive woman I'm making some sort of pass at you. The fact is that I'm quite happily married. Does that ease your mind?'

Joanna registered the lie, but was less shocked by it than she felt she ought to be. 'Then why are you doing all this?'

Matthew smiled. 'Because you're a neighbour. Because you've got a gorgeous singing voice. Because – forgive me – because I think, having injured your back, you could do with a little help.'

'A little help! You're ...' She lost track of what she was going to say, distracted by his comment about her voice. 'You're bloody well taking over my life!' she concluded feebly.

He winced. 'Not deliberately, I assure you. I was simply going to say, if you'll let me have your keys I'll get someone to sort out your car problem.'

'You're doing it again!' Joanna raised her eyes to the heavens, almost choking on her exasperation. 'You are quite the smuggest, most infuriating human being I have ever met. You seem to believe that I'm totally incapable of doing anything for myself!'

'Smug?' He looked hurt. 'I can't help it if my inner humility just doesn't show. Anyway, about your car – I think you'll agree that it's not driveable?'

'Of course it isn't!'

'OK. But you'll need some sort of transport by Monday, to get to work. Can you get your car fixed by then?'

'I don't know. Probably not.' She wouldn't be going to work on Monday, but that was definitely none of his business.

'I can. I know a man.'

'I'm sure you do. Another bloody expert, I suppose, like your bloody physio?'

'He *is* very good,' admitted Matthew. 'And a big advantage of leaving it to me is that you could go indoors and have a proper rest.'

'You are quite insufferable, you know that?' Joanna foraged in her handbag and fished out her car keys. 'Here. And don't you dare pay the man yourself!'

'Naturally.' His face was perfectly solemn. 'I'll call you this evening and give you a progress report.'

After he had gone Joanna felt an enormous sense of relief. She sat in the big armchair in her drawing-room, leaned her head against the chair back, and let the tensions ease out of her neck and shoulders. Matthew Clements was quite right: she needed a rest. In particular, she needed a rest from Matthew Clements. There was just so much unflappable efficiency a girl could take.

An hour later, stretched out on the sofa, half-asleep and comforted by the undemanding sounds from Classic FM, she was jolted awake by the bleeping of the phone. She started to rise, then changed her mind as her back protested. She didn't want to talk to anyone, anyway. The answering machine could cope with it.

The machine whirred and clicked and finally spoke.

'This is Matt Clements,' the now-familiar voice said. 'Just to let you know that the mechanic has taken away your car, and left you a courtesy car to use, since your own vehicle won't be ready before Tuesday, at the earliest. The car is a Citroën, and it's parked in your space at the end of the road. I'll put the keys through your letter-box. I hope you're resting, and that the rest is doing you good.'

A few minutes later she heard the keys rattle through the letter-box. Matt had written a note to go with them. *Here's the number of the car workshop. Ask for Mack. If you give him your insurance details and the police crime number, he'll sort it all out for you.* She was slightly disappointed that he hadn't signed it. She was quite curious to see what his signature looked like. His writing was something of a surprise. She would have associated his methodical nature with a small, neat, square hand, but Matt's writing was both jagged and expansive, full of odd curlicues and flicks of the pen.

Now that she had rested she began to feel a little more charitable towards the man. He meant well. And he couldn't help being a tidy-upperer. In his own way, he was quite interesting. He was certainly different, that was for sure. A bloke who can tell you you're attractive and your voice is gorgeous, and then not make a pass at you is quite a rarity. Perhaps they could be friends after all.

In the middle of her reverie she suddenly remembered something. She sat up gingerly and switched off the radio. 'Bugger, bugger, bugger,' she said, rhythmically in time with the music. She had promised to go into school that afternoon and pick up her belongings.

When she had collected the exercise-books and written notes for whatever poor sod had to take over her duties, she rang Mrs Milner. Yes, Mrs M said, she would be there to help. She was really distressed to hear about Joanna's accident, and before she rang off, she said 'Get Well Soon', in a voice that suggested she feared the worst.

It was obvious that Mrs Milner knew nothing about Joanna's

suspension; and Joanna was suitably grateful. 'God bless you, Piers Atherton,' she muttered. 'You may be a selfish, ambitious slave-driving sod, but at any rate you know how to be loyal.' The thought cheered her enormously. If someone like Piers could stand by her, surely she could count on the loyalty of her real friends? That was what she was determined to believe, anyway.

The courtesy car was OK, but its very existence reminded her of the venomous graffito on her beloved Ford. The memory was depressing, and the nearer she got to the school the lower her spirits became. However, when she got there she was surprised at how busy the place was, and how different the atmosphere seemed from the normal working day. It was unnervingly quiet, for one thing, considering the number of people about, but the big difference – the one that made the school so eerily unfamiliar – was its air of cheerful friendliness. She supposed it was because the place was full of volunteers, rather than conscripts.

Clearing the little cupboard-like office she had used for pastoral work took hardly any time at all. She left her few coloured prints and the potted plant for the next occupant, and when she had tidied up the files and emptied the drawers of the desk she had only half-filled the cardboard box she had brought. The pile of exercise-books which she had crammed into the box, she had left in the staff room with a note for the head of department. The burden she had to carry home was far lighter than the one she had brought.

Standing in her tiny office she was suddenly overwhelmed by the conviction that this would be the last time she would be here – that she would never see the place again. The thought had been there, unacknowledged, from the beginning – she had decided to leave the prints and the plant *for the next occupant*. It was ludicrous, of course – the stupid accusation by the Tanner boy was bound to be cleared up in a couple of days, and she would be back at work as normal – but the feeling wouldn't go away. Hard on the heels of this foreboding came another unwelcome thought: if she didn't ever come back, would anyone miss her? Maurice Banks probably would, but what about the kids? Would they feel that she had deserted them – let them down? Probably not, she decided with a wry smile. Kids were pretty tough and unsentimental on the whole.

When she got back to the secretary's office, Mrs Milner had gone home, and a woman Joanna had never met before took the keys and locked them away.

Unbidden, the memory of Darren Palmer and his book-token came into her mind, and with it the recollection of her own anger and frustration at having to disappoint the boy. Well, now she was discovering for herself what it was like to feel helpless, to be pushed around by forces outside her control. On impulse, she pulled writing paper and an envelope out of her cardboard box. She addressed the envelope to the school secretary.

> Dear Annie, she wrote, I meant to give you this on Friday, but with one thing and another, I forgot. It's a part-payment from Darren Palmer towards the summer camp at the Windgate. I understand he earned most of it himself, doing a paper round and cleaning cars, etc. He won a book-token in a competition, and sold it for cash – he's that keen! I don't know what the final cost will be, of course, but I'm sure he'll work hard to make it up. He's a good kid. I meant to have brought this to you in person on Monday, but obviously I can't. Warm regards, Joanna.

She tucked the letter into the envelope and added a cheque for a hundred pounds. There were a few untruths in the note, but she didn't care. She had made a gesture, and it felt good.

In the car going home, she sang a few bars of 'Hear Ye, Israel', which was probably in the wrong key but had a satisfyingly Mendelssohnian ring to it.

CHAPTER 8

For the second night in a row Joanna needed to take pills in order to sleep. The moment she closed her eyes her head began to ache with anxiety. Why had the wretched Nick Tanner made such a monstrous accusation about a teacher he had never even met? But more worrying still, why had he made that disgusting phone call? Could it be that he was mistaking her for somebody else? He didn't use her name: he called her "miss". Had another teacher seduced the boy and borrowed her name? Or was it somehow connected with all the publicity she had received after the *Elijah* concert?

Who had passed on the gossip to Patrick Pringle? And how many other people had heard it? Even if she was cleared, would any of the mud stick? She had no answers to any of the questions, but they nagged relentlessly at her. It seemed an age before the sleeping pills took hold and swamped the turmoil in her mind.

In the morning she felt terrible. Somehow she forced herself to do her back-stretching exercises, then showered, dressed, and tried to settle down with the Sunday papers; but she simply couldn't concentrate. She felt as if her head was stuffed with wet cotton wool. Even the knowledge that she had no marking to do, no lessons to prepare for Monday morning, failed to cheer her. Nick Tanner haunted her like a sickness of the mind, blighting her day.

Gloomily, she stared out of the window at her garden. It was a beautiful spring morning, fresh with dew and sparkling in the sun: the sort of day to lift any heart. But not her heart; not this day. In fact, she thought it was really perverse of the weather to look so cheerful when she was feeling so grey.

Next door Matthew Clements was standing in his garden, staring intently at something at his feet. He was standing so still that she didn't notice him at first. When she did, some unexplained impulse made her hurriedly throw on a coat and scarf and step outside. His smile did more than the weather could to lighten her heart.

'You're looking better,' he said; which was obviously an exaggeration. 'But shouldn't you be resting?'

'I'm going for a walk,' Joanna said brightly. 'Janice recommended walking as the best exercise I could do.' The moment she said this she convinced herself that Ms Pounder would have used those very words, had she thought of it.

'Ah.' If Matthew noticed the hint he showed no sign of taking it up. Frowning, he continued his contemplation of the flower-bed. Joanna realized that she would have to lead the conversation.

'Doing a spot of gardening?' she asked brightly.

'Gardening? Oh Lord, no. I don't know the first thing about it. No, I was fascinated by this sorry-looking plant here. Is it dead, or just shamming? Everything else in the garden looks positively frisky, but this poor fellow appears to have shuffled off his mortal coil. I mean, he's so thin and emaciated, I can't even guess what he might have been in life.'

Joanna felt ever so slightly smug. 'It's an Aronia.'

'Get away!' Matt was visibly impressed. 'An Aronia, eh? Quite apart from the fact that I don't know what that is, I'm blowed if I know how you can identify it from this stunted twig.'

'I watched Mr Gelson put it in,' Joanna confessed. 'I told him at the time it wouldn't take. I tried to grow one in my previous garden, but the soil here is just too chalky and dry – the Aronia hates that. You might save it with lots of mulch and liquid fertilizer, but I wouldn't bank on it.'

'Mulch?' Matt handled the word carefully, as if it might be dangerous. 'I don't really see myself as a mulcher. I'm afraid I must let poor Aronia go to that great herbaceous border in the sky. Should I yank it up now, or wait until dark?'

'Bite the bullet,' Joanna advised. 'Delay just makes it harder.'

'Right,' Matt said a moment later. 'I too am about to take a walk. Should we walk together?' Which showed that, given time, he could take a hint as well as anybody.

They climbed up the raised bank of the Causeway, and walked along the canal towpath, since Matt wanted to see how the work on the bridge was progressing. As usual on a fine Sunday morning, there were plenty of people strolling up there, although at this end the canal was little more than a wide, shallow ditch crammed with scrubby vegetation, with not a glimmer of water to be seen. Further out, beyond the new bridge and Oughton Lock, where the urban sprawl gave way to open fields, the watercourse was in better condition, though both banks were thickly overgrown with bush and bramble. Not many people walked as far as the old lock house at Oughton, and only a few hardy souls braved the spiny thickets beyond.

Matt was as enthusiastic about the canal as a child with a new toy. He praised everything: the vision and daring of the eighteenth-century architects, the craftsmanship of the stonemasons, the sheer brawn of the diggers and earth-movers – the "navigators", as he called them. And, of course, the cunning of the engineers. 'The first thing they had to be sure of,' he told her, 'was the water supply. Not only did they have to fill the channel, they had to top it up constantly. Every time a lock opened, more water was lost downstream. That's why the Causeway is where it is.'

'There's a water supply there?'

'The Alder Brook. The stream that gave Aldersgrove its name. But of course, in hot weather the stream occasionally dried up, so they had to have an emergency supply. They dug a huge underground reservoir.'

'In Aldersgrove?'

'Just outside. In Knowley Hill.'

'I never knew that. Is it still there?'

'Indeed it is. The local water company owns it now.'

They walked on in silence for a while, Joanna looking at the scruffy, unkempt channel and trying to see the beauty that so inspired Matt. 'And you're going to restore all this to its former glory?' she asked.

He laughed. 'I doubt it. My firm's been hired to do a preliminary survey of the whole sixteen-mile stretch, assess the work to be done, and make some estimate of the likely cost. The first thing I had to tell them was that the whole exercise was pointless unless they completely rebuilt the Canal Road bridge. The old bridge was really struggling to cope. It had been shored up and patched so much over the years that it was just a sad old mess.'

'I understand that new bridge is your design?'

'Yes.' He tried to sound modest, but it didn't work. His face grew quite pink with pleasure. 'I love bridges,' he said warmly.

But when they reached the bridge Joanna realized that in its present state its charm depended entirely on her imagination. Two dense thickets of scaffolding faced each other across a sea of mud surrounded by vast machines, heaps of stones and metal, and a random scattering of portable sheds.

Matt was clearly entranced by the sight. The work was progressing really well, he told her; and he tried to explain, with graceful gestures of his arms, how the two structures would inch towards each other and meet gloriously in the middle. His enthusiasm was so intense that she suspected he would be quite content to spend the rest of the day in happy contemplation of the view.

But after only a few minutes he turned away from his bridge and looked solicitously at her.

'How are you feeling? Would you like to turn back now, or walk on a little further?'

'Let's go on. I'm sure it's doing me good.' The uncharitable thought crossed her mind that what he really wanted was to view his bridge from the other side, but she couldn't complain about that. After all, she had practically bullied him into accompanying her. This was what she had wanted from the moment she had seen him from her window. But to be brutally honest, it wasn't particularly *his* company she needed. Just company.

They walked on in silence, Matt carefully adjusting his pace to hers. To her surprise he didn't look back at his bridge or even comment on it. He seemed perfectly content to be quiet. Occasionally he glanced at her face, as if he was about to say something; but each time he decided against it.

Soon they reached the edge of the town, where the warehouses, workshops and housing estates gave way to open fields. Joanna exclaimed with pleasure at the sight. The sun was warm on her back; in the clear light the speckles of fresh green leaf in the hedgerow glittered like tiny jewels. There were lambs in the fields, as bouncy, excitable and shy as nursery children, and in the tangled undergrowth of the old water-channel, she noticed for the first time scattered clusters of marsh-marigold, primrose and periwinkle, shining in the sun like new paint. She pointed them out to Matt, cheerfully aware that she was winning a totally undeserved reputation as a horticulturalist. He was impressed, and said so, but tactfully didn't press her for more information. Instead, possibly prompted by her more relaxed mood, he said: 'I'm sorry I talked so much shop, back there. I got carried away. You must have been very bored.'

She was quick to reassure him. 'No, not at all. It was very interesting. I'm so envious of people who are really in love with their work.'

'Envious?' He was puzzled. He obviously didn't know how to respond. Embarrassed, he let the matter drop, and they walked on again in silence.

Joanna, too, was puzzled. She had the feeling that something important had just been said, and she had missed it. It took her several minutes to work out what it was; and with the realization came a rush of emotion that took her quite by surprise. Of course! All that ebullience, all that enthusiasm for the work he was doing, had been bottled up inside him! He needed to share it with someone! He needed someone who would understand what his work meant to him, rejoice in his triumphs, bring comfort to his disappointments.

She felt a sudden rush of warmth towards him, of fellow-feeling. She remembered, after the *Elijah* concert, the heady feeling of success, the congratulations, the exhilarating knowledge that she had excelled herself. And afterwards, the dejection at coming home to an empty house, the loneliness, the frustration, the restlessness. Yes, she and Matthew Clements had something in common, after all.

But the fellow-feeling was simple friendliness, nothing more. His wasn't the sort of face that quickened the pulse. He was personable enough, but she just couldn't imagine seeing him across a crowded room and feeling that the evening was enchanted. So long as there was some emotional distance between them she could feel comfortable in his company.

She was pleased to see that there were far fewer people along this stretch, where the path was uneven, overgrown with grass and weeds, and here and there barred with brambles and waist-high nettles. However, judging by the unlovely litter of beer-cans, cigarette packets and other debris on each side of the path, it was not completely neglected. Matt asked her several times whether she wanted to turn back, but by this time she had convinced herself that the walk really was doing her good, and she pressed on determinedly to Oughton Lock.

Where the lock itself had once been nothing was left but a deep pit, more than half-filled with cans and plastic bottles, and surrounded by a sagging barbed-wire fence. In stark contrast, on the bank at the far side of the pit stood an impressively huge tangle of blackthorn, sparkling with blossom.

The lock house itself was still standing: doorless, windowless, but with most of the roof intact. Though derelict, it still had its uses apparently, for as well as the obligatory piles of discarded beer cans, its floor was generously littered with used condoms.

Below the lock the outline of the old canal was much clearer. Long stretches of the canal walls were plainly visible though the dense tangle of weed and scrub; and in the centre of the channel the forest of reeds parted here and there to show pools of clear water.

There was a little huddle of machinery on the other side of the waterway: a tractor, a bulldozer and some earth-moving equipment; and Matt hurried to explain their purpose.

'We're blocking off a hundred-yard section of the canal just here,' he said. 'We'll pump out the water, clear the silt and debris and have a look at the canal bottom. If the lining is in good condition – as I hope – it will cut millions off the cost of repair.'

Joanna wasn't sure that she wanted to see order imposed on the scene of picturesque decay, but she smiled tactfully. 'Will it take long?'

'Two or three weeks. It depends on how long it takes to pump the water out. We're putting the pumps and the generator down there, as far away from the town as possible, because of the noise.'

Joanna nodded, but she hadn't taken any of it in. The towpath here was muddy and pot-holed, and she was having to pick her way very carefully. But soon their way was barred by a thick jungle of bramble and ground-elder, and they had no choice but to turn back. Matt was determined not to monopolize the conversation on the return journey.

'Tell me about the Mendelssohn concert. Did you really step in at the last moment?'

'I didn't have a lot of notice,' Joanna admitted. 'I mean, I'd read in the papers that Amelia de Courcy wasn't in the best of health, but I assumed that her agent would supply another soprano in her place. I still don't know why that didn't happen. In the end, I had just over twenty-four hours to get ready. I did a piano rehearsal with Patrick – our conductor – the night before, and an orchestral rehearsal the next morning.'

'You were very impressive. I assumed you were a professional singer until I was told otherwise.'

'It was what I always wanted to be. It didn't happen.'

'Why not?'

She remembered from their first meeting how direct his questioning could be. The very abruptness of his tone sounded like a criticism. She bridled slightly. 'It just didn't.'

'Sorry, sorry.' His apology was as abject as he could make it. 'I didn't mean to pry. It's none of my business.' Which was exactly what she was thinking.

She relented. 'Look, I'm not being coy. But it's a long story, and I expect it would bore you to distraction.'

'I'm sure it wouldn't. But I would like to understand one thing: surely, with your kind of talent, you could turn professional tomorrow?'

'If I wanted to starve, you mean,' she said mildly. 'I don't have contacts, an agent, a patron – or even a repertoire. Also, I need more training.'

'I see,' he said, obviously not seeing at all. 'But you must have had some training. You couldn't have sung that concert by the light of nature.'

'No.' She sighed, realizing that he was determined to draw the story out of her. 'I was taught music by my grandmother – well, she wasn't actually my grandmother, she was my grandfather's second wife. I spent a lot of my childhood with them, because my father was in the Army, and spent most of his career overseas. Gran was a professional singer, and much younger than Grandad, who was a high court judge. They lived in a huge house in Hampstead. Grandad taught me the piano, and Gran showed me how to sing. The years I spent with them were by far the happiest years of my life.'

Her voice faltered a little at the memory, and Matt gave her a minute or two to recover her composure. 'Look, you just can't leave it there,' he said. 'How did you get from a mansion in Hampstead to a cottage on the Causeway in Aldersgrove?'

Joanna made a wry face. 'It wasn't planned. I was unlucky, and I made some silly mistakes. You really don't want to hear the sordid details.'

'Of course I do,' Matt said candidly. 'But don't talk about it if you don't want to.'

But surprisingly, Joanna found that she did want to. 'I suppose it all began when I met Rose Kelsey—'

'Rose Kelsey!' Matt exclaimed, startled. 'I've heard of her.' He checked himself. 'I'm sorry. Please go on.'

'Rose came to the Hampstead house to coach Marie – my gran – for an important recital. She stayed with us for several days, and Gran coaxed her into giving me a few lessons.' Joanna paused, affected by the memory. 'I can't begin to tell you what it was like. "Inspirational" is such a feeble word for Rose's effect on me. She showed me that when you get a musical phrase right – I mean really, truly right – you stop being plain, ordinary Joanna Godwin, and become …' she halted in mid-stride and turned to face him, her fists clenched with the frustration of trying to express herself properly, 'You become the music itself. Can you understand that?'

He nodded soberly. 'I think so.' And it suddenly occurred to her that she was demonstrating just the kind of enthusiasm for her music that he had over his beloved bridge. The thought distracted her, and she resumed walking in silence. He prompted her: 'So that's where it began. And then?'

'Well, then, I nagged my parents to let me study at the Manchester Art Academy because I knew that Rose taught there, but my father refused to countenance it.'

'Why was that?'

'It was personal, I suppose. He resented Gran's influence over me, for a start. He didn't get on with her – she was his stepmother, after all – and he was always uncomfortable with strong-willed, intelligent women. He wanted all women to be like my mother – pretty and fluffy and feather-brained. Anyway, he insisted that I got a "proper" education first, and so I was packed off to York, where I picked up a rather poor third in maths, along with a rather poor husband.' She smiled ruefully at the memory. 'My first big mistake. Lewis was so incredibly handsome, I was totally besotted at first sight. He was studying law, and he told me he intended to be a famous barrister; but I wouldn't have cared if he'd told me he planned to be a famous axe-murderer. I wanted him, and I was determined to have him. We were married within the year, which may explain why I got such poor exam results.'

Matt was listening intently. 'And what did your parents think of all this?'

'Shrewd question,' Joanna said drily. 'They were appalled – my father particularly. "He's an empty vessel," he said several times, but it took me a year and a half to understand what he meant. You see, I adored Lewis – but not half as much as Lewis adored Lewis. He was vain, egotistical, and quite incredibly stupid. He flunked his exams, of course – so badly, that the university advised him not to bother trying again. Even before graduation day I knew I had made a ghastly mistake.'

'So you divorced him,' Matt said in his usual blunt fashion. 'Was it a messy divorce?'

'Look, I wish you'd stop being so brusque. I feel as if I'm being cross-examined here.'

'Sorry, sorry.' He looked genuinely contrite. 'I don't mean to be rude. It's just that I'm impatient to know what happened next. Please go on.'

'Well, Lewis and I didn't split up immediately. We moved to Manchester – I was determined to study with Rose Kelsey if I possibly could. I hadn't given up my ambition, you see. Lewis just tagged along, because he couldn't think of any alternative. We rented a flat, and I got a job with Social Services. Lewis had several jobs – he never managed to hold one down for longer than six weeks. He got bored, or someone insulted him, or the manager's secretary made a pass at him – something always went wrong. Anyway, I could never save up enough money for singing lessons – particularly when I discovered that Rose Kelsey lived out at Aldersgrove. What was worse was that after about a year I was finding my job as a social worker intolerable. I simply couldn't cope on a daily basis with all that ignorance, cruelty and poverty out there. I hit rock bottom, though, when both of my grandparents died within weeks of each other. The judge went first, and then my lovely gran. I can't remember what strain of flu it was that year; but it carried them both off. I was desolate.' She fell silent again, and for once he didn't prompt her with another question. Surprisingly, when she took up the story, she sounded quite cheerful.

'But then, just as I was at my lowest ebb, I had two strokes of luck. First, Lewis got a job as a salesman in a menswear shop – one of the big stores. In no time at all he was spotted by a company executive as a potential male model for their new style range. They tried him out, and he was an instant hit. Fashion photographers swooned over him. In fact, one of them – a very rich and famous lady indeed – swept him out of my life. So, to answer your question, no the divorce wasn't very messy.'

'A stroke of luck indeed. And the second one?'

'My gran left me all her books and sheet music. And quite a lot of money. Enough to buy a little house here, and start studying again with Rose Kelsey.'

'That all sounds too good to be true,' Matt commented wryly. 'Something tells me the Man in the Suit is about to make his entrance.'

'Gerald Dudley, yes. It's hard to believe that I could make the same mistake twice in so short a time, only worse. Much, much worse.' Joanna winced, not at the memory, but because her back had suddenly begun to ache again.

Matt registered the grimace. 'Are you OK?'

'Yes. My back's getting stiff, that's all.'

'You're nearly home. A hundred yards, no more.' Which she could see for herself, but she appreciated his concern and encouragement, none the less. He addressed no more questions to her, but watched her attentively, as if worried that she might stumble. However, he was clearly determined to hear the rest of her story, and said so with his usual directness. 'You must lie down and rest now,' he said sternly. 'And when you are properly rested, you must come round to my house and tell me all about your Big Mistake while I cook a meal for you.'

She was amused and exasperated at the same time. 'Stop ordering me about!'

'I wasn't. I was making a suggestion. You oughtn't to be mucking about in the kitchen in your state. And you owe me the rest of your story. You can't leave me in suspense like this.'

'Can you cook?' It seemed unlikely.

'All men can cook. A bit. I bet even Gerald the Suit could cook something.'

'Don't remind me of Gerald's cooking. He'd use every damned utensil in the kitchen, and never wash up a thing. And everything he dished up tasted as if it had been pickled in salt.'

'Hah!' Matt dismissed Gerald's efforts with a wave of his hand. 'No contest. Tonight, I shall prepare for you a fish soup, a pasta thing with salad, accompanied by a wine hand-picked from my own cellar; and for dessert, a creamy-custardy thing with liqueur in it.'

Joanna was intrigued in spite of herself. 'A pasta thing?'

'A speciality of mine.'

'And a creamy-custardy thing?'

'You'll love it. I can't remember its name, but it's Italian.'

Joanna showed reluctance for form's sake, but there was never any possibility that she would refuse. She really didn't want to spend the evening on her own; and Matt Clements wasn't such bad company, after all.

And the bonus was, that there wasn't the slightest hint of any sexual spark between them. He had told her very firmly that he was happily married; which, even if it was a lie, meant that he didn't fancy her. And she certainly didn't fancy him.

CHAPTER 9

'You've been in the wars, mate,' Mr Guest observed unsympathetically.

Jack Dabdoub shrugged. 'Just a knock.' The cut in his forehead had only needed six stitches, and his lower lip was hardly swollen at all.

What really hurt was that Bottersley had lost 48:16, and not one of the Grimston team had been crippled or even badly scarred.

'All in the day's work, I expect.' Mr Guest clearly had his own ideas about the daily grind of the private investigator. 'Look, I'm sorry to contact you on a Sunday, but I'm off out of town for a couple of days, and I wondered if you'd made any progress?'

Dabdoub had been less than enchanted at being called out on a weekend, but he cheered up when he realized he could bill this Aussie hot-shot for another 500 quid. 'We've made a start,' he mumbled. This was true in the literal sense. So far, he had made three phone calls on his client's behalf. 'I know the name of the officer who led the murder inquiry. He's retired, but I hope to track him down and talk to him some time next week.' He made haste to squash any false hopes. 'It's only a fishing expedition, mind. He's hardly likely to put his hand up and say, "By Golly, I reckon I banged up the wrong guy!" But somebody on his team may have raised the possibility that Tares had an accomplice. What I hope to find out is why they were convinced there wasn't one.'

Mr Guest's frown added more creases to his leathery forehead. 'Yeah. Your young partner here hinted that you tend to look on the negative side. So basically you're telling me there's nothing to report?'

'Not entirely.' Tony, who had put far more hours into the investigation than his boss had, was quick to intervene. 'We've opened up a very interesting line of enquiry. For a start, we've discovered what your mother did for a living.'

'What was that?' Mr Guest's face darkened yet further, as if he expected some scandalous revelation.

'She was an investigator,' Tony said smugly, savouring the moment. 'She worked for what was then called the Department of Social Security. She investigated benefit fraud.'

'You've lost me, son,' Guest admitted. 'What did she do, exactly?'

Tony was in his stride now, enjoying himself. 'There are people,' he said solemnly, 'who claim the dole while they are in gainful employment. They defraud the state. Your mother hunted them down and brought them to justice.'

Guest took time working it out. 'She was a snooper?'

'She was doing a valuable job – saving taxpayers' money.'

'Yeah.' Guest wasn't altogether happy at what he was hearing. As an entrepreneur, he was all for private enterprise, but on the other hand he could see that his ma was doing a job that needed a lot of bottle. 'You're saying that she could have made enemies in her line of work?'

'It's a possibility, and as far as I know it's one that the cops didn't look at. Once they'd built the case against Melvin Tares – fingerprints, stolen goods, eye-witnesses – they were happy to wrap it up.'

'Eye-witnesses?' This was news to Guest.

'He was seen outside the apartment house on the day of the murder.'

'Was there anyone with him? Did the eye-witnesses say?'

'No. He was seen running away, and he was alone.'

Mr Guest didn't like what he was hearing. 'So it looks like this Anita Mons article was a load of bullshit?'

'I raised that possibility right at the start,' Dabdoub said sourly.

Tony brushed the objection aside. 'If, say, two guys have committed a murder, surely their first instinct is to split? If they're gonna run, surely they'd run in different directions?'

'Yeah, OK. So, did these eye-witnesses see anyone else running away? Or acting suspiciously?'

'That's something I'd like to find out,' Tony said. 'Once the cops had fixed on Tares, they didn't ask that kind of question.'

'This guy Tares – was he one of the guys my ma was after?'

'Not for benefit fraud. He wasn't on the dole. He was a low-level crook who did enforcement work for a pair of brothers who ran a drugs-and-prostitution racket.'

'And he was into burglary as well?'

Tony shook his head vigorously. 'No, that's one of the things that make his conviction look dodgy. He had no previous record – for burglary, or anything else. His connection with the Ganja brothers only surfaced after he was banged up. And another curious thing: there was no sign of forced entry into your mother's flat.'

'You're saying my ma let him in?'

'That's what the cops assumed, though they could never explain why she would do that. But suppose—' Tony was becoming more animated by the minute, 'suppose there *was* an accomplice, and that accomplice was someone your mother knew and trusted? That would explain why she let them both in.'

Dabdoub was becoming interested in spite of himself. 'Wait a minute. You seem to be suggesting that this was a planned killing – made to look like a burglary gone wrong. And that would mean that somebody had a motive for murdering Mrs Guest. Any ideas about what that might be?'

'Not yet,' Tony admitted. 'What I'd like to do, is to look through her work files – her list of suspects, and see if I can find any links to the Ganja Brothers.'

'How the hell are you going to do that?' Dabdoub scoffed. 'We're talking over seven years ago. Those files are long gone.'

Tony held his ground. 'Well, I was wondering …'

Guest was on his wavelength. 'She left a lot of papers, yeah. There could be something in there. I put everything she had – furniture, clothes, papers, the lot – in store. I couldn't cope – I didn't know what else to do.'

Tony was jubilant. 'So, the lead we're looking for could be in her private papers. I reckon it's the best chance we've got.'

Charlie Brain, Dabdoub thought. Lateral thinking, or what? 'I was going to ask you what had happened to your mother's effects?' he said artlessly.

'I'll fix it so you have access.' Guest was slightly mollified, but still full of questions. 'These eye-witnesses – did they pick Tares out from an identity parade, or what?'

'No. What happened was, that the body wasn't discovered for two days. It was a cold trail. The police put out a TV appeal, and got a response. Three people saw a big guy running away from the scene – and one of them got the registration number of his car.'

'And remembered it two days later?' Dabdoub was his usual sceptical self. 'That's some memory.'

'Maybe it was a customized number – I don't know the details. Anyhow, once the cops got Melvin Tares the conviction was a formality. They got his fingerprints and hairs at the murder scene, a smear of the victim's blood on his shoe, and some of her jewellery in his possession. He was a sitting duck.'

'And nobody even raised the possibility that someone else might be involved?'

'Not at the trial, certainly. I don't know whether the cops ever considered it.'

Mr Guest sat silent for a while, brooding on what he'd heard. Now that Dabdoub knew how rich the little man was, he found him strangely impressive. 'Well like you said, it's early days,' Guest observed, eventually. 'It looks to me like you got three trails to follow. My ma's papers, the lead detective on the case, and these so-called eye-witnesses. Get to it. When I get back I'll lean on this Anita Mons character, see if she knows more than she's telling.'

'She's a journalist, Mr G,' Tony said, scandalized. 'She'll protect her sources, come what may.'

Mr Guest flashed him a quick, razor-edged smile. 'We'll see. You got your methods, sonny, and I got mine.'

CHAPTER 10

The fish soup turned out to be a lobster bisque, and it came out of a tin. Joanna, her appetite sharpened by a couple of glasses of dry sherry, pronounced it delicious. She looked round the room with interest.

'These little houses all look alike from the street, but inside they're all different. This kitchen, for instance, seems bigger than mine.'

'Does it?' Matt took away her plate and put out clean glasses. 'You wouldn't have said that when I first moved in. I had to put most of Mr Gelson's furniture in store. There was barely room to breathe in here.' He poured wine for them both. 'Now, there is going to be a pause while I create my pasta thing. Relax, drink your wine, and tell me the rest of your story. You had just inherited some money and music, moved to Aldersgrove, and were studying with Rose Kelsey. Then?'

'Then it all went pear-shaped. Rose recommended that I join the local choral society – she had a high opinion of Patrick Pringle, the musical director – and there I met Gerald Dudley.'

'The Suit?'

'The very one. He joined shortly after I did, and caused such a flutter in the dovecotes as you wouldn't believe. Soon it seemed that every woman in the neighbourhood was swooning at the very thought of him. He was tall, handsome in that boyish, floppy-haired way that English women find so irresistible, drove a flash car, wore expensive suits, smiled a lot, – and most important of all – he was practically unattached.'

'Practically?'

'His wife had left him, and he was jolly nearly divorced, he said. Too good to be true? Of course he was. He courted me assiduously from the beginning. "Love at first sight," he told me. He was charming, witty – and refreshingly intelligent. Quite different from poor Lewis, though handsome in the same sort of way, I suppose. When he said that his greatest thrill would be to support my singing career, I realized that he was the perfect man for me. The bonus, of course, was that every woman in the vicinity was green with envy.'

Matt was busy preparing salad. 'But you didn't marry him?'

'No. His wife was being difficult over the divorce, he said. We bought a house jointly in Church Lane, and moved in together.'

'Church Lane? Isn't that the posh area of Aldersgrove?'

'Of course. Nothing but the best for Gerald. My share of the cost took every penny I had: the proceeds from selling my little house, and the money in my bank account.' She waved a hand, as if she was trying to wipe the memory away. 'I know, I know. Don't look at me like that. I was in love. I had taken leave of my senses.'

Matt said nothing. He arranged the salad in bowls and put the chopping-board away. Silently, he refilled both their glasses. Joanna nodded her thanks. 'It's a sordid little tale. I'm sure you're bored with it already.'

Matt didn't answer her directly. 'My pasta thing is almost ready,' he said. 'I usually eat it with a hot crusty roll.'

'That sounds fine to me.'

'Good.' He started ferrying things to the table.

Joanna stared into the dish. 'Fettuccine.'

'Yes.' He looked worried. 'Don't you like fettuccine?'

'I think I'm going to like this. Smells great. *Fettuccine casa Clementi*.' The wine was definitely lifting her mood. 'What's the sauce?'

'I don't know if I can dignify it with a name. It's got ham and mushrooms in it, and some other stuff. I take the view that if you start with olive oil and garlic, it's going to turn out OK.' He sounded casual, but she noticed that he watched her carefully as she tasted the food, and looked relieved when she smiled her approval.

The moment seemed innocuous enough, but it seemed to mark a distinct shift in their relationship. Joanna felt a little flutter of panic at the back of her mind. This man she was chatting to so comfortably was not an old friend, someone she had known and trusted for years. He was a stranger. Forty-eight hours ago, she hadn't even known of his existence. What's more, he had lied to her about being happily married. It wouldn't do to relax too much in his company, not until she had worked out what his agenda really was. As a first step she resolved to go a bit easier on the wine.

She thought again how fortunate it was that Matt didn't have the kind of looks that appealed to her. His hair was more wiry than floppy; and his face wasn't boyish at all. It was a sad face, really, she decided. Except when he smiled. Then he looked quite different, as if he had changed faces with someone else. However, smiling or serious, he wasn't her type. So that was OK then.

Matt let her enjoy her food without interruption for a few minutes, then resumed the conversation in his usual direct fashion.

'What did Gerald Dudley do for a living?'

She hesitated, unsure whether she was flattered or annoyed by his curiosity. 'He called himself an investment adviser. His speciality was arranging mortgages for low-income clients. But he had other irons in the fire – office refurbishment, rent collecting, and so on.'

'I see. I suppose, when you bought the Church Lane house, you both employed the same solicitor?'

'Yes. A personal friend of Gerald's. Another crook. How did you know?'

'It's a classic stitch-up. It would have been much harder for Dudley to cheat you if your interests had been properly represented. With a lawyer on his side, it was all ridiculously easy. Let me guess. You agree to buy the house jointly – on a fifty fifty basis; and you put in your half of the purchase money. But when the time comes to pay up, Gerald is temporarily short of the readies, because—'

'Because his wife is being difficult over the divorce settlement,' Joanna muttered bitterly.

'Exactly. So Gerald has to take out a mortgage – which, his lawyer explains, has to be a joint mortgage, because the house is jointly owned. So now, having put all your money into the house, you are legally responsible for half of Gerald's debt.'

'Which doesn't matter, because he loves me, and I would trust him with my life.' In a strange way, Joanna actually found herself enjoying this cynical, to-and-fro dialogue. She was eating heartily between sentences, and occasionally waving her fork in the air to emphasize her points. 'Do you know, for nearly six months, I believed myself to be deliriously happy? I moved in all my furniture, including my piano – a lovely little Bechstein. There wasn't much of Gerald's stuff – problems with the divorce settlement, of course. But that didn't matter – life was rich and full of promise. The only fly in the ointment was having to ask Gerald for housekeeping money – I hadn't a bean of my own.' That memory was painful, and her cheerfulness began to evaporate. 'Perhaps if I hadn't flown so high, the fall wouldn't have been quite so sickening.'

'When did you find out that he had borrowed a lot more on the mortgage?' Matt had watched her changes of mood with interest, but didn't comment on them.

'Not until the end of that year. And even then, I didn't really appreciate what was happening, because I was in such agony over the break-up of our relationship. I started to suspect that he was having an affair – and I was right, of course – but I was ashamed of my jealousy. I tried to stop myself nagging at him, but I couldn't. I lost sleep, I lost weight; I looked like a haggard zombie. In the end he just moved out, just went, without a word of warning. I never got to speak to him directly again. Afterwards, we communicated solely through lawyers.'

Matt was stony-faced. 'By this time, Dudley had borrowed more than the house was actually worth?' It was not really a question.

'Not only that, but he hadn't made any mortgage repayments after the first couple of months. You can guess the rest. The bank foreclosed; and after a forced sale, I was still in debt. I had to sell my piano.'

'So in short, he made love to you and then cheated you of all your money?'

She was becoming used to his bluntness, but it still made her blink. 'I couldn't have put it better myself. Except that it misses out the worst part – the cruelty, the contempt, the humiliation. The suspicion that he had hated me from the very beginning.'

'Strange, that.' Matt helped himself to more wine and pushed the bottle towards her. 'Do you suppose he had heard about your grandmother's legacy, and imagined it greater than it was?'

'I try hard not to suppose anything of the kind.' Joanna winced. 'It's bad enough that he cheated me. To imagine that he planned it and carried it out in cold blood is really sickening. You must think I'm a total mug.'

'No, I don't think that. Anyone can be conned by a really convincing crook. Is Dudley still around?'

'He's not in gaol, if that's what you mean. He moved away some years ago – to somewhere in Surrey, I believe. But oddly enough, he's in Aldersgrove right now, I've heard. God knows what he's up to. Something evil, I expect.'

Matt's interest in her was real, no doubt about it. He pressed on relentlessly: 'You say that Dudley cheated you out of all your money. How did you survive?'

Joanna took her time answering. 'Why do you want to know?'

Matt held up his hands in apology. 'Sorry, sorry. I was so absorbed, I forgot my manners. Please don't talk about it if it would distress you.'

'Distress me?' Joanna realized that he hadn't answered her question, but allowed herself to be distracted. 'I don't know about that. The fact is, I've never discussed it with anyone. No-one's asked me the question before. How did I survive? The short answer is that my father rescued me. The irony is that he was probably looking to me for emotional support. But at the time I was in such agony over Gerald that I hardly registered Dad's suffering. I was so sorry for myself that I hadn't any sympathy to spare for anyone else.'

Matt raised his eyebrows at that, but said nothing. After another pause Joanna began again, speaking quietly and abstractedly, as if to herself. 'My father adored my mother. They were teenage sweethearts, they married young; and even after more than thirty years of marriage he still thought he was the luckiest man alive. He hated being separated from her, even for a day. She accompanied him on all his overseas tours, whenever it was humanly possible.'

'You told me that you spent much of your childhood with your grandparents.'

'Yes. Unless you understand how devoted my parents were to each other, it's hard to make sense of the rest.' In spite of her resolution, Joanna felt she needed another healthy swig of wine. 'About eight years ago – more or less – my mother began to suffer stomach pains. She went to her doctor, who diagnosed an ulcer, and gave her some pills, which sorted out the problem. A few months later, Dad took her on holiday to America. They had been out there for a couple of weeks – got as far as the Grand Canyon, I believe – when her stomach pains came back, and this time, the pills only seemed to make matters worse. She was whisked into hospital, and in a very short time they told Dad that she had cancer. It was operable, they said, but – this being America – it was expensive. Dad had no travel insurance, so he had to find the money himself. After the operation she went into a convalescent home – which also cost money. She lived for another ninety-five days – I know that, because my father mentioned it a thousand times. When she died, he brought her home to England – and the day after her funeral, he had a stroke.' Joanna's voice faltered, and she took a few moments to recover herself. 'It didn't affect him too badly – his speech was a little blurry, and his memory played him tricks, but his physical co-ordination was OK. Emotionally though, he was a mess. He simply didn't know how to cope without my mother. He couldn't bear to live in the house they had shared, so he sold it, and moved up here, to be near me, his closest relative. It was he who bought number seven, next door.'

Matt looked as if he was trying to keep up. 'At that time you were still living in Church Lane?'

'Just about. I was still fighting to hold the relationship together. I couldn't bring myself to face reality. But in the end I had to. Gerald broke my spirit and left me penniless. I moved in with my father, thanking God I had some refuge to go to.'

'What did your father think about Gerald Dudley?' Matt stood up and began clearing the table. Joanna offered to help, but he waved at her to sit down.

She shrugged. 'I don't know. I don't think he really registered what had happened to me. He grew more and more confused and irrational. He was obsessed with the idea that the National Health Service was responsible for my mother's death – if only they had got the diagnosis right, he kept saying, she would be alive today. He blamed the government for the shortcomings of the NHS; and he said he was ashamed to belong to a country that could let such things happen. He wrote angry letters to the press, which were never published because they were so incoherent. My friends would tell me they'd seen him walking along the street gesticulating angrily and muttering to himself.'

'Didn't he get help from anyone?' Matt was busy at the stove, holding an egg-whisk in one hand and a bottle in the other. 'There are plenty of organizations out there offering support to ex-servicemen.'

'I think he was too bitter and resentful to turn to anyone. He was pleased when I moved in with him. He welcomed the company, but apart from letting him talk endlessly about my mother, there was little I could do to ease his misery. Unbelievably, things got even worse. The War Office wrote to him that they had miscalculated his pension, and had been paying him too much. They would have to adjust the payments. It wasn't a huge reduction – in fact it was so insignificant, I wondered why they bothered – but to my father, it was a betrayal, a rejection. He was cruelly hurt. He sent back all his medals. And he said he'd make them pay, though what he meant by that, I can't imagine. He had another heart attack, which left him semi-paralysed. When he died, a few months later, it was actually a relief – to both of us.'

She was distracted by the arrival of Matt's 'creamy-custardy' pudding in glass bowls. 'That looks like zabaglione,' she said.

'Does it?' He eyed the mixture with new respect. 'You're good at remembering the names of things, aren't you. Fettuccine, aronia, periwinkle – and now this. You take one look at this featureless yellow blob, and pronounce it zabaglione. How come you can recognize all this esoteric stuff, but not remember faces?'

'It's a handicap,' she admitted humbly. 'Some people are colourblind, some are tone-deaf. I forget faces. It's probably a genetic flaw. I bet there are millions of people out there with the same problem.' Now that he had stopped cross-examining her about her life she was determined not to give him another opportunity. 'You said you rented this place to be near the reconstruction work on the canal. Do you live far away?' She took some pleasure in imitating his directness of manner.

'I've got a place in Cheshire, a few miles outside Wilmslow. It's not all that far away, but I didn't fancy commuting. And this house happened to be available.'

'"A place in Cheshire". That sounds rather grand.'

He acknowledged her teasing with a wry smile. 'It's an old farmhouse. I've made some improvements, but it still needs work. I wouldn't call it grand.'

'And your wife – she has a career, too?'

He translated the sub-text good-naturedly. 'You mean, why isn't she here with me? She's in Devon at the moment.'

'On holiday?'

'In a way. She's been ill, and now she's convalescing.'

'Convalescing?' That wasn't what Janice Pounder had said. 'I'm so sorry. You must miss her.'

'Yes.' He didn't seem put out by her questioning, but he obviously wasn't going to volunteer any information. To her surprise, he had yet another question for her. 'So you inherited your house from your father?'

'Yes, bless him. He didn't own anything else – I guess my mother's medical bills must have been horrific – but he left me the house. I still had to work for a living, but at least I had a roof over my head.'

He frowned slightly, as if something she had said puzzled him; but it seemed that his curiosity was satisfied, at least for the moment. But now that he had run out of questions he had also run out of conversation. He seemed abstracted, as if his mind had wandered onto other topics, and for the first time that evening their talk became stilted and desultory. She sensed that he had become bored and, after another awkward silence, she announced that she ought to be going.

Infuriatingly, he was prompt to agree. 'Ah yes. A working-day tomorrow,' he said brightly; to which she responded with a non-committal smile.

But as she was leaving she glanced in at the open door of the drawing-room, and came to an abrupt halt. 'You've got a piano!' she said accusingly.

She sounded so indignant, that he was instinctively apologetic. 'It's not a very grand one, I'm afraid. Just a little upright.'

'It's one of those Japanese jobs.' She stepped into the room for a closer look. 'I know that make. Costs a fortune and sounds like a concert grand. You never told me you could play!' She knew it was unreasonable of her to be so irritated with him, but she couldn't help it. On Friday, he had let her rabbit on about the canal, when he knew all about it, and today she had waxed lyrical about music, assuming he was just another tone-deaf punter, when all the time he was a pianist himself! And judging by his competence in other fields, he was probably a bloody good one! He really was the most infuriating man she had ever known.

'I'm sorry – I thought you knew.' If Matt thought she was being illogical, he showed no sign of it. 'I mean – your living-room is just the other side of that wall. You must have heard me practising.'

'Never.' She relented, but only a little. 'You must have done it while I was out.'

'I expect so.' He seemed to be humouring her. 'Actually, I'm glad to hear you say it. I expect my poor efforts would drive a proper musician crazy.'

She laughed, her irritation gone. 'You really don't do modesty very well at all, Matthew Clements. I bet you're a corker at the keyboard.' She was pleased with the phrase, and giggled at her own wit. 'Anyway, I ought to be apologizing to you. Like you said, I'm just the other side of that wall. Hearing me go through my scales and vocalizes must be absolute hell for you.'

For one heart-stopping moment she thought he was going to agree with her; but of course he made the only correct response. 'Not at all,' he said gallantly.

Naturally he insisted on seeing her home, which involved escorting her to the end of his front garden, and waiting by her front gate until she was safely inside her own house. On the way she debated with herself how she would respond if he attempted to kiss her goodnight, and decided that it would be churlish to resist too strenuously, though she would be careful not to be too encouraging, either, but in the event her planning was unnecessary. He didn't offer to embrace her and, as far as she could tell, the idea never even crossed his mind.

He did express the hope that her back would soon get better, and he mumbled something about really enjoying her company, but on the whole his attentiveness and courtesy made her feel like a particularly frail maiden aunt. She rewarded him with her most charming smile, but she couldn't help thinking that it was bloody infuriating not to be kissed when one had made up one's mind to put up with it.

Later she examined her face closely in the mirror as she removed her make-up. Perhaps she was getting old.

Matthew Clements stacked the dishwasher, and settled down in an armchair with a large brandy. There were things he needed to think about. His relationship with Joanna Howard had developed so quickly, and out of such an unpromising beginning that he felt he had been improvising his response to her from minute to minute, and getting it wrong more often than he got it right. The sharpness of her hostility towards him at that first encounter in Buchanan's had put him on the back foot right at the start, and it seemed that he had been trying to catch up ever since. Her excuse for snubbing him – that she was hopeless at remembering faces – seemed pretty shaky at the time; even if it were true, he took little comfort from it. The brutal truth was that she had taken an instant dislike to him, and everything he had done from that moment sprang from his bloody-minded determination to make her change her mind.

With hindsight it was obvious what an idiot he had been. Wounded pride, or something equally puerile had made him behave like an idiot. He hadn't been straight with her. He had pretended ignorance when he knew all the facts; he had lied to her – by implication, if not directly, and worse, the remark about his wife Mary was an outright lie, and a really stupid one.

And then, all the effort he had put in, trying to impress her! Bullying Janice Pounder, bribing Mark at the garage, boasting about his bloody bridge! Just thinking about it made him cringe. All that, just because a pretty woman had told him, in effect, to piss off? He needed his head examined.

And yet, and yet ... It was really hard to face up to the truth. He was a rational man, yet what he was feeling wasn't rational at all. A reasonable man doesn't fall idiotically in love at first sight. That was for poets and madmen. Well, he wasn't a poet, so he must be mad. He was certainly confused.

He could still remember, with all the clarity of a digital recording, his first sight of her. She was hurrying down the garden path, on her way to work. She greeted him with the kind of absent-minded politeness one offers to the virtually invisible, and passed on. And in that one heart-stopping moment his life changed. He had no explanation for it; but there was no point in denying it. From that moment on he had been behaving like a man obsessed. He had hung about in the garden every morning in order to say hello; he had gone to concerts, not for the music, but just to look at her, and when at last he had the chance to make her acquaintance, he had leapt at it like a trout to a fly.

And now he was hooked. If only she had turned out to be stupid, or bigoted; if only she had a voice like a squealing tyre; if only there was something about her that he could dislike or despise, he could argue himself out of this infatuation. But as it was she was so goddam perfect that every minute he spent in her company just made him more besotted.

Reluctantly he tried to face the facts. Quite apart from the fact that he hadn't yet resolved the problem of his marriage, Joanna just didn't fancy him, and probably never would. If he tried to court her, he would face nothing but disappointment. Sweet reason told him that his best plan was to go away and forget all about her.

His glass was empty and he poured himself another, trying to persuade himself that it would make him less maudlin. Unsurprisingly, it didn't work. To hell with sweet reason, he thought suddenly. Whatever I do, I'm not going to forget her. I'll just stick around and hope, and maybe she'll get used to me.

It wasn't a particularly dynamic plan but it gave him some comfort. His mind at last moved on to other things.

One thing in particular had been bothering him all weekend. It was the photograph in Joanna's house. It stood on the sideboard in her kitchen, and he had found himself looking at it in those embarrassing moments when the undersized fellow in the baseball cap was gabbling about having to break into her house to go to the lavatory.

It was a snapshot of two military-looking gents wearing Norfolk jackets and carrying shotguns, as if for grouse-shooting. It wasn't until afterwards that it occurred to him that there was something odd about the photograph. Several things in fact, unless his memory was playing him tricks. He would really like to take a closer look at that photo.

Another thing that had stimulated his curiosity was Joanna's description of her father's last few years. Something there didn't quite ring true, but again, he couldn't quite put his finger on what it was. It probably wasn't anything important, but he knew it would chafe his mind until he had investigated it.

Finally, there was the piano. Now that really was a mystery.

CHAPTER 11

'N*o, shut up and listen to me. I had to do it, I'd got no choice. And now you've got no choice. You've got to help me, just like last time.*

... Why? Well, let's just say for old times' sake, know what I mean?

... Yes, you are. You're as deep in it as I am, and you know it. It's not just my neck on the block here, Sunbeam. For God's sake, this whole bloody thing was your idea. I don't know why I ever listened to you. I ought to have done it my way, quick and simple. But no, you had to complicate things because you think you're so fucking clever.

... Yeah, yeah, don't go on. It's done, and that's it. You tell me, what else could I have done?

... No, they won't. We'll do it just like last time. Just tell me the details, so we get our stories straight.

... No, tell me now. Tomorrow could be too late. Come on, think! You're supposed to be the brainy one.

... Yeah, that'll do. Let me just write that down. Bet you wish that last bit was true, eh?

... What? What about him?

... No, he won't. He's not that bright.

... What do you think I'll do? I'll deal with it.

... I said I'll deal with it. What's the matter with you? You going soft, or something?

... Look, just forget it. I told you, I'll sort it. Actually, I've already got it in hand.

... Relax. So long as you an' me stick together, we'll be OK. But if one goes down, we both go down. Just like old times, eh?

... No, it's not blackmail, it's just the way things are. But talking about the way things are, I'm dead skint. I don't even have enough money to buy a decent smoke. How about it, partner? Two or three hundred quid would – Hello? Hello?

CHAPTER 12

After some discussion, it was agreed to hold the meeting in an upper room of the Aldersgrove Child Protection Unit, a branch of the social services with its own offices on Corporation Street. It was to be a formal meeting, chaired by the director of the CPU, Mrs Lucy Olivier; with her assistant, Mr Ken Stanley, taking notes. Ms Philippa Crouch was also present, quietly seething with resentment at the fact that her fellow officers, though considerably junior to her in age, were infuriatingly senior to her in rank.

These three were joined by three police officers: Detective-Inspector Theresa Burgage, Sergeant Dewbury and WPC Kylie Barrel. The senior officer was a slim, elegant woman in her early forties; the sergeant, ten years older, was balding and running to fat; while the constable was a broad-shouldered, square-faced young woman with a mouth like a bullet-hole.

Mrs Olivier welcomed them all and got down to business. 'You all know why we are here. Mrs Joanna Howard, a teacher at the Jas Priestley School, has been accused of sexual misconduct, persisting over several months. Her alleged victim, Nicky Tanner, was at one time in her care. This is a serious allegation, and of course must be investigated, but,' she addressed herself to Inspector Burgage, 'bear in mind that your department and mine have different priorities. Ours is the welfare of the child; yours is to bring offenders to justice.'

'I don't see that our separate duties need collide,' Burgage observed coolly. 'But we must also bear in mind the number of false accusations made in recent times, and reported in prurient detail in the newspapers. The tide of opinion is turning – and against the children. If we decide to proceed against Mrs Howard, we must be absolutely certain that we have a cast-iron case.'

The sergeant snorted derisively, but offered no other comment. Load of bleeding hearts, the lot of them. Not one with half his experience. Blind as bats. It wasn't hard to see where this was going to end up.

Lucy Olivier registered Dewbury's reaction, and her face wrinkled in distaste. Macho Neanderthal, she thought. More belly than brains. Dewbury's misogyny was well known: the story was that when his wife divorced him one of her complaints had been that he treated her like a slave; his response was that since God made Adam first the male was clearly superior to the female. He was a class warrior, too; convinced that Theresa Burgage and virtually every officer senior to him had been promoted over him because they were posh and he wasn't. He reserved his deepest dislike, though, for clever women. They made him feel inferior, which was not merely unfair, in his opinion, it was unnatural.

Mrs Olivier ignored him and turned to her co-worker. 'Philippa, I think you should begin. You had contact with the family, and were the first to raise the alarm. Perhaps you could just sketch in the background for us?'

Ms Crouch sat up straight and took some papers from her yellow folder. 'Nick Tanner first came to our attention about eighteen months ago. He and his mother and stepfather – Briony and Fred Steen – were then living in rented accommodation in Dovebridge. A neighbour of theirs reported to us that Fred Steen was often the worse for drink, and in that state frequently beat up his wife and stepson. We investigated this report, and as a result the child was put on the At Risk register. Nick, then aged thirteen, attended the Jas Priestley School where Mrs Howard was a teacher. He got into trouble through striking a male teacher, and came close to being expelled.'

'Excuse me,' the interruption came from Inspector Burgage, 'do we have any details of this assault on the teacher?'

Philippa Crouch shook her head. 'Not to hand, I'm afraid. The school will have some record of it, I'm sure.'

'But your department didn't interview the teacher in question?'

'No.' Ms Crouch sounded defensive. 'I know that he resigned soon after, as a result of the incident, and quit the profession.'

'What's your point, Theresa?' Mrs Olivier wanted to know.

'No criticism intended,' the inspector murmured. 'I was merely wondering about the circumstances. If this case comes to court we can be sure that the defence will make a big play about this incident and the boy's aggressiveness. It's common in abuse cases for the defence to paint the victim as the villain. It would be useful if we could convincingly show that the teacher provoked the boy in some way.'

'I take your point.' However, Mrs Olivier's tone managed to convey her opinion that the point was insignificant. 'Please carry on, Philippa.'

'Yes. Mrs Steen had made representations to us that her domestic situation would be much improved if the family had better accommodation. Our group considered this to be a reasonable proposition, and we managed to persuade the council to offer them a flat on the Wickerbrook Estate in Aldersgrove. Fred Steen got a job at the local hospital as a security officer, and Mrs Steen assured us that the situation regarding domestic violence had definitely improved. We were able to take the boy off the At Risk register. Unfortunately, Nick was just as disruptive at his new school as at his previous one.'

Philippa Crouch paused, and looked up as if she had brought her narrative to a close. Mrs Olivier gently reminded her that there was more to come. 'And your next contact with the family was ...?'

'Yes. About three weeks ago Mrs Steen got in touch with me, in a very agitated state. She wouldn't discuss it over the phone, but when I got to her home she told me that her son had confessed to having had a sexual liaison with Mrs Howard, which had begun in July last year and continued up to the present time.'

'Did you speak to the boy himself?'

'Yes. He was reluctant to talk to me – insisted that what had happened was not a seduction, but a love-affair. He told me several times that he loved Mrs Howard, and expected to marry her as soon as he came of age.' Philippa Crouch became quite animated as she finished, confident that she had saved the best for the last.

But Mrs Olivier had a point to make. 'You say the boy was reluctant to accuse Mrs Howard. Would you say his reluctance was genuine or feigned?'

'Genuine, I'm sure. He was really embarrassed; I don't think he would have spoken at all, if his mother hadn't insisted.'

'Thank you. Just for the sake of completeness, will you tell us what action you took, subsequently?'

'I made a report to the director, and at the next team meeting it was decided to inform the head teacher and the police of the situation.'

Mrs Olivier moved on briskly. 'I understand that the headmaster immediately suspended Mrs Howard from duty?'

'That was my understanding. At any rate, she is not at school today, but apparently the staff have been told that she is on sick leave.'

'That could be a diplomatic move on the head's part. Very good. Thank you, Philippa.' Mrs Olivier addressed herself directly to Theresa Burgage. 'That is the background. Now to particulars. I talked to the Tanner boy myself, in the presence of his mother, with Mr Stanley and Ms Crouch monitoring the interview from an adjoining room. With the mother's permission, I made a recording of that interview, which I would like you all to hear.'

'You got the kid on tape?' Dewbury was indignant. This woman was appropriating police work. 'Is it admissible in court?'

Mrs Olivier shrugged to show her indifference, and Ken Stanley took it upon himself to answer. 'We don't see why not. There were three witnesses besides the mother; and I took the precaution of taking two simultaneous recordings, so that I could give Mrs Steen a copy.' He lifted a compact tape-recorder from the floor and placed it in the centre of the table. Lucy Olivier took up the narrative.

'To answer the sergeant's point directly, this isn't a statement in the strictly forensic sense. I simply wanted to get the boy's story in his own words, and in as much detail as possible. For two reasons: I wanted to know whether his story was plausible and could be corroborated; and I wanted it recorded in case he changed his account later on.' She nodded to Ken Stanley to begin.

Before pressing the play button Ken Stanley felt it necessary to explain something. 'I've skipped the first few minutes of the tape,' he said. 'It's just the date, and the identification of all present. It took rather a long time, because Nicky was reluctant to say his name out loud.' He started the tape, and stood by the machine for a moment, his hand hovering over the volume control.

The first voice they heard was Lucy Olivier's.

MRS O: Well, Nicky, have you finished your Coke? Want another?
NICK: (mumble) No, you're all right.
MRS O: Good. Now, if you're ready, would you tell us about the first time you met Mrs Howard?
MRS STEEN: Now you go easy on him, missus. No bullyraggin', d'you hear? He's upset. He's got to go and see his dad in hospital tomorrow. He's proper poorly, poor man.
MRS O: His father? I'm so sorry, Nicky. I didn't know—
NICK: My real dad. Not old sloppychops.
MRS STEEN: Nicky!
MRS O: Look, I had no idea about ... If you want to do this another time—

MRS STEEN: No, now we're here, let's get it over with. Go on, Nicky. Tell them what you told me.

NICK: Aw, Mum, I don't want to get nobody in trouble. We love each other.

MRS STEEN: Don't talk such bloody rubbish. Get on with it.

MRS O: We understand your concern, Nicky. We're not trying to cause trouble. We just want to get at the truth. Now, when did you first meet Mrs Howard?

NICK: I seen her round the school, but I wasn't in her class. The first time we did it was at Darwen Lowe Farm.

MRS O: That was on the school outing, right?

NICK: At the farm, yeah. She only joined right at the end. Yeah, I will have another Coke.

MRS O: Here you are. Now, take your time. Start at the beginning and tell us exactly what happened.

NICK: I got the flu real bad. That was on the Friday before we were going home on the Sunday morning. They put me to bed in a room in another building, away from the others. The doctor came on Saturday and gave me some stuff. I stayed in bed all day. Miss – Miss Howard came to see me in my room that night. She told me that Miss Bell had gone home early because of an accident, and she'd come to help out just for the one night.

MRS O: Miss Bell was one of the teachers in charge of your group, is that right?

NICK: Yeah. Miss Howard had been with the other lot, at Wingate Camp. They packed up before us.

MRS O: I see. What happened next?

NICK: She fussed around, and made me take a couple of pills. She asked me how I was feeling, and I said not too bad. Then she said she'd look in later, when the other kids had gone to bed, and bring me a hot drink. I think I dozed a bit, because she seemed to come back quite soon. She had a couple of glasses on a tray, and she'd changed.

MRS O: Changed? What do you mean?

NICK: Into a dressing-gown. A black one, with a criss-cross pattern on the pocket. She smelled really nice. She said she'd made me a hot drink, and it looked so good, she'd made one for herself. She had a candle on the tray, as well. She lit it, and turned out the light. She said it was nicer, sharing a drink by candlelight. Then she sat on the bed, and we clinked glasses. It was very nice.

MRS STEEN: (inaudible)

MRS O: Please stay calm, Mrs Steen. We—

MRS STEEN: I said I'll kill the bitch! He's only fourteen!

NICK: What's that got to do with it? It's my life.
MRS O: Now, now, don't let's get into an argument, we'll only waste time. Please go on, Nicky. Tell us about the drink.
NICK: She said it was lemon and honey with hot water and a little whisky. I said it seemed like quite a lot of whisky to me, and she laughed. Then, while we were drinking, she put her hand under the bedclothes.
MRS O: What did you do?
NICK: Nothing. She said she wanted to see if I still had a fever. She undid my pyjamas and put her hand on my chest. Then she slid her hand into my trousers and stroked my thing.
MRS O: Your thing? You mean your ...?
NICK: My dick. She played with my dick. She called it my thing.
MRS O: Did you try to stop her?
NICK: No. I liked it. It was nice. It got big and she pushed the bedclothes right back, and she said ooh what a lovely thing, and she bent over and put it in her mouth. I said Oh Miss, because I was getting too excited, and then she got on top of me, and that was the first time we did it. I came very quick the first time, but the next time took longer. She told me I was quite a man.
MRS O: Did she stay with you all night?'
NICK: No, after the second time she got out of bed and went away. She took the glasses with her, but she left the candle burning. She said shall we do it again, and I said Oh yes, and she said it's got to be our secret, else they'll stop us. Well, she didn't need to tell me that.
MRS O: And did you do it again?
NICK: Yes. Lots of times. We were in love.
MRS O: Where did you go?
NICK: Lots of places. Knowley Castle, the lock house down the canal. Mainly her house.
MRS O: You went to her house?
NICK: Lots of times. Only after dark, though.
MRS O: What can you tell us about her house?
NICK: It's not very big. The stairs are at the back. She's got a green eiderdown with little roses on it, and pillows to match. She's got a photo of two gangsters in her kitchen.
MRS O: Gangsters?
NICK: Yeah. Big, ugly blokes with moustaches.
MRS O: How do you know they're gangsters?
NICK: 'Cause they got guns. Both of 'em. Shotguns.
MRS O: I see. Anything else you can tell me about?
NICK: No ... Yeah. She's got a spare toilet in the bathroom, with a tap on it.

MRS O: A bidet?

NICK: Wharrever. (sniggers) Anyroad, most of the time we was in the bedroom.

MRS O: Yes. Thank you, Nicky; you're being really helpful. Now, just so I get it straight: the first time was last July, in Activities Week?

NICK: Yeah.

MRS O: OK. Apart from that one time, can you remember any other specific dates when you and Mrs Howard ... um, did it?

NICK: Any what?

MRS O: Actual dates, Nicky. It would help us if we knew exactly when these ... er ... meetings took place.

NICK: I dunno. There was lots of times.

MRS O: I understand that. But – well, did you have a regular date? Every Thursday, for instance?

NICK: No, it wasn't like that. She'd give me a wink, and I'd know we were on for that night.

MRS O: I see. But what happened when you left the Jas Priestley and went to another school?

NICK: What do you mean?

MRS O: Well, your new school was ten miles away from hers. How did she tip you the wink then?

NICK: Lots of ways.

MRS O: Like what?

NICK: She'd send me a message.

MRS O: How did she send it? Through the post? A phone call?

NICK: Yeah. Sometimes one, sometimes the other.

MRS O: Did you keep any of her letters?

NICK: 'Course not.

MRS O: Did she phone you at home?

NICK: I dunno. I can't remember.

MRS STEEN: Here, what is this? Who's the guilty party here? This isn't any fun for the lad, you know. Are you calling him a liar?

MRS O: I'm sorry, Mrs Steen. I was just trying to jog Nick's memory. I've nearly finished. Just one more question.

MRS STEEN: Get on with it then.

MRS O: Nicky, what's Mrs Howard's first name?

NICK: What?

MRS O: The woman you love and want to marry. What's her first name?

NICK: Er ...

MRS O: You've been lovers for eight months, Nicky. Funny you never asked her what her first name was.

NICK: I did. You're putting me off.
MRS STEEN: Stop bullying him. You're putting him off.
MRS O: Sorry, Nicky. Are you saying you can't remember?
NICK: 'Course I can. It's – it's Joan.
MRS O: Joan? Are you sure?
NICK: That's what she told me, anyway. I dunno if it's true.
MRS STEEN: Now that's enough. We come here in good faith. You're not going to bully our kid any more.
MRS O: No, of course not. Mrs Steen, may I ask you a question?
MRS STEEN: What?
MRS O: This affair has been going on for a long time. When did you first become aware of it?
MRS STEEN: I got my suspicions weeks ago. He'd stay out 'till all hours, and come home stinking of cheap scent. I could tell he'd been with somebody – I do his laundry, you know. Only I thought it was some girl, and I was afraid he'd get her into trouble. I went on at him and on at him, and finally it all come out. I couldn't believe it. I went to the Social and complained.
MRS O: Thank you, Mrs Steen. And Nicky. You've both been very helpful.

Ken Stanley leapt to his feet and turned off the machine. 'That's it, except for the end-tape idents.'

Sergeant Dewbury's whistle broke the silence. 'Stone me!' It was hard to tell whether he was appalled or amused.

Inspector Burgage was looking sombre. 'Something tells me this is going to be very messy,' she said.

'What!' Dewbury couldn't believe his ears. 'It's bloody open and shut, to my mind. Play that tape in court, and any jury in the land'll convict the bitch.'

'Maybe.' Burgage was conceding nothing. 'Lucy, I couldn't help noticing that your tone changed about half-way through that interview, and your questions got much tougher. Was that deliberate?'

'I hadn't planned it that way, if that's what you mean,' Mrs Olivier said. 'What doesn't come over on the tape is the boy's manner: the expression on his face, his body-language. I suddenly got the feeling that the kid was enjoying himself too much: mocking me, laughing up his sleeve.'

'You thought he was lying?'

'I wouldn't put it as strongly as that. There's a lot of detail in his story that is open to corroboration – the detail of the dressing-gown, for instance, and his description of Mrs Howard's house; but I couldn't help noticing that he was absolutely specific about some things, yet really vague about others.' Mrs Olivier sighed and leaned back in her chair. 'To be absolutely honest, as the interview went on, I was struggling to stay impartial. In my entirely unprofessional view, the child is a ghastly little oik. If he and the Howard woman did have sex, I wouldn't like to bet on who seduced whom.'

'It's still a crime,' Burgage said mildly. 'The adult has to bear the responsibility, especially since this particular adult was in a position of trust.'

'I know, I know. I'm just glad that the pursuit of justice is in your hands and not mine. Now, unless you have any questions, I'd like to get back to my office. Ken has a copy of the tape and a written transcript for you. I would be grateful if you would let me know how your investigation progresses and naturally, if we learn anything, we'll pass it on.'

As soon as the social workers had left the room Dewbury rounded on the inspector. 'Look, let's not pussyfoot around. Why don't we pull in this Howard bitch and lean on her a little?'

Burgage threw him a withering glance. 'Don't you listen to a word I say, Sergeant? There's been a spate of these accusations lately, most of them malicious. Delinquent kids have a go because they reckon the balance of power has tilted their way and against the teachers. Mrs Howard is a high-profile citizen; I'm not going to proceed against her until I've got a rock-solid case.'

'High-profile?' Dewbury sneered. 'I've never heard of her.'

'She distinguished herself at a concert the other week. It was written up in all the papers.'

'I must've missed that. What group is she with? The Molesters?' He cackled loudly at his own wit.

WPC Barrel was not amused. In fact, her expression was slightly glazed, as if she was having trouble keeping up. 'There's things in the kid's statement that we can investigate, ma'am,' she said tentatively. 'That stuff at Darwen Lowe Farm, for instance – I mean, I suppose somebody has confirmed that the kid did have the flu, and that Mrs Howard was called out that night?'

'Philippa Crouch checked that out,' Burgage said. 'But you're right, Kylie. There's a lot of detail that we need to verify.' She ticked them off on her fingers. 'The black nightie with the criss-cross pattern, the green eiderdown; the bidet – that's the kind of thing a working-class kid would notice – and the photo of the guys with guns. If we can find those things in the woman's house we're starting to build a case. So you and I, Constable, are going to have a little nosy round. In the meantime, Sergeant, there are a couple of things you can do. Talk to Mrs Howard's neighbours – discreetly, mind! – and find out if anyone has seen the Tanner boy sneaking in and out of her house. Also, bear in mind that if she *is* a child-molester this incident is unlikely to have been a one-off. See if you can dig up any evidence that she has shown an unhealthy interest in any other boys.'

'Talk to the other teachers, you mean?' The sergeant obviously didn't relish the prospect.

'Start with them, but keep your ears open for any gossip around town. It's not a big place: strange behaviour rarely goes unnoticed.'

'OK.' Dewbury was sulking, and made no attempt to hide it. 'Any chance of a bit of help?'

'Afraid not. The resources just aren't there, Sergeant. We three ought to be able to manage it between us. Particularly if it's as open and shut as you think.'

Dewbury's worst fears were confirmed. These women – these *professional* women – were closing ranks before his very eyes. No way were they going to see one of their own kind go to the wall. One of them had actually called the boy – the victim, mind you! – a ghastly little oik! And Inspector Bloody Burgage had called him "a working-class kid". Call that impartial? He could see all too clearly what was going to happen. The Howard bitch would be tipped off, the evidence would disappear, the poor kid would be discredited and probably wind up in some young offenders' institution. These upper-class university tarts stick together. That was why he – the copper with the most experience – was being elbowed off the case.

But Benjamin Dewbury knew a trick worth two of theirs. He would grease the wheels of justice in his own way.

CHAPTER 13

Joanna answered the phone without thinking. 'Hello?'

'Joanna? Oh, I thought you'd be at work. I was all geared up to leave a message on your answering machine.'

'No, I'm taking a few days off.' Joanna crossed her fingers. 'What is it, Rose?' She was intrigued; she hadn't spoken to Rose Kelsey, her singing teacher, since the day after the Mendelssohn concert.

'Hang on, that changes things. Wait a minute.' The line went dead for more than a minute. Then: 'Does that mean you're free right now?'

'Free for what?'

'Well, um, free to come over here for half an hour or so. I have someone here who would dearly love to meet you.'

'Rose, you're being very mysterious. Who is it?'

'No, I don't want to spoil the surprise. Do come, there's a dear.'

'How could I refuse? Look for me in about twenty minutes.' In truth, it was a welcome diversion; Joanna was already feeling aimless and fidgety at the long empty day stretching before her. Rose couldn't have chosen a better time to spring her surprise, whatever it was.

Her mood changed when she stepped outside and saw the courtesy car in her parking space. She had momentarily forgotten – or subconsciously put out of her mind – the damage to her own car, and the sight of the Citroën was an unwelcome reminder of her predicament. All the fears that she had been trying to suppress flooded into her mind. The accusation had been horrible enough; but the vandalism of her car pushed the horror of it into another dimension. She had deliberately tried to ignore the implications of it, but now she had to face the brutal fact: Nick Tanner's accusation wasn't just a random piece of mischief-making. For some unfathomable reason the kid was out to get her. She couldn't think why, and she couldn't think what to do about it.

But there had to be something she could do. After her visit to Rose Kelsey she would sit down and think about the problem seriously. As she drove away she remembered that she still hadn't phoned Mack, the helpful garage man.

Rose Kelsey's house was on the outskirts of town, overlooking the fields that sloped down towards Oughton Lock. It was a big house, comfortable rather than stately, and she shared it with her sister and a devoted cook-housekeeper, who cosseted them both as if they were royalty.

Rose had the front door open before Joanna stepped out of the car. 'Welcome, welcome!' she cried, beaming. 'Come in, come in!' She led the way, not into the drawing-room, as Joanna had expected, but upstairs to her vast studio, where a slim, elegantly dressed woman sat at the smaller of the two pianos, marking a musical score with a pencil. 'Here she is!' Rose announced happily, though it wasn't immediately obvious which of the two women she was referring to. 'Joanna Howard – Angela Bonneville. Now, I'll leave you two to talk, while I go and sort out Mrs Triffid. You're both staying to lunch.' She waved her arms about extravagantly. 'Now don't argue. I want to hear all about it!'

'She doesn't waste time on idle chat, does she?' The slim woman chuckled. 'Still, I'm sure you know her as well as I do. I'm Angela Bonneville, by the way.'

Joanna was overcome with shyness. 'I heard Rose say it, but I couldn't bring myself to believe it. Angela Bonneville? Here in Aldersgrove?'

'I used to live here. In fact, I still own a house here, though the only time I get to use it is when I'm recuperating after a long tour.'

Still shaken, Joanna made haste to apologize. 'I'm sorry if I overreacted. I'm just not used to meeting the ultra-famous. Rose really should have warned me. As you've probably gathered, I'm a huge fan of yours. I think your records are fabulous.' She checked herself: nervousness was making her babble.

Angela laughed: a deep, throaty sound, incongruous from so slim a frame. 'Rose is my oldest friend, but she can be very naughty sometimes. As for your reaction, I thought it was charming. And very flattering. Most people, when they meet me for the first time, say "Ah, you're the pianist," as if I didn't know what I did for a living.' She took a pace backward, and put a finger to her lips as if she was examining a work of art. 'The truth is, Mrs Howard, that I'm a fan of *yours*. Not only do you have a lovely voice, but you are even more beautiful close up than from a distance.'

Joanna gasped. She felt elated and embarrassed all at once; and the only response she could manage was to go very red in the face. Miss Bonneville pretended to ignore her reaction, and went on: 'I was fortunate enough to hear you sing at the Mendelssohn concert, and I badgered Rose to set up this meeting. I have a favour to ask.'

'Oh?'

'Yes. I don't know whether you have heard of a singer called Christina Hauptmann?'

It was like asking a priest if he'd heard of the Pope. Hauptmann was already being called the voice of the decade, with the critics comparing her favourably with classical divas such as Milanov, Tebaldi and Los Angeles. 'Yes,' Joanna said weakly, 'I've heard of her.'

'We got quite pally in New York, and – well, to cut a long story short, she's asked me to accompany her on her next recording. This is quite a challenge for both of us. She hasn't done a *lieder* recital for years, and I'm not what you would call experienced as an accompanist. Another complication is that her schedule doesn't give us much rehearsal time. So I wondered if you would be kind enough to help me out?'

Joanna's mouth was dry. 'In what way?'

'Singing, of course. I'd like you to rehearse the programme with me.'

'Me?' This couldn't be happening. 'You want me to sing for you?'

'I would be really grateful. There is so much I could learn from you.'

Joanna felt a trembling in the pit of her stomach. 'Do you mind if I sit down?'

Angela was instantly contrite. 'Sorry, sorry! I'm so clumsy when I get excited. The moment I heard you, I knew you'd be perfect. Christina has what I call a "Mozart" voice – and so do you. And then, when Rose told me you were a pupil of hers, I was convinced. This is Fate. God sent you when I needed you most.'

'Ms Bonneville—'

'Call me Angela, please.'

'Angela ...' Joanna hesitated, gradually regaining her composure. 'I'm just a small-town girl. This is heady stuff for me. Of course I want to sing for you. But it's hard for me to take in. What could I possibly teach you?'

It was Angela's turn to struggle to explain herself. 'I'm nervous about tackling vocal music. I'm used to the voices of the orchestra – the fiddles, the oboes, the horns – and I feel I understand them. But the human voice – the oldest and greatest instrument of them all – is a mystery to me, and I am in awe of it. It can do so much!'

'I guess you're talking about voices like Christina Hauptmann's,' Joanna commented wanly.

'As I said, working with her is going to be a big challenge. I want to be really well-prepared. That's why I'm asking for help. I need a singer – a real singer, a fellow musician – to work with me, and show me the ropes. I want to know how you breathe, how you arrive at a tempo, how and why you give different colours to different words. Who is more important to you, the poet or the composer? And how, in God's name, do you give stature and relevance to a piece that is only twenty-four bars long?'

Joanna realized that the last question was both a clue and a test. 'A miniature can be a great work of art, and so can a short song. A singer merely interprets the song; if it's not great, she can't make it so. If it is great, and she's up to the challenge, its stature reveals itself.'

'Bravo!' Angela clapped her hands in delight. 'I knew we would hit it off. Do say you'll help me?'

Joanna could hardly speak. 'I'd be honoured,' she croaked eventually.

'Thank you, thank you. I expect you've guessed the composer we have in mind?'

The twenty-four bar song was a giveaway. 'Hugo Wolf?'

'Yes. Christina wants to start her programme with nineteen songs from the *Italienisches Liederbuch*. Now you know why I need help.'

To be sure she wasn't dreaming, Joanna was compelled to spell it out. 'You – Angela Bonneville – want to rehearse nineteen songs from Wolf's *Italian Songbook* with me?'

'Please.' Angela hurried on, as if she feared Joanna would refuse. 'Of course, I would pay you for your time.'

Joanna shook her head. 'You must know I would do it for nothing.'

'Sure, but that doesn't seem right. Look, I don't know what to offer, and you don't know what to ask. Why don't we ask Rose to arbitrate for us?'

Relieved, Joanna was quick to agree, and Rose was happy to oblige. She suggested a fee based on her estimate of the work involved, and her suggestion was accepted without discussion. It was a sum that made Joanna's eyes widen, and over lunch she couldn't resist doing a quick mental calculation. On a daily basis, the fee made her teacher's salary look meagre. It hardly seemed fair, and she ought to feel guilty about it, but what she actually felt was a fierce joy.

It was only when she was driving home that Joanna began to appreciate the full irony of her situation. If she hadn't been suspended from work she simply wouldn't have the time to work with Angela. By trying to destroy her, the wretched Tanner boy had given her the most exciting adventure of her life.

She was still giddy with excitement when she drove into the Causeway and parked the Citroën. But the euphoria drained away when she realized that the two women waiting outside her house were police officers.

Jack Dabdoub's first business in Devon was concluded well before midday, and he had time to write up his notes and have a pub lunch in Exeter before driving to Sidmouth to interview Detective-Superintendent Brian Curry, retired. He had never met Curry, but he had made some discreet enquiries among the superintendent's ex-colleagues in Manchester, and he thought he had learned enough to be able to handle the man. 'Solid' was the word most people had used, which might or might not have been a compliment, but what everyone was agreed on was that Curry was scrupulously honest. 'He niver 'ad the imagination to be owt but' was the opinion of one young detective.

When the ex-superintendent opened the door of his little terrace house Dabdoub's first impression was that the man was seriously ill. The old policeman's face was deeply tanned, but gaunt and hollow, as if the skin had been shrink-wrapped around the skull. He seemed pleased to have a visitor, though, and he ushered Dabdoub into a tiny parlour which smelled strongly of wet wool and air-freshener.

'Tea?' he enquired; and without waiting for an answer, scuttled off, to return moments later with a huge silver tray loaded with scones, cream, strawberry jam, crockery and a massive brown teapot. 'There, lad. Now you know you're in Devon. Back home, it 'ud been a pikelet and a pot o' meat-paste.'

'Home?' Dabdoub queried. 'Do you miss Lancashire, then?'

'Ay. Well, yes and no. Miss the people; don't miss the weather. Mind you, it rains just as much down here as it does up there. The rain's just a bit warmer, that's all. Anyroad, now that my wife's gone I don't give a bugger where I live. My daughter and my grandchildren live down here, so the choice is made for me.'

Dabdoub steered the conversation towards the matter in hand. 'Chris and Andy send their regards, by the way.'

'Oh, you talked to them, did you? And they told you I'm a dull old stick who did everything by the book. I'm not ashamed of it, laddie. I reckon on balance I did more good than harm.'

'I believe you. I just want to tap into your recollection of a case you handled about eight years ago. The murder of a woman called Carole Guest.'

'Melvin Tares,' Curry said promptly. 'Probably the stupidest lout I ever put away. He was a right wally. He left his fingerprints at the scene, he had the victim's blood on his clothes and the victim's jewellery in his flat. It couldn't have been an easier collar if he'd taken an ad in the papers. Speaking of which, is this on account of that Anita Whatsername article?'

'Yeah. Has she been in touch?'

'Twice. The first time she asked me if I'd convicted the wrong man, and the second time she offered to buy my story.'

'What did you say?'

'No, both times. I also told her that I'd never taken a bribe in my life, and I weren't about to start now. That's true, by the way.'

'I don't doubt it,' Dabdoub assured him. 'Like I said, it was the Mons article which started this particular hare. My client's hired me to find out if there's any truth in it.'

'No, there ent. It's all bollocks. That's what I told the Mons woman, and that's what you can tell your client. Who is your client, by the way?'

'George Guest. He's Carole Guest's son.'

'Ay, well I can see why he could get all churned up over the idea that his mother's killer got away with it. That Anita Mons has got a lot to answer for.' Brian Curry took a long swig of tea to calm himself down. 'That article of hers – what does it amount to, anyway? A low-life who's shared a cell with Tares thinks of a way to make a crust. He contacts a crusading journalist who's looking for a crusade. He spins her a yarn, which he knows she can't check, because Tares is in an isolation ward. Dear Anita rushes into print anyway, with a story that nobody else can challenge, because she won't reveal her sources. And what's the result? The police get smeared, judges look foolish, and the victim's relatives are forced to relive their agony. It's bloody unfair, that's what it is.' He leaned back in his chair, breathing hard and looking exhausted. 'Have another scone.'

'Thank you.' Dabdoub took his time, letting the other man relax. 'Tell me how you got onto Tares in the first place? He hadn't any previous, as I understand?'

'We got lucky. As you probably know, the poor woman was lying dead in her flat for two days before the alarm was raised. We put out an appeal on the nine o'clock news – any information, however insignificant, et cetera – and this woman gave us the registration number of Tares's car. After that, it was just routine.'

'This woman remembered the registration number after two days?'

'Yeah. It was the date of her father's birthday, or something like that. Anyway, it gave us Tares, and forensic gave us the rest. I don't remember an easier case.'

Dabdoub finished his scone and smacked his lips in appreciation. 'Super—'

'I'm retired; you can forget all that shit. Call me Brian.'

'Thanks. Brian, I need to pad out my report a bit. Tell me, did you ever consider the possibility that there could have been an accomplice?'

' 'Course we did. But we couldn't pick up any leads. The witness who gave us the car number was adamant that Tares was alone when she saw him. And Tares himself didn't cough up any names. If that story in the paper was right, why did he take the rap for somebody else?'

'Good point,' Dabdoub conceded. 'This witness – the one who saw the car – did she actually identify Tares?'

'No, she never saw his face. But once we were on to him and showed his picture around we found three people who were willing to swear he'd been in that apartment block that morning.'

'And these other witnesses – did they notice any other strangers or suspicious-looking characters around that day?'

'Nothing that checked out. We got a phone call from an old guy who told us we should investigate a sinister-looking woman who spent a lot of time in the pub with Mrs Guest – "plying her with drink", he said. He told us that women who get drunk in public are capable of anything. They ought to be locked up, he said, flogging's too good for 'em. When you make a TV appeal, a hell of a lot of the calls you get are from weirdos or barmpots.'

'But you had to check it out, all the same?'

'Oh, ay. The sinister woman turned out to be a pretty little office-girl, thin as a whippet. She told us that yes, she had met Carole Guest in the pub a few times. She got chatting to the older woman because she didn't feel comfortable being in a pub on her own. I asked her if they had become friends, and she said not really. Mrs Guest drank a bit too much, she said. The pub landlord confirmed that. "She'd come in three times a week and get maudlin drunk", is how he put it.'

'So the old guy got that bit right – Mrs Guest did get drunk in public. Quite often, it seems.'

'True, but the info didn't get us any forrader with the murder investigation. And before you ask, yes, we did check that the girl had an alibi. She'd accompanied her boss on a business trip to Liverpool that morning.'

'I'd like to talk to her,' Dabdoub said. 'Apart from my client, I don't know a single soul who knew Mrs Guest when she was alive.'

Curry chuckled. 'Trying to stretch the investigation out a bit, eh? Your client must have deep pockets.'

'He has,' Dabdoub admitted. 'But even more important, he wants to see effort for his money. If he thinks I've skimped anything, he'll chop me off at the knees. What's the girl's name?'

'I can't remember. I'll find out for you. But she may have got married and changed her name. She wasn't a bad-looking kid.'

'Thanks, Brian, you're a star. Just because I'm poking around into this old business doesn't mean I think you got it wrong, by the way. I'm just trying to put my client's mind at rest.'

'Nay, I don't mind. You've got to make a living, just the same as the rest of us. They tell me you used to be a copper at one time.'

So the old guy had done his own bit of checking up, Dabdoub thought. Old habits die hard. 'For a while,' he said. Absent-mindedly, he licked a blob of jam from his knife. 'But my wife told me I had to chose between her and the job. So I quit the job. She left me anyway. She said I'd no right to call her bluff like that.'

Brian Curry looked sad. 'Ay, it's no joke being a copper's wife. My Elsie was a saint. Have another scone, why don't you?'

'I don't mind if I do.' Dabdoub helped himself cheerfully. 'Why do you suppose Carole Guest let her killer into her flat?'

'I've no idea. Maybe he spun her some tale.'

'Do you think they'd become acquainted, somehow? We know she spent a lot of time in the pub. Maybe, like the office lassie, he chatted her up there?'

'Maybe, but I doubt it,' Curry said, without humour. 'He isn't what you would call a ladies' man.'

'Gay, you mean?'

'Gay, bent, ginger, pixie – I never know what this week's label is. 'The man's a homosexual.' Curry's narrow face darkened with distaste.

Hurriedly, Dabdoub changed the subject. 'You reckon robbery was the only motive?'

'What else? Her jewellery was found in his flat.'

'Well, Mrs Guest's job was investigating welfare fraud. Could there be a connection?'

'If you can find one, you're a better man than I am. Melvin Tares was a scumbag, but he wasn't a dole cheat. He worked as a bouncer in a late-night drinking-club.'

Dabdoub was learning nothing new, but then he hadn't expected to. 'Brian, you make the whole case sound like a stroll in the park. I haven't your experience of course, but nothing in our line is ever that neat. Didn't your investigation turn up anything at all that was odd or out of line?'

Curry started to deny it, but then changed his mind. 'Well, there was one irritating loose end. Scattered round the body were lots of glass beads from the necklace that Mrs Guest was wearing when she was killed. The forensic guys found blood and tiny fragments of skin on some of them. Most of the blood was the victim's, but there were a few microscopic spots that the lab boys said were somebody else's. Unluckily for us, they didn't match Tares's blood-group either.'

Dabdoub's interest quickened. 'So there could have been somebody else in the room?'

'It's possible, I suppose, but it's not really conclusive either way. If there had been another suspect in the frame we could have broadened the inquiry, but there wasn't. We made full disclosure of all that stuff to the defence, and they couldn't get any mileage out of it either.' Curry was anxious to let Dabdoub know that everything had been done by the book.

Dabdoub wrote *Beads?* in his notebook. It wasn't a very promising lead, but it would be something to think about on the long drive home. 'I guess that just about wraps it up,' he said. 'Brian, I can't tell you how grateful I am. You understand that all this is confidential. Everything you've told me goes only to my client, nobody else.' He paused, studying the older man's face. 'Look, I don't want to cause offence, and I took on board what you said earlier, but my client said I should offer to pay you for your time. He suggested a couple of hundred quid. I could make it out to your favourite charity, if you like.'

'Make it out to my daughter,' Curry said, smiling. 'She ain't a charity, but she is my favourite.'

Before he went Dabdoub thought of another question. 'Did you ever find the murder weapon?'

'No. We found some brass knucks in Tares's flat, but the pathologist said they didn't match the impact wound. He couldn't describe the weapon for us. He just said that the instrument – whatever it was – was heavy, and domed, like a small mushroom, or the back end of a peen hammer. He told us the force of the impact fractured the hyoid bone. But he also said that the hyoid bone can become quite brittle with age.'

'By gum, you've got some memory,' Dabdoub said admiringly. 'You've dredged all that up from eight years ago?'

'Nay, I looked it up only yesterday. I got a call from my old division, wanting to pick my brains. There's been a copy-cat killing: young woman bashed in the throat. Mugged in the street outside her flat.'

'In Manchester?'

'No, in one of those dormitory towns to the south-east. Aldersgrove, I think its name is.'

CHAPTER 14

The woman who identified herself as Detective-Inspector Burgage was elegantly dressed, fashionably slim and only a few years older than Joanna herself. Burgage's companion, WPC Barrel, was a very different prospect: dumpy, whey-faced, with hair like a Brillo pad and a mouth that looked like a mistake. Joanna welcomed them into her house with as much grace as she could muster.

Burgage got straight down to business. There had been a complaint, and it was her duty to investigate it. With Joanna's co-operation the interview need not be unnecessarily prolonged. She personally hoped that the matter could be sorted out with the minimum of fuss.

Her friendly manner seemed just a little too calculated, and Joanna was instantly suspicious of it. She determined to be on her guard.

'You have been told about the allegation against you, I believe?' Burgage asked.

'Yes.'

'And your response?'

'That it is nonsense. To my knowledge, I have never even met the boy.'

Burgage picked up on her answer. 'To your knowledge?'

Joanna bit her tongue. 'The Jas Priestley is a big school. What I meant was, that I never taught Nick Tanner. I may have passed him in the corridor, but since I don't even know what he looks like, I didn't register his presence.'

'OK.' Burgage registered the resentment in Joanna's response. 'So, your answer, in brief, is that the boy is lying?'

'Yes.'

'Why would he do that?'

'How do I know?' Joanna shrugged and spread her arms. 'Officer, what you have to realize is that we teachers are wide open to malicious accusations from the children under our supervision. The kids aren't stupid: they can see how vulnerable we are. They know that in the present climate of opinion they are going to be believed rather than us. To the ill-disposed child that's an open invitation to make trouble.'

WPC Barrel made an unexpected intervention. 'I reckon the boot could be on the other foot.'

The young policewoman's voice was so thin and squeaky that it took Joanna a few moments to work out what she had said.

'What do you mean?'

'Well, in the present climate of opinion,' Barrel mocked Joanna's accent, 'who are people going to believe – the posh, professional lady, or the ignorant, delinquent kid from a poor family?'

The hostility in the woman's attitude was so blatant, that Joanna felt a small shiver of apprehension. These people were more disposed to believe the boy than her. She answered slowly, choosing her words with care.

'Then it clearly behoves the independent mind to be absolutely even-handed. To base decisions on facts rather than prejudices. Class prejudices in particular.'

Burgage nodded, clearly undismayed at seeing her subordinate slapped down. 'I couldn't agree more. Let's stick to facts. You were one of the teachers in charge of the activities week at Wingate Camp, is that right?'

'Yes.'

'What happened after the Wingate Camp broke up?'

'Happened? We saw that the kids got home safely, that's all. They'd had a great time, and they were very happy kids.'

'Good. And after that?'

'After that? Nothing. I had the rest of the summer holiday to look forward to, and I planned to veg out. I was knackered.'

Inspector Burgage nodded encouragingly. 'Was that the end of your activities week involvement?'

Joanna was puzzled by the question. 'Yes, of course. What are you getting at? I thought you were investigating Nicky Tanner? He wasn't at Wingate.'

'We know that. Tell us what happened that weekend – after you had closed down the Wingate Camp.'

'I went home.'

'Are you sure? Please try to remember, Mrs Howard, this is important. You brought the children back to Dovebridge on the Saturday morning. Then what?'

Joanna stared hard at the inspector. She felt that the questions were designed to trap her in some way, but she couldn't figure out how. 'I haven't the faintest idea what you're getting at.'

Burgage sighed. 'What I'm getting at, Mrs Howard, is that you didn't go home. You went to the school group at Darwen Lowe Farm.'

'Oh, that!' Joanna shook her head. 'I'd forgotten all about it. Yes. There was a mini-crisis. Cynthia Bell, one of the teachers with that party, had to rush off home – her husband had broken his leg, or something – and they needed a replacement, just for their last night in camp. As I'm sure you know, each group has to have a minimum number of staff in attendance. As I was the only woman available, I got lumbered with the job.'

'Tell us what happened?'

'Nothing much. I went home, had a bath, got into some clean clothes, then drove up to Lowe Farm in the afternoon. It's only about forty miles away. I organized supper – the kids love a big fry-up on the last night – and then we gradually got them quietened down and settled for sleep. The two blokes – my colleagues – scuttled off to the boozer, and I baby-sat until they got back. The next day, we brought that lot home. It was all very routine stuff. Why are you so interested in it?'

Burgage didn't answer directly. 'At Darwen Lowe Farm, was one of the children taken ill?'

'Yes, poor sod. He got flu symptoms, so they quarantined him in the stables. That sounds a bit primitive, but in fact the stables have been converted into quite nice bedrooms. I checked up on him, took his temperature and gave him a couple of aspirin. He was very sorry for himself, but I figured he'd last till morning.'

'What was the name of the boy who was ill?'

'I've no idea. I knew hardly any of the kids in that group.'

WPC Barrel, who had sat grimly silent since her last interjection, fidgeted in her seat and suddenly spoke. 'Excuse me,' she said, her voice thin and harsh. 'Can I use your toilet?'

Joanna winced inwardly at the thought of that sluglike young woman in her bathroom, but she couldn't decently refuse. 'Of course. Through there and up the stairs. It's the first door you come to.'

When her assistant left the room, Inspector Burgage scribbled something in a notebook. As she wrote, she asked casually, 'Will you be involved with the school's summer camp this year?'

'I suppose so, unless somebody else comes forward. Surprisingly few people are prepared to do it. Unless, of course, it's a foreign trip – they're much more popular.'

'So I should imagine.' Burgage smiled and put the notebook down on the table, holding it open with her hand. 'I want to talk some more about the Darwen Lowe Farm group. You say you don't remember the name of the boy who had flu?'

'No.'

'Isn't that unusual? Surely someone mentioned his name?'

'If they did, it didn't register. I told you, I never taught that group of kids. Look, I was with them from three o'clock on Saturday afternoon until ten-thirty on Sunday morning. There wasn't time to memorize their names, even if there had been any point to it.'

The young policewoman came quietly back into the room. Joanna was startled. Subconsciously, she had been listening for the sound of her lavatory being flushed; she was almost certain that she had heard nothing. She tried to convince herself that she had been mistaken, but she had an uneasy suspicion that she was being tricked in some way. Constable Barrel nodded at her superior as if confirming something, and sat down as smug and silent as ever.

Inspector Burgage again wrote in her notebook, this time at some length. When she had finished, she seemed in no hurry to continue. 'So,' she said after a pause, 'you had no idea that the boy with the flu was Nicky Tanner?'

Joanna simply stared at her, too astonished to speak.

Burgage looked at her directly. 'Would you like to recast your statement that you had never even met the boy?'

'No! He was just a sick kid. It didn't matter to me what his name was. I gave him a couple of aspirin and left him to sleep.'

'That isn't what he says.'

'I don't care what the little sod says. He's the one who's lying.' Joanna's voice rose with her temper. 'Why does everyone persist in believing him and not me?'

The inspector ignored the question and asked one of her own. 'Do you ever go to Knowley Hill?'

'The place the locals call Knowley Castle? Yes, I've been there a couple of times, to pick blackberries. Why?'

'And what about the old Lock House at Oughton? Have you ever been there?'

'Yes.' Joanna didn't ask why this time, and was surprised when Burgage supplied an answer.

'Because they are two of the places where, according to Tanner, you and he had sex. But – again, according to him – intercourse mainly took place here, in this house.'

Joanna gasped, acutely aware that she was red in the face, and that her responses were sounding more and more like bluster. 'This is ridiculous! I just cannot believe that I am sitting here and listening to this garbage! Can't you people see how ridiculous this is?' She paused, breathing hard, trying to collect herself. 'Just think about it for a minute. I have friends in this town, a social life, a respectable career. Do you really think I'm stupid enough to put all that at risk for the sake of a sly bunk-up with some snotty teenager? And even if I were that crazy, I'd have to be totally off my head to do it here! We are a close little community in this street. How do you suppose that I could possibly carry on an affair like that without my neighbours noticing?'

Burgage stared at her impassively. 'I can't answer for your state of mind, Mrs Howard. But I can tell you that one of my officers has questioned your neighbours on that very point. And more than one witness is prepared to state, on oath, that on several occasions they have seen a schoolboy surreptitiously entering and leaving your house under the cover of darkness.'

'Wait!'

The two police officers were practically out of the door before Joanna managed to gather her wits and call them back. They exchanged glances as they turned to face her; and WPC Barrel in particular had a very satisfied glint in her eye. Oh God, Joanna thought despairingly, they imagine I'm about to confess. Well, they're going to be disappointed.

'I want to ask you something,' she said.

Burgage nodded encouragingly. 'Go ahead.'

'These nocturnal visits that the neighbours witnessed – when did they happen?'

'There were several of them, over an eight-month period.'

'But on what specific dates? Can you tell me?'

'Not at this moment. It is hardly necessary, is it? The boy says he came here: the neighbours say they saw him. That evidence seems compelling enough.'

'Not to me,' Joanna said grimly. 'The boy is lying; the neighbours are mistaken. I'll prove it to you, if you'll only name some definite dates.'

'You mean you'll cook up an alibi,' Barrel sneered. 'That won't get you off the hook.'

'I'm merely pointing out that this bit of your argument is curiously imprecise. "Several occasions over an eight-month period", I think you said. And yet you can't pin down a single one of those occasions exactly. You might call that evidence compelling, I call it vague.' Joanna was pleased to see that Inspector Burgage was looking slightly rattled.

'I'm sure that we shall pin down some definite dates as the investigation progresses,' Burgage said. 'One or other of your neighbours is bound to remember. How would that information help you?'

Now she had come to the point, Joanna found it difficult to explain without embarrassment. 'Because then I could show that the person who was here on that night was not Nicky Tanner, but someone who might be mistaken for him.'

'Another school kid, you mean?' Barrel cut in harshly.

'No. A friend of mine. He is – not very tall, and slightly built. In the dark, he could easily be mistaken for a tall teenager, particularly since he tends to wear the kind of cap that school kids favour.'

'You're making this up!' Barrel almost shouted.

'Don't be a fool!' Joanna snapped back. 'Do you think I don't know you'll check it out?'

'Indeed we shall,' Burgage assured her. She had recovered her poise, and was looking keenly interested. 'Your neighbours insisted that this person was being quite furtive. "Sneaking about", was how one of them put it.'

'I can explain that. My friend wanted to keep our relationship secret.'

'A sexual relationship, I take it?'

'Yes.'

'Ah. A married man?'

'No; a colleague from school – another teacher. Sexual liaisons among the staff are discouraged, if not actually forbidden. Our head teacher is particularly severe on transgressors. That's why my friend was being discreet – or furtive, as you put it. He was protecting his career.'

'You certainly make it sound plausible,' Burgage said judiciously. 'This friend of yours – is he still on the staff at the Jas Priestley?'

'Yes.' Joanna was reluctant to continue, but she knew she was committed. 'His name's Tom Short.'

'*Short*?' WPC Barrel yelped with laughter. 'You're telling us you're having an affair with a midget called Short?'

'No, right now I'm trying to hammer some sense into a blockhead called Barrel,' retorted Joanna, crossly. She turned to the inspector. 'Tom is certainly sensitive about his height, but it's a cross he bears with a lot of dignity. I hope he's not going to be subjected to that kind of crass gibe.'

'You mean the constable's or yours?' enquired Burgage. 'You certainly know how to make friends and influence people.' However, she looked as if she had enjoyed the exchange. 'We have to interview your friend, of course, and we always do our best to be courteous. At the same time, it's my duty to point out to him that the penalties for perjury are very severe.'

Joanna was suddenly much more self-confident. She felt that the argument was at last going her way. 'Good. I hope you point that out to Nicky Tanner as well,' she commented. 'Or don't you apply the same rules to lying little toe-rags?'

'She's a slippery customer that one, and no mistake,' WPC Barrel said, as soon as they got outside. 'But I reckon we've got her bang to rights. The kid's description of her bathroom and bedroom is spot on. And did you notice the picture of the guys with shotguns? That fits with the kid's story as well.'

'Yes.'

'Mind you, I'll give her full marks for imagination. That tale about having it off with a short-arse called Short! What did you make of that, ma'am?'

'I think it's so bizarre it's probably true. We'll have to see what this Tom Short says about it. If he confirms her story, that knocks a big hole in the neighbours' evidence. We've got a long way to go yet, Constable. Mrs Howard pin-pointed the one weak spot in the case.'

'Which is?' Barrel's tone made it more of a contradiction than a question.

'That apart from the Darwen Lowe farm incident, Nick Tanner hasn't given us one definite date on which intercourse took place. He told us where, but he was really vague about when.'

'Yeah, but ...' Barrel clung obstinately to her conviction, 'maybe he was trying to protect her. He says he loves her; he doesn't want her to go to gaol. It was his ma who forced him to make that statement in the first place.'

'It's an interesting theory,' Theresa Burgage said, unconvinced. 'But I'm afraid you and the sergeant will have to handle this investigation without me for a while. I have to go and help out with another case.'

'Something important?'

'You could say so. There's been a murder on the Wickerbrook Estate.'

CHAPTER 15

The police called again the next day. Different ones this time. They introduced themselves as Detective Constables Bailey and Cope of the Greater Manchester CID, and they just wanted a quick word, if Joanna wouldn't mind?

If they had been told about Nick Tanner, they were too polite to mention the fact. Their interests lay elsewhere. Did Joanna happen to know a woman called Elizabeth Nair?

'Lizzie Nair? Of course I do. She's my cleaning-lady.'

'Ah, yes.' They nodded in unison and exchanged glances. The one called Bailey continued: 'Can you tell us when you last saw Miss Nair?'

'Saw her? Why? What's all this about?'

'Just answer the question, please, Mrs Howard.'

'Not so long ago. Two weeks, I think. No, not quite two weeks. A week last Wednesday.'

'You haven't seen your cleaning-lady for over a week?'

'No.' Joanna looked from one young man to the other. Such bland, unlined faces. They were watching her so keenly that she had a panicky feeling that they were waiting for her to recognize them. 'You weren't by any chance at the Jas Priestley, were you?'

'The what?'

'The school in Dovebridge.'

'No, Mrs Howard.'

She had said the wrong thing. Referring to their lack of years offended their dignity. Hurriedly she got back to the subject in hand. 'Lizzie cleans this place on Wednesdays. I only actually see her during the school holidays. During term-time I leave her money on the kitchen table, along with a note if there's anything special I want her to do. She's worked for me for more than a year.'

'Who lets her in when you're not here?' Bailey asked.

'She has her own key.'

'That's very trusting.'

Joanna smiled. 'She's very trustworthy. She's never given me any cause for misgivings.'

'But she wasn't here last Wednesday?' DC Cope looked curiously around the room as if checking for dust.

'No, she didn't turn up last week. She was cross with me. She's a very sensitive girl.'

'Why was she cross with you?'

'Oh, the week earlier, I had left her a note reminding her not to smoke in my house. She had never done it before, but I came home to find the house reeking of cigarette smoke. To a non-smoker, the smell is quite disgusting.'

'Is that so?' Bailey sounded quite surprised. 'So she took umbrage, did she?'

'Indeed. She rang me that night, saying I was just looking for an excuse to sack her. She had promised me not to smoke in my house, and she was a woman of her word. Was I calling her a liar? I just said, Lizzie, the house stinks of smoke and there's cigarette ash on the kitchen floor. At that, she burst into tears, called me a stuck-up bully, and banged down the receiver.'

'So you didn't really expect her to turn up last Wednesday?'

'Oh, I thought she'd cool down and get over it. She's touchy and insecure, but she's genuinely good-hearted. She doesn't like to admit she's in the wrong, but then, who does?'

The two young men had lost interest in this line of questioning. Cope tried another tack: 'To your knowledge, did Miss Nair have any enemies?'

'Enemies? I don't imagine so. She's terribly shy, on account of her speech impediment. I can't imagine how she could offend anyone.' Joanna suddenly registered the past tense. '"Did she?" *Did* she? Listen, I think it's about time you levelled with me. What's this all about?'

Bailey shrugged. 'Elizabeth Nair was murdered on the Wickerbrook Estate on Sunday night.'

'Murdered! Lizzie?' Joanna was horrified. 'What happened?'

'She was mugged. Someone struck her down and stole her handbag. We've no reason to believe it was premeditated, but we have to check out all her acquaintances, just in case somebody out there had a grudge against her. So,' he smiled apologetically, 'we have to ask, as a matter of routine, where were you on Sunday night, about nine o'clock?'

'Sunday? I was having dinner with my next-door neighbour at number eight.'

'Very good.' Both men scribbled in their notebooks. 'And your neighbour's name?' Cope asked.

'Clements. Matthew Clements.'

'Fine. Thank you, Mrs Howard.' As one, they rose to leave. 'You've been very helpful.'

After they had gone, Joanna sat for some time staring blankly into space, unable to take in what she had just heard. Lizzie Nair murdered! Killed, apparently, for nothing more than the few pounds she had in her purse! The mindless wickedness of it was too appalling to contemplate.

Lizzie had never allowed anything like familiarity or intimacy to flourish between her and her employer. Her speech defect made her overly-sensitive to other people's attitudes towards her, and she reacted to anything she perceived as mockery, or worse still, pity, with bitter resentment. She and Joanna had quickly developed a cool, matter-of-fact way of dealing with each other which, although seemingly dispassionate, was as close to real friendship as Lizzie would allow. All the same, Joanna had pitied the girl for the cruel way life had treated her. And now she wept at the cruel way her life had ended.

The phone rang, and she had to dry her eyes and pull herself together. It was Mack, the friendly garage-man, to say that her car was repaired and he would bring it round straight away, if that was convenient? It was a welcome diversion, and she was pleased to see her little car again, looking shinier and tidier than she had ever seen it before.

At last she felt able to begin work on the Hugo Wolf songs. She was pleased to see that the first one on her list began simply enough: a five-bar phrase in G minor, right in the meaty part of her voice. In fact, she could see at a glance that the whole song lay comfortably within her range. This was going to be a doddle.

An hour later she was in despair. She had sung the song through a dozen times, not attempting the accompaniment, but marking in the harmonies at crucial points, and she hadn't the faintest idea how to perform it. The music and the words seemed to pull in opposite directions. Was it sad, or was it sardonic? Gloomy, or funny? Why the hell should she slow down in the middle of the German word for "bed"? Trying to control her panic, she moved on to the next song, which again was comfortably within her range. And this one, she decided, was definitely light-hearted, in spite of the words. The more she sang, the more confident she felt; every breath she took seemed to lift her spirits like some stimulating drug. She worked, with a few breaks to clear her head, for more than three hours; and only stopped when the phone interrupted her again.

The voice was relentlessly cheerful. 'Hi, Joanna darling, somebody told me you'd be at home. What's the matter? You sick, or something?'

'Sort of, Alicia.' Alicia Quinton was one of the altos in the choir, and one of Joanna's oldest friends. 'I'm off work right now with a bad back.'

'A bad back? Darling, I know the most marvellous osteopath. Moonie, his name is, can you believe it? But he's magic, honestly. I'll give you his number.'

'No, it's OK. My girl – Janice Pounder – is jolly good.'

'Never heard of her,' Alicia said decisively. 'You've got to be careful, darling. There are lots of charlatans about.' She barked with laughter. 'That's what I'm calling you about, actually.'

'Osteopaths?'

'No, silly. Charlatans. Does the name Gerald Dudley ring any bells?'

Joanna carefully put down the receiver, pulled a chair towards her and sat down. She picked up the phone. 'Alicia?'

'Yes?'

'Make my day. Tell me the bastard's dead.'

'Far from it, darling, very far from it. In fact, he's here, in Aldersgrove.'

'Yes, I'd heard that. Where is he? At the Royal Oak?'

'No, no. He's staying with your friends – and his friends – the Brays.'

'With Betsy? How could she? I mean – Christ, everyone knew what hell I went through with that bugger. How could she possibly invite such a pig into her home?'

'Steady on, old thing. Woo, woo.' It was the sound Alicia made to soothe her young children, and she laboured under the delusion that it worked with everybody. 'You've got to remember that it was you who introduced him into our little circle. You told us, if I quote you correctly, that the sun shone from his immaculate backside.'

'Lord, woman, do you have to remind me what an unmitigated idiot I was? That was another world, another me. That bastard introduced me to depths of misery beyond my worst nightmares.'

'Well, anyway,' Alicia's tone made it plain that she thought Joanna was being over-dramatic, 'the rumour is that Shona's thrown him out.'

'So soon?' Joanna laughed without humour. 'I guess she didn't have as much money as he thought.'

'Oh, come on, darling. Woo, woo. That's a bit cruel.'

'No it isn't. I know that smarmy sod inside out. Right, dear, thanks for the warning. I'll just stay out of circulation till he's gone away again. I've got stuff to do, anyway.' She was longing to tell someone about the prospect of working with Angela Bonneville, but she was afraid that Alicia would interpret it as boasting. Patrick Pringle had mentioned that some of the women in the choir had been bitchy about her after the Mendelssohn concert, and warned her to keep a low profile.

'Just one other thing,' Alicia said. 'If Betsy gets in touch, don't tell her I've told you about Gerald, will you?'

Joanna felt a faint stirring of alarm. 'Why would Betsy get in touch? I've hardly spoken a word to her for ages.'

'You know Betsy. She's as sentimental as a Victorian ballad. Gossip has it that Gerald's been sobbing on her shoulder about his poor, wretched, empty life without the only woman he has ever loved.'

'Alicia,' Joanna said coldly, 'you are joking, aren't you? Tell me you're just winding me up?'

'Just repeating gossip, darling. All I can say is, don't be surprised if Betsy's got her matchmaking hat on. She always used to say that you and Gerald were the perfect couple.'

'The woman's a cretin. And Gerald's a monstrous hypocrite. I don't suppose you know what his private name for Betsy was, when he was living with me?'

'No, darling. Do tell.'

'Big-Bum Bessie.'

'I don't believe you.'

'It's true.'

'How awful!' Alicia was obviously delighted. 'You must admit, he could be very witty when he chose. And charming.'

'Charming, hell. If that creep shows his face round here I'll do him a serious mischief. Tell Betsy that.'

'No, I don't think I'll tell Betsy anything of the sort, darling. I mean, she did swear me to secrecy. I think I'll just retire to the sidelines and watch the action.'

Which, Joanna reflected, was exactly Alicia's style. Stir the pot and watch it bubble. There was no real malice in her, but she loved a little vicarious excitement. 'Alicia?'

'Yes?'

'Gerald is a greedy and unscrupulous swine, but he's not a complete fool. He knows I'll never have him back. So he's up to something. What is it?'

'I don't know, darling. But don't forget, he's very vain. He might think he can talk you round.'

'No way. He's not that stupid. And I've no intention of talking to him. You might pass that round the grapevine.'

'Of course, darling,' Alicia said insincerely. 'Got to go now. Stay in touch, eh? 'Bye, darling.'

The phone rang again seconds after Joanna had put down the receiver. It was Alicia again. 'Darling, darling, I quite forgot to ask you – is it true? The news, I mean? I can hardly believe it. Is it true?'

Joanna felt sick. She had been dreading this moment. Someone from the school must have been gossiping. 'Is what true, Alicia?'

'What I've just heard about that girl, whatsername, your cleaning-lady. My neighbour's just told me that she's been found in a back alley on the Wickerbrook with her throat cut.'

'She's been murdered, yes. The police have just been round here. They're interviewing everyone who knew Lizzie They didn't say anything about her throat being cut.' Joanna spoke quickly, half-ashamed of the relief she was feeling.

'Yes, but isn't it too ghastly for words? Almost on our doorstep.' Alicia lived in one of the more affluent parts of town, about as far away from the Wickerbrook Estate as it was possible to be. 'I tried her out, you know, after you took her on, but it didn't work out. She was much too surly for me, and I couldn't understand a word she said. Did the police say who did it?'

'They thought it was probably a mugger.'

'How awful. I really can't understand these people. I think they do it just to be nasty.'

CHAPTER 16

Jack Dabdoub phoned Matt early on Wednesday morning to make his report. 'Basically, apart from the move to Devon, the situation is exactly the same. She seems perfectly happy and in good health. I was only able to talk to her for a few minutes, and I took a snapshot of her, which I'll put in the post. You'll see she's put on some weight. She said to tell you that she prays for you, and that she believes Saint Praxted has you in his special care.'

Matthew sighed. 'Saint who?'

'Praxted, I think. I may have got the name wrong; I'm not deeply into saints. Be grateful. I doubt there's many folk in Lancashire with Saint Whatsit on his team.'

Matt wasn't amused. 'You say she's in good health – and she's happy?'

'Yeah.' It was Dabdoub's turn to sigh. 'Look, do you want to go on with this operation? I report to you every month or so, and it's always the same. She isn't coming back, Matt. And the Rev Whosis isn't going to turn her out as long as you keep sending that monthly cheque. Be honest with me, chum: do you really want her back? If you do, you're going the wrong way about it.'

Matt didn't answer the question. 'You're sure she's happy?'

'Yeah.' Another thing Dabdoub was not deeply into was subtlety. 'She's nuts, but she's happy. I told you, nothing's changed from last time. And the time before that. She's not coming back, Matt.'

'So you keep saying.'

'So what are you going to do?'

'What I've been doing for the past year or so. What else can I do?'

'You could divorce her. She'll be happy so long as she can stay with the Rev Whatsit's holy fellowship. All you have to do is to write the cheques.'

'No.' Matt sounded unhappy but obstinate. 'Divorce wouldn't change anything. I would still need to know that she's all right. As long as nothing changes, that's fine. But if things do change, and she's in trouble, I need to know.'

'OK, OK.' Dabdoub responded to the tension in his friend's voice. 'All I'm saying is that right now you don't have a marriage. It may not matter to Mary, but I reckon it matters to you. So what happens if you fall for somebody else?' Dabdoub had a vivid memory of a gorgeous brunette on Matt's arm at the Rugby Club.

'I can't,' Matt said simply. 'I may not have a marriage, but I do have a responsibility.'

There was no point in arguing with the guy. 'Well, fine,' Dabdoub said, shaking his head. 'It's your money.'

There was just time before the briefing in the Incident Room for Sergeant Dewbury and Constable Barrel to report developments to Inspector Burgage.

Dewbury went first. 'The Howard woman's alibi just blew away. The little guy – Tom Short – denies any involvement with her at all. As for sneaking round to her place under cover of darkness, he says that's just plain ridiculous.'

'Would he be willing to swear to that in court?' Burgage wanted to know.

'I asked him that. He was a bit evasive, but eventually said yes, if he had to, but he'd much rather be left out of it. He didn't want to be associated in any way with such a disgusting case, he said.'

Burgage started to get angry. 'So you told him what the case was about?'

'No, I didn't. I was really careful not to. But he seemed to know all about it.'

'Yes, I suppose the rumours are starting to circulate. But Mrs Howard struck me as an intelligent woman. It seems odd that she should offer an alibi that is so easily disproved.'

'Playing for time?' WPC Barrel suggested.

'Time to do what?'

'Well, maybe she intended to nobble the Tanner kid, get him to change his story.'

Burgage smiled without humour. 'Right, Kylie. That's something for you to check out. Is there anything else you want to say about Tom Short, Sergeant? Did he strike you as being honest and reliable?'

'I'm not sure. I reckon he's hiding something. He started to say something about a telephone call, and then backed off, saying he was confusing it with something else. He surely looked confused. He's a prickly guy, probably on account of his being so little.'

'Well, either he's lying or Mrs Howard is,' Burgage said. 'And if she's lying, then the case is pretty well wrapped up. I'm amazed that she should take such a risk.'

Dewbury was scornful. 'Nay, she's guilty as sin. Folk like her never expect to get caught. When they are, they're too flustered to think straight. I reckon it's time to bring her in and charge her.'

Burgage ignored that. 'Did you dig up anything, Kylie?'

'Yes, well it occurred to me,' Barrel said virtuously, 'that if Mrs Haitch was shagging the Tanner kid, she might well have tried it on with some of the other boys.'

'Christ, you haven't been questioning the pupils at the school?' Burgage was aghast.

' 'Course not. Like you said, we've got to tiptoe round this case in kid gloves.' It was a pretty conceit, and Barrel was proud of it. 'No, I chatted to some of the admin staff at the school; they always know what's going on. And I found that our Mrs Howard had paid a hundred quid to take one of the boys on holiday next summer. A kid called Darren Palmer, who had been on a school trip with her last summer. The school secretary said it was an unusual arrangement, which was putting it a bit mild, I'd say.'

'Sounds promising,' Burgage conceded. 'Talk to this Palmer boy, find out what's going on. But be tactful. Keep tiptoeing round in kid gloves.' She glanced at her watch. 'I've got to get over to St Gregory's right now. Keep digging, both of you. I don't think the CPS will buy the case on what we have so far. We need a clincher.'

Dewbury made an obscene gesture at her retreating back. 'Bloody kid gloves!' he snorted. 'She just can't bring herself to believe that a posh professional woman could stoop to shag a working-class kid. She's just dying to bury this case and let the Howard bitch off.'

Kylie Barrel shrugged philosophically. 'She's the boss. She calls the shots.'

The sergeant looked crafty. 'Not all of them, my duck. Not all of them.'

Dabdoub wished they could hold these conferences somewhere else. He was sick of sitting in his office and wanted a change of scene. He had generously offered to trek over to his client's hotel suite to make his report, but George Guest had turned down the idea flat. It was almost as if he suspected Jack of having designs on his mini-bar; which, Dabdoub thought, just showed you the kind of person he was.

So now George Guest sat bolt upright on a hard chair in Dabdoub's office, generating energy and inquisitiveness like a radioactive squirrel, while Jack and Tony made their reports.

Jack went first. 'I talked to ex-Superintendent Curry, the officer who led the murder investigation. He simply confirmed what we already knew: the evidence against Melvin Tares was overwhelming. I asked him whether they had considered the possibility of an accomplice, and he said of course they had, but all their enquiries that way came to a dead end.' That wasn't the happiest phrase in the circumstances, but Dabdoub only realized that after he had said it.

Guest was not pleased. 'So that's it? That's the police story, and you swallowed it whole?'

'No, there are some holes in it, but I don't know how significant they are. They can't explain, for instance, why your ma should have let Tares into her flat in the first place. There's no evidence at all that she knew him beforehand. Then, although the police found your mother's jewellery in Tares's flat, they didn't find the murder weapon. If he didn't expect to be caught, why did he dispose of the weapon? Also, the forensic team came up with something they couldn't explain.' Dabdoub repeated what Brian Curry had told him about the blood and the fragments of skin on the beads around Carole Guest's body. 'It was a puzzling detail, but it didn't really prove that somebody else was with Tares in that flat. Without corroborative evidence it didn't actually prove anything.'

George Guest stared at him beady-eyed. 'Well, did they follow it up properly? Did they check the DNA?'

'DNA? No, I can't see 'em doing that. We're talking over eight years ago, remember. DNA tests weren't routine and they were expensive. The police wouldn't go to that trouble unless they had a real suspect to match it against.'

Tony saw that their client was not pleased with this answer. 'Jack, I know that it's only a tiny detail, but it does keep open the possibility that

Tares wasn't acting alone. And the upside of that is that the police will still have those beads filed away with the rest of the case evidence. So if *we* find a real suspect, we can match him against real DNA evidence.'

Guest nodded vigorously. Tony had the kind of attitude he approved of. 'Before we go any further, I'd better chip in my two cents' worth. I had a long natter with that Anita Mons. Now, that is one very sassy sheila. I thought she'd play hard to get, but in fact she was keen to talk to me. She's got an eye for a story, that girl. Her pitch was this: that if she wrote up the interview with me, making a big play out of my quest for justice, that might jog a few memories, or even spook the real murderer into an indiscretion.'

'Or it might create a queue of con men outside your door with dodgy information ' Dabdoub commented drily.

'Maybe, but we had to make a trade. She wouldn't give me anything unless I gave her something.'

'So what did she give you?'

'She swore to me that the guy she'd talked to – the bloke who'd shared a cell with Melvin Tares – was fair dinkum. He had repeated to her what Tares had said to him. Tares said that someone else had done the actual murder, and that all they had been sent to do, was to scare the old woman off. No—' He anticipated Dabdoub's question, 'he didn't say why they wanted her scared. The killing wasn't meant to happen, that's what he kept saying.'

'But if he didn't do the killing himself why did he keep quiet at the trial?'

'Apparently he was told that if he grassed his accomplice, somebody close to him, would be killed. But if he took the rap there would be a pot of money waiting for him when he came out.'

Tony pressed the point home. 'So when he found he was dying, both the threats and the bribes were worthless. He might as well tell the truth.'

Dabdoub was unconvinced. 'So why tell another con? Why not tell the authorities?'

'Because,' Guest said, po-faced, 'the other con was his lover.'

'Yeah, I see.' Dabdoub yielded the argument. 'Brian Curry told me Tares was gay. So, did Miz Mons tell you the name of her informant?'

'No. She said – and I believe her – that the guy won't say another word while Tares is alive. He wants his lover to end his days in peace. When Tares is dead, he'll sell his story to the highest bidder.'

'How romantic.' Dabdoub mimed being sick. 'Well sir, I don't see that you really need us any more. Once Melvin pops his clogs his lover will reveal all, and the perpetrator will be brought to justice. All's well that ends well.'

Guest's wrinkled face screwed up tight. 'Every book I've read says that you private eyes are a cynical mob. Why don't you want to see this through with me?'

Dabdoub clasped his turnip head in both hands. 'Because I'm ashamed to take your money, Mr Guest. We're not giving you what you want. Anita Mons is closer to solving this case than I am.'

'No, no.' Guest was alarmed. 'I was told you were the best, and I believe it. Please stay with me. I haven't told you the rest. Anita Mons told me that her informant accidentally used the word "she" in describing the murderer. When she questioned him about it the guy said he was just being camp: everybody in his world was a "she". Mons didn't buy it. She thinks the murderer could be a woman.'

As usual, Tony could see a positive angle. 'Maybe the woman was someone Mrs Guest knew. That would explain why she let her into her flat.'

Dabdoub fell silent, staring down at his desk.

'What is it?' Guest was instantly alive to Jack's change of mood.

'Tony could be right,' Dabdoub said slowly.' It fits in with something Superintendent Curry told me. Apparently your ma was a regular at a local pub. Curry got a tip-off that she'd been seen in there several times in the company of another woman. The informant described the other woman as "sinister". I assumed what he meant was that she was a stranger – not a local girl, I mean.'

Guest was excited. 'Do you think this woman could be the murderer?'

'No, no, don't jump the gun. The police investigated her and drew a blank. She was some bloke's secretary, and on the day of the crime she was away with her boss on a business trip.'

'But you just said that Tony could be right!' Guest insisted. 'Now you're saying he's wrong.'

'No, what I'm suggesting – and it's only a hypothesis – is that if your ma chummed up with one woman in a pub, maybe she got acquainted with another one? One that the police didn't find out about?'

'That's pretty far-fetched.'

'I know it is. I just said as much. I'm trying to find an answer to the question: why did your mother let Melvin Tares into her flat?'

Tony joined in. 'The way I see it, Tares and the woman have to be working together. The woman strikes up an acquaintance with Mrs Guest and they become friendly. The woman calls on Mrs Guest, who lets her in. The woman subsequently opens the door to Tares. If Anita Mons is right, the couple were there to put the frighteners on the old lady.'

'Which suggests they were working for someone else,' Dabdoub said. 'Which further suggests that the crime had something to do with Mrs Guest's job.' He held up both hands in warning. 'Don't forget this is pure guesswork. We haven't a shred of proof. We've just built up a whole scenario on the idea that a woman might be involved. But we could be dead wrong. And even if we're right, we haven't the faintest idea who this woman is.'

'I reckon you've got a dead negative attitude, matey,' Guest said bluntly. 'Let's accentuate the positive here. A few days ago we had nothing. Now we've got a hypothesis. What do scientists do with a hypothesis? They test it until it either pans out or goes down the toilet. So that's what we're gonna do.' He glared at Dabdoub, daring him to disagree. 'Now, we haven't yet heard from our young colleague here. What have you got for us, cobber?'

Tony looked abashed. 'Not a lot, I'm afraid. I waded through all the papers you gave me, and I only turned up one thing that seemed out of the ordinary. As far as her work was concerned, she kept on hand only the barest records of cases she was actually working on. I suppose her previous cases were filed in her office at the DSS. I couldn't access those.'

'So what was the one thing that was out of the ordinary?' Guest asked.

'This.' Tony produced a sheet of paper. 'I photocopied it to show you, although I'm not sure how significant it is.'

Dabdoub and Guest looked at the paper together. It was a list of thirty-odd names all bracketed together, and outside the bracket a single name: Joseph Godwit. At the bottom of the page, Carole Guest had written: *What's going on?*'

'What do you make of it?' Guest asked.

Dabdoub shrugged. 'Joe Godwit was a builder. Did a lot of renovation work on council flats, stuff like that. This looks as if he was using lump labour.'

'Lump labour? What's that?'

'Casual labour: not registered, not on the books. Joe pays them in cash, gives them time off to claim unemployment benefit. The workers don't pay income tax, and Joe doesn't pay national insurance contributions, and doesn't waste time on paperwork. If he was really doing it on this scale, Joe would be saving himself around a thousand quid a week.'

'Cripes!' Guest looked appalled, but there was a note of admiration in his voice. 'So why didn't she report it?'

Dabdoub let the question hang in the air for a moment. 'One can only guess,' he said calmly.

'Holy Moses!' Realization came slowly. 'What are you trying to say? That she was blackmailing this Godwit guy?'

'We don't have any proof of that. But if we're looking for a motive for murder, that's certainly a possibility.'

'So where do we go from here? How do we get at this Joe Godwit?'

'We don't. He died about four years ago.' Dabdoub tried to soften the blow. 'Don't forget, we're in the realms of conjecture here. I've given you my interpretation of this list. But I could be wrong. It's another hypothesis that has to be tested.'

Guest didn't appreciate hearing his own words being thrown back at him. 'I want a full report on this Godwit guy. I want to know if he was connected in any way with Melvin Tares.' He pointed at the paper. 'My mother wrote those words: "What's going on?" Well, that's what I want to know. What the fuck was going on? You guys had better come up with some answers.' His face looked even darker and more wrinkled in his rage. He growled something unintelligible and stalked out of the room.

Dabdoub watched him go, then closed his eyes and leaned back in his chair. 'He's an exhausting little bugger, ent he? Sparky as a bloody firecracker. He don't give a feller time to think.'

'You practically told him to sack us,' Tony said resentfully. 'That's not very professional, is it?'

'Is he for real, do you reckon?' Dabdoub wondered aloud. 'Do people actually say things like "fair dinkum" and "cobber" in real life? I thought that was comic-book stuff.'

'You're a right racist, you,' Tony said. 'He's a sad little millionaire who wants to know what really happened to his mam.'

'Oh, ay?' Dabdoub wasn't listening. He lolled back in his chair, looking half-asleep. 'He shouldn't have rushed off like that. I was just on the verge of thinking something interesting.'

Tony mocked him. 'Oh, ay? What were you thinking?'

'I was thinking,' Dabdoub said dreamily, 'that we might just have a chance of cracking this case after all. I noticed something in that list you found. It's only a little thing – a tiny thread, you might say. If we give it a gentle tug, the whole thing might unravel before our very eyes.'

'Something on that list?' Tony was intrigued, as his boss meant him to be. 'You mean a name?'

' 'Course I mean a name, you great wally. There's nowt but names on it. Leslie Tanner. Small-time burglar. Had a nickname. Toolbox Tanner they called him, 'cause he wore overalls and carried a toolbox when he went out on a job. Drove a really manky-looking van, which was not a bright thing to do if you're working the drums in a posh neighbourhood. No-one who saw that van ever forgot it. It landed him in pokey more than once, but he never really got the message.'

'So what's this guy doing, working for a builder?'

Dabdoub opened his eyes and sat up. 'You're beginning to catch on, laddie. Whatever Tanner was doing for Joe Godwit, it wasn't laying bricks. George's ma was right: there was something going on. Something worth killing for.'

CHAPTER 17

Detective-Superintendent Teddy Giles of the Greater Manchester Serious Crimes Squad had set up an incident room in St Gregory's Church hall. He was a tall, dapper, stiff-backed man, who looked like an Army officer in civvies. His long, serio-comic face with its high-domed forehead and big, dark-brown eyes was not unattractive, Theresa Burgage thought. She had never met him before, but she knew and respected his reputation as a dogged, patient man who got results.

But right now he was looking harassed. 'Where the hell is everybody?' he growled. 'Is this all we're going to get?'

Burgage looked suitably apologetic. 'I'm afraid so, sir. We're short-staffed anyway, and this flu epidemic has knocked us for six. These are all the people I can spare.'

'Oh, well.' Giles had learned to be philosophical about such setbacks. 'The fewer men, the greater share of honour, eh?' One thing he hadn't learned was that few police officers shared his fondness for Shakespearean quotations. This one was received with baffled looks from the men, and resentful stares from the women. He pressed on: 'Let's bring everyone up to speed, shall we? The victim was Elizabeth Nair, aged thirty-four, unmarried, living in a flat on the Wickerbrook Estate. Unemployed, but did casual work, when she could get it, as a cleaner. Her body was found just before 6 a.m. last Monday, by the workmen coming to empty the rubbish bins in this waste disposal area.' Giles pointed to a rough ground plan pinned up on a notice board. 'As you can see, it's just a rectangular space, enclosed on three sides by blank walls. There are six refuse chutes set into the walls, each serving a different level, delivering rubbish into large, wheeled bins which are emptied every day. The body was found here,' he tapped the drawing, 'in front of bin number four. The cause of death was two heavy blows to the throat with a blunt instrument, possibly a hammer. Time of death somewhere between nine p.m. and midnight. No handbag or purse has been found, either with the body or in the victim's flat, so at the moment the favourite theory is that this was a spur-of-the-moment mugging. Someone saw an opportunity, and took it.'

'Someone who just happened to be carrying a hammer?' one of the detectives murmured.

'The doc didn't say it definitely was a hammer, just that it was a possibility,' Giles shot back. 'But I take your point. Some guy could have been prowling the area with a weapon, looking for a victim. You're suggesting that the existence of a weapon implies premeditation?'

'Something like that,' DC Bailey agreed. 'Do we think that this is drug-related?'

'It's the first thing that comes to mind. We know that plenty of drugs are traded on that estate, especially among the kids. OK, let's open this out a bit. Sergeant, you were in charge of the house-to-house. What did you turn up?'

The sergeant, one of Giles's own squad, shrugged. 'Not a lot, sir. Nobody we talked to admitted seeing or hearing a thing. There are about ninety families on that estate, and we've managed to speak to about half of them. So far, apart from her immediate neighbours, we've found very few people who knew Ms Nair, or even knew *of* her. It seems she was dead shy, on account of her speech impediment. The local kids used to make fun of her; that's the only thing people remember.'

'Thank you, Sergeant. Keep at it. It's a lousy job, but it's got to be done.'

'I know that sir. We should finish the job today, in any case. You'll have our report first thing tomorrow morning.'

'Good lad. Once more into the breach, dear friend, as the Bard has it. That's the spirit.' Someone at the back of the room laughed, but Giles wasn't sure it was the kind of laugh he wanted to hear. He ignored it and turned back to Detective Bailey. 'Right, Bill. What have you got for us?'

'Nothing much to the purpose, I'm afraid,' Bailey said. 'We found an address book in Nair's flat, and Eric and I checked out the names in it. It wasn't a long job, because it wasn't a long list. Most of the people on it were women Nair had worked for as a cleaner. The rest were mainly useful contacts – doctor, plumber, hairdresser, stuff like that. There were only three people on the list who could be called friends. One was an old widow lady who lived in the next block. She told us that Lizzie Nair would run errands for her, do her shopping, and sometimes sit and chat with her in the evenings. My guess is that they became acquainted because the old lady herself has a pronounced stammer. There was probably some fellow-feeling there. At any rate the old girl was inconsolable at the news. Next up was a bloke who lived in Blackpool – apart from the doctor and the plumber, the only male on the list. We phoned him, and he said yes, he'd gone out with Lizzie a few times, but he hadn't seen her for thirteen years or so. He was now married, with a couple of kids. The last one on the list was another neighbour, lived on the floor above hers. Fernie Brent, her name is.'

'Fernie?' Giles looked shocked. 'What kind of name is that?'

Bailey spread his hands. 'I just report the facts, guv, I'm not responsible for them. We had a long chat with Fernie. She told us straight up, she's out on licence: she was released half-way through a two-year stretch for her involvement in a robbery. She's living with her married sister on the Wickerbrook, and her parole officer has fixed her up with a job at Buchanan's store.'

'So what's her connection with Elizabeth Nair?' Giles asked.

'Pretty casual, according to Fernie. They were on nodding terms on account of seeing each other on the estate; but they only got acquainted when Fernie broke up a crowd of kids who were baiting Lizzie about her stammer. After that, they formed a kind of friendship, mainly, I gather, instigated by Lizzie. Fernie said she felt sorry for the woman. They did a few things together – went to the pictures, visited the pub, but by Fernie's account they were never really close. She was horrified by the murder, but we could tell she wasn't actually heartbroken. It wasn't like she'd lost a close friend.' Bailey paused and consulted his notes. 'She told us what everybody else had told us: that Lizzie Nair was a shy, insecure person with no real friends.'

Superintendent Giles was determined to cover all bases. 'Did you rate this Ms Brent person as a suspect?'

Bailey looked at DC Cope before he spoke. 'We asked her where she was on the Sunday night, yeah. Like most people in that situation, she looked flustered, had to think about it. Then she told us that she had spent that evening – from about eight o'clock until after midnight, with an old friend – a bloke she had worked with some years ago. From the way she said this, I got the impression that she had had sex with the guy, which, after a year in stir, was not unlikely.'

'Did she give you the name of this guy?'

'Yeah. We haven't contacted him yet, but we're on to it.'

Giles had to be satisfied with that. 'OK. Did any of the people you interviewed tell you whether Ms Nair had a boyfriend?'

Cope and Bailey both shook their heads. 'Quite the opposite, guv,'

Cope said. 'We got the impression she was too shy and uptight for any kind of sexual relationship.'

'I was afraid you would say that,' Giles said gloomily. 'It leaves us with a problem. Forensics are still working in that flat, but they've given me some preliminary findings. The sheets on Ms Nair's bed are liberally stained with semen. Your impression notwithstanding, it seems that our Lizzie was being shagged by someone.'

Angela Bonneville's house was not far from Rose Kelsey's, and it was about the same size, but it was markedly different in style. It was the difference that money makes. Angela clearly had neither the time nor the inclination to choose her own furnishings, so she had turned the job over to professionals. The result, in Joanna's opinion, was exquisite, but faintly unreal, like a stage setting for a drawing-room comedy. The drawing-room she was standing in had, besides tastefully matched wall-paper and fabrics, a picture-window view of an elegant formal garden. She looked round in vain for something that wasn't in perfect taste.

The other difference from Rose's establishment was the quality of the service. Joanna had no idea how many servants there were in Angela's house, but she had already seen the maid and the gardener: and she was convinced that there were many other hands at work below stairs, making sure that Angela's life ran as smoothly as possible. These were the rewards of success, Joanna thought, and for a moment she allowed herself to day-dream about her own hopes. But she wouldn't have a home like this, she decided. It was just like living in a posh hotel.

Angela rushed into the room, full of apologies. 'Sorry, sorry! I was on the phone to my agent, and she's such a chatterbox. Perhaps you'll forgive me if I tell you that I mentioned your name to her, and she's quite intrigued. When we're ready we'll get her over to listen to you.' She waved aside Joanna's attempt to thank her. 'Come through into the workshop, and let's get started.'

"Workshop" seemed an odd word for Angela to use, but Joanna saw at a glance that it was appropriate. It was a large, high-ceilinged room, with a gleaming Yamaha grand at the window end, flanked by book-cases and cabinets packed with sheet music, but apart from a rectangular space in the centre the rest of the room was packed with a bewildering array of electronic gadgetry. There were several micro-phones, recording equipment, a control board that looked as if it belonged in the cockpit of a jumbo jet, a keyboard synthesizer, four loudspeakers, two computers and a stack of metal boxes bristling with dials, knobs and switches. At intervals around the room, swags of heavy grey material hung from ceiling to floor. 'Sound-absorbing curtains,'

Angela explained. 'At the touch of a button, I can turn this place into an acoustically dead room.' She was amused by her visitor's wide-eyed expression. 'Sportsmen and women watch videos of themselves to sharpen up their performance. I do the same thing with sound-recording. But apart from that, I just love playing with these toys. When I get tired of the concert circuit, I'm going to retire and try my hand at composition.'

Joanna was growing more apprehensive by the minute. Angela's energy and enthusiasm seemed inexhaustible; it was obviously going to require a tremendous effort to keep up with her.

But for all her bounce Angela was not insensitive. When she had settled herself at the piano and arranged her music she looked up with a sympathetic smile. 'Nervous?'

'Yes, very.'

'Me, too. Let's do it.'

After that, nothing mattered but the music. The first song was over so quickly that at the end they stared at each other, startled and exhilarated. 'Cripes!' Angela muttered. 'What was that?'

'It was fun,' Joanna said breathlessly.

'Fun for you, my fine feathered friend. I was playing like an elephant on stilts. Hang on a minute.' She flicked off strings of triplets at incredible speed. 'Right. "*Nein, junger Herr.*" Do you think she means it?'

'Oh, yes. She's not bluffing. But she's confident she can bring him to heel. That little pause before "*nicht wahr*?" is just enough to tell you she's on top of the situation.'

'I'll take your word for it. I liked the way you handled the rubato, by the way.'

Joanna blushed with pleasure. 'Thank you.'

'Wow.' Angela leaned forward and reverently touched the page, running her fingers along the lines as if she was reading Braille. 'Hey, this is going to be fun. Let's do more. Lots more. Ready?'

'Yes.'

'Have at you, then.'

They worked all afternoon, rehearsing each song over and over, then discussing, experimenting, arguing and agonizing over each one. Joanna's confidence grew, not least because Angela treated her as an equal, constantly asking 'Am I too loud?' or 'Do we breathe here?' and once, in a moment Joanna knew she would cherish for the rest of her life, saying 'Cripes, girl, that was bloody marvellous!' They stopped only when the effort of concentration became too great, and even then they put the work aside reluctantly. For Joanna, stopping was like waking from a dream. While they had been rehearsing she had focused completely on the music, but now that it was over the excitement of the whole experience flooded her heart and mind with an overwhelming joy. For years she had known what she wanted; now she knew where she belonged.

That same afternoon Jack Dabdoub, his feet sore from tramping the mean streets of one of Manchester's grottier suburbs, was busy cursing Anita Mons under his breath. The bloody woman had completely undermined his negotiating position. That morning she had printed a follow-up article about Melvin Tares, making a big dramatic play about the victim's father and his quest for justice; which would have been OK if she hadn't mentioned – twice – that George Guest was an Australian millionaire. Although she hadn't mentioned Dabdoub by name, every snout in town seemed to know he was on the case, and that one word – millionaire – meant that he was having to pay exorbitant rates for information, most of which he was sure was unreliable.

And now even Andrei the hacker, the most readily corruptible kid on the block, was refusing to co-operate without a down payment of a hundred quid, with another 200 on delivery. 'Is illegitimate, what you ask,' he said primly.

'It's never stopped you before,' Jack said.

'Big risk. I could screw up in gaol.'

'We say wind up in gaol,' Jack told him. 'You wouldn't screw up, Andy lad. You're too clever.'

'Is true,' Andrei admitted modestly. 'So, one hundred pounds, yes? In cash?'

Dabdoub handed the money over. 'Here's the names. Make it snappy, will you?'

The youth frowned. 'Snappy? Who is snapping what?'

'Just be as quick as you can, eh?'

'This cannot be rush.' Andrei's artistic soul was affronted. 'When I am ready, so?'

'Yeah, OK.' Dabdoub was tired and wanted to go home. 'Godamighty, I don't know why I bother with you.'

Andrei beamed and swished his shoulder-length hair from side to side. 'Because I'm worth it,' he murmured provocatively.

When she drove to her parking spot on the Causeway, Joanna was pleased to see Matt Clements standing in his garden, particularly since she was dying to tell someone about her afternoon with Angela Bonneville.

'Do come in and have a drink,' she called. 'I haven't thanked you properly for rescuing me last weekend.'

He seemed slightly taken aback by the enthusiasm of her greeting, but he was obviously happy to see her again. 'I'd like that very much,' he said. 'Just give me a minute or two to change out of these muddy clothes. I've been on-site all afternoon.'

When he knocked on her door a few minutes later he was carrying a bottle of champagne. 'Something tells me this is a celebration,' he said.

She clapped her hands with pleasure. 'How clever of you! How did you guess?'

'The way you look. You're on a high about something. I guess your back is feeling better.'

'Much better, thank you. I feel fine.'

And yes, she was on a high, she told him. She felt wonderful. They sat in her little kitchen and sipped champagne, and he watched her, smiling, as she chattered on about Angela Bonneville – of course, he had heard of her – and about her house, and her workshop, and her gleaming piano, and her hi-tech toys; and about Hugo Wolf and his songs; and best of all, about just being there, singing, and being accompanied by a genius. 'But Angela's not at all intimidating,' she assured him. 'She laughs a lot and says things like "cripes" and "crikey"!' She badly wanted to tell him Angela's comment about her being bloody marvellous, but she didn't want to seem boastful. All the same, flushed with happiness and champagne, she wanted to share everything with him. He said little, but smiled and nodded encouragingly, and let her rattle on. Gradually her speech slowed, and she began to feel tired and deflated. He was quick to recognize her change of mood.

'You're running out of steam. Would you like me to leave?'

'No.' She had wanted someone to share the high with her, and she didn't want to be alone now the reaction had set in. 'Please stay. I can't finish the champagne all by myself.'

'Good.' He took the hint and refilled her glass. 'I've been hoping for a chance to talk to you.'

'What about?'

'Well, for one thing, I was curious about that photograph on your sideboard. The two gents with shotguns.'

She smiled. 'The one on the right is my father. The other one is his best friend, Peter Crawford-Webb. They were in the Army together.'

'Do you mind if I have a closer look?'

'Go ahead.'

Matt took the photograph down and examined it. 'Where was this taken, do you know?'

'Oh, that would have been at Peter's place in Yorkshire – a massive

Victorian pile called Ginsley Hall. I only went over there once, about thirteen years ago, and even then most of the place was virtually falling down. Peter lived in a three-bedroom apartment in the west wing. That was all he could afford to maintain, he said. He was a funny old stick. His wife died young, and he never remarried; in fact, by the time I met him he seemed the stereotype of the crusty old bachelor.'

'Did they shoot often?'

'Quite often, after they retired from the Army. Mum and Dad would go up there mid-September, and stay for about a month. It wasn't just shooting; there was fishing, riding, golf – and mother always took her sketch-pad and water-colours.'

'Sounds idyllic.' Matt was only half-listening. 'Any idea who took this photograph?'

'My mother, I suppose. Why do you ask?'

'Well, they're both togged up in shooting-gear, and their hats have got their ear-flaps down, as if there's a jolly cold breeze blowing, and yet they're obviously indoors. Posed like that, you'd expect to see a stretch of moorland behind them, not a simple wall with a picture on it.' Matt cocked his head appreciatively. 'Quite a nice picture too, I'd say.'

Joanna took the photo from him. 'Oh, that's Georgie.'

'Georgie?'

'That's what Peter called it. "My Georgie", he would say. I assumed it was the name of the horse. He loved that picture.'

'One can see why.' Matt took the photo from her and replaced it on the sideboard. He stared at it for a moment longer, frowning slightly. 'Was that your father's gun?'

'Oh no, they both belonged to Peter. Dad didn't have a shotgun. Mother wouldn't allow guns in the house.' Joanna was intrigued. 'All these questions. What's so special about that photo?'

'I don't know.' Matt seemed unable to tear his eyes away from it. 'There's something odd about it, but I can't work out what it is.'

'You just said – they're wearing their hats indoors.'

'No, it's something else.' Matt gave up and abruptly changed the subject. 'What branch of the Army was your father in?'

'He was a sapper.'

'An engineer?' Matt was pleased. 'So he was a practical kind of chap?'

'Very. He did all the decoration and repairs in this house himself.' She saw the glint of interest in his eye and expected another flood of questions, but instead he changed tack yet again. 'Are you hungry?'

'What? No.' She had second thoughts. 'Actually, yes. I wasn't until you put the idea into my head. Now, I'm bloody ravenous.'

'Let me take you out to dinner.'

'You fed me on Sunday. I owe you a meal.'

'You've had a busy and exciting day. You don't want to cook, and neither do I. On the other hand, I do want to go on talking.'

'Well …' She was tempted, but she felt she ought to object.

'I know a place,' he said.

She laughed. 'I'm sure you do. And it's bloody perfect, no doubt.'

'The food's good, and the place isn't crowded mid-week.'

She yielded, but not gracefully. 'Oh, all right. But we go Dutch, OK?'

He pursed his lips doubtfully. 'Can one go Dutch in a Thai restaurant?'

She liked the place. The Oriental decor was not too garish, the lighting was not too bright, and the tinkling music was distant enough to be pleasantly undemanding. Sensibly, they had arrived by taxi, so that they could continue to drink champagne if they wanted to, and after a short discussion they agreed that it would be the wisest option. She thought the food was marvellous, and said so several times, in rising tones of delight, as one dish succeeded another. She no longer felt tired and deflated; the memory of her afternoon with Angela Bonneville kept flooding her mind with happiness. Knowing that Matt would not despise her vanity, she finally confided to him that Angela had actually praised her singing at one point; she could tell by the expression in his eyes that he was almost as pleased as she was herself. It was an evening quite unlike any other in her experience. She knew that Matt adored her – in spite of that pompous little lie about not being sexually attracted to her because he was happily married – but he wasn't being a pain about it. He was a sensitive guy: he obviously realized that she didn't fancy him and had settled for just being a good friend. Which was great. She could relax, allow herself to be thoroughly spoilt, and wallow in the memory of her golden afternoon.

If she hadn't been feeling a little tipsy she might have approached the subject with more delicacy, but she knew him to be a plain, blunt fellow, so he would appreciate her directness. 'Tell me about your wife,' she said.

'Ah.' He swallowed hard, and fiddled with the stem of his wine glass in a blatant attempt to give himself time to think.

'You told me you were happily married,' she prompted him.

'Yes, well, that was at least half-true. I am married.'

'But your wife has left you.'

He moved his head to one side, as if he was physically dodging the question. 'I suppose so.'

I've drunk too much, Joanna thought. I ought not to be talking like this. But she ploughed on anyway. 'You suppose so? That doesn't sound like you at all, Matthew Clements.'

He sighed. 'I'm sorry I lied to you. I spoke without thinking.'

Joanna realized that she had made a bad move in getting him to admit that he had lied. Now, he was free to admit that he had fancied her all along, and start to court her in earnest. That wasn't what she wanted at all.

'The truth is ...' Matt began, then paused and started again. 'My wife Mary has had a bad couple of years. The trouble began when she miscarried, late in pregnancy.'

Joanna now wished she hadn't started this. 'Your first child?'

'Yes. Soon after the miscarriage she became severely depressed; and neither counselling nor medication seemed to help her. Then, one afternoon, she had an accident. She drove her car into a tree.' His voice was flat, matter-of-fact. 'She was taken to hospital badly concussed and with broken ribs. She was unconscious for thirty-six hours. The injury left her with slightly impaired hearing and occasional episodes of blurred vision. And of course, her depression became worse.' Matt was now speaking so quietly that she had to strain to hear him. 'The doctors suggested that she might benefit from a spell in a convalescent home, and indeed, after a couple of weeks there she did seem a little happier. She had become friendly with another patient, who by chance was also called Mary, and who had also suffered the loss of a child. The two women were able to comfort each other where nurses and counsellors had failed.' He broke off, looking rueful. 'I'm sorry this is so long-winded.'

'No, I'm interested. Really.' All the same, she hadn't bargained for such a pathetic story. It was putting quite a downer on the evening.

'Well, one day Mary told me that she wanted to leave the nursing home and go to a retreat with her friend. She was so positive about the prospect – I hadn't seen her look so animated for months – that she convinced me that this was her path to recovery. She talked about peace and meditation, and self-discovery. I was pleased for her. The only drawback was that I wouldn't be able to visit her – at least, not until she felt "ready", as she called it. Well, that was OK; I could cope with anything, if it would help to pull her out of that awful depression. Now, I had assumed that she was going to some conventional religious community – a priory, or some cloistered sisterhood somewhere, but it turned out that she and her friend were going to a commune in Dorset known as the Phalanstery of the First Sacred Light, run by a guy called Othniel Tophet, who called himself the Acmic Hierophant of the Sacred Light.'

Joanna gaped. 'You're making this up!'

'I wish I were. She had forbidden me to visit her, but she wrote to me regularly at first. They were rambling, not very coherent letters, but they gave me hope that she was gradually coming out of her depressed state. Then the tone of the letters changed, and it became clear that she had got religion in a big way. But it wasn't conventional Christianity, or indeed any recognizable orderly creed. It was just a mish-mash of myth, miracle and magic. This world was just a bad dream, a nightmare; all the goodies were stored up in the next world. All you had to do to enter Paradise, according to the Acmic Hierophant, was to believe fifty impossible things before breakfast.' Matt made no attempt to hide the bitterness in his own soul. 'Inevitably, I got a final letter: she wasn't coming back to me. She was determined to spend her life in the service of the First Sacred Light. Shortly after that, I got a letter from Othniel Tophet, setting out the monthly cost of a permanent stay in the commune.'

Joanna waited for him to go on, but it seemed that was the end of the story. 'But – are you saying you just left her there? Didn't you try to get her back?'

'Of course I tried. But the truth was that if I had forced her to leave the commune she would have been miserable. She was happy – genuinely happy – where she was. The Acmic Hierophant meant more to her than I did.'

'So, you pay for her to stay in that commune?'

'Yes. I check on her welfare every month or so. A private investigator – Jack Dabdoub, the fat fellow you met at the Rugby Club – keeps an eye on her.'

Joanna was confused. Was Matt weak for simply accepting the situation, or strong for putting his wife's happiness before his own? The only conclusion she could come to was that he was unlike anyone else she had ever known.

'That's one of the saddest stories I've ever heard,' she said.

'Don't let it spoil your evening. It's my problem, not yours.'

But Joanna wasn't prepared to leave it there. 'But what are you going to do?'

'Do? Mary is my wife. She's my responsibility. She's happy now, but suppose she loses this new-found faith? Where would she turn if I desert her?'

Joanna wasn't entirely satisfied with that answer. It was OK so long as she wasn't attracted to him. But what if things changed? Looking at the breadth of his shoulders, and the depth of concern in his eyes, she wasn't at all sure that things would always stay as they were.

CHAPTER 18

The briefing in the incident room on Thursday morning was short and unsatisfactory. The investigation into the death of Elizabeth Nair was completely stalled. House-to-house enquiries had drawn a blank, the search of Nair's flat had turned up no obvious clues, and the results that were coming in from the forensics lab provided more questions than answers.

'We have evidence from fingerprints and DNA that three people have been in that flat recently,' Superintendent Giles announced. 'Nair herself, her friend Ms Brent – the gal who has form for robbery – and one other, an as yet unidentified male. Obviously, our priority is to find that man. If Nair was in a sexual relationship, then someone, somewhere, must have seen them together. And before you ask, no, this guy's DNA isn't on file. So far as we know, he's got no previous.'

One of the younger officers made a sour face. 'Sir, are you saying what I think you're saying?'

'I'm afraid so. Tomorrow night, we'll put out an appeal on the local news, and hope for a response from that; but for now, we've got to go over the same ground again, and ask specific questions about Lizzie Nair's boyfriend.' He raised his voice over the chorus of groans. 'By the way, did anybody check Ms Brent's alibi? We don't want to leave any stone unturned.'

Cope and Bailey exchanged glances. 'Not yet, sir,' Cope said. 'We haven't been able to catch the guy at home. Hopefully, we'll get to talk to him today.'

'OK. Right, get to it everyone. Photos of the victim are on the desk by the door. Show them around, and see if you can jog somebody's memory. Good luck.'

This last remark prompted some ribald comment as the officers filed out, but Giles had no doubt that his men would do a thorough job. It was boring, routine work, and the likelihood was that it would end in failure. The investigation would be wound down and the case would be shelved along with all the other unsolved crimes. Giles had learned to be philosophical about it all. Win some, lose some. So long as you had done your best, you could sleep easy.

He was aware that one of the uniformed cops had lingered behind the rest, and was regarding him speculatively from the far side of the room. He was a burly, weather-beaten man, who looked as if he had at least twenty years' service under his belt. But he was still in uniform, with no stripes on his shoulder which, in Giles's opinion, meant that he was either stupid or unambitious. He was one of the local men, but there was something about him that was familiar. 'Don't I know you, Constable?'

'We worked in the same nick, ten years ago,' the man said. 'Joe Lolly.'

'Joe Lolly, of course!' Giles lied automatically, ever the diplomat. 'How are you doing, Joe?'

'OK. I transferred out here because this is my wife's home town. It's a friendly little place.'

'So it is, so it is. Well, it's nice to talk to you again, Joe.'

'Thank you.' Joe hesitated, unsure how to continue. 'There was something you said at that first call that set me thinking. The victim was killed with two sharp blows to the throat with a hammer, you said.'

'No.' Giles corrected him. 'I said something like a hammer. The actual impact wounds were made by a metal domed object about two inches across – like the head of a hammer.'

'Yes, sir. But it's not likely that the weapon was an actual hammer, is it? I mean, to hit someone in the throat with a hammer takes some doing, if you think about it.'

If Giles was getting impatient with the man he didn't show it. 'OK, Constable, it probably wasn't a hammer. We don't know what it was.'

'Well, sir, I think I might have an idea about that. Did you ever hear of a thing called the China cosh, or sometimes the Hong-Kong cosh?'

'No, I never did. What is it?'

'I've got a drawing here, which will give you a rough idea. It's easier than trying to describe it.' He showed the superintendent a page of his notebook. 'It's basically a bar of lead that fits into the palm of the hand. This narrow curved bit hooks over the forefinger, while at the other end the bar balloons out into a curved shape like a thick mushroom. It weighs over a pound. Obviously, you could do a lot of damage with a downward blow; but a karate chop to the throat would be even more effective.'

Giles was definitely interested. 'I've never seen anything like this. Where did you get it?'

'I haven't actually got one sir. I drew that from memory. Back in the mid-nineties, there was a street war in the Whalley Range area, and the local prostitutes were caught in the middle. They got aggro from kids, gang bullies, and some of their rougher clients. One of the pimps issued these things to his string of toms for self-protection. He said he imported them from China, hence the name, but they looked home-made to me. Anyway, the toms never used them, to my knowledge. A pound of lead is a lot to carry in your handbag, and anyway most of the girls were expert in the use of the hatpin. So in the end they were happy to hand over these lead things without much trouble.'

'I'm not sure what you're trying to tell me, Joe,' Giles said, losing patience a little. 'I've never seen these things before. Are they still in use or not?'

'I'm sure they're not generally in use, sir. I think we confiscated most of them. But since we didn't know how many were in circulation, we couldn't be sure that we got them all.'

'So what you're saying is that one of these things could still be in existence, and our killer could have used it?' Giles's tone made it more of a dismissal than a question.

Joe was not insensitive: he recognized a brush-off when he heard one. But he had a stubborn streak. 'There was something that made it stick in my memory, sir. About that time – eight years ago – an elderly social worker was killed in her flat—'

'Yes I know all about that. I've talked to the officer who led that investigation. The MO was strangely like this one – a blow to the throat with a domed metal object. But apart from the way the victims died, the cases seem quite different. That one was eight years ago, twenty miles away, and anyway, they caught the guy who did it.'

'But they never did find the murder weapon,' Joe said.

'True, Constable, and we haven't found the murder weapon in this case, either. What you're saying is that the instrument used in both cases could be something like this Chinese whatsit. I take your point, Joe, and I'm grateful for your input.'

Again Joe refused to take the hint. 'There's another thing,' he said.

Giles's patience was wearing thin. 'Is it relevant?'

'I think so, sir. You'll have to judge for yourself. The man who was sent down for the murder was an enforcer for the Ganja brothers—'

'The Ganja brothers died years ago, man!'

'Just hear me out, sir. The pimp who supplied these things to his girls paid protection money to the Ganjas. There's a possible link, d'you see? The enforcer and the pimp might well have met in the way of business.'

Giles spelled it out slowly. 'Melvin Tares could have picked up one of these coshes from the pimp and used it to kill the old woman, yes?'

'The weapon fits the forensic description, and Tares could easily have got his hands on one.'

'OK, I'll grant you that it's possible. So, on the back of that, your theory is that one of these weapons is still around, and was used to kill Lizzie Nair?'

'I know it's a long shot, sir. But the medical report says an unusual weapon was used, and this is an unusual weapon. We also know that only a limited number of them were made and circulated.'

'I see where you're headed, Joe, but I don't fancy our chances of tracing that rogue weapon. Melvin Tares is banged up, and the Ganja brothers are history.'

'I know the Ganjas were killed in the street wars of the nineties, sir. But I don't remember hearing that any prostitutes were killed.'

Giles took a moment to catch up. 'You think that some of these toms – the ones who got these China coshes – are still out on the streets?'

'I think it very likely, sir.'

'But they must be ancient!'

'Most of that particular string will still be under thirty, sir. But in any case, age isn't a barrier. Many handicapped clients prefer a motherly type.'

Giles made a wild gesture with his hands as if he was trying to push that image out of his head. 'I'm beginning to wish we hadn't started this conversation. If I understand you, you're suggesting that one of these girls – women – might just give us a pointer to what happened to this rogue weapon. Or are you saying that one of them might be a murderer?'

For the first time Joe showed a trace of diffidence. 'I wouldn't have brought it up if we had any solid leads on this one, sir. And this is a pretty feeble straw to be clutching at. But one of those women might just remember if anyone showed a particular fancy for these Chinese coshes.'

'But we've no proof that this is the kind of weapon that was used in either murder.' All the same, Giles was still weighing the possibilities. 'Did you know these women?'

'All of them sir. Never had occasion to nick any of 'em, though.'

'So there might be a touch of goodwill there, you reckon?' Suddenly Giles was in a good humour. 'Right, Joe, you've talked yourself into a job. Get over there and see what you can find. Only don't tread on any toes, d'you hear?'

'I've still got mates at the local nick, sir. It won't be a problem. And it shouldn't take long.'

Giles suddenly thought of something else. 'Listen, there's a P I called Jack Dabdoub looking into the Carole Guest case for some crackpot client. It might be worth sharing your theory with him, in case he's got anything interesting for us. Hang on a minute, I'll find his number.'

Joe grinned broadly. 'No need, sir. I know young Jack well. We're in the same rugger team. I'll give him your regards, shall I?' As he was leaving, he met Inspector Burgage in the doorway and stood aside for her. 'Ma'am,' he said cheerfully, but she was in too much of a temper to return his greeting. She strode across the room and threw herself into a chair across from Giles's desk.

'That bloody man!' she burst out, her face scarlet with fury.

Giles regarded her with some interest. She was rather magnificent when her blood was up, he thought. Like some powerful jungle animal, though he couldn't quite think which one. 'Which bloody man would that be?' he enquired mildly.

'Sergeant bloody Ben bloody Dewbury!' Burgage rocked forward and backward in her chair, breathing deeply and noisily.

'What's he done?'

But it was some little time before she could calm down enough to tell him just exactly what Sergeant Dewbury had done.

The first phone call Joanna had that morning was from Piers Atherton. 'Bad news, I'm afraid,' he said without preamble. 'I have to make your suspension official. I'm meeting the governors this afternoon. After that wretched article, I have no choice. Have you any idea who's behind it?'

'I'm sorry, Headmaster, I'm not with you. What article is that?'

'You haven't read this morning's *Voice*?'

The *Aldersgrove and Dovebridge Weekly Voice* was the local newspaper. 'No, I haven't looked at any of the papers yet.' The truth was that Joanna hadn't been up very long, but she didn't want to confess as much to Atherton.

'It is quite vile,' Atherton said. 'If it weren't for the fact that your name is not specifically mentioned I'm sure you would have excellent grounds for a libel suit. Have the police contacted you?'

'Yes. I denied the charge, and I had the feeling that the senior officer believed me.'

'Good, that's very good. And have you been in touch with your union district officer yet?'

'Ivor Griffiths? Not yet. To tell the truth, Headmaster, I thought this whole farcical episode would simply blow over.'

'Well, it hasn't,' Atherton said bluntly. 'And now the press has got hold of it, it looks like turning into a very nasty mess indeed. Already the police have been making a thorough nuisance of themselves at the school, and the staff are getting rattled. We're chronically short of staff anyway, because of budget cuts and the flu epidemic. I could really do without this extra hassle, Joanna!'

'It's Nick Tanner's fault, not mine, Headmaster,' Joanna pointed out coolly.

'I know, I know. I could strangle the little sod.' Atherton paused and gave his characteristic double cough, to pull himself together. 'Contact Griffiths ASAP. Enlist as much help as you possibly can, Joanna. I fear you're going to need it.' He rang off abruptly, as if he was afraid of saying something he might regret.

Joanna hurried to the front door, to pick the papers off the mat. There was no need to search for the article. The *Voice* had given it pride of place, on the front page:

WHY DON'T THEY DO SOMETHING?

Angry Parent Accuses Authorities of Negligence.

(A Special Report by Monica Rawe, Crime Correspondent.)

Child abuse must be one of the vilest crimes known to man. It is almost too disgusting to contemplate, and many people would ridicule the idea that it could possibly exist in such a quiet, law-abiding place as Aldersgrove.

Yet, according to Mrs X , a respectable, hard-working mother (for legal reasons I am not allowed to disclose her name), her son has suffered regular sexual abuse from one of our local teachers for more than eight months! Mrs X says that the police and the welfare services have known about it for ages, and they have more than enough evidence to convict, yet they are taking no steps to bring the guilty party to justice. As Mrs X rightly says: "Why don't they do something? Do they think they can ignore us just because we're working-class?" Some of us might think she has a point.

Deviant Sexual Practices

I have seen a transcript of a taped interview between the authorities and the child in question, and it is by far the most shocking and disgusting thing I have ever read. The most dreadful thing is that the child – a boy barely fourteen years old! – is so completely under the influence of this middle-aged seductress as to be totally besotted with her. Not only did she regularly ply the boy with strong liquor, but she introduced him into deviant sexual practices too nauseating to think about, let alone describe. And he declares himself to be in love with her! The truth is – to judge by his own confessions on tape – she has left her evil mark on him for life.

Intimate Detail

I have to say, having read the boy's story with its wealth of intimate detail, that for me it has the ring of truth. There are facts in it that the child could not possibly have known by hearsay. Also, he did not volunteer the information – it was wrung from him by the pleas of a desperately worried mother. And, as his mother points out, what can he possibly gain from lying?

I pride myself on keeping an open mind: I believe devoutly in the principle that a person is innocent until proven guilty. But I also believe that justice delayed is justice forgone. Today, Mrs X is going to work, as she does every day – cleaning other people's houses for £4 an hour. The middle-aged woman who has corrupted Mrs X's son is temporarily suspended from duty – on full pay, of course. That sort of "punishment" is what you and I would call a holiday. Is this what our society has come to? Can this really be British justice?

Numb with shock, it took Joanna some time to register that the phone was ringing again. This time it was Ivor Griffiths, her union representative.

'Joanna? I've just been speaking to Piers Atherton. This article in today's *Voice* – is it really about you? There can't be any truth in it, for heaven's sake?'

'It's a false, malicious accusation, Ivor.' Wearily, Joanna began to recount the whole sorry tale, beginning with the interview with Atherton and Philippa Crouch. Just recalling it all made her depressed. But sadly, she couldn't tell from that sceptical Welsh lilt in Ivor's voice, whether he believed her.

Betsy Bray held out the phone, her face positively glistening with excitement and curiosity. 'It's for you, Gerald. The police.'

Gerald Dudley had prepared himself for the call, although he had half-convinced himself that it wouldn't happen. He took the receiver from her. 'Yes?' he said languidly. Then, a little more sharply, 'Yes, this is he.'

Betsy smiled to herself as she moved quietly out of the room, though not out of earshot. She had always admired Gerald's masterful way of putting subordinates in their place.

Dudley knew that his hostess would be eavesdropping, and was careful to shape his end of the conversation for her ears. 'One moment, officer. Would you mind telling me what this is all about? Ah yes, I see ... No, that won't be necessary. I shall come to you ... Not at all ... Your name again? ... Well, Detective Bailey, I'm sure you appreciate that this is a matter of extreme delicacy, and I would wish that any statement I may make be treated as entirely confidential ... Of course I understand ... Very well then, expect to see me within the hour.' He put down the phone and stood with his hand on the receiver, apparently lost in thought.

For form's sake Betsy waited a couple of beats before re-entering the room. 'Is everything all right?'

Dudley gave a hopeless shrug. 'It's all right for *me*,' he said, laying heavy stress on the last word.

'Oh gosh.' Betsy put both hands to her mouth. 'It's that *Voice* article, isn't it? It's about *her*: I knew it as soon as I read it. Golly, Gerald, you knew her better than anyone; it's only natural that they would want to question you. What will you say?'

Gerald sighed. 'The truth, Betsy. What else can I say?'

'Yes, well of course. And you're one of the few people around here who's in a position to know the whole truth. But you're so incredibly loyal. And don't tell me you're not still carrying a torch for her, for I won't believe it.' It suddenly occurred to Betsy that if she didn't stop talking Gerald wouldn't have a chance to tell her what she wanted to know. 'I mean, poor Joanna couldn't possibly ... I mean, those things in the newspaper, they couldn't possibly be ... Could they?'

Absent-mindedly, Gerald pulled his brier pipe from his pocket. He rarely smoked it, but he liked to clamp the stem between his teeth and flex his jaw muscles. 'The Joanna I knew,' he said sadly, 'was a highly-sexed woman.'

'Well, we all knew that, my dear. But this cradle-snatching – well, golly, that's a bit too rich. Isn't it?'

Gerald looked deep into Betsy's eyes. 'She liked to experiment.'

Betsy laughed nervously. 'Oh?' She would have liked to ask for details, but it didn't seem quite the thing. 'Yes, but – young boys? Surely she never ...?'

He took the pipe from his mouth and examined the bowl as if he was wondering why there was no tobacco in it. 'Betsy, my love, you are one of Joanna's staunchest friends. Are you sure you want to hear all this?'

'Yes,' Betsy said bravely. 'A friend's a friend for a' that.'

Dudley didn't even try to make sense of that remark. He waved a hand in the general direction of the local newspaper. 'All I will say is that all this comes as no great surprise to me.'

'Really? You mean that even when she lived with you, she ... with little boys?'

'No, no, of course not,' Gerald said hurriedly. 'But she talked about it. Frequently. I used to hint that I thought it was an unhealthy interest, but she laughed and called me a prude.'

'Good Lord!' Betsy sat down heavily. 'Honestly, I would never have guessed.'

'That's because you always think the best of everyone, my dear. But there were straws in the wind, even back then. For instance, why do you suppose she gave up a perfectly good job in the social services to take up teaching? In a boys' school?'

'How awful!' Betsy was shocked to the depths of her bourgeois soul. 'Is this what you're going to tell the police?'

Gerald chewed the stem of his pipe. 'Betsy, I am not going to volunteer anything. If the police ask me a specific question, I shall give them a specific answer. What I hope and pray is that they won't ask me the wrong questions.'

'Ones that incriminate Joanna, you mean?'

'Yes. And – I know I don't have to say this, but I will – this conversation is our secret, Betsy. Not a word to another living soul. Please?'

'Of course, my dear. You really didn't have to ask.'

'Thank you.'

'For what?'

'Oh, I don't know.' His eyes were moist. 'Thank you for being you. One in a million. No, correction: totally unique. You're a giddy marvel, Betsy.'

'Get away with you.' But she glowed inside, nevertheless.

'Yes,' he said. 'I promised to be at the police station within the hour. But thank you again for your wise counsel.'

Betsy moved to the window and watched him get into his car and drive away. Then she picked up the phone. 'Alicia? Yes, it's me. My dear, you were quite right about that article: it is about *her*. But listen, you don't know the half of it....'

Theresa Burgage felt she was losing the battle, and feared she was on the brink of losing the campaign. 'It's too soon,' she insisted. 'And that bloody *Voice* article didn't help.'

Peter Walker, of the Crown Prosecution Service, didn't agree. 'We needed a kick up the backside on this case, and that article provided it. Next week the Voice is going to publish a shitload of letters about how we're failing to protect our innocent children, blah, blah, blah. We need to act before that happens. Have you searched the woman's house?'

'Not yet,' Burgage said.

'Do it. Pick up that black nightie and the other stuff the kid mentions in his statement. We've got more than enough to charge this woman. The clincher, in my view, is that she told a stupid lie about her nocturnal visitor being that Mr Tom Short-arse.' He looked around the room. 'We have got that aspect sewn up, haven't we? Speak, somebody.'

Sergeant Dewbury spoke. 'Tom Short absolutely denies any sexual involvement with Mrs Howard. I've got his sworn statement to that effect.'

Theresa Burgage butted in. 'On the other hand, Short could be lying to protect his job. We know that inter-staff relationships were frowned upon.'

'He perjures himself, he goes to gaol,' Walker said. 'I'm sure somebody pointed that out to him?'

'I did,' Dewbury said. 'He's a shifty bugger, but I reckon he'll stick to his story.'

Walker smiled. 'So far so good. Now, there's a suggestion in these notes that Howard was making advances towards another boy – Darren Palmer. Any developments about that?'

WPC Barrel sat slumped in her chair. With an effort, she raised her head and said wearily: 'I'm trying to arrange an interview with the kid. I'm having bit of a problem there. I need a responsible adult present, but his mother's got the flu, and his father refuses to co-operate. I'm hoping the mother will be well enough for me to see her tomorrow.'

'You're not looking too bonny yourself, Kylie,' Burgage said. 'Are you OK?'

'Yeah.' Barrel leaned back again. 'Bit of a headache.'

'That time of the month, eh?' Walker said without sympathy. 'OK. For the sake of completeness, we'll wait for your report on young Darren. Meantime, get the rest of the paperwork tidied up. Failing any major developments, you should be able to make the arrest over the weekend, and get her into court early next week. Let's get it sorted before the national press get their teeth into it.'

'You don't think the *Voice* article will prejudice the case?' Burgage addressed the question to Walker, but she was keeping a very beady eye on Sergeant Dewbury.

Walker shrugged. 'It doesn't name either Howard or the kid. I reckon it's probably OK. In any case, we can't unpublish it. If we wrap the case up promptly, we won't give this Monica Rawe bitch another chance to have a go at us.'

'This is a small town,' Burgage pointed out. 'A lot of people will have already worked out that the article refers to Mrs Howard. When the word spreads to the vigilante element, she could be subjected to abuse.'

'Tough.' Walker curled his lip. 'She should have thought about that before she started messing about with little boys.'

Burgage muttered something under her breath.

'What was that?' Walker asked sharply.

'Nothing.' Burgage realized that there was no point in arguing with the man. He and Dewbury seemed to be pursuing some personal agenda; but whether it was from simple misogyny or some deeper motive, she couldn't determine. 'I should just like to say, on the record—' she glanced towards WPC Barrel, to make sure that she was paying attention – 'that I think an arrest at this stage would be premature. I personally am not convinced that all the witnesses are reliable.'

'Objection noted.' Walker put his hand to his mouth and pretended to yawn. 'Fortunately, Inspector, your conscience need not be troubled. Just send me the file, and I'll take the responsibility for any action. I shall also make sure that your scruples are prominently chronicled in my case report.' Satisfied that he had had the last word he gathered up his papers and left, taking Dewbury with him. Before the door closed behind them, the sergeant made a comment about "bleeding hearts" that had them both sniggering like adolescents.

CHAPTER 19

Gerald Dudley smiled his most winning smile at the two policemen. 'I hope this isn't going to prove too embarrassing, gentlemen. Would you mind telling me what young Fernie has been up to this time? I know that in recent years she's gone off the rails a bit.'

'It's really just routine, sir,' Bailey said. 'Ms Brent isn't being charged with anything. We just need to confirm her statement that she was in your company last Sunday night.'

'Yes, I can confirm that.'

'All night, sir?'

Dudley looked sheepish. 'Well, not exactly, officer. We met about nine o'clock, had a spot of supper in a restaurant, and I took her home in the wee small hours. She's living with her sister and brother-in-law, you know. She told me she's on parole, but she assured me that she wasn't under curfew. I hope she was telling me the truth?'

'So far as we know.' Bailey finished making a note. 'Which restaurant was it, sir?'

'The Potifar, on Knowley Road.'

'Would they remember you there, Mr Dudley?' Cope took up the questioning.

'I don't suppose so for a minute. But I paid by credit card. Does that help?'

'That'll do nicely, sir. Can you be more specific about the time you took the lady home?'

'Not to the minute. But it was pretty late. Nearly three o'clock, I imagine.'

Bailey asked delicately: 'You weren't in the restaurant until three a.m.?'

'Of course not.' Dudley leaned back in his chair and massaged his brow with his fingertips. 'Look, gentlemen, I'll be absolutely frank with you. After supper, Fernie and I drove up to the picnic area on Knowley Hill, and had sex in the back of my car. She was pretty keen, I can tell you. Remember, she's been in prison for the last year. In telling you this, I am relying on your utmost discretion. For one thing, I am married; for another, I don't want to lose the respect of my friends in this town.'

Cope and Bailey looked at each other for a moment in silence. Cope recovered first. 'I take it that you and Ms Brent had known each other previously?'

'She was my secretary five years ago, when I had an office in Manchester. And if you are asking whether we had carnal knowledge of each other back then, the answer is yes. Neither of us ever contemplated a permanent relationship, but we are both liberal-minded, modern people.'

'Er, yes.' Bailey looked slightly stunned. 'I understand that you now live down South, sir. May I ask if you came up here on purpose to see Ms Brent?'

'God, no!' Gerald was highly amused. 'I didn't even know she was in Aldersgrove. I'm up here visiting old friends. I bumped into Fernie quite by chance in Buchanan's store. She looked as if she needed a spot of cheering up, and so I asked her out. For old times' sake, you understand.' He gave the policemen a knowing look. 'Now, are you chaps going to tell me what this is all about? What's young Fernie supposed to have done?'

'She's not really under suspicion, sir,' Bailey said. 'We had to eliminate her from our enquiries, that's all. Like we said, just routine.'

'Jolly good. Well, I can see it's no use trying to prise information out of you fellows.' Gerald stood up and shook hands with both of them. 'I trust you to be just as discreet about my affairs, what?'

'Of course, sir.' Bailey took it upon himself to answer, since he could see that Cope was biting his lip and incapable of speech. 'Thank you for your co-operation.'

Both detectives managed to keep their faces straight until Dudley was out of the room, then Bailey, who was the more controlled of the two, held his hand over Cope's mouth, and slowly counted to ten. 'Now!' he said, and released his partner, who collapsed against the wall, shaking and bubbling with laughter. 'Godamighty!' Cope yelled. 'God-a-fucking-mighty! Is that guy for real?'

Bailey grinned, then laughed aloud, infected by his partner's reaction. 'Salt of the earth, laddie. Stiff upper lip. Straight bat, and all that rot, what?'

'No, but seriously ...' Eric Cope spoke slowly, still weak from laughter, 'have you ever, in your born days, encountered such a pompous prat?'

'He's a prime contender for the top prat title, no doubt about that,' Bailey conceded. 'But let's get professional about this. Did you believe him? Would a jury believe him?'

Cope slowly calmed down, breathing hard. 'Oh yeah. Yes to both questions. He's a prat, but when it comes down to it, I believe him *because* he's a prat.'

Sergeant Dewbury was disappointed to find Joanna at home. He would have liked the excuse to batter the door down. 'We have a warrant to search these premises,' he told her, and stood aside to let the uniformed officers in. He ignored her protests, and strode after the squaddies, barking orders.

Joanna was acutely aware that the police cars outside her house were attracting attention. Already Mrs Whalley was peering over her fence, and other neighbours were congregating in the Causeway. She stood helplessly by while the police ransacked her house, leaving a trail of disorder in their wake. Dewbury stubbornly refused to answer any of her questions, or indeed to offer any response other than to wave a sheet of paper under her nose.

When Matt Clements knocked at her door and strode into her house, her relief was so great that she could have embraced him on the spot. She tried to tell him what was happening, but he seemed to understand without explanation. What was more, he had brought a camcorder with him, and he followed the policemen from room to room, ostentatiously recording their every movement.

Dewbury went puce with indignation. 'What the hell do you think you're doing?' he shouted. 'Get out of here!'

'This isn't your house,' Matt countered, pointing the camera at the sergeant's face. 'I'm here with the owner's permission. What I'm doing is making a record of your activities.'

'I've got a warrant to search this house,' Dewbury blustered.

'I'm not stopping you. I'm just taking pictures.'

'I could arrest you for obstructing our enquiries.'

'But my camera will show that I'm doing no such thing. Just carry on, Constable. Let the record show that you and your men behaved with scrupulous fairness and propriety.' He swung the camera from the sergeant's face to the slew of papers on the living-room floor.

Dewbury, although he was loath to show it, was impressed by Matthew's air of authority. 'Yeah, well, just watch it,' he mumbled lamely, and followed his men upstairs.

As soon as he was out of sight, Matt pushed the camcorder into Joanna's hands. 'Hold the fort a minute,' he said, and then, to her surprise, he ducked into the kitchen, picked up the photograph of her father from the sideboard, and ran with it out of the front door. He returned seconds later, and took the camera from her. 'I'll explain later,' he panted. 'If they ask about the picture, you've just sent it to the War Museum.'

And Dewbury did ask, an hour later, when he thrust into her hand a written statement that he was taking away a black négligé and a duvet-cover as evidence. 'There was a photo here, of two blokes with shotguns. Where is it?'

'It's gone,' Joanna said. 'What business is it of yours?'

'It's evidence, woman,' Dewbury snarled. 'Where is it?'

Joanna pretended to think. 'At the moment, it is possibly with the archivist of the Royal Engineers. Or it may have been passed to the War Museum. Or possibly to the Records Office. I really don't know where it is just now.' The last bit at any rate was true, Joanna thought. 'The gentlemen in the photograph were war heroes. One of them was my father. What's your claim to fame, Sergeant? Bullying women?' It was a cheap shot, but it was worth it to see Dewbury swell like the frog in the fable.

Goaded as much by the suppressed sniggers of his men as by Joanna's taunt, Dewbury controlled his voice with difficulty. 'Mrs Howard, I'm going to put you where you can't corrupt innocent children. Your lies about your friend Short have back-fired on you. He flatly contradicts your story, and is prepared to swear to that in court.

So enjoy your liberty while you can,' He congratulated himself on his self restraint. He didn't have the gift of the gab, like these poncy bourgeois scroungers, but by God he said what he meant.

As soon as the police had gone, Joanna turned on Matt. 'Look, don't think me ungrateful, but do you mind telling me what the hell you're doing here? And what was all that to-do about my dad's photograph?'

Matt raised his hands in apology. 'I should have got here earlier. When I saw what was happening, I had to improvise. Sorry.'

Joanna hardly heard what he was saying. 'It's about that bloody article in the *Voice*, isn't it?'

'Yes. The Tanner boy made a statement to the police, which somebody leaked to Monica Rawe, a free-lance journalist. The *Voice* only agreed to publish after Rawe had signed a contract indemnifying the paper against a possible lawsuit.'

'How do you know all this?'

'I've just come from the *Voice* office. Richard Radcliffe, the proprietor, is a friend of mine.'

'Of course he is!' Joanna clicked her tongue and rolled her eyes upward. 'Dear God, Matthew Clements, is there anybody of consequence in Lancashire you don't know?'

Matt ignored the interruption. 'Richard showed me a transcript of the boy's statement. It mainly focuses on an incident at the Darwen Lowe Farm, during the summer vacation.'

'The police questioned me about that. It's all rubbish.'

'Tanner goes on to say that you and he have been in a sexual relationship ever since. He says he's in love with you.'

'He's a lying little shit. He obviously hates me.' Joanna noticed with alarm that the group outside her gate had not dispersed now the police cars had gone, but stood staring at the house like spectators at a pageant. It took an effort of concentration to understand what Matt was saying. 'What? What was that again?'

'I said, the most damning part of his evidence is his description of the interior of this house. He mentions your black négligé, the pattern on your duvet, the bidet in your bathroom, and the photograph of your father and his friend.'

Joanna stared at him. 'That's not possible. That brat has never been in my house.'

'I believe you. So, consider the implications. The boy's accusation wasn't just an indiscriminate act of malice. Somebody put him up to it. Somebody who *has* been in your house.'

'But,' Joanna was becoming distraught, 'dozens of people have been in my house! All my friends. I had a house-warming party, with more than thirty people here. Are you trying to tell me that one of those people – my friends – has done this to me? Why, for God's sake?'

'I don't know, and I'm not going to speculate right now. The point is that the police have just searched your house for evidence that confirms the boy's story; and as far as they're concerned, they've found it. Which means, unless I miss my guess completely, that they plan to arrest you.'

'What!' Joanna's voice sank to a whisper. 'You're trying to frighten me!'

'Quite the opposite. I'm telling you what to expect, so you won't be afraid of it. If the police charge you, they've got to show their hand, and then you can refute their case item by item.' Matt was looking directly at her, willing her to listen.

But Joanna was still shaking. 'They're going to put me behind bars!'

'No, that isn't how it works. They'll summon you to appear before a magistrate, and the magistrate will refer the case to the Crown Court, which means that the case won't be tried for six months or more. He may take away your passport, but he'll certainly grant you bail.'

'And that's supposed to be good news? Can't you see what six months under suspicion will do to my life?'

'That won't happen. We'll get at the truth long before that. I'll get Jack Dabdoub onto it. He's the best, so he tells me.'

Joanna wasn't to be comforted. 'Don't you see? If the police charge me I'll never be clear of the accusation. Even if I'm acquitted people will say oh, she got off on a technicality, or she bribed the jury, or seduced the judge. Someone, somewhere, will always think of me as that teacher who fucked underage boys.'

Matt spoke slowly and forcefully. 'Look, you haven't got time to wallow in self-pity. The future is the future. Your problem right now is how to get through the next few days. A lot of people in this town will have worked out that the article was aimed at you, and in a place this small everyone will know before the day is out. You've got to face the fact that more unpleasantness is on the way.'

'Are you telling me I've got to run away and hide?'

'I don't think you should stay in this house. Too many people know where you live. Look at that group out there. At the moment, they're just staring and gossiping. But as the word spreads more people will join them. And the bigger that crowd gets, the nastier it's going to be, particularly since I believe the guy who leaked that statement to the press will soon be out there rabble-rousing.'

Joanna glanced out of the window again, and recoiled as if avoiding a blow. 'Matt, you're terrifying me. What am I to do?'

'Move in with me.' He held his hands up as if in surrender. 'Sorry – I didn't mean that the way it sounded. What I mean is – here's the key to my back door. I've made a gap in the fence between our back yards. If there's any sign of trouble out there, you can slip into my house unnoticed. And you can slip back in here again once the coast is clear.'

'I can't believe this is happening to me,' Joanna said miserably. 'I've done nothing wrong. Why am I having to skulk about like a criminal?'

'We've got to play for time, my dear.' Instinctively, Matt reached out and took both her hands in his. 'Up to now you've been thinking of this as just childish malice – a mindless prank. But it's obviously more than that. Somebody out there hates you – or fears you.'

'But why? What have I done?'

'I don't know the reason. I don't know if there *is* a reason. Crazy people have crazy motives. Right now I just want to be sure you're safe until we find out exactly who and what is behind all this.'

'You keep saying "we", as if we're some sort of partnership. What makes you think I can't handle this on my own? Why are you always trying to sort out my problems?'

He looked pleased at this small show of spirit. 'Let's not argue, Mrs Howard. I want to help you. Just accept it.'

She began to relax a little. 'Just trust you, you mean? I'd be happier if you showed a bit of consistency. "My dear", one minute, and "Mrs Howard" the next. Make up your mind, can't you?'

Matt felt his cheeks growing hot. 'Sorry, I didn't mean to be over-familiar.'

'Oh, really?' It was cruel to tease him, but she rather enjoyed it. 'Never mind. Tell me why you nicked my pa's photograph? Was it just to keep it out of the hands of the police?'

'Well, partly.' Matt was still embarrassed. 'But mainly because I want to examine it a bit more closely.'

'Why?'

Matt was looking positively shifty. 'Please – can we discuss this later, when we've sorted out more pressing problems? If I tell you my theory about that picture, you'll think I've gone stark staring mad. For now – take my key; escape to my house if you need to. Meantime, I'll get Jack Dabdoub to investigate this whole sorry mess. If anyone can sort it out, he can.'

But Dabdoub wasn't available. 'Sorry, Matt, no can do,' he said. 'I'm in the middle of something else, and it's just beginning to get ripe. This Mrs Howard – that's the gorgeous chick you brought to the club?'

'Yes. Jack, she really needs help right now.'

'I'd like to help, truly. Tell you what, Matt: write down all the details you have about the case, and fax them over to my office. I'll look them over when I have time, and I'll get onto it as soon as I'm free.'

And with that, Matthew had to be content.

As soon as Matt left, Joanna tried to contact Tom Short. She knew that he had been hurt and offended by their break-up, and bitterly angry over her outburst at their last meeting, but she couldn't believe that he would carry his resentment so far as to lie to the police about her. It must be Dewbury who was the liar. She felt sure that Tom would have an explanation if she could just speak to him for a few minutes. But she couldn't reach him. She left messages at the school and on his answering service, but she couldn't shake off the irrational conviction that he would ignore them. She told herself it was silly to worry about it, but she worried, nevertheless.

There was no response from Tom Short, but at five o'clock in the afternoon the anonymous phone calls began. After the first two incoherent diatribes, spite-ridden litanies of "slag", "bitch", "whore", "tart", and some expletives Joanna had never heard before, she let the answering machine take the strain. As the calls flooded in, she grew more and more depressed. It seemed as if the whole of Aldersgrove was queuing up to tell her that she was too disgusting to be allowed to live.

Then at last, she heard a familiar voice. She clicked off the machine and spoke. 'Yes, I'm here. Patrick! How nice to hear from you! You wouldn't believe the hell I've been going through since that poisonous article in the *Voice* this morning. I've had abusive phone calls, people shouting in the road outside, visits from the police. I can't tell you what a relief it is to hear from a friend.'

Patrick sounded wary. 'I'm not exactly the bearer of good tidings, dear heart. The thing is that next week's choral rehearsal – well, to be blunt, the committee wants you to stay away from all our meetings, until this unpleasantness over the child abuse thing is cleared up. Practically all the altos have resigned or threatened to resign over the issue. The phone's been virtually white-hot all afternoon. Sorry, and all that,' he added, after a pause.

Joanna gasped with shock. She felt chilled, as if she had been drenched with icy water. 'Patrick, what are you saying? Those women are my friends: I've known many of them for years. They surely can't believe that I'm guilty of – of those libellous things in that wretched paper?'

He sounded interested. 'Are you going to sue them for libel? The article doesn't mention your name.'

'Yet you've just told me that scores of my so-called friends believe that it's about me.'

'Yes, but that's because …' Patrick halted guiltily in mid-sentence.

'Because what, Patrick? You can't leave it there.'

'Well, it's your oldest friends, the ones who know you best, who are saying that, well, you know …'

'No, Patrick, I don't know. What, exactly, are they saying?'

'That they're not surprised. That they noticed when they first met you, years ago, that you showed an unhealthy interest in young boys.'

'Dear God!' There was a taste in her mouth as bitter as wormwood. 'All these years I've made the mistake of liking those people. And you, Patrick, whom I've always counted as one of my dearest friends – what do you really think of me?'

'Sweetie, I honestly don't care if you're Arthur or Martha. And as you know, I don't consider an interest in young boys is at all unhealthy.' He thought she might be amused at that, but she didn't respond. He added, more soberly: 'I respect your talent. I always have.'

'Thank you.' But she still felt bitter. 'You realize that I can't come to choral practice ever again?'

He obviously hadn't realized that. 'I'll miss you. What will you do for music?'

She took a smug satisfaction in telling him. 'I'm rehearsing with Angela Bonneville.'

'What!' He sounded as much shocked as surprised.

'Angela's planning a recital with Christina Hauptmann. She's using me as a stand-in for the great lady.'

'Angela Bonneville?' He seemed to have trouble taking it in. 'You're working with Angela Bonneville? How come?'

'She asked me. She heard me at the Mendelssohn concert.'

'Sweetie, take care! That woman is not your friend.'

'What? What are you talking about?'

'God, you're such a simpleton sometimes! Angela Bonneville was the woman Gerald Dudley was living with, before you came on the scene. He ditched her – quite cruelly – for you.'

'No. Gerald was separated from his wife when I met him.'

'That's what he told everybody, lovey. But he was never actually trapped into matrimony until Shona Moneybags came along, to supplant you. At the time his roving eye fell on you, dear, he was comfortably shacked up with la Bonneville; and she was not pleased to be dumped, believe me. So now, out of the blue, she's made your acquaintance? I don't know what she's up to, darling, but believe me, it's nothing to your advantage.'

CHAPTER 20

To: Mr George Guest, Suite no.11, Majestyk Hotel
Subject: Investigation Update, as requested.

Dear Mr Guest
Following our discussion in my office, I concentrated my initial enquiries on Joseph Godwit.

Godwit owned or controlled three companies: Godwit & Co, Builders; J G Demolition & Clearance; and J G Developments. He employed a small permanent staff, augmented by casual labour. We persuaded an ex-employee of his to talk to us, and, as we guessed, Godwit regularly operated a tax fraud. All his workers – except for a few very highly paid craftsmen – were unregistered, paid in cash and given time off to claim the dole. This was just the kind of scam that your mother was employed to uncover.

In the mid-nineties Godwit had several building projects on hand at the same time; judging by what our informant told us, over £25,000 in cash was being handed over every week. Where did that money come from? It could hardly have been in Godwit's business account, since those workers weren't officially on his books.

Then we had our first real break. Our informant told us that the cash was delivered to the site manager every Friday by a bloke driving a scruffy old Ford van. The bloke was always in grotty overalls, and he carried the money in a large metal toolbox.

The pieces were beginning to fit together. Mrs Guest's list included a man called Leslie Tanner, who was certainly no builder. He was a burglar, and a notoriously incompetent one. Tanner was so well known to the police that they gave him a nickname – Toolbox Tanner – because he did his housebreaking wearing overalls and carrying a large metal toolbox, under the impression that the disguise made him invisible. Unsurprisingly, he spent most of his adult life in gaol. In fact, he was usually back inside less than six months after his previous release. Except, oddly, for the period from 1993 to 1998.

It didn't take us long to work out how Les Tanner had spent those five gaol-free years. He had been a bagman for the Ganja brothers.

The Ganja brothers, (real names: Ephron and Jethro Makereddy) headed the most powerful criminal gang in Manchester during the mid-nineties. As the name suggests, they began by trafficking in marijuana, but they soon expanded into hard drugs and other rackets, like extortion and prostitution. Their activities generated a lot of cash: not the billions of the global drug-dealers, but quite impressive by the standards of local street-gangs. The police estimated that in their heyday the brothers were raking in about £3m a year.

Since Melvin Tares was also associated with the Ganjas we concluded that the building scam had been part of a money-laundering operation. The cash Tanner handed over to Joe Godwit was 'dirty' money from the Ganja brothers' drug-dealing. In due course Joe would return 'clean' money – less his commission – to the Ganjas.

It's easy to see why the Ganja brothers would be alarmed by your mother's activities. Although the building scam could only have been a small part of the gang's money-laundering process, a full-scale police inquiry might uncover the whole operation. Also, money-laundering is generally a white-collar crime. People other than the Ganjas would be involved – outwardly respectable, professional people, with reputations to protect. They too would feel threatened by Mrs Guest's investigation.

If Tares was acting under instructions, we have no way of knowing whether he was sent to intimidate Mrs Guest, or to silence her. Nor do we know whether he was alone, or was with an accomplice. On the other hand, if our hypothesis is right and Tares was under orders, then the people who sent him are as guilty as he.

You will infer from all this that the investigation is growing much wider – and potentially more expensive – than anticipated. Please let us know how far you wish us to go with it.

Work in progress: Superintendent Curry, the lead officer in your mother's case, has promised to send me a copy of his notes, but they are not yet to hand. Also, an old acquaintance of mine, Constable Joe Lolly, has contacted me with some theory about the murder weapon used on Mrs Guest. I am meeting with him later today. Les Tanner is currently in gaol again; I hope to interview him as soon as it can be arranged.

I enclose a detailed account of our expenses so far. I am sure you will understand that our informants and technical assistants provide their services only on the understanding that they will remain anonymous, so they are referred to in the accounts only by initials, not necessarily their own.

Assuring you of our utmost efforts on your behalf,

J Dabdoub.

Tony watched his employer's face anxiously as Dabdoub slowly read through the letter. 'What do you think?'

Dabdoub grunted. 'You've got a right lawyer-like hand. Nobody in their right mind will believe I wrote this load of bull.' Nevertheless, he scrawled his signature at the bottom of the page.

CHAPTER 21

Darkness began to fall, but Joanna resisted the temptation to switch on the lights. In the gathering gloom, she watched as the knot of people outside her gate gradually dwindled away until only Mrs Whalley remained, smoking her cigarettes down to the last millimetre and wheezing like a rusty bellows. At last, either because she had run out of fags or because of the increasing cold, she shuffled off to her own house.

Still Joanna sat in the dark. The abusive phone calls had tailed off, and she closed her eyes, welcoming the remission. When the phone rang she ignored it, leaving it to the answering machine. Then she heard Angela Bonneville's voice:

'If you're there, Joanna, please pick up. If not, please call me as soon as you can. I've only just heard—'

Joanna picked up the phone. 'I'm here.' Her throat felt constricted and dry. Talking was an effort.

'Joanna!' Now that she had made contact Angela seemed unsure how to go on. 'That thing in the *Voice* this morning …'

'Yes, it was about me, and it was all lies,' Joanna croaked harshly, not trying to hide her bitterness and frustration. Patrick's phone call had soured her feelings towards Angela Bonneville.

'I believe you. I think we should meet as soon as possible. I really would like to talk to you.'

'About Gerald Dudley?' Joanna was determined to show that she couldn't be deceived any longer.

But Angela was unfazed. 'Of course. Did you know he's been spreading vile rumours about you today? He told Betsy Bray that the reason he left you was because he discovered you were a paedophile. And dear Betsy has passed that on to all her friends. In the strictest confidence, naturally.' She waited a moment, but Joanna was feeling too sick to respond. 'Joanna, whatever animosity you feel towards that man is as nothing to the way I feel about him. I know he treated you badly, but believe me, he treated me ten times worse. Please come and see me.'

Joanna was confused. 'I can't see what we could say to each other. I wish you hadn't lied about wanting to rehearse with me. That was cruel. I have never knowingly harmed you. I didn't know about your relationship with Dudley.'

'No! No!' Angela said vehemently. 'That wasn't a lie. I don't lie about music, believe me. I think your voice is great. I wanted us to share something – something that we both care about. I wanted us to become friends.'

'Why?'

'Because there is something else I want to share with you. But I don't want to talk about it over the phone. Please come over here soon. Tomorrow?'

'You won't expect me to sing, will you? I really don't feel up to it right now.'

'No, we'll just talk. And I'll show you my toys.'

'OK.' Joanna shifted uneasily in her seat. Sitting in the dark was becoming oppressive and, worryingly, her back was beginning to ache again. 'If I haven't been arrested before then.'

'That pig!' Angela said forcefully. 'It wouldn't surprise me if he's behind this whole charade. I'd like to string him up by his thumbs.'

'His thumbs?' Joanna croaked malevolently. 'I've got a better idea.'

'Good girl!' Angela barked her deep, throaty laugh. 'That's more like it.'

Jack Dabdoub met Joe Lolly in a pub just off Market Street. He didn't think that Joe's ideas about the so-called Chinese cosh were particularly interesting, but he was happy to relax over a pint or two and swap gossip with an old friend. It didn't take them long to agree on one thing: that, apart from the fact that both victims had been killed by a blow to the throat, there didn't seem to be any connection between the murders of Carole Guest and Lizzie Nair. It was interesting that Joe had managed to find a link between Mrs Guest and the Ganja brothers, but Jack had already got there by another route. He told Joe about the progress of his investigations, in rather more detail than he had passed on to his client; in return, Joe described the meagre findings of the Lizzie Nair murder team.

It was a pleasantly sociable evening, both men agreed, but it was a dead loss as far as useful information was concerned. Still, since that was what they had both expected, they were not too disappointed.

The report from Superintendent Curry had arrived at Jack's office by special delivery late that afternoon. Jack took it with him, intending to read it at home. But after a few beers he wasn't in the mood for more work. He poured himself a stiff whisky and watched a cop show on television.

Matt paused briefly outside Joanna's house, looked from left to right along the street, then opened the gate and started down the path. Joanna had the door open before he reached the step.

'Thank God.' She felt she had never been so pleased to see anyone in her life. 'Did I say I could handle this on my own? I take it all back. I've been going quietly crazy, sitting here all alone in the dark.'

'Sorry I've been so long. I had stuff to do.' For the first time since she had known him, Matt actually sounded worried. 'There's something very nasty going on in this town. You can't stay here tonight.' He reached up and slid the bolt on the front door. 'Do these downstairs windows have security locks?'

'Yes.'

'I'll just check them.' He strode into the living-room and examined the windows one by one. 'Good. Let's go. Oh – before I forget: take this. Keep it with you at all times.'

'A mobile phone? Why?'

'Press this button – no, I'll show you when we've got some light.' He took her arm, urging her out of the room. 'I'll explain it all in a minute. For now, I just want to get you somewhere safe.' He pushed her through the kitchen to the back door. 'Now – have you got the key? My key, I mean – the key to my back door?'

'No, I—'

Matt swore under his breath. 'Then get it, woman! Quick as you can!'

Impressed by his urgency – he had never before called her "woman" – she ran back and blundered about in the dark. 'Got it!'

'Come on!' Once they were in the yard he pointed her to the gap in the fence. 'Use my key. I'll follow you in just a minute.' Once outside he locked her door and wedged a length of wood under the handle.

Even in his own house Matt found it difficult to relax until he had closed the curtains and double-locked the front door. 'Do you mind if we sit in the kitchen for a while?' His eyes were dark with anxiety.

'Of course not. What's the matter? You look as if you were expecting a siege.'

'Something very nasty is going on,' he repeated. 'The pub down the street—'

'The Waterman's Arms?'

'Yes. That pub is usually as quiet as a churchyard on Thursday nights. Tonight, it's packed – crowded with rowdy teenagers, mainly, but there's a middle-aged couple, a man and a woman in there, brandishing copies of the *Voice* and talking at the tops of their voices.'

Joanna shuddered. 'About me?'

'Yes.'

'But that article doesn't mention my name!'

'I know. This is a set-up. That crowd didn't turn up at the pub by accident. Someone's organized the whole thing. Those kids are being plied with free booze and harangued by paid rabble-rousers. Come closing-time, they're going to fall out of that pub roaring drunk and itching to make trouble.'

'And they'll – what? Come to my house and shout abuse?'

'Probably.'

'And since I'm not there, they'll have to content themselves with painting smut on my door, throwing stones at my windows and trampling on my flowerbeds?'

'It's possible. We'll deal with that later. Right now, you have to face the fact that this threat to you is being deliberately orchestrated. Somebody hates you enough to make your life here intolerable. Who?'

'I don't know! I haven't knowingly injured or cheated anyone. Nobody has any reasonable grounds for this kind of animosity. It's just crazy!'

Matt nodded, as if she had confirmed something. 'Then whoever it is has just made a big mistake,' he said. He looked at his watch. 'Plenty of time. Are you hungry?'

'What? No.' She was much too wound up to eat. 'You're always asking me if I'm hungry. Do I look as if I'm wasting away or something?'

'No, it's just that I'm starving. I'm going to phone for a take-away. If you *were* hungry, would you prefer Chinese or Indian?'

'I'm not hungry.' But she could see he was going to be persistent. 'Chinese.'

'OK. I'll get some for you, in case you change your mind.' He picked up a leaflet from the sideboard and began marking it with a pencil.

It was strange, she thought, how his nervousness and anxiety had dropped away from him in the space of just a few minutes. Suddenly, he was relaxed and confident again, and there was a light in his eye that might almost be mistaken for excitement. And, what was just as strange, his self-assurance was catching: she could feel her own courage flooding back, because – and this was another mystery – she was sure he would make it all come right. He was her own personal tidy-upperer.

'Let me see that menu,' she commanded suddenly. 'I've changed my mind.'

He grinned at her, unsurprised. 'Here. And while you're choosing, let me fix you a drink. Sherry?'

'I'll have what you're having.' She felt reckless.

'Gin it is, then. Look, I've got loads of phone calls to make. Why don't you make yourself comfortable in the sitting-room and watch the telly? I'll bring your drink through in a minute.'

She wandered through into the sitting-room, but she didn't turn on the television. She was much more interested in Matt's Japanese piano. There was a small but varied collection of sheet music in a cabinet nearby; she was gratified to see that most of it – the Mozart and Beethoven selections particularly – was in simple arrangements, easily within her technical compass. At first she was dismayed by the instrument's brilliant tone, which seemed harsh and over-loud; but she discovered that it was very responsive to gradations of touch, and soon she was coaxing a very pleasant sound out of it.

Matt had entered the room, holding her drink. When she came to the end of the piece, he shook his head in admiration. 'That was ...' he paused, wanting neither to falsely overpraise or offensively underpraise. 'I could never make it sound as good as that,' he said; which was neither more nor less than the truth.

She took her glass, and raised it in salute. 'I like your house. Somehow, it seems more spacious than mine.'

'Yes.' He turned to go out of the room, then checked in the doorway. 'We must talk about that sometime.'

'Why not now?'

'I've still got phone calls to make. Supper will arrive in about half an hour. We'll talk then.'

Forty-five minutes later supper arrived, and they began to talk. Matt began.

'Tell me about your father.'

'I've already told you. He left me the house next door. He went a bit peculiar after mother died.'

'Was he good at practical things? Things like carpentry, brick-laying?'

'Of course. He was a sapper. He used to boast that he never ordered any soldier to undertake any task he couldn't perform himself.'

'Good.' Matt ate enthusiastically. 'In his will, did he mention that photograph of him and Colonel Crawford-Webb?'

'Not in his will, no. His solicitor handed me a letter. In it, Dad said that he hoped I would keep that picture with me always, as a memento of happy times.'

'Did he say anything else?'

'Yes, but I can't remember what it was. I've still got the letter somewhere. I can dig it out and show you, if you like.'

'Later, yes.' Matt got up and left the room, returning in a few moments with the photograph. 'Here. Now, tell me what you notice about this picture?'

'What I've always noticed: my father and his friend in shooting gear.'

'Why are they wearing their hats indoors?'

'Why not? They've just come in, or they're just about to go out.'

'Their boots and gaiters are quite muddy.'

'That answers your question. They've just come in.'

'You said you thought your mother might have taken the photo. Didn't she mind muddy boots in the house?'

Joanna shrugged. 'Well, it wasn't her house.'

'It was Colonel Crawford-Webb's house, then?'

'Yes, of course. Why all these questions? And what's all this got to do with the size of these rooms? You're being very mysterious.'

'Yes, I suppose I am.' Matt chewed thoughtfully. 'The trouble is that there are many things here I don't understand. And when I find a bizarre puzzle, I tend to imagine outlandish answers.'

Joanna was getting impatient. 'Now you've gone from the mysterious to the downright weird. What's bizarre about that snapshot of my father?'

'Everything,' Matt said simply. 'It's a mock-up: a composite of several different photographs. It's cleverly done; your father was very artistic as well as being technically efficient.'

Joanna picked up the photograph and studied it carefully. 'How can you tell?'

'The light is all wrong, for one thing. Look at their faces. It's obvious from the shadows on their cheeks that the light is falling on them from their left-hand side. The gleam along the gun barrels tells us the same thing. Now look at the picture behind them. The shadow of the frame is clearly visible on the wall – and it's on the wrong side. The light on the wall is coming from the opposite side from the light on the men.'

'Well, since it's indoors, the light sources could be anywhere,' Joanna argued.

Matt wasn't convinced. 'Possibly, but I don't think the shadows would be quite so sharp. Anyway, that's not the only thing. How far in front of the wall do you think they're standing?'

'Hard to say. Three or four feet, possibly.'

'Yes. Now, look at Colonel Crawford-Webb's gun. You can see every detail of the decorative plate by the breech mechanism and the trigger. You can even see part of the maker's name. It's all in really sharp focus.'

'So?'

'Now look at the picture on the wall. Again, it's so sharp, you can practically see the grain of the crayon strokes. If your mother took that photograph, she must have been really skilful to get that depth of focus.'

'Are you saying it's impossible?'

'No, I'm asking you to look at your father's right foot.'

Joanna treated him to her most devastating glare. 'God, you're infuriating! Why don't you just tell me what the hell you're talking about?'

'Your father's right foot is about six inches back from his left foot,' Matt pointed out mildly. 'But the image is very slightly blurred. The foreground is in sharp focus, and so is the background, but the bit in the middle isn't. It would take a very cute camera to do that. The picture is a mock up: a sort of clever collage.'

'Well, all right.' Joanna held the picture at arm's length and studied it critically. 'So Dad had a bit of fun with it. Does it matter?'

'Only that your father mentioned it specifically. There must have been scores of other family photographs about. Why did he go to so much trouble over this one? Why specially bequeath this one to you? Why not a picture of him with your mother? You told me how much he adored her.'

'I did wonder about that myself.' Joanna looked sad for a few moments, affected by memories. She collected herself with an effort. 'But he was quite doolally at the end.'

Matt smiled. 'Not as much as you think.' He was about to go on, but he was interrupted by a rhythmic ring on his doorbell. 'That'll be the twins,' he said enigmatically. 'Excuse me.'

The size of the two young men who followed him back into the room was truly awesome. Taller even than Matt, they had shoulders like oxen and forearms like legs of mutton. They ought to be heavyweight boxers or night-club bouncers, Joanna thought, except that they've got the rosy cheeks, twinkly eyes and curly hair of little choirboys. Identical choirboys, at that. They stood shoulder to shoulder, grinning down at her like two massive bronzes poured from the same mould.

'Mrs Howard,' Matt said formally, 'let me introduce Tristram and Lionel, colleagues of mine at work.'

'Low-paid lackeys is what he means,' one of the boys said. 'Downtrodden proletariat. Otherwise known as trainees getting so-called work experience. Good evening, ma'am. I'm Lionel, and this ugly fellow here is my younger brother Tristram.'

'We've seen you before,' Tristam said. 'At the Rugby Club. But we didn't get introduced. Which just shows you the kind of chap we have to work for.'

'And we've read about you in the paper,' Lionel added.

'Really?' Joanna's face stiffened and went pink.

'Rather. About how you stepped into the breach at that concert. That was really cool.'

'Icy cool,' Tristram agreed. 'Stupendously sub-zero.'

'Thank you,' Joanna said weakly.

'OK boys, that's enough showing off.' Matt announced the end of formalities. 'Tell me the state of play.'

The twins glanced at each other, and it was Lionel who answered. At least, Joanna thought it was: they had changed positions, and she was no longer sure which was which. 'Big Dave is already here, with his truck,' he said. 'Ben is with him. Little Dave and Ali are in the other truck, round the corner. Alec and Ernie are building something in next door's garden.'

'My garden?' Joanna said sharply. 'I hope they're not flattening my flower-beds.'

'They wouldn't do that,' Tristram assured her. 'They both love gardens. They're middle-aged,' he added, as if that explained everything.

Matt looked at his watch. 'Half an hour to closing time.'

'I wouldn't bank on it,' Lionel said. 'I looked in the pub on the way over. It's absolutely packed, and getting very rowdy. The landlord was looking pretty nervous. It wouldn't surprise me if he decided to close up early. Or try to.'

'The sooner the better,' Matt said. 'Did you spot the ringleaders?'

'I clocked the one you mentioned – a puny little guy in spectacles and a vulgar suit. He won't give any trouble.'

'Good. Now you guys go out and keep the troops cheerful. I'll come and join you in a few minutes. Tell everybody to take it easy when we get down to business. I don't want any mindless violence.'

Tristram grinned. 'OK, skipper. I take it mindful violence is OK?'

With the twins gone the room seemed larger. Joanna still looked slightly dazed. 'Is there any chance of you telling me what's going on?' she asked plaintively.

'All will be revealed very soon,' Matt told her. 'Where's the mobile phone I gave you?'

'Here.'

'Good. I want you to keep it by you at all times. If you need to contact me quickly, just press this button.'

She couldn't resist mocking him. 'And you'll come running?'

'Something like that.'

'That's silly.'

'Then humour me. It's just a precaution.' Matt stood in the hall and swapped his coat for a black donkey-jacket. 'I'm going out now. I don't expect this to take long. If you want to watch the fun, do it from an upstairs room. But don't show yourself, there's a good girl.'

The upstairs room that overlooked the Causeway was Matt's bedroom; Joanna examined it curiously. All it told her was what she knew already: Matthew Clements was compulsively neat and tidy. The bed was large – almost too large for the room – but whether it was Matt's own, or part of the rented furniture, she couldn't tell. The walls were quite bare of pictures, but in the centre of the chest of drawers was a framed photograph of a round-faced woman with long, dark hair. Matt's wife, she supposed. She studied the picture for a long time. The face was smooth, unlined, childlike, Joanna thought, but the gentle smile on the lips was not reflected in the dark, troubled eyes. Joanna put the photograph back carefully in its place. She tried hard to put aside the unworthy thought that sprang to her mind: *she's not half as pretty as I am*. All the same, facts are facts, she thought comfortably.

'Here they come!'

Tristram's warning was unnecessary. The noise of the drunken crowd as they spilled out of the Waterman's Arms was loud enough to be heard all over town, let alone the length of the Causeway. 'OK,' Matt said. 'Let's get this done as fast as possible. You two know what to do. Just don't mark him, understand? We don't want any trouble with the police.'

'Sure, boss.' Tristram held up his massive hands as if in surrender. 'Look – kid gloves.'

But Matt was already talking into his mobile phone. 'Dave? Right – get into position, but stay well back until Big Dave signals. Afterwards you'll have to reverse out, so get Ali to keep an eye on the rear end. Don't be tempted to run any of the buggers over. We don't want any blood on the pitch.' He pocketed the mobile and called over the fence. 'Alec? Ernie? All set?'

'Ay.' Two bulky shadows moved in the gloom. 'It'll be like coney-catchin' wi'out the ferret,' one said. 'O'ny …'

'What?'

'Well, once they're in the net, shouldn't we disable 'em, like?'

'Look, lads, I don't want anybody seriously hurt. Go easy on the rough stuff, eh?'

'Righty-ho, squire. Put 'em out of action gently, like. That'll tek some thinkin' on.' They melted back into the darkness, snuffling with suppressed amusement, like schoolboys sharing a secret joke.

The mob outside the pub was beginning to get organized. Some were rehearsing a chant, which grew in volume and confidence as more people joined in: 'Pae-do! Pae-do! Out! Out! Out!' There was a lot of drunken shouting, and shrill screams of laughter. In the upstairs room, Joanna shivered and stepped back from the window as she heard – or fancied she heard – her own name in the braying noise. Someone began to harangue the crowd through a loudhailer: 'Whadder we call women what corrupt our kids? Filthy slags, that's what we call 'em. Whadder we call 'em?'

'Filthy slags!' screamed the crowd.

'I can't 'ear yer!'

'Filthy slags!'

'Right! And whadder we say to filthy slags?'

'Out!' roared the mob. 'Out! Out! Out!'

Horrified, Joanna saw that some of her neighbours were standing in their gardens, watching the advancing crowd. Old Mrs Whalley hobbled down the path in a dressing-gown and pink plastic shower-cap, brandishing her stick. She was shouting something, but whether it was encouragement or abuse was impossible to tell.

The noise increased in volume: the mob was on the move. 'Pae-do! Paedo!' The chant rose above the cacophony of sound, the mindless, drunken oaths, the jeering, the cat-calls. 'Out! Out! Out!' One girl, supported by two youths almost as drunk as she was, was laughing and shrieking like a madwoman. As they drew closer, Joanna shrank back into the shadows. Her stomach was churning, and she felt sick with fear and shock.

A man ran forward of the rabble. He was short and pot-bellied, and he carried a loudhailer. He pointed at Joanna's house and raised the hailer to his mouth. 'We want you out, slag!' he bellowed. 'Out of this street, out of this town, out of this country! Baby-molester! Your kind are filth!' He beckoned to the rest to catch up with him. 'Whadder we call ...' he began, then broke off, holding his hand in front of his eyes. 'What the fuck ...?'

The man and his followers were suddenly bathed in light, first from the right, then from the left. They slowed to a halt, and the chant tailed away into a string of angry obscenities. They stood confused, blinking and turning from side to side, shading their eyes.

A moment later Joanna saw the cause of their dismay. Two massive trucks were inching along the Causeway from opposite directions, their headlights blazing. They were high-sided tipper-trucks, the kind she had seen in the Derbyshire quarries. They moved very slowly but inexorably towards the mob, the roar of their engines sounding very loud in the sudden silence.

The laughing girl began to shriek with terror. The two youths let go of her and she staggered backwards into the darkness at the far side of the road. The man with the loudhailer also backed away, his spectacles flashing as he turned his head from side to side. The two trucks ground their way forward until they were no more than twenty yards apart, then stopped, their engines throbbing with dull menace.

The crowd now turned their protests against the truck drivers, demanding at the tops of their voices to know what the hell? and threatening all kinds of retribution if the truckies didn't piss off and mind their own business.

Strangely, the man with the loudhailer didn't join in. In fact, he was nowhere to be seen.

The lights on the right-hand truck flicked off and on. Its engine revved noisily, and it moved forward inch by inch for a few yards, and then stopped. A moment later, the other truck did the same.

'Christ, they're going to crush us!' someone yelled. Panic set in. People milled around aimlessly, barging into one another, unsure which way to run. Then, another distraction: 'It's raining!' several voices cried in melancholy chorus.

But it wasn't raining. There was a garden sprinkler wedged into the fork of Mr Gelson's eucalyptus tree, and now a thick jet of water arched high into the air and fell into the cramped area between the trucks. The engines roared and the headlamps moved closer. Cold, wet and sobering fast, the crowd scattered as best it could. Several diehards, determined not to leave without committing some mischief, broke into Joanna's garden and ran towards the house, planning, at the very least, to break a few windows.

They didn't get far. Within minutes, a dozen half-drunk youths were lying flat on their faces, struggling to get up only to fall down again. Joanna watched as the bulky figures of Alec and Ernie moved sedately from one prostrate form to another, kneeling on this one's back, pressing that one's face into the damp soil. She couldn't see exactly what they were doing, but it certainly persuaded the intruders to leave quietly. Some of the youths were limping badly, she noticed.

Then, as if by magic, it was all over. The Causeway was empty, except for the two trucks, which slowly rolled away towards the High Street. The sprinkler stopped, and Matt reached up to take it down from the tree. Alec and Ernie folded up a huge square of rope netting like two washerwomen folding a blanket. Ernie collected some debris into a sack. Mrs Whalley hobbled indoors. The little man with the pot-belly emerged from the shadows without his spectacles and his loudhailer, and half-limped, half-hopped back towards the pub. The twins, Alec and Ernie and four other men assembled under the street-light, and Matt joined them. There was a lot of laughing, back-slapping and shoulder-punching, then they all huddled together in a tight little circle, like conspirators. Joanna couldn't see what they were doing but she suspected that money was changing hands. The group separated and set off in different directions. The twins bowed in her general direction, and waved cheerily before trooping off into the night.

Matt came in looking tired and grim-faced. 'I guess they won't be back in a hurry.'

'I hope they never come back at all,' Joanna said fervently. 'I've never been so terrified in my life. Those men – the lorry drivers, and the men in my garden – are they all your employees?'

'They've all worked for me, at one time or another, but they're not all on my payroll. Big Dave and his son are independent contractors. What we all have in common is the Rugby Club.'

'Have you done this sort of thing before – breaking up riots, I mean?'

'Never. We had to improvise. We guessed that some of the mob would try to vandalize your house and garden, so we fixed up a reception for them. Alec and Ernie really enjoyed themselves. They'd rigged up a spread of wide-mesh rope netting – the kind of thing you see on Army combat courses. You have to pick your way through it very carefully, or it tangles your feet. It's hard enough when you can see it, but in the dark it's virtually impossible.'

'I saw lots of men fall down, but I couldn't see what Ernie and Alec were doing.'

'They were removing the enemy's shoes.'

'What!'

'I told them not to injure anybody, so they decided the best way to deal with those hooligans was to take their shoes off. It worked a treat, they told me. Really took the stuffing out of those grotty little thugs. Later, Ernie collected all the footwear into a sack and put it in the Salvation Army bin.'

He was trying to make light of the incident, but Joanna could see that his face was still drawn and sombre.

'I'm beginning to lose count of the number of times you've rescued me,' she said. 'I don't know how to thank you.'

'No need.' He took off his coat and started to sit down, then changed his mind. 'I need a drink. You?'

'No, thank you. If the excitement is all over, I guess it's safe for me to go back to my house?'

'Sure. But keep me company a little longer, will you?' He seemed to be having difficulty in deciding what to drink. In the end, he poured himself a tiny measure of whisky, and came back to sit facing her. 'That was a very ugly business,' he said. 'Half of those guys were mercenaries.'

'Mercenaries? What do you mean?'

'I mean that somebody paid them to come round here and make trouble. That little guy with the megaphone is a professional agitator. He gets paid to organize demos like this one. He has a core group of troublemakers, and they swell their ranks by plying bored kids with free booze.'

'You said earlier that you thought the protest was being deliberately orchestrated. Are you now saying that someone actually paid them to come and make trouble?'

'Yes.'

'Why, for God's sake? Who would do such a thing?'

'I don't know why.' Matt looked glumly at the whisky in his glass, but made no attempt to drink it. 'However, the twins took the megaphone guy for a little walk along the canal path. They swear they didn't hurt him – not enough to leave marks, anyway – but after about a hundred yards of trotting along in the dark, he became quite chatty. So, although I don't know why, I do know who.'

'What do you mean?'

'I know who paid them.' He lifted his glass and drained it. 'It was your friend in the natty suiting. Dudley. Gerald Dudley.'

CHAPTER 22

The unfamiliar noise gave Joanna a moment of panic. It was a bleating sound, penetrating, yet oddly muffled, and it came from her handbag. Her pulse was still racing as she dug out the mobile phone. 'Yes?'

'Did you sleep?' It was Matt's voice. It had to be: no-one else had the number.

'Hardly at all,' she said bitterly. 'I woke up a dozen times, thinking I could hear that bloody mob. And in between naps I was mentally roasting that swine Dudley on a spit.' That was a lie: she had lain awake wondering why Matt hadn't invited her to his bed. He had wanted to, she was sure of that, but he hadn't. Perfect bloody gentleman.

'I slept badly, too. I couldn't help wondering whether Dudley had more mischief planned.'

'God, I hope not!'

'Look, I have to go in to Manchester today. Why don't you come with me? I don't feel happy leaving you on your own all day.'

'I won't be on my own. I'm going to visit Angela this afternoon. Apart from that, I'll just stay here. I don't fancy facing the good citizens of Aldersgrove just yet.'

Matt sounded gratifyingly disappointed. 'OK. But please keep your mobile handy at all times. I need you to stay in touch.'

'Need?'

'Don't quibble. You know what I mean. Oh – if you're staying indoors, what about supplies? Do you need me to do any shopping for you?'

Joanna hadn't thought about that. 'Hell, I suppose so. The basics, anyway – milk, bread, tea, eggs. You don't think I've got to stock up for a siege, do you?'

'I hope not. Anyway, you've got the key to my place. I've got a freezer full of junk. You won't starve if you stick with me, kid. I'm off to Buchanan's. Now would be a good time to charge up your mobile.'

As she was putting the mobile down the house phone began to ring. The caller was so unexpected that Joanna didn't at first know who it was.

'Hi, Joanna?' the voice said. 'This is Cynthia.'

'Hi,' Joanna said vaguely. The name was familiar, but she couldn't immediately place it.

'Sorry, did I wake you?'

'No. I've been up for ages.' Suddenly, Joanna identified the voice. Cynthia Bell! The shyest and most reticent of her colleagues at the Jas Priestley; the one who never loitered in the staff room after working hours, but scurried off to her husband like a little homing pigeon. 'Cynthia! What a surprise! How are things?'

'At work? Chaos. Athers is going potty. We're four staff short, and the only supply we can get doesn't know her fanny from her funny-bone.'

The comment was so out of character from Cynthia Bell that Joanna gasped aloud. 'So how come you can find the time to phone me in working hours?'

'Fiendish cunning, my dear. You don't want to know the details. Look, how are you?'

'As you would expect. Being suspended is no fun, believe me. What are people saying about me, over there?'

'No surprises. The bitches are being bitchy, the saints are being saintly, and the morons are being moronic. An everyday story of teaching folk. Oh, and I forgot to say, the plods are plodding. In ever-diminishing circles.'

'Cynthia,' Joanna said gratefully, 'you are a breath of fresh air. Correction: you are pure oxygen. Do you know, apart from Atherton no-one else from school has been in touch since this awful business began?'

'Don't be too hard on us, Joanna. The work is killing us. At the end of each day we're too knackered to be proper human beings.'

'All the same it's a relief to hear a friendly voice. Thank you.'

'Look, nobody in their right mind is going to believe a little snot like Tanner. I had to teach the little bugger, and given the choice, I think I'd rather have been burnt at the stake.'

'Tell the cops that.'

'I have, my duck. The only one who seemed to have more sense than a stuffed dinosaur was a woman.'

'Detective Inspector Burgage.'

'That's the one. Too pretty to be a policeman. Look, I've got to go, and I haven't told you my news. Have you got the morning paper?'

'On the table in front of me. I haven't even looked at it yet.'

'Check out the Forthcoming Marriages. Surprise, surprise! Got to go, sorry!' She rang off hurriedly, as if she had been caught out in some misdemeanour.

Joanna turned over the pages. The item was on a page she normally ignored, so if she hadn't been prompted she would have missed it. But there it was, in the second column:

Mr T W Short – Miss F Buchanan.

> 'The engagement is announced between Thomas, younger son of Mr and Mrs Jeremy Short of Dovebridge, Lancs, and Fiona, only daughter of Sir Craigie and Lady Buchanan of Buchanan Hall, Aldersgrove, Lancs.

At last, Joanna was able to make sense of Tom Short's behaviour. If he really had won the heart of the heiress to the Buchanan fortune it was no wonder he was so desperate to distance himself from the scandalous Joanna Howard. Sir Craigie Buchanan was not only famously rich and notoriously mean, he was also known to have severely Calvinistic views about sexual morality. The slightest breath of scandal would wreck Tom's chances completely. Joanna knew enough about her ex-lover to believe that he would perjure himself ten times over rather than risk losing the Buchanan millions.

She admitted a reluctant admiration for the brass neck of the guy. All the time he was carrying on his affair with her he must have been courting Fiona Buchanan! That's why their affair had to be a secret! And only last week, practically on the eve of announcing his engagement to Fiona, he had been trying to get into Joanna's bed! He had a nerve, that was for certain.

In the light of this development Joanna accepted that it would be futile to approach Tom Short just now. He would simply deny everything.

It was only with hindsight that she could appreciate how careful he had been, during their months together. He had left behind no photographs, no letters, no personal items whatever. Now she thought about it, his courtship of Fiona Buchanan must have begun before his affair with Joanna. No wonder the deceitful little sod had insisted on absolute secrecy!

After a few minutes' thought she rang the police station and asked for Inspector Burgage. To her surprise, she got through immediately. This seemed a good omen, and she enthusiastically passed on the news about Tom Short's engagement. 'So you see, Tom has a very strong motive to lie about his affair with me. Fiona's a rich girl; Tom doesn't want to lose her, and he knows that the Buchanans would chuck him out on his ear if they so much as suspected his involvement with me.'

Theresa Burgage chuckled. 'Nice try, Mrs Howard. You're telling me that our vertically-challenged friend was dallying with two dollies at the same time?'

'Yes.'

'But he denies it.'

'Of course he does. He's got a lot to lose.'

'I understand your point, Mrs Howard. But don't you see, the burden of proof is on you? Your neighbours don't back you up, and Mr Short flatly contradicts you. Show me something. Where are the billets-doux, the love-tokens, the birthday-cards, the photographs? Most love-affairs leave some traces behind.'

'Yes. I thought I had some letters and cards and stuff, but I can't find them.'

Burgage sounded uninterested. 'You mean you've lost them?'

'Well, I ...' Joanna hesitated, aware that she sounded as if she was improvising. 'I think Tom took them. He knew I would find out about Fiona some day.'

'So he removed the evidence, in case you blackmailed him, is that what you're suggesting?'

'No. I don't know what was in his mind. He was obsessive about secrecy, that's all I know.'

Burgage decided to end the conversation. 'OK. If that's all ...?'

'No, wait!' Joanna was excited. 'I've remembered something! I gave Tom Short a key to my house! Surely that shows he was more than just a casual acquaintance?'

'It doesn't prove anything, if it's just your word against his,' Burgage said cautiously.

'But it isn't! My next-door neighbour, Matthew Clements knows that Tom let himself into my house in my absence! He'll swear to it!'

'OK. I'll look into it,' Burgage said. But judging by her tone, she wasn't going to make it a priority.

Just before midday, Detectives Bailey and Cope were driving down the long hill from Knowley village, when Cope noticed something.

'Hey! There's that place,' he said, pointing to a sign. 'That restaurant – the Potifar.'

'So? You feeling hungry? Looks a pretty swanky caff to me.'

'It's the place that guy Dudley went to. Since we're here, why don't we check it out?'

'What's the point?' Bailey was thoroughly bored with the investigation, which seemed to be going nowhere. 'Dudley showed us the bill and the credit-card slip. He was there all right.'

'Yeah, but you know what Farmer Giles is like. He likes things nicely rounded off. Let's get ourselves some Brownie points. It won't take a minute.'

But in fact it took the best part of an hour, and they left looking puzzled and thoughtful. 'Was that meant to be English?' Bailey complained. 'I reckon I missed two words out of every three.'

'Maybe, but we got the drift all right. Let's go and tell the boss.'

Angela Bonneville answered the door herself. 'I've given the staff the afternoon off,' she told Joanna. 'Told them to go away and enjoy themselves, whether they wanted to or not. Cook's left us some sandwiches, though. Come and have a quick bite, then I'll show you the gear. I hope you're a quick learner. We've only got a couple of hours before the curtain goes up.'

'You're talking in riddles, and I'm not up to it,' Joanna said crossly. 'Yesterday was horrible, and today isn't shaping up much better. Driving here, I was sure that at any minute somebody would point at me and shout abuse. My whole body feels raw and painful, as if I'd been flayed. I'm just not in the mood for light conversation.'

Angela led the way into the kitchen. 'I haven't invited you here for light conversation. This is deadly serious, I assure you. Sit down while I make us some tea.' She busied herself at a side counter, and with her back to Joanna, said, 'I hear that Gerald Dudley paid a crowd of hooligans to stage a demo outside your house.'

'What! Where did you hear that?'

'And I also hear that the demo was thwarted by members of the Bottersley Rugby Club.' Angela laughed. 'For a poor defenceless female, you have some remarkably beefy friends.'

'No, I mean how do you know that it was Dudley who organized that demo?'

Angela carefully carried the tea-tray to the table. 'I know everything about Gerald Dudley's movements,' she said calmly. 'I have him watched. Night and day.' She waited for Joanna's response, but Joanna merely stared at her wide-eyed. 'About a month ago,' Angela continued, 'I hired an agency to check on Dudley. I knew he was short of money, and I wanted to know why. I soon learned he's in a lot of trouble. He gambles, and he's in debt to some very aggressive loan sharks. He's got through Shona's fortune, and she's suing for divorce. About a couple of weeks ago he came up here. I followed him; that's really why I'm here. He's obviously up to something, but I don't yet know what it is. But I'm pretty sure you're involved.'

'Me? Why? I haven't seen the man since he upped and left me penniless.'

'All the same, he laid out hard cash to have you harassed by that mob. This is a guy who's dead broke, remember. He can't afford luxuries. It looks to me as if he was desperate to run you out of town.'

Joanna was distraught. 'That doesn't make any sense. He cheated *me*. Why should he be the one with the grudge?'

'Search me.' Angela poured tea and pushed a cup across the table. 'The thing is, you're the one person in the world who can help me. The one person who loathes Gerald Dudley as much as I do. The one person I can trust. And the bonus is, that you're a talented musician, and I like you. Very much.'

'You're flattering me,' Joanna said. 'And that makes me nervous. Tell me why you set a private detective on Dudley in the first place?'

'Oh, my dear, I thought you must have guessed by now.' Angela sipped her tea. 'Because he's been blackmailing me for years.'

'Well?' Sergeant Dewbury asked. 'When are we going to do it?'

'When I'm ready.' Theresa Burgage no longer bothered to hide her dislike of the sergeant. She knew he gossiped about her behind her back, and was unsubtly insolent to her face. He was a sly, lazy misogynist, too stupid to see that it was perilous to make an enemy of a senior officer. Dewbury didn't know it yet, but his future was not looking rosy.

'What are we waiting for?' the sergeant persisted. 'We've got the evidence from her house, and the interior is just as the kid described it. Dammit, the neighbours have actually *seen* the kid going in and out. And that demo last night – that just shows the public is losing patience. They want to see justice done.'

'And so do you, Sergeant, it seems,' Burgage said drily. 'What do you know about that demo?'

'Only what I heard. There was a ruckus outside Howard's house. Ordinary folk – good, honest people – hate these bloody child-molesters.'

'But why pick on Mrs Howard? She wasn't named in the *Voice* article.'

'No, but she's the only local teacher on suspension. It don't take a genius to work it out.'

'No.' Burgage's tone was deceptively mild. 'I wonder how they knew she was suspended from duty?'

'Search me. This is a small town. News gets around.' Dewbury felt he was winning the argument. 'Come on, ma'am. We've got more than enough to convict this scrubber. Let's bring her in.'

'Not yet.' Burgage sounded calmer than she felt. Dewbury's choice of words scalded her mind. 'Mrs Howard phoned me this morning. She suggested a plausible reason why Tom Short should lie about his relationship with her. We need to check that out. Also, CPS suggested that we need to get a statement from the boy Darren Palmer, to round out the investigation.'

'I thought Kylie was on to that,' Dewbury said.

'Kylie is really sick with the flu, didn't you know? Somebody else will have to do it.'

'Not me,' the sergeant said hastily. There was football on the box that night, and he had a TV dinner and a six-pack of lager waiting for him at home. 'I've promised to visit my mother this evening. She's poorly.'

Burgage, who knew that Dewbury and his mother had been on terms of bitter loathing for years, scowled unsympathetically. 'Then I'll have to see to it myself. Tomorrow, if we've got the paperwork in order, we'll put it up to the CPS. Another day won't harm.'

'I suppose not,' Dewbury said reluctantly. He turned to go, but before he reached the door, Burgage said casually: 'I suppose you've heard the rumour?'

He half-turned, and looked back at her. 'What rumour?'

'They say there's going to be an internal inquiry into who leaked that tape to the *Voice* reporter. The District Commander is said to be hopping mad about it.'

Dewbury froze for a moment, his mouth hanging open. 'Waste of time,' he said, recovering his composure. 'Them reporters never reveal their sources. It's like a religion with 'em.'

'Ye-es,' Burgage said doubtfully. 'But that girl isn't a real reporter, is she? She's more like an apprentice. I mean, suppose for a minute that Mrs Howard is acquitted? I reckon she'd sue the paper, and the balloon would really go up. Everybody would be desperate to expose the idiot who leaked that tape, just to have a scapegoat. Somebody's head would roll, for sure.' There was no mistaking the relish in the inspector's voice, as she laid out this scenario. Dewbury didn't bother giving her an argument. He fled.

Everything she had just said was pure fabrication, but Burgage didn't see any harm in giving the sergeant something to worry about over the weekend. Smiling for the first time that afternoon, she picked up the phone and asked the operator to put her in touch with Darren Palmer's parents.

Dudley grinned up at the surveillance camera above the front door. Typical cheapskate rubbish, he thought. He could spot a dummy camera a mile off. He was still smiling when Angela opened the door. 'Long time no see,' he said predictably.

'Not long enough,' Angela said tartly. 'Come in.'

'The house is empty, right?' Dudley was cautious. 'No faithful retainer lurking in the cellar?'

'Search the place if you like,' Angela said carelessly. 'But ask yourself: why would I want a witness to this grubby transaction?'

'Yeah, good point,' Dudley conceded. 'We wouldn't want anybody else to know about your grubby past, would we?' He made a detour round the entrance hall, opening doors and peering into rooms. 'Hey, this is pretty classy. You're still doing well for yourself, I see.'

'No thanks to you.' Angela led the way into the drawing-room. 'Let's get this over with. Did you bring the letters?'

'Not so fast.' Dudley threw himself into an armchair and grinned up at her. 'Aren't you going to offer me a drink?'

'No. I want you out of here. Just the sight of you makes me want to throw up.'

'Ooh, bitchy.' He carefully filled his pipe and lit it, closing the lighter with a snap and a flourish, like an actor in a bad movie. 'Just be careful, darling. Insults like that can come very expensive.' He tapped the pipe-stem against his teeth. 'And talking of money, you still owe me. Last month's instalment didn't arrive.'

'No.' Angela retreated and sat down, her back to the window. 'And it won't. That arrangement is over, finished. I'm making you an offer for those letters. Take it or leave it. I want you off my back.'

'You said as much over the phone.' He leaned back and trickled smoke out of the side of his mouth. 'But sweetie, you seem to forget who's in charge here. I like the arrangement as it is. Think of it as an insurance premium: you pay me every month, and I keep those randy letters safe for you. Actually, now I see what a rich little bitch you are, I reckon you're getting off cheaply. What say we double the premiums? Starting now.'

'Do you think you can blackmail me for ever?'

'No, darlin`. Just for the foreseeable future.'

Angela closed her eyes and sat silent for a couple of minutes, her head bowed. Looking up, she said quietly, 'And what if I never pay you another cent?'

'Well, dearie ...' Dudley's pipe had gone out. He made a fruitless attempt to relight it, then deliberately tapped out the dottle onto the carpet, and stirred it with his foot. He took his time answering. 'Well, dearie, then I should have to sell those letters to the highest bidder. I reckon one of the tabloids would pay handsomely for them.'

'Do you think so? I'm a humble pianist, you know, not a pop star.'

'You're famous enough. And anyway, you're not the only one involved. What about that dirty old frog who wrote them? He's even more famous than you are. He won't want to see his dirty linen hanging out in public. *Quel scandale*, eh?'

Angela sighed. 'He's dead. I don't have to protect him any more.'

'What!'

'I told you. He's dead. The situation has changed.'

'Yeah, well.' Dudley was thinking hard. 'What about his wife, then? Poor old cow. Do you really want to blight her twilight years?'

'No. Which is why I'm making you an offer.' Angela sat up and her voice hardened. 'You really don't get it, do you? You don't have any leverage any more. As far as I'm concerned, your bloodsucking days are over. I've already notified the police that those letters were stolen from me, so no reputable newspaper is going to touch them, let alone pay a fortune for them. You're pathetic, you know that? You come here to bully me, and all the time you're up to your eyeballs in debt, to people who'll take your flesh if they can't get their cash out of you.'

'How do you know that?' Now Dudley was genuinely alarmed.

'I know lots and lots about you, Gerry. I know you've been spreading lies about a local schoolteacher, and that you even laid out money you can't afford on a rent-a-crowd to harass her, you mean-minded sod. I even know your real name. If you had any money I might be tempted to blackmail *you*. Just think how Betsy Bray would react, if she knew your family name was—'

'Shut up!' Dudley had begun to sweat. 'Look, I could make photocopies of those letters and send them to all your friends and all the music critics. That would take the smile off your face.'

'Indeed it would, Gerry. It would embarrass me for months and months. But the embarrassment would gradually die away. On the other hand, you wouldn't make a single penny out of the exercise. Take my offer. Bird in the hand, and all that.'

'No!' Dudley leapt to his feet and shook his fist at her. 'I'm buggered if I'll be bullied by a slag like you! I'll publish those letters if it's the last thing I do!'

'Go ahead.' Angela looked bored. 'Publish and be damned. If what I hear about those London loan-sharks is true, your next defiant gesture will be made from a wheelchair.'

'Bugger you.' He subsided sulkily into the armchair and began chewing on a fingernail. 'I'll make you sorry for this.'

'Calm down, dear.' Angela's tone was mocking. 'I'm not being cruel or unreasonable. I'm still willing to buy those letters from you.'

'How much?'

'Fifty thousand dollars.'

'What!' Dudley's face was purple with anger. 'You bloody cheapskate! Is that what your reputation's worth? Is that all you're prepared to pay for that poor old widow's peace of mind? God, you're disgusting!'

Angela went on as if he hadn't spoken. 'Twenty thousand cash, in euros. The balance in bearer-bonds and a bank-draft, drawn on the First Farmer's Bank of Illinois. As you know, bearer-bonds can be turned into cash at any American bank. And they're a lot easier to carry than a case full of money.'

'Euros?' he was momentarily distracted. 'Euros, for God's sake?'

'Think about it,' Angela said patiently. 'I don't imagine you're in a hurry to go back to London. Shona won't let you into the house, and the debt-collectors will strip you of every penny you've got. On the other hand, with cash in your pocket, you could nip over to France, swan around like an English milord – you're good at that – until some gullible French heiress falls under your spell.'

'France, eh?' Gerald was visibly attracted by the idea.

'Or Spain. Or Italy. There are rich women all over the world. America might be good.'

'American women?' He pulled a face. 'I don't think so.' He seemed to have accepted without question the premise that he would have to make money out of some woman or other. 'Look – you're not the only one who checks things out. I know about the apartment in New York, and the house in London, as well as this place up here. You're worth millions, kiddo, and if you think I'm going to settle for a measly fifty thousand bucks, you're out of your mind.'

'OK.' Angela sighed and smoothed down her skirt.

'OK? OK what? I've just told you your offer is unacceptable. I refuse it.'

'OK.' Angela rose. 'Then we've nothing more to talk about. I'll show you out.'

'Wait a minute! You've forgotten who you're dealing with, sweetie. You're here on your own, and you've just let me know that you've got an untraceable fifty grand lying around. What's to stop me taking the cash and keeping your precious letters? Now I think about it, I'll be able to sell them in France, all right.'

She shrugged and strolled to the window. 'You know, I never really appreciated how incredibly stupid you are. Did you really believe I would trust you? Why do you suppose I invited you here? Into my house?'

He was beginning to lose his bluster. 'You tell me.'

'Because it's a trap, Gerry-boy. You walked into it, but you can't walk out unless I let you out. If you attempt to open the front or back doors – or any of the windows – without entering the code on the hidden key pad, the security guards will be here within ten minutes.'

'You're bluffing,' he said uncertainly. 'That security camera outside is an obvious fake.'

'True. The thing that looks like a camera is an ornament. The tacky ornamental owl over the door is a camera. Your sadly sagging features have been faithfully recorded, believe me.'

Her composure totally unnerved him. 'Look,' he said menacingly, 'I've got photocopies of all the letters, you know.'

'Of course you have, you pathetic fart. And I now have a recording of you threatening to blackmail me. "For the foreseeable future", I think you said.'

'What!' His eyes darted comically from side to side. 'This room is bugged?' He made it sound like a betrayal of a holy trust.

'The whole house is bugged, *sweetie*.' Angela laid a heavy emphasis on the last word. 'But just appreciate the drama of the situation. I'm making you an offer you can't refuse.'

'Bitch!' was the best Dudley could come up with in defeat. 'Fifty grand is peanuts to you,' he said resentfully.

'But not to you, alas. Give me the letters.'

'Show me the money.'

'Letters first. Then I'll tell you where the money is.'

Dudley pulled a slim packet from an inside pocket and handed it over. Angela took the letters to the window and examined them carefully one by one. 'Right,' she said, without looking at him. 'The money's in a briefcase behind that door.' She left him to figure out which door she meant.

Dudley brought the briefcase into the room and emptied the contents onto a low table. Kneeling down, he flicked through the bundles of notes and then counted the bundles. 'The euro's worth about a dollar, right?'

'More on a good day. But if you're going to spend them in France the exchange rate's academic.'

'So you're telling me that this little baby,' he brandished one of the notes, 'is worth three hundred bucks?'

'Yes. It's a convenient way to carry a lot of cash. There's a couple of thousand in smaller denominations to tide you over until you get that banked.'

'Yeah, OK, but what am I supposed to do with these?' He held up the thick wad of printed paper.

'Any big American bank will cash them for you. You'll have to show identification and fill in a form, but it shouldn't be a problem unless you get greedy. They're for comparatively small amounts, which shouldn't raise any suspicions.'

His shoulders slumped, and he began to stow the money back into the briefcase, arranging the bundles and lining them up with fastidious neatness. When he had finished he stood up and faced her, looking both resentful and frightened, like a whipped dog. 'Well,' he said vaguely, 'that's it, then. No hard feelings, eh?'

'Of course there are hard feelings, you moron!' Angela snapped cruelly. 'Just go, will you? I'm sick of the sight of you.'

She opened the front door and let him out. He took a few steps, then turned and looked at her, frowning. 'You opened that door without entering a code,' he said. 'You told me there was a hidden key pad.' He began to tremble with fury. 'You liar! You—' The heavy door slammed in his face. He opened his mouth to shout, then turned to look nervously over his shoulder at the street. He didn't want to call attention to himself. He bent down and pushed at the flap of the letterbox. 'Bloody cheat!' he called softly through the open slot. It made him feel better but not much. He marched swiftly to his car, his back stiff with indignation.

Angela looked up at the hidden camera. 'Wasn't that fun?' she said, chortling her throaty laugh. 'I hope you got it all?'

Joanna came down the stairs a few minutes later, and joined Angela in the drawing-room. 'That was so much easier than I thought it would be,' she said. 'That equipment is fantastic. I even got some great close-ups when he started to sweat. Anyway, once you got him into that armchair, it was a piece of cake. Golly!' She shook her head and shuddered melodramatically. 'To think I actually had a relationship with that man! He's so gross!'

'He was better-looking when he was younger, and a lot more subtle,' Angela commented. 'Even now, he has a certain greasy charm. We might still find him tolerable if we didn't know what an utter pig he is.'

'Never! When his face came up on that screen, I was so angry I thought I was going to faint. Then the whole thing was like watching a play. Why on earth did you give him all that money?'

'I had to give him something. I wanted those letters back.'

'But he told you he's made copies. He might circulate those, just to be nasty.'

'He might. But he's a lazy fellow, more motivated by profit than revenge. If he can't make money out of those copies he'll lose interest. Also, I now have a video of him offering to blackmail me "for the foreseeable future". I don't think he'll risk going to gaol.' Angela suddenly barked with laughter. 'Sorry, sorry. I just thought of something funny.'

'What?'

'Never mind. I'll tell you later.' But her eyes still sparkled. 'Do you want me to tell you about those letters?'

'Only if you want to.'

'I think I do. I've never told anyone before.' She turned her head and looked out of the window. 'When I was seventeen I won a scholarship to go to Paris and study piano technique with a very eminent teacher – some said, the best in the world. He was more than twice my age, but I fell for him on sight. We became lovers, and we wrote passionate letters to each other. He destroyed mine – he was married, you see – but I kept his. The affair ended, as it was always destined to do, but gently, and with that painful sweetness you only feel when you're very young.' She paused, her face alight with memories. 'Anyway, years later, when I ought to have known much better, I took up with Gerald. When we lived together he went methodically through my possessions – I'm sure you remember that habit of his – found the letters and stole them. I've been buying his silence ever since.'

'For the sake of your French lover?'

'For the sake of a great and well-loved teacher, yes.' Angela pulled a large handkerchief from her sleeve and blew her nose energetically. 'Well, that's over and done with. I need some Bach. How about you?'

'I …' Joanna was flustered. 'I don't really feel up to singing at the moment.'

'No, I don't mean performing, I mean listening. I've got a super old recording of Grumiaux playing Bach concertos. Nothing like Bach for clearing the cobwebs out of the mind. Afterwards, we'll go somewhere and eat drink and be merry. What do you say?'

'Fine.' But Joanna had something on her mind. 'May I ask you something?'

'Go ahead.'

'Why did you really ask me here? You could have easily set up that recording equipment to operate itself. You didn't really need me for that. You knew you had Gerald over a barrel; he's desperate for money, and as you pointed out, yours was an offer he couldn't refuse. So you just wanted me here as a spectator. But why?'

'I was coming to that,' Angela said, discomfited. 'Eventually.' For a moment, it seemed as if she was unsure how to go on. 'I wanted you on my side. I knew you hated Dudley, and I wanted you to understand why I hate him, too.'

'I do understand, and I am on your side. But why is it so important?'

'Because I might have to ask a big favour of you.'

'All you have to do is ask. What favour?'

Angela drew her breath noisily through her teeth. 'I might have to lie to the police. And I'd be really grateful if you would back me up.'

CHAPTER 23

Betsy Bray hurried out of the kitchen as soon as she heard Gerald's key in the lock. 'That policeman – Bailey – rang again. Wanted to talk to you.'

'What about?' Dudley put the briefcase on the floor, and flexed his arm.

'Oh, nothing important. I was able to sort it out for him. Is that a new briefcase? I haven't seen that before.'

'No – I mean, yes, fairly new. So what, exactly, did the fellow want?'

'Oh, poor chap, he'd lost his notes. About his interview with you, I mean. He said he remembered you saying you went to a restaurant last Saturday night, but he couldn't remember what it was called. "Oh," I said, "that'll be the Potifar on Knowley Road." "Are you sure?" he said. "Oh, yes," said I. "I was with him. And a jolly nice meal it was, too." Then he paused – writing it all down, I suppose – then he said: "And would you mind telling me your name, miss?" Miss! Well, I shrieked! "Thank you very much, kind sir," I said, "but I'm old enough to be your mother, I bet. I'm Mrs Betsy Bray of Church Lane," I told him, and he apologized for his mistake, but my voice sounded so young, he said. What a nice young man. It was a pleasure talking to him. So, you see, I've sorted it all out for you.'

'Thank you, Betsy. You're a true friend.' Dudley's lip trembled, and he looked away, avoiding her eyes.

'Gerald! My dear, whatever's the matter? You look – gosh, are you ill, or something?'

'No, I'm all right. It's …' He swallowed hard. 'It's bad news, I'm afraid. Look, promise me you won't tell a soul?'

'Well,' Betsy looked doubtful, 'I don't have any secrets from Ronnie, you know.'

'No, of course not. But I would be mortified if this ever got out. Please – not a word outside these four walls. Promise?'

Now Betsy was goggle-eyed with curiosity. 'Not a word, Gerald. You know you can trust me.'

'It's Shona,' Gerald said sadly. 'I expect you've heard that we're having a trial separation?'

Actually, Betsy had heard that Shona had thrown him out, but she didn't think this was the time to mention it. 'Yes. I was so sorry.'

'I knew she was awfully cut up about it, but I never thought …' Gerald broke down again. 'Oh, God, it's so awful! She slashed her wrists. Last night.'

'Oh, dear Lord! She's dead?'

'Someone found her just in time, thank goodness. She's in hospital now. Very weak, of course, but … Betsy, I must go to her.'

'Of course, my dear. You must fly.'

'No, I'll drive down, it'll be quicker in the end.'

'No, I didn't mean …' Betsy flapped her hands in her agitation. 'I'll help you pack.'

'Thank you, but …' he regarded her soulfully, 'I'd rather be alone for a few moments.'

'Of course.' But she had to do something. 'I'll put up some sandwiches and a thermos for you. It's a long drive.'

In less time than she would have believed possible he was gone, his suitcases thrown carelessly into the boot, and his new briefcase propped in front of the passenger seat. Betsy smiled wanly as she waved goodbye, and spent a tearful half-hour tidying his room.

Afterwards, she made herself a cup of tea, settled herself in her favourite chair, and picked up the phone. 'Alicia? The most awful thing has happened to poor Gerald, you wouldn't believe …'

Jack Dabdoub was feeling crabby. He'd made a special effort to get to the practice at the club that afternoon, and really put his back into the boring training routine. But then, right at the end, after all that stretching, trotting, sprinting and bashing into padded dummies, they'd announced that the Wackstone fixture had been cancelled. Some pusillanimous excuse about half their team being down with the flu. Right bunch of softies. He really wanted a game, too. He'd had a frustrating couple of days, and he needed to work off some aggression. Beating up a few of those Wackstone lard-arses would have been just the ticket. Rugby was a hard-contact sport, and for Dabdoub the sport was in the contact – the harder the better.

Another irritation was to find out that he had missed a really memorable barney in Aldersgrove the night before. To hear that old fart Ernie Rainer tell it, eight of them had beat the living daylights out of about fifty drunken yobbos who were on the rampage down by the canal. The old fool was exaggerating of course, but the boys had obviously enjoyed some sort of rumble, and inexplicably, Dabdoub, arch-rumbler, had not been invited. It was a sad world when so-called friends could be so stingy as to keep all that aggro to themselves.

Sulking, he had asked Matt about it, but Matt was spitting tacks because Dabdoub still hadn't read through the info about the Howard woman. For a supposedly gentle guy, Matthew Clements could fix you with a look that made you feel like something that lived under a damp rock. Still, no point in arguing with him; you can't expect sweet reason from a guy in love.

Now he was back home, Dabdoub felt restless and bad-tempered. He didn't want to think about the Carole Guest case; he had been thinking about it too hard for too long. It buzzed around angrily in his brain, like a bee in a bottle. The trouble was that the case had stalled and Dabdoub had no idea how to get it moving again. He had dug up a lot of background stuff, but George Guest was only interested in one thing: did Melvin Tares have an accomplice when he murdered George's mother? And for all his intelligence-gathering, Dabdoub was no nearer solving that than when he had first laid eyes on his client.

Resentfully, he laid out on the table all the paper work he had brought home, and arranged it into three piles. The smallest heap was the few pages of notes he had made of his talk with Joe Lolly. Then the fax from Matt, about Mrs Howard, and finally, the massive file that Tony had prepared – he called it a 'dossier' – on the Carole Guest murder. Tony had bulked it out only the day before, with a heap of newspaper-cuttings and a transcript of the trial of Melvin Tares.

Muttering to himself, he went into the kitchen and poured himself a stiff whisky. After a moment's thought he carried bottle and glass back to the table.

Someone had once told him that if you study a problem just before going to sleep you often wake up with the answer in your head. It was probably rubbish, but when you're desperate anything was worth a shot. Making sure that the whisky bottle was comfortably within reach Dabdoub reached for Matthew's fax, and began reading.

Teddy Giles forced himself to stay calm. His nerves were tingling, and his copper's intuition was telling him that this was a major breakthrough; but he was determined to see the whole picture before getting his hopes too high. 'Run it by me again,' he said. 'Start with the girl.'

DC Bailey scribbled a few headings on a notepad before he spoke. 'As we said in our first report, Fernie Brent was a friend of Elizabeth Nair – one of the few friends Nair had. She's on parole; she's living with her married sister on the Wickerbrook Estate, in a flat in the same block as Nair's apartment, and her parole officer got her a job at Buchanan's. Fernie told us that she didn't know Lizzie Nair well, but she felt sorry for the woman. She was pretty sure that Nair didn't have a boyfriend, and she couldn't imagine that she had any enemies.'

'I remember all that,' Giles said. 'And her alibi for the night of the murder was that she had spent the whole evening with an old business colleague.'

'That was this guy Gerald Dudley. She told us that she had worked for him years ago, when he ran a business in Manchester. Dudley had since retired and gone to live down South, but he happened to be in Aldersgrove for a visit. They met by accident, she said – he had spotted her in Buchanan's, and made a date.'

Giles interrupted again. 'Has this Dudley got form?'

'We ran his name through, sir, but we didn't find anything.' Bailey glanced down at his notes. 'We contacted him last Wednesday, and he came into the nick to make a statement. He confirmed what Fernie

Brent had told us – that they'd had a slap-up supper at the Potifar restaurant; he produced this bill and the credit-card slip as proof.' He pushed the papers across the desk.

'He let you keep this?'

'Practically insisted on it. He added that afterwards they had driven up to Knowley Castle and had a spot of nookie in the back of his car. Fernie had hinted about something along those lines in her statement.'

Teddy Giles was shocked, but tried not to look it. 'What was your opinion of this Dudley chap?'

Detective Cope laughed. 'He's a plonker. A right wally.'

'He comes over as a kind of wrinkly Hooray Henry,' Bailey said. 'Tries to act the gent, but he's about as convincing as a hand-knitted wig. We had him down as a prat, but he could be smarter than we thought. I would have bought his story if it hadn't been for Eric here.'

'No, he'd convinced me all right.' Cope took up the narrative. 'We were driving down Knowley Hill, and I saw this sign – the Potifar – and I said, hey let's go tidy up that loose end, or something like that. Just to make things look neat, you know? I thought it would only take a few minutes. It took bloody ages.'

'There was only one bloke there at that time of day,' Bailey explained, 'and his English wasn't good. He was Greek, I think.'

'Ah.' Giles brightened. 'Anyway, what he said was Greek to you, eh?' but no one shared his amusement. '*Julius Caesar*,' he explained, but their faces remained blank. 'Oh, never mind. Go on.'

'We had about a dozen words between us,' Bailey said, 'so most of the interview was in sign language.'

'Just like bloody charades,' Cope said, rolling his eyes.

Bailey went on: 'We were getting nowhere until I showed him the bill; then the fellow livened up. "Nay, nay," he said, over and over, shaking his head and grinning like a monkey. "Nay, nay."'

Cope joined in: 'Finally, we worked out that what he meant was "Yes, yes." The poor bugger had got it the wrong way round. Then he kept saying "Pop, pop," and pretending to pull a cork out of a bottle. I mean, if you'd seen it on the telly, you'd of been in tucks.'

'Well, to cut a long story short,' Bailey said, 'the fellow remembered that customer, because he had bought two bottles of their most expensive champagne. It was on the bill, see? And he described the customer – he did a lah-di-dah, stage-door-johnny act that got Dudley down to a T. Then we asked him about the girl. He seemed to understand the word "girl", but he looked sideways at us. We did more mime – long hair, bosoms, and that – and he kept shaking his head and saying something like "You nick her?" and we said no, she wasn't in trouble, we just wanted to know what she looked like. "Madam?" he said. "Yes, madam," we said. "Ah, nay, nay," he said, "Madame," and he laughed and made great big curves in the air with both hands. "Madame Roly-poly." He kept saying "Roly-poly": it was the one English word he was dead certain of, and he knew what it meant, all right. Boss, Fernie Brent is as thin as a fiddle-string. You couldn't possibly call her roly-poly.'

'After that,' Cope added, 'we rang his landlady, a Mrs Bray, and she told us that she was the one with Dudley at the restaurant, that Saturday night. We haven't seen her yet, but I'll lay odds she's a right roly-poly.'

'So Dudley was lying, eh? Good work lads.' Giles knew it was too early to celebrate, but with a case this frustrating, any lead was a ray of hope. 'Let's get him in and find out why.'

Dabdoub skimmed through the notes that Matt had sent him, and put them to one side. Joanna Howard looked to be having a rough time of it, but if the kid was lying, then sooner or later his lies would be exposed. If the kid wasn't lying, well ... in that case, the woman needed a good lawyer more than she needed Jack Dabdoub. He reached for the second pile of papers, and took a sip of whisky.

He started to read, then changed his mind and turned back to the fax. There it was, right at the beginning: the trivial detail that was niggling at the back of his mind. Sighing, he reached for the phone, and jabbed irritably at the key pad. 'Tony? I know it's late, but I need to ask you something. You were planning to investigate Les Tanner: did you get anywhere with that?'

Despite the lateness of the hour Tony sounded alert and cheerful. 'Yes, Jack, I was just writing up the report. I saw him today.'

'Saw him? In gaol, you mean?'

'No, he's out on compassionate grounds. He's dying, Jack. Cancer. He's in a hospice just outside Derby. I went down there and bluffed my way in, told him I was writing a book about the Ganja brothers, and offered to pay him for an interview. He was pleased to have someone to talk to. I was with him all afternoon.'

'How is he?'

'Very poorly, Jack. All yellow and shrunken. He knows he's dying. The nurses in there are just doing their best to ease him out as painlessly as possible. But like I said, he was pleased to have company.'

'So what did he tell you?'

'Well, nothing about Mrs Guest – he just looked blank when I asked him about her. But you were right about him being a bagman for the Ganjas. He was really proud of that job. It made him feel important. He would do the rounds with his sister-in-law, and they would hand the money over to a couple of guys in one of those little offices round the back of Piccadilly. The sister-in-law was the girlfriend of one of the guys, so Tanner said.'

'Did he give you any names?' Dabdoub asked.

'Yes. Wait a minute.' Tony rustled some papers. 'Here we are: a solicitor called Gordon Cracknel, and a money-lender called Gerald Dudley. I guess they were in charge of the money-laundering. When the gang broke up Cracknel scarpered overseas, according to Tanner.'

'Yeah.' Dabdoub wrote the names down. 'I'm not sure this is getting us any closer to Carole Guest's killer. I just wish some of the dots would join up.'

'I know, Jack. I'm sorry. I wrote down a couple of other things he told me, but I don't think they're relevant to the murder, either. Do you want to hear them now, or wait for my report?'

'Tell me now. And afterwards, remind me that I want to ask you something.'

'OK. Well, I found out that Les Tanner hasn't had many visitors. But he has had a couple. And the very first guy to call was Gerald Dudley.'

'The money-lender? What did he want?'

'Money, apparently. There was quite a lot of confusion around the time that the Ganja brothers were killed; and Dudley believes that Tanner stashed away quite a lot of Ganja cash during the kerfuffle. Tanner swears that he didn't collect any money during that time, because it was too dangerous to be on the streets. Anyway, Dudley made quite a scene at Tanner's bedside – pleading, saying he was desperate, and what use was the money to Tanner anyway? When the sob-stuff didn't work, he started to get so abusive that the nurses turned him out. The other visitor, three days ago, was his son.'

'His son?' Dabdoub perked up. 'Was his name Nicky? Nicky Tanner?'

'Yes. How did you know ?'

'His name cropped up just now. Go on. Tell me what Tanner said.'

'Oh, he got quite emotional. Said he hadn't seen his kid since his divorce, five years ago. Said he was sure that Nicky's stepfather ill-treated the boy. Shed a few tears. But just before I left he cheered up. He winked at me and whispered that he'd "seen the boy right".'

'What do you think he meant?'

'My first thought was that he *had* nicked some of the Ganja money, and was going to leave it to his son. But I really don't know. He just winked and said "I seen the boy right." So, what was the other thing you wanted to ask me?'

'You've answered it, Tony, thanks a lot. Get some sleep, eh?'

Dabdoub finished off the dregs of whisky in the glass. He picked up the bottle and took it into the kitchen, returning with a jug of water. He had a lot to do, and he needed a clear head. Some of the dots were joining up. At last.

Theresa Burgage finished her report, printed out three copies, and shut down her computer. With a start she realized that Superintendent Giles was sitting at the far end of the room, watching her. 'Gosh, Teddy, you made me jump!'

'Sorry. I was waiting for you to finish. You're working late.'

Burgage smiled wanly. 'We're terribly short-staffed. I'm just trying to keep up.'

'Well, if you're done, do you fancy a drink and a bite to eat?'

'Again?' She fluttered her eyelids in mock surprise. 'People will begin to talk.'

'Good. Let's go.'

She picked up her coat. 'You're sounding very chipper. Has something happened?'

'Yes. We've had a break, just now. We caught out one of our witnesses in a lie.'

'What a coincidence.' She caught up with him and linked her arm through his. 'I just found out that one of our witnesses is a liar, too.'

The music made her restless. It was beautiful, and Grumiaux's phrasing was sweetness itself, but her mind kept wandering onto other things, particularly the bizarre scene she had witnessed between Angela and Gerald Dudley. She still couldn't make sense of it, and Angela's cryptic comment about possibly having to lie to the police made her uneasy. She liked Angela's company, but right now she couldn't face spending the rest of the evening with her. Last night's fracas had been frightening, and had made her nervous about going to a public place. She made a lame excuse about having a headache, and made her escape.

But once she was in the car she realized that she didn't want to go home. She was still restless: she wanted to be on the move. If she went home now, she would just walk up and down in her little house like a caged animal. She wondered briefly if she should ring Matt on the mobile he had given her. His company would be all right. He knew how to be with her without crowding her. But she was ashamed to beg for his help yet again. It seemed unfair. She was pretty sure she knew how he felt about her, but she really couldn't make up her mind how she felt about him.

She drove around aimlessly for a while. The light was beginning to fade, but the sky was clear. It wouldn't be full dark for another forty minutes or so. Suddenly, she knew what she wanted to do – simply to get away from Aldersgrove, if only for a few hours. At the next main road she came to, she turned and headed south.

Detective Cope angrily banged the phone down on its cradle. 'This is a bloody waste of time, Bill. The bloke's scarpered. He could be anywhere.'

'Was that the wife you were talking to?' Bailey asked.

'Yeah. She doesn't know where he is, and she doesn't give a toss. He ain't going back to her, that's for sure.'

'So he lied to his landlady, you reckon?'

'I reckon he's a compulsive liar. He's probably forgotten what the truth is. Anyway, I've had enough for tonight. Farmer Giles has gone home. What are we staying here for?'

'Good point, Eric. I dunno about you, but I'm gasping for a pint.'

It was nearly eleven o'clock before she turned for home. It had been a strange evening. Driving with no purpose other than to escape from Aldersgrove for a few hours had induced in her a curious sense of detachment from reality. The road, and the sights along the road, came to seem artificial, like the graphics in a computer game. Some images stood out sharply in her mind; but even these had a touch of artifice about them, as if they had been carefully constructed for her benefit. She had stopped the car and climbed a tussocky knoll on a hill near Buxton to watch the gaudy sunset, with massive banks of scarlet and gold, shrinking minute by minute to a thin, purple smudge. The wind up there was invigorating but chilly; she didn't realize how cold she was until she got back into the warmth of the car.

Later the moon came up, and along one stretch of road, running alongside a broad stream, white wisps of mist drifted ghostlike through the thin trees. She was past it in a minute; but the image stayed etched in her mind, like an illustration from a book of fairy-tales.

Soon she was in the hills. The road was full of unexpected twists and turns, and she grew tired, finding it increasingly hard to concentrate. In the next village, she pulled into a lay-by opposite the church, moved into the passenger seat, and took a nap.

She woke to the sound of singing. The singing had woven itself into her dream and for a few minutes she was disorientated, half-asleep and bewildered by her surroundings. She had no idea how long she had been asleep, but once she was fully awake she felt alert and refreshed. She opened a window to let in more sound and a blast of cold air. The noise was a choir practice, she decided: good sturdy English singing, with more enthusiasm than finesse. She found it oddly comforting, though she couldn't think why it should be so. She stretched out in the seat and savoured the clean air and the final rousing choruses of an unfamiliar hymn.

In another little town she took her old Barbour jacket out of the boot and huddled in it against the cold, sat on a wooden seat in an empty car-park and ate fish and chips out of a paper bag. She was hungry, but the size of the portion defeated her and she had to throw half of it away.

Out of nowhere the memory of poor Lizzie Nair came into her head. How was it possible that such a harmless, pathetic creature could be murdered just for the few pounds in her purse? In Aldersgrove, of all places? The wickedness of it chilled her more than the bitter east wind. Once again she sought the warmth of her car and began the drive home.

From time to time she tried to convince herself that she ought to be thinking hard about her predicament and how to cope with it, but her mind simply shied away from it all. Since this nightmare began she had been at the mercy of chance, battered this way and that like a ping-pong ball. Her feeble attempts to fight back, to defend herself, had simply been brushed aside. She couldn't bring herself to believe that this state of affairs would change. The police would either arrest her or clear her; and nothing she could say or do would affect their decision one way or the other. She had to make herself accept that.

She was still troubled by her relationship with Angela Bonneville. Was Angela just using her as part of her revenge on Gerald Dudley? Working with Angela had been one of the most exhilarating and exciting experiences of Joanna's life; the thought that it might be based on deceit was unbearable.

She drove slowly; it was midnight when she got back to Aldersgrove. The streetlamps at the far end of the Causeway were broken again, but on a Friday night that was no surprise. No houses overlooked that area at night, so it was a popular target for vandals.

Another irritation was the white van left on the pavement opposite the Causeway parking area. There was just enough room to squeeze her car past it into her parking-slot; but it was a tiresome chore so late at night. She switched off the engine and the lights. She was home. She just wished she felt happier about it.

As she picked up her handbag she suddenly remembered the mobile phone Matt had given her. She had switched it off when she got to Angela's house, and had forgotten to switch it back on again. It hardly seemed worthwhile to switch it on now. It was late, and anyway she had got home safely. On impulse, she fished the mobile out of the clutter of her handbag and stowed it in a pocket of her Barbour. She got out of the car and locked it, and as she straightened up she heard a sound behind her: the squeak of rubber on asphalt. She turned quickly, heart thumping. 'Who's there?'

'Hello, miss.' Whisky fumes gusted towards her.

She couldn't see his face, shadowed under the long peaked cap, but she knew the voice. She had heard it on the answering machine and it was branded horribly in her memory.

Nick Tanner.

CHAPTER 24

Jack Dabdoub read on into the night. He didn't expect to solve the case: he merely wanted to form some sort of a plan for the next stage of the investigation. So when the answer presented itself his mind wasn't ready for it, particularly since it came from such an unlikely source. He almost missed it. Then, certain that he must have made a mistake, he back-tracked, and hunted through the sketchy notes he had made at his meeting with Joe Lolly. He found the place, and compared it with the page he had taken from Brian Curry's statement. He had made no mistake: the two statements coincided almost word for word. 'Jack,' Dabdoub muttered to himself, 'I really believe you've cracked it! By George, you've cracked it!'

Now that he had made the break-through, he quickly scanned the rest of the material. Some details were missing, but the broad outline was clear enough. He was confident that he now knew who had killed Carole Guest.

He had just started to read the transcript of Melvin Tares's trial when he suffered the second shock of the evening. He groaned aloud. 'Hell! I should have read this before! Oh, hell!' He grabbed the phone and tapped out a number. There was no answer, so he had to search in his book for Matt's mobile number. 'Matt! I thought you'd be at home.'

Matt sounded tired. 'I'm still in the office. I'd got some drawings to finish. What's up?'

'Is Mrs Howard with you?'

'No, why should she be? I expect she's at home, asleep.'

'Check, will you? Ring her up.'

'What! Jack, what's got into you? It's the middle of the night.'

'Look, I've got no time to explain, but I believe she could be in serious danger. Ring her up, will you? Please?'

Matt was bewildered, but he responded to the urgency in his friend's voice. 'OK. Wait there.' He rang back a few minutes later: 'She's not answering her home phone, and her mobile's turned off. I asked her particularly to keep it switched on. Jack, what's going on? Why is she in danger? Should we contact the police?'

'Look, I don't want to waste time. And there's always the possibility that I'm panicking unnecessarily. Let's just get over there as fast as we can. Is your car handy?'

'Yes.'

'OK. Pick me up outside my office as soon as you can. I'll explain on the way. Move it, will you?'

As Dabdoub scrambled into his car, Matt said, 'Jack, you're scaring me. What the hell's going on?'

Dabdoub struggled to get the seat-belt round his considerable bulk. He was out of breath and anxiety made him bad-tempered. He glowered at his friend and swore under his breath. 'Why the hell didn't you tell me that Joanna Howard had been a witness in a murder trial?' he said balefully.

Blackness. No glimmer of light anywhere. A darkness so absolute that it possessed her completely, body and mind. It confined her, squeezed her, pressed down on her like a leaden weight. It was frightening and yet, as the tiredness pulled her back down into sleep, it was oddly comforting.

She woke slowly, reluctantly. Her face felt numb. She hovered on the edge of consciousness, neither completely insensible nor fully aware. Time had no meaning. She drifted in and out of a deadly lethargy, not knowing whether the blank intervals lasted for minutes or hours.

Thoughts moved sluggishly in the fog that enveloped her mind. She knew she would die if she just lay there, but although her arms and legs were now free she couldn't get them to move. She hadn't even the energy to cry for help; even if she could form the words her cheeks were too stiff and her tongue too numb to utter them. She lay on her back, weak, cold and hopeless. Tiredness crept up on her. The next wave would carry her away for good.

'I didn't tell you because I didn't know about it,' Matt snapped back. 'What murder trial?'

Dabdoub was still fidgeting with his seat-belt. 'A woman called

Carole Guest was murdered in a Manchester suburb eight years ago,' he said. 'Joanna Howard happened to be at the murder scene on the day it happened, and her evidence led to the arrest of the guy who was eventually convicted of the murder.'

'She identified the murderer, you say?' Matt was puzzled.

'She saw the guy running away from the apartment block, yes.'

'That isn't making sense, Jack. Joanna Howard is hopeless at remembering faces. She'll tell you so herself.'

'She didn't identify the guy. She remembered the registration number of his car. Or most of it, anyway. At the trial the judge asked her why she was so certain she had remembered the number correctly, since she wasn't asked about it until several days later, and she said it was because …' Dabdoub swallowed hard, and prepared to quote verbatim, 'the last three digits and the registration letters made up the catalogue number of the Saint Matthew Passion by Johann Sebastian Bach, which she happened to be studying at the time.'

Matt took a little time to absorb this information, and drove the next mile in silence. He was still confused. 'You said all this was eight years ago. If the murderer was convicted, why is Joanna in danger now? Is this guy out of prison?'

'I'm not sure the murderer *was* convicted,' Dabdoub said quietly. 'I think Mrs Howard saw the real killer that day, but still doesn't realize it. The really bad news is that the killer saw her.'

The pain hit her without warning. It writhed inside her, gnawing spasmodically, as if a serpent was trying to bite its way out of her stomach. Suddenly she was choking, drowning. With an effort that used up every ounce of her energy, she rolled onto her side and vomited, bile scalding her throat.

At the edge of her vision the darkness was now smudged with grey. The greyness wavered, formless and indistinct. She closed her eyes, and the greyness was still there, behind her eyelids. But with her eyes closed, she felt that her brain was spinning, faster and faster. The dizziness was terrifying. She knew with a dread certainty that if she let go, if she let her brain spin out of control, she would die. She opened her eyes, and fought the dizziness grimly, panting with effort. The turmoil in her head slowed, gave way to a dull lassitude. Her whole body went slack and sleep overwhelmed her again.

Matt raced back to the car. 'She's not there,' he panted. 'But the front door is open, and the whole house reeks of cigarette smoke. The place has been ransacked. I don't know what's been stolen, but her drinks cupboard has been raided.'

Dabdoub now looked very worried. 'Where does she keep her car?'

'Down there, at the end of the street.'

'OK. Have you got a torch?'

'In the car.'

'Get it. Let's go.'

Matt got to the parking area well before Dabdoub. 'Her car's here,' he called. 'And it's unlocked.'

Dabdoub touched the car bonnet. 'The engine's still warm. It's been used within the last hour. Is the key in the ignition?'

'No. But it stinks of booze in here.' Matt shone the torch around. 'The back seat is damp.' He leaned closer and sniffed. 'It smells as if someone has been splashing whisky all over it!'

Dabdoub crowded closer, trying to see over Matt's shoulder. 'What's that on the floor? Pills?'

'Looks like it.' Matt picked up the three capsules and held them out in the palm of his hand. 'Do you know what they are?'

'No.' Dabdoub looked uneasy. 'But I'll lay odds they're barbiturates or Rhohypnol.'

'You think she's been drugged?'

'Yes, I do.' Dabdoub took the torch and began examining the ground near the car. 'Drugged and abducted.'

She didn't know if it was the cold that woke her, but she was bitterly cold. Her whole body shook uncontrollably. She was lying face downward now, and the uneven ground under her cheek was gritty and coated with slime. She became aware for the first time of the vile stink all around her: her own vomit, stale urine, rotting food. She knew she had to move or die. This was her last chance. She lifted her head, and the greyness wavered, stilled, took form. A doorway. Painfully, she began to crawl towards it.

'Abducted?' Matt was panicking. 'I don't understand. Why would someone kidnap her? I mean—'

'I know what you mean,' Dabdoub said edgily. 'If someone was out to silence her, why didn't they do it on the spot? Why go to the trouble of drugging her and carrying her off? There must have been two of them, by the way; I don't see how one person could have held her down on the back seat of that car and forced pills and whisky down her throat.'

'Two of them?' Matt paced up and down restlessly. He pulled his mobile from his pocket and punched in a number. 'I bet one of them was that sod Dudley.' He listened impatiently for a response from the phone. 'Damn! Why in God's name did she turn the bloody phone off?'

'Gerald Dudley?' Dabdoub was surprised. 'Yes, that's a possibility. What made you think of him?'

'He paid a mob of kids to demonstrate outside Joanna's house last night. He's got some kind of grudge against her. Jack, we've got to find her!'

'Yeah. I just wish I knew how,' Dabdoub said.

She reached the door before her strength gave out. Blood pounded in her head, a heavy, insistent beat that seemed as if it would go on for ever. As she eased forward her hand slipped and she fell across a stone step. Something stabbed into her ribs. Moaning in pain, she fumbled into a pocket and found what was hurting her. It was a little block of metal and plastic. She couldn't see it properly, and she had no idea what it was, or how it had come to be in her pocket. Dizziness blurred her vision again. She fainted, and the thing dropped from her hand.

Matt was getting frantic. 'What are you doing?'

'Phoning the police,' Dabdoub said. 'We have to get help.'

'It's going to take hours to persuade them to do anything, and then it'll be too late.' Matt knew he was being unreasonable, but anxiety and frustration were driving him crazy. 'There must be something we can …'

His mobile phone rang.

He snatched it from his pocket and looked at the display. 'It's her! Hello? Yes?' he almost shouted into the phone. 'Joanna, is that you? Hello? Hello?' He threw an anguished glance at Dabdoub. 'She's not answering!' He started walking aimlessly in a circle. 'Where are you? Are you all right? I can't hear you! Hello! Hello!' He kept walking, head bowed, clutching the phone tightly to his ear.

'Don't ring off,' Dabdoub said urgently. 'Don't lose the connection.'

Matt was getting more and more distraught. 'Nothing! I can't … Why isn't she answering?'

'Perhaps she can't,' Dabdoub said soberly. 'Let me listen.'

Matt handed over the phone. 'What can we do? Can we trace the call?'

Dabdoub held up his hand. 'Quiet!' he closed his eyes and listened intently. 'What's that sound?' he said, turning the receiver from his ear.

'Sound?' Matt looked dazed, his wits scattered.

'There's a thumping sound. Like a machine.'

Matt clamped the phone to his ear again. He stood silent for a full minute, concentrating hard. His eyes widened. 'Yes, by God! It's the old … I'd know that sound anywhere!'

'The old what?' Dabdoub called, but Matt was already on the move, running towards the canal footpath.

He found the body ten minutes later. It was lying face down beside the path, blood trickling from the gash in the back of its head. There was a broken whisky bottle under its arm, and the ferns and bracken round about was spattered with blood. Dabdoub lumbered up, panting hard. 'Jesus!' He was appalled. 'Who's that?'

Matt was reluctant to touch the body. 'I don't know. I've never seen him before. We'd better get the police.'

'He's only a kid.' Dabdoub bent down and touched the youth's throat. 'There's a pulse here. He's alive. We need an ambulance. Where are we?'

'On the canal towpath, just above the new bridge. Tell them the nearest access is from the end of the Causeway.' Matt waited until Dabdoub had rung the emergency service and passed on the information. 'Jack, I'm going to leave you here. Joanna's along here somewhere. I've got to find her.'

'Sure. But tell me – you recognized the sound on the mobile. What was it?'

'Oh, it's the old generator. We're draining the canal below Oughton Lock, and the genny is running the pumps.'

'You recognized the sound of your generator?' Dabdoub was impressed.

'That old boy has a funny, hiccupy rhythm. You can't mistake it. It's like a signature.' Matt was anxious to be off, but Dabdoub had a point to make. 'We can hear that generator from here, right?'

'Yes.'

'So,' Dabdoub said brightly, 'if you ring her number, either she'll answer or her phone will bleep. Either way, you'll have a homing signal.'

The phone rang at 5.30 in the morning. Theresa Burgage groaned. At that hour it had to be bad news. Unless it was a wrong number. She prayed for it to be a wrong number. 'Yes?'

'Inspector? Sorry to disturb you, but I knew you'd want to hear this. The boy Nick Tanner has been found down by the canal, with his head bashed in.'

'Dear God!' Burgage sat up quickly, then wished she hadn't. She felt dizzy, and her head ached abominably. She had enjoyed her evening out with Teddy Giles, but she had drunk too much. 'Is he dead?'

'No, but he's in a bad way. He's in Emergency right now.'

She grabbed the notepad and pencil she kept by her bed. 'Whereabouts along the canal was he found?'

'Near the new bridge, on the town side. We've got two men watching the site until the CID arrive.'

'That's the stretch by the Causeway, right?' *Near Joanna Howard's house*, was the unspoken thought.

'Yes, ma'am.'

'Have you notified the boy's parents?'

'We've tried to contact them, ma'am, but they both work nights. The stepfather works at the hospital, on the maintenance staff, so he may have been told by now. But the mother works for an office-cleaning agency, and we haven't reached her yet. But I did speak to someone who says she's the boy's aunt. She's on her way to the hospital now.'

Her head was spinning, and she found it hard to concentrate. 'Have we got anyone up at the hospital?'

'Not yet, ma'am. There's no-one available. You know how stretched we are.'

Burgage knew only too well. 'OK. I'll get in as soon as I can. I'll go down to the canal first, and talk to the guys there.' She was trying to remember where she kept the Alka Seltzer.

'Wait, ma'am, I haven't finished!' The duty officer sounded agitated. 'There was another incident along the canal last night. A Mrs Joanna Howard was found unconscious on the steps of Oughton lock house. She's in hospital, too. The medics say it looks like a drugs overdose.'

'Oh, my God!' Burgage said again. The implications of the situation were swamping her mind. 'How is she?'

'Not too good, they say.'

'I'm on my way.'

But the moment she got out of bed she knew she was in trouble. Her legs felt weak, her throat was sore, and her head felt as if it was being squeezed in a vice. With an effort she made it to the bathroom, and there stared disconsolately at her haggard reflection in the mirror. This was no simple hangover. She was coming down with the flu.

The doctor was young, dog-tired and irritable. 'Are you sure these are what she took?' He jiggled the pills in the palm of his hand.

'No, I'm just telling you what the guy who found her said.' The ambulance paramedic was just as young as the doctor, and just as tired. 'She was in that old ruin down by Oughton lock. She was filthy – that place stinks like a sewer – and pretty well covered in her own vomit. I reckon if she hadn't thrown up she wouldn't have lasted this long.'

'Oh, that's what you reckon, do you?' The doctor didn't like subordinates trespassing on his territory. He looked unsympathetically at his patient. 'Booze and barbiturates. Shit, I hate bloody would-be suicides worse than alkies or druggies. Selfish sods. Get her pumped out and put her on a drip.' He stamped away, his shoulders slumped with fatigue.

The nurse and the young paramedic exchanged rueful glances. 'Bad tempered little bugger,' the nurse muttered, loud enough to be overheard.

The paramedic tried to take a generous view. 'I suppose he's overworked, what with this flu epidemic and all.'

'It's not that.' The nurse tossed her head. 'He's pissed off because the junior nurses have just voted him creep of the year.'

'I can see how that could sour a person's outlook,' the paramedic said. He looked at the still figure in the bed. 'Look after her, will you? I was at her school. She was the only teacher I really liked.'

CHAPTER 25

Jack Dabdoub spent a fruitless hour at the police station waiting to give a statement. He told the officer at the desk that it was important, but she was obviously stressed and distracted by the stream of phone calls that constantly interrupted her. There was nobody available at the moment, she told him; a lot of their staff were in Manchester, policing the big match; there had been a serious incident during the night, on the canal bank, and several officers were down with the flu. 'So it's a bit chaotic just now,' she explained, in case Dabdoub hadn't noticed.

After an hour, Dabdoub gave up. He had done his best. He handed his card to the girl at the desk. 'I'm going home,' he announced. 'I'll be in my office on Monday, in case anyone's interested.'

The girl nodded, glanced at the card, and did an elaborate double-take. 'Private investigator?' She stifled a guffaw. 'You've made my day. You mean, like Lord Wimsley and Hercule Parrot?'

'Not exactly.' Dabdoub had met this reaction many times before.

'I know what it is!' The girl was enjoying herself hugely. It had been a dreary day and she needed a good laugh. 'You've just solved a dastardly murder that's baffled us poor plods for years!'

Dabdoub winked and tapped his nose with a fat finger. 'Funny you should say that,' he said.

As soon as Matt was sure that Joanna was out of danger he had her moved to a private ward. He was surprised at how easy it was to arrange: one swipe of his credit card and the deed was done. He was practically out on his feet, but he still had things to do. He went out of the hospital and made several calls on his mobile. Then he went back in and sat patiently by Joanna's bedside until he had satisfied himself that she would be all right. Not trusting himself to drive, he took a taxi home, threw himself into bed and was asleep within seconds.

With Theresa Burgage calling in sick, it fell to Teddy Giles to do the preliminary investigation into the attack on Nick Tanner while keeping the Nair murder inquiry going. Luckily, there was plenty to work on, and the clues came in thick and fast. Also, as Sergeant Dewbury was quick to point out, there was really only one prime suspect in the frame. They had found a tyre lever with blood and hair on it in the boot of Howard's car; there were fingerprints on the whisky bottle near the body that might well be Howard's; and in Howard's house there were fingerprints that could belong to Nicky Tanner. He had to wait for confirmation from forensics of course, but the obvious conclusion was that Howard had tried to kill Nick Tanner, and then attempted to take her own life. He read through the transcript of the boy's taped interview and the subsequent inquiry, and he had to admit that the woman certainly had a motive for wanting the kid out of the way. Her reputation and her livelihood were on the line. He tried to imagine the state of mind that would lead a person to murder and suicide. Madness. There was no other word for it.

Dewbury was pressing for a quick arrest. 'If we'd brought her in last night, like I wanted, this would never have happened. I still don't understand what we're waiting for."

'Right now, we're waiting for the forensic reports,' Giles said. 'There's no hurry: the woman's still in hospital.'

'Yeah, but we've got nobody up there watching her. She could scarper at any minute.'

Giles didn't respond to this. There was something else on his mind. 'Tell me, Sergeant, was it you who leaked that kid's statement to the press?'

'No, 'course not!' Dewbury denied it loudly and indignantly. 'Though I can't see it's done us any harm. It's flushed her out into the open, hasn't it?'

'Are you trying to say,' Giles asked quietly, 'that it was pressure from that article that made the poor woman try to kill Nick Tanner? If so, whoever leaked it has a lot to answer for.'

A surgeon came out of the operating-room in his scrubs and approached the group of people waiting in the annexe. 'Mr and Mrs Tanner?'

'Steen,' the man said. He was wearing overalls with the hospital badge on the pocket. 'Mr and Mrs Steen.'

'Nicky's my son by my first marriage,' one of the women explained.

'Sorry.' The surgeon felt a surge of pity for the little group. The stepfather was holding up all right, but the two women looked grey and stricken. 'Your son has been prepared for surgery, and is being brought up to theatre now. He is suffering from a depressed fracture of the ...' he was about to use technical terms, but changed his mind, 'of the back of the skull. The operation to correct it is likely to take some time – possibly several hours. I suggest that you go home and get some rest. We'll contact you as soon as there are any developments.'

'Is he – I mean, he isn't going to die, is he?' the other woman asked. 'I'm his auntie,' she added, as if to explain her concern.

'He's in good hands,' the surgeon told her. 'Possibly the best in the country. I really believe we can save him.'

'Yes, but what about afterwards?' the aunt persisted. 'Will his brain be OK? Will his memory be OK?'

'I don't want to speculate about that,' the surgeon said. 'Our priority now is to save his life. His rehabilitation will be in the hands of another team of doctors.'

'What I'm getting at,' the woman said, 'is that maybe tomorrow Nicky can tell us who did this dreadful thing?'

The surgeon found the question rather shocking. The woman ought to be praying for her nephew's recovery, not thirsting for revenge. 'I doubt that,' he said stiffly. 'I'm afraid you'll have to accept the fact that Nicky's recovery is going to take some time.' He stayed a few moments longer, uttering encouraging platitudes, then hurried back to the operating-room. The PR exercise had left him ruffled, as usual. He had no objection to healing the poor and ignorant, but he really didn't enjoy talking to them.

Kylie Barrel was back on duty, telling anyone who would listen that this new flu virus was an absolute bastard, and she was still feeling as weak as a kitten. Although Superintendent Giles found her company almost as disagreeable as Dewbury's, he chose her to go with him to the hospital to interview Joanna Howard. 'I need someone to take Howard's fingerprints. Best if a woman does it,' he offered by way of explanation, and was pleased to see that his decision had rendered Dewbury quite livid with fury.

Before he set out Detectives Cope and Bailey came in to report. 'We've no idea where this guy Dudley is,' Cope said. 'He spun some yarn to his landlady about his wife being ill, and having to go home; but that was a lie. He's gone somewhere, but we dunno where. We've been trying to interview Fernie Brent again, but her nephew's in hospital, and her brother-in-law says she's too upset to talk to anyone. He says we're harassing her because she's got a prison record.'

'Keep after her,' Giles said. 'Dudley's disappearance looks suspicious; and it seems they both lied about their whereabouts on the night of the murder. We need to know the truth of it. Harass her if you have to. Let her know we're serious.'

Bailey said: 'We've been kicking around the idea that Dudley might be Lizzie Nair's phantom lover. Maybe the two have a history. Maybe she was blackmailing him. That could be a motive for murder. And he somehow persuaded his ex-employee Fernie to cover for him.'

Giles was unimpressed. 'That's a lot of maybes, Bill. Let's get a few facts in, eh?'

Bailey shrugged. 'It was only an idea.'

'And Lord knows we en't got many of them,' Cope added.

There were a lot of flowers in Joanna Howard's ward, and more people than Superintendent Giles expected to see. Besides the staff nurse there were three women and an exceptionally tall and broad shouldered young man. No-one introduced themselves, not did anyone look particularly welcoming. He found himself apologizing for the intrusion and showing his warrant card to a row of unimpressed faces. However, the three women – Rose, Angela and Celia, he gathered from their affectionate farewells – tactfully departed, leaving only the nurse and the massive young man. Neither of these persons could be persuaded to leave, but they did retire to the far end of the room, where they sat and watched the proceedings with undisguised suspicion.

Giles sent WPC Barrel back to the station as soon as she had taken Joanna's fingerprints. He sensed a deep-seated hostility between the two women, and quickly decided that the policewoman was a liability. He apologized to Joanna yet again and asked her if she felt able to answer a few questions?

'Do I have a choice?' Joanna's throat hurt, and her voice was no more than a whisper. She made no attempt to be civil: she had learned to treat the police as the enemy.

'The questions will have to be answered sooner or later,' Giles said patiently. 'I don't want to play games with you, Mrs Howard. Let me tell you right away that you are suspected of trying to kill Nick Tanner and of attempting to do away with yourself.'

Shock made Joanna speechless for a moment. 'Kill Nick Tanner?' she croaked at last. 'The little sod tried to kill me!'

Giles stared hard at her. 'I'll tell you the evidence we have so far,' he went on calmly. 'We know you had a motive for hating the boy, after he revealed your relationship. We know that a neighbour saw a woman and a young boy enter your house at about ten o'clock last night. We have found Nick Tanner's fingerprints in your house and in your car. We found a tyre-lever in the boot of your car, with Nick Tanner's blood and hair on it.'

'A tyre-lever? I don't own a tyre-lever!' Joanna's voice cracked with the strain.

'Are you sure?'

'Officer, I subscribe to a breakdown service. I wouldn't know how to change a wheel, let alone a tyre!'

Giles was impressed by her vehemence. He remembered Theresa Burgage saying that she greatly preferred Joanna Howard to the people accusing her.

'Tell me about your movements last night.'

'I got home shortly after midnight, and—'

'I'm sorry to interrupt you,' Giles said, 'but you got home from where, exactly? Had you been out to a cinema, perhaps? Or visiting friends?'

'No, I'd just been driving around.'

'On your own?'

'Yes. I had been under a lot of strain lately, and I wanted to escape for a few hours.'

'I see. Roughly how long did you drive around?'

'About five hours, I suppose.'

Giles raised his eyebrows at that, but made no comment. 'Thank you. Please go on.'

'As I said, I got back to town about midnight. The two streetlamps at the far end of the Causeway were out, and there was a white van in the street opposite the parking area. It made it quite awkward to get my car into its slot.'

Giles interrupted again. 'A white van? Had you seen it before?'

'I wouldn't know. They all look alike to me.'

'Did you get its number?'

'No. I didn't even think about it. I got out of the car, and was about to lock it when I heard someone approaching. It was Nick Tanner.'

'How did you know who it was? You said many times that you had never even met the boy.'

'When he spoke I recognized his voice. He had left a disgusting message on my answering machine.'

Giles made a note. 'Then what happened?'

'Someone grabbed me from behind and put a pad over my mouth. I struggled, but he was too strong for me. I passed out.'

'You said "he". Are you sure it was a man?'

'I assumed it was. Whoever it was, was very strong. Anyway, when I came to, my hands and feet were bound, there was tape over my eyes and a cloth in my mouth. I was on the back seat of a car.'

'How did you know that, if you were blindfolded?'

'My hands were tied behind me. I could feel the buckle of a seat-belt. Then, when two people squeezed in on either side of me, I heard the car doors close.'

'Was it your own car?'

'I don't know. I think so.'

'Then what happened?'

'They took the gag out, and one of them pulled my hair, tilting my head back. They held my nose until I had to open my mouth to breathe. They put pills in my mouth, but I managed to spit some of them out. They poured whisky into my mouth; I had to drink or drown. More pills, more whisky. I felt myself going under, like sliding into a black hole. After that, nothing, until I came to in hospital.'

Superintendent Giles took his time writing it all down. 'Did either of them say anything while they were doing this to you? Did you hear their voices?'

'Look, all I remember is that I was terrified. I knew they were going to kill me.'

'So then you passed out? Is that all you can tell me?'

'Yes. No – whoever it was reeked of cigarette smoke. Their clothes, their breath.'

'An awful lot of people smoke cigarettes, Mrs Howard.' Giles looked unhappy. He didn't want to bully the suspect, but his softly-softly approach was getting nowhere. 'I have to advise you that it is in your own interest to tell me all you know now, rather than have it come out later.'

'I have told you exactly what happened,' Joanna said wearily. It seemed that the police were determined to disbelieve every word she said.

'I see. Then how do you explain the fact that one of your neighbours saw you and a young boy entering your house at ten o'clock last night?'

'It wasn't me!'

'Oh, no. You were out motoring in the dark. All on your own.' The superintendent laid on the sarcasm.

'How old is this witness of yours?' Joanna demanded. 'How good is her eyesight? Can she see in the dark?'

It was a shrewd thrust. Giles had been told that Mrs Whalley was elderly and more than a bit doolally. He tried again: 'We have evidence that Nick Tanner was in your house. The door wasn't forced. So who let him in, if it wasn't you?'

'It wasn't me,' Joanna repeated.

'So you say. But perhaps you can understand why I have some difficulty in believing you. Now, you were found at Oughton Lock. How did you get there?'

'I don't know. I told you, I was unconscious.'

'So your assailants must have carried you there?'

'I suppose so.'

'Carried you more than a mile, over rough ground, in the dark? Why would they go to all that trouble?'

'Superintendent,' with an effort Joanna recalled the man's rank, 'we both know that isn't really a question. It's just another way of calling me a liar. You believe I planned to kill the Tanner child and then commit suicide, and you're trying to persuade me to confess to it. And while you're wasting your time with me, the real culprit is walking free.'

Giles wanted to say that he was just doing his job, but he was afraid it would sound like an apology. 'As I said, you had an obvious motive for hating the boy.'

Joanna sighed in exasperation. 'You must think I'm a crazy woman. Let me ask you a question. Your witness says that I took Nick Tanner into my house late at night. So, if I had planned to kill the boy and commit suicide, why didn't I do it in the comfort of my own home? Why on earth would I traipse a mile down the fucking canal in the dark with pills, a whisky-bottle and a tyre-lever?'

Teddy Giles didn't attempt to answer that one. But he acknowledged to himself that the lady had a point.

Jack Dabdoub strolled round to his office in the late afternoon. He had slept well, eaten hugely at an all-day-breakfast café, and he had the warm, smug feeling of a job well done. He had been lucky, of course, but as he was to say to Tony many times: 'The harder I work, the luckier I get,' which, as Tony was often to respond, was neither true nor original.

The only message on his answering service was from Matt, to say that Joanna was OK, and was now in a private ward. Nothing from the Aldersgrove police station. Dabdoub wasn't surprised; the duty officer had probably binned his card as soon as he was off the premises.

He phoned his client's hotel, and was told that Mr Guest was dining out and wasn't expected back until late. Jack left his name, and said he would ring back next day. He rang Matt at home. 'How is she?'

'She's OK,' Matt said. 'Badly shaken, but I'm told she got very stroppy with the policeman sent to question her. That's a good sign, I reckon.'

'Sure. Is she safe?'

'So far. The twins are over there. Tristram's up in her room, and Lionel is keeping an eye out in the lobby.'

'Good. I'm coming over there now, OK? I ought to talk to the chief plod, not that I expect any thanks for doing their job for them. And even if they believe me, which I doubt, it'll take 'em days to get the kind of proof they'll need.'

'Jack, you're making me nervous. How long do you think Joanna's life will be in danger?

Dabdoub didn't see any virtue in beating about the bush. 'Until we nail this killer, laddie,' he said.

The phone call took Superintendent Giles by surprise. 'I thought you were at death's door, love,' he said.

Theresa Burgage warmed to his concern. 'Frankly, I feel ghastly. I'm really glad you can't see me right now. Look,' She knew he was going to say something gallant, and didn't want to be sidetracked, 'Kylie Barrel has just phoned to say that you've interviewed Joanna Howard today.'

'Yes.'

'Did you read my report?'

'I'm sorry?'

'My report. I interviewed Darren Palmer last night. I left the report on my desk.'

'I'm sorry, it doesn't seem to have reached me as yet. Is it important?'

'I think so. Young Palmer told me he has a paper round in Aldersgrove which includes the Causeway. So he knows where Joanna Howard lives.'

'And?' Giles massaged his brow; it had been a long day, and he was getting a headache.

'And Darren told me that he had often seen Tom Short leaving Howard's house in the early hours of the morning. Now, Darren recognized Tom, because – well, because everybody in the school knew the short Mr Short, but Tom didn't know Darren, because Darren wasn't in his class. So, you see, Joanna Howard was telling the truth, and Tom Short was lying. The case against her just doesn't hold up. Nicky Tanner's accusation was a malicious falsehood.'

'No, but ...' Giles's headache was getting worse, 'somebody tried to kill Nicky Tanner last night. If it wasn't Joanna Howard, who was it?'

'I don't know, dear.' Burgage leaned back against the pillow. Her head was swimming. 'But, Teddy ...'

'Yes?'

'One thing I do know. You'll get it right in the end.'

A girl in a million, Teddy Giles thought.

At 5.30 p.m. Nicky Tanner died. The operation had seemed successful; but soon after he had been moved into intensive care his condition began to deteriorate. His family was notified and Mr and Mrs Steen, with Mrs Steen's sister, arrived at Nick's bedside only minutes before he died. Because the hospital staff was overwhelmed by the volume of work, it was another half-hour before the police were informed.

'Mr Indispensable.' Joanna smiled up at him. 'It seems I just can't manage without you. That's yet another thing I have to thank you for.'

'I just hope I got it right,' Matt said. 'I picked out the sort of stuff I thought you might need, and packed it all into these suitcases. You can tell me if I've missed anything, and I'll go back for it.'

'I'm sure it'll be fine. How is the house looking?'

'It's a bit of a mess. There's some broken glass in the kitchen, and there's a thin grey mist of fingerprint powder over much of the furniture. But the front door's OK. I left the place secure.'

'I'm sure you did. Thank you.' But thinking about her house had left her depressed.

'So,' Matt said, too heartily, 'how are you feeling?'

'Well, apart from a sore throat and a bruised midriff, I feel OK.' Joanna picked fretfully at the sheet. 'I really don't want to stay here any more. The nurse overheard the police interrogating me, and saw them take my fingerprints, and since then she's been as nervous around me as if I was Jack the Ripper.'

'That's fine. The doctor says you can leave as soon as you feel up to it.' Matt had only just heard the news of Nick Tanner's death, and was reluctant to pass it on until Joanna was safely out of the hospital.

'Yes.' She was still picking at the sheet, avoiding his eye. 'I thought I might stay at a hotel for a day or two.'

'A hotel?'

'I don't think I can go back to my house just yet. The police have ransacked the place, and that awful child has been in there. I just can't face it at the moment.'

Matt had anticipated this and had a suggestion to make. 'Why don't you stay at my place in Cheshire? It's quiet, and you won't be disturbed.'

'The old farmhouse you're renovating?' His suggestion was so predictable she nearly laughed aloud.

'Yes. Mrs Coolley – she lives in the cottage next door, and she and her daughter look after the place while I'm away – will make up a bed for you, and generally take care of you. Stay as long as you like.'

She demurred at first, but in fact the idea was very attractive, and she was consumed with curiosity, so she allowed herself to be persuaded.

'Boss?' Tristram raised himself stiffly from his chair by the window. 'I guess you won't be needing us any more?'

'Just hang on a minute or two longer, will you?' Matt said. 'I want to go down to the lobby and see if Jack Dabdoub has arrived.'

'And if you wouldn't mind standing guard outside the door,' Joanna added, 'I can get dressed and make myself presentable.'

Dabdoub had arrived; Matt found him pacing to and fro near the reception desk. 'Have you heard about the kid?' Dabdoub asked without preamble. He was looking tense and agitated.

'Yes, but I haven't told Joanna yet.'

'Good.' But Dabdoub didn't explain why it was good. 'Don't bring her down yet. I'm waiting for someone.'

'Who?'

'Nobody you know. Is that one of the twins over there?'

'Lionel. He and Tristram have been standing guard all day.'

'Good,' Dabdoub said again. He did some more pacing. 'God, I hate hospitals. Being without my mobile is like losing a limb.' He saw a burly figure pushing through the glass doors, and visibly relaxed. 'It's OK. You can bring her down now.'

Matt carried one of her cases and Tristram the other. Matt told her that they had only one stop to make, at the reception desk, to let the clerk know of her departure. But it was only now that she was on the move that she realized just how weak she was. In the lift going down she leaned against the wall and closed her eyes. Her head was swimming. When the lift grounded she took Matt's arm for support and gathered all her strength for the long walk to the car.

She was half-way across the lobby when the shout went up. 'There she is! Bitch! Murderer!' Hazily, she saw three people running towards her: a man and two women. They were shouting at her: 'Murderer! Murderer!' the sounds echoing crazily round the bare walls. Matt dropped the suitcase and shook her hand from his arm. He stepped forward, braced himself, lowered his shoulder, and let the larger of the two women run into him. The woman bounced off him, winded, and fell backward. On the other side, Tristram ran at the man and took him out with a flying tackle that had the two of them skidding yards across the polished floor. The other, slimmer woman stopped in front of Joanna. 'Remember me?' she whispered.

'No.' Joanna backed away. Shock had cleared her head: although she didn't recognize the woman's face, she recognized madness when she saw it. The woman followed close, pushing at her with her left hand. 'You killed him, you slut!' she shouted. 'Murderer!' Measuring her distance with her outstretched arm, she swung her right hand across her body.

Joe Lolly caught her wrist on the backswing, and pulled it towards him. Caught off balance, she stumbled, and Dabdoub, following behind, took her other arm and locked it behind her. Joe prised open her right hand and took a metal object from it. 'A Chinese cosh, if I'm not mistaken. That's a collectors' item, that is!'

Dabdoub leaned close to the woman's ear. 'Fernie Brent, I presume? I've been looking for you.'

Sergeant Dewbury was livid with rage. 'You've what?' he shouted. 'Constable, do you know who she is? Her sister's child has just been murdered! Can you blame her for having a go at the woman responsible?'

'She attacked Mrs Howard with a dangerous weapon,' Joe Lolly said stubbornly. 'I have reason to believe that she is implicated in the assault on Nicky Tanner. I had to bring her in.'

Dewbury wasn't listening. 'If you had the brains of a dead bug, you'd realize that the Howard woman is the prime suspect for the Tanner killing. If she'd killed your kid, wouldn't you take a swing at her?'

'Sergeant, I—'

'Let her go!' Dewbury thrust his head forward belligerently.

Joe tried to be reasonable. 'Shouldn't you check with Superintendent Giles first? Isn't he in charge of the investigation?'

'He's gone home, and Burgage is sick. I'm in charge.'

'Then perhaps you ought to hear what Mr Dabdoub has to say. He's waiting at the front desk.'

'Mr who?'

'Dabdoub.'

'Who the hell's he, when he's at home?'

'A private investigator. He says he has some important information.'

'Jesus!' Dewbury's jaw clenched and his face became even redder. 'Do you think I'm going to be told how to do my job by a bloody amateur? Tell him to piss off and let the woman go.'

'Sir?'

'Are you deaf, Constable, as well as stupid? Turn her loose. That's an order. Let the poor woman grieve in peace.'

CHAPTER 26

Although three days had passed Joanna was still nervous. 'Has she been caught yet?' she asked.

'It's only a matter of time,' Dabdoub said. 'She's broken her parole, and she hasn't got a passport. The police have got her picture and her fingerprints; and if she's not caught by the weekend George Guest is going to offer a reward for her capture. That ought to do the trick.'

'Is that what you're waiting for, a reward?' Matt asked. 'I'll lay odds you know where she's gone. I haven't forgotten that sneaky trick you played at the hospital.'

The three of them were sitting in the big kitchen of Matt's farmhouse. Dabdoub had told his story to the police and to his client, George Guest; and he felt that he owed it to Joanna to tell it a third time.

'Sneaky trick?' Dabdoub was hurt.

'You used Joanna as bait. You knew that woman would try to attack her.'

'I didn't *know* it,' Dabdoub protested. 'I guessed it might happen. That's why I wanted Joe Lolly on hand. He was the only one of us who could positively identify her.'

'How did he know who she was?'

'He had interviewed her on that first house-to-house session. And he knew about her because she was out on licence, and Joe was pally with her parole officer. It was really quite fitting that Joe should make the arrest. He was the one who really cracked the case.' He grinned at their bewilderment. 'It was Joe who first saw a possible link between the murder of Lizzie Nair and that of Carole Guest, eight years earlier. The MO was similar, he thought; and so maybe the same kind of weapon was used in each case. The trouble with his theory was that there was no way of checking it or proving it. But because he had raised the possibility I took a closer look at the police investigation of both cases. And there it was, sticking out like a molehill on a bowling green.' He paused savouring the moment. 'In both cases the police investigated Fernie Brent because she was acquainted with the victim. And in both cases she was eliminated from the inquiry because she had a cast-iron alibi. But in both cases, the alibi was provided by the same person. Gerald Dudley.'

'Gerald Dudley?' Horror reduced Joanna's voice to a whisper. 'Are you saying he was involved in two murders?'

'He was an accessory, yes. Look, I'd better tell it from the beginning. Ten years ago organized crime in Manchester was pretty well in the hands of one outfit called the Ganja family. They handled drugs, prostitution, protection, extortion – and they made a mint of money. Dirty money – it needed laundering. That job was undertaken by three apparently respectable businessmen – Dudley, a mortgage broker; Joe Godwit, a builder; and one G. Cracknel, a solicitor.' Dabdoub broke off. 'Sorry – did you want to say something?' This to Joanna.

'That name – Cracknel,' Joanna said bitterly. 'He was the one who helped Dudley to swindle me out of my money.'

'That figures,' Dabdoub said. 'Anyhow, I won't bore you with the details, but those three cleaned up the Ganja money through property deals, fake mortgages, stuff like that. Now, the cash was collected from the dealers, pimps, shopkeepers and so on, by a squad of three – Les Tanner, a small-time crook; his sister-in-law, Fernie Brent; and a thick-eared thug called Melvin Tares. The cash was handed over on alternate weeks, to Cracknel or Dudley.'

Dabdoub paused again, to add a caution to his narrative. 'From here on, I have to guess at some of the details, but the main picture is clear enough. One of the money-laundering schemes involved paying some of Godwit's workers in cash, and allowing them to claim unemployment benefit. This is where Carole Guest became involved. Her job was to track down benefit fraud; and I reckon so many building workers being sacked at once attracted her attention. Someone – possibly Godwit himself – registered her curiosity, and Fernie was dispatched to find out what she knew. Fernie struck up an acquaintance with Carole in the pub, and somehow persuaded her to blurt out her suspicions about the building scam.'

Matt interrupted at this point. 'Most of that is guesswork, right?'

'Yes, and I haven't finished yet. My theory is that Melvin Tares and Fernie were sent to visit Carole Guest, to scare her off – or possibly to buy her off. What seems to have happened, is that Fernie lost her temper and killed her.' Having got that part of the story over, Dabdoub continued in more confident tones. 'Now, we're on more solid ground. You turned up at that apartment block that morning, Joanna. You must have arrived very soon after the murder took place.

You saw Melvin Tares running to his car, and you memorized the number plate.'

'BWV 224,' Joanna said promptly. 'It just so happened that I was studying the Matthew Passion at the time.'

'Very appropriate,' Dabdoub murmured, and was gratified to see Matt blush like a schoolgirl. Joanna didn't seem to have noticed. At any rate, her expression didn't change. 'But,' Dabdoub continued, '—and I admit I'm guessing again – you must have seen a woman there at about the same time?'

'No. Well, yes – the car-park was full, and I saw this girl getting into her car. I asked her if she was leaving, and she said she was. I took her slot.'

'So you talked to her? You saw her face?'

'Yes.'

'What did she look like?'

'She was young.'

'Could you describe her face?'

'No. It was just a face. I'm not very good at faces.'

'What colour was her hair?'

'I've no idea.'

Dabdoub sighed heavily. 'That girl was Fernie Brent. She didn't know you were no good at faces. She had been expecting you to recognize her ever since she saw you in Aldersgrove and recognized you.'

Joanna wasn't following the logic of this. 'Why should it matter whether I recognised her or not?'

'I'll come back to that in a moment,' Dabdoub said. 'Let me go back to the trial. It was your evidence, plus lots of forensic detail that put Melvin Tares in gaol. Now, if Tares hadn't actually struck the blow that killed Mrs Guest, why did he take all the blame? Why didn't he incriminate Fernie?'

'Because he was threatened? Or bribed? Or both?' suggested Matt.

'I think threats were used, but not against Tares. Remember, he was homosexual, but that wasn't generally known at the time. It's not the sort of thing you advertise if you're a muscleman for a gangster. But I bet Fernie knew. And I bet she threatened to kill Melvin's partner, if Mel didn't keep schtum.'

'It's plausible,' Matt agreed. 'But it's still guesswork. But what about Joanna's question? Why was Fernie Brent so scared of being recognized?'

'Because she had lied to the police: told them she was nowhere near Carole Guest's flat on the day of the murder. Joanna was the one person who could blow Fernie's alibi out of the water.' Dabdoub took a deep breath. 'All this talking is thirsty work.'

'Beer?' Matt was already on his feet.

'That depends. Not out of the fridge, is it?'

'I keep some warm especially for you. Bottled brown ale.'

'All right then,' Dabdoub said ungraciously. 'It'll have to do. Now then,' he took a long swig from the bottle, 'let me digress for a minute. Shortly after Tares had been tried and convicted, Gerald Dudley appeared in Aldersgrove and joined the choral society. And unless I'm very much mistaken, Joanna, he courted you very assiduously?'

'Oh, God!' Joanna looked sick. 'You're going to tell me he chatted me up just to find out what I knew about Fernie Brent?'

'I think so. Cheating you out of your property was just a bonus.'

'Wait a minute!' Matt was following the argument closely. 'If he spent any time at all with Joanna he would know all about her inability to remember faces. He'd realize that she wasn't any threat at all.'

'Exactly. He probably told Fernie that, but that was years ago. She may have forgotten, or simply disbelieved it. We're talking about an unstable, psychopathic personality here.'

Joanna shivered, remembering her narrow escapes. 'Go on. Let's get this over with.'

'OK. The first time Fernie realized that you were in the neighbourhood was when she picked up Nicky from the school camp at Darwen Lowe Farm. She obviously recognized you immediately. It must have been a tremendous shock to her. At any rate, she spent the next few months avoiding you, which was something of a problem since she worked at the check-out counter at Buchanan's.'

'So that was why there was always chaos whenever I went to the store!' Joanna said.

'That's right. The moment Fernie spotted you she high-tailed it to the ladies' loo. Luckily for her, Buchanan's is such a chaotic place anyway that she got away with it. So, things were comparatively stable until Anita Mons wrote that article about Melvin Tares. That set the cat among the pigeons. The idea that the inquiry into Carole Guest's murder might be reopened gave Gerald Dudley a nasty fright, too. He was an accessory, remember: he had given Fernie a false alibi, knowing that she was a murderer. To be honest, I think that his immediate fear was that the article might provoke Fernie into murdering Joanna here. He guessed that if that happened Fernie would be bound to be caught, and the subsequent investigation would uncover everything, including his involvement in the Guest murder. He raced up to Aldersgrove to try to control Fernie. He was planning to come up here anyway, to try to raise some money.'

'I know all about that, too,' Joanna muttered. 'But if you're trying to convince me that he was ever concerned about my welfare, forget it.'

'No, Gerald's agenda had no room for anyone but Gerald. But when he got to Aldersgrove he saw that there was a ready-made scheme available. By that time Fernie had seduced her nephew Nicky, and was conducting a full-blown affair with him.'

'Was that pun intentional?' Matt asked.

'I wouldn't have noticed if you hadn't mentioned it.' Dabdoub scowled and took another swig of warm beer. 'The point is that it was easy to persuade the kid – who was besotted with Fernie by this time – to make the accusation against Joanna. Gerald's idea was to drive Joanna out of town.'

'It damn nearly worked, too,' Joanna growled.

'It might have worked if he and the girl had kept the idea simple. But they had to tart it up with corroborative detail. Fernie knew that a neighbour, Lizzie Nair, worked for Joanna as a cleaner. She befriended Lizzie, and persuaded her to let her into Joanna's house.'

'She was a smoker!' Joanna exclaimed. 'I smelled cigarette smoke in my house, and blamed Lizzie for it! And when I was tied up in the car, the only thing I registered was the stink of smoke!'

Dabdoub had finished the bottle, and looked at it thoughtfully until Matt took the hint and swapped it for a full one.

'For some reason – possibly because Lizzie was overjoyed to have someone as a friend – she lent Fernie the key of her flat. We can only guess at Lizzie's motive, but Fernie's was clear enough – it was a place where she and Nicky could go to have sex without fear of discovery. Superintendent Giles told me they actually used Lizzie's bed. Tragically, it all went wrong – Lizzie came home unexpectedly and caught them at it. One of her cleaning jobs had been cancelled, apparently.'

Joanna was aghast. 'My God – that was probably because I sacked her! Or rather, she had a tantrum and walked out on me.'

'I dunno.' Dabdoub looked sombre. 'What I do know is that the discovery was Lizzie Nair's death-warrant. Fernie had to kill her to keep her quiet. The consequences, if Lizzie had blabbed to Nicky's mother, didn't bear thinking about. Even if she escaped physical injury Fernie would be back in gaol quick as a flash. So she planned quickly. She knew that Lizzie emptied her trash into the refuse chute every evening about nine o'clock. She jammed the chute on that level, knowing that Lizzie, orderly soul, would carry her rubbish down and put it into the bin at the rear of the building. When Lizzie turned up on cue, Fernie cut her down with two swift chops to the throat, like killing a rabbit.'

'Poor girl. She had a rotten life. And to be slaughtered like that, by someone she thought was her friend – it's just too cruel.' Joanna shook her head sadly.

Dabdoub shifted his huge bulk uncomfortably. He had let himself be carried away by his description of Lizzie Nair's murder, forgetting that Joanna had known her quite well. 'Anyway, Fernie turned to her old mate Gerald for an alibi, and with their history there was no way he could refuse. He did his best on the spur of the moment, but he knew that if the police bothered to check it he was in dire trouble. He was panicking, and wanted to leg it at the first opportunity. His problem was that he hadn't any money. This is where Les Tanner comes into the story. Les had been released from gaol early, on compassionate grounds. In fact, he was dying. Gerald was convinced that Les had appropriated some of the Ganja brothers' cash, and so he dashed to Tanner's bedside to try to coax some of it for himself. He failed; but actually he had been right about the cash. Les had over two thousand quid on him; and when his son Nicky came to see him on his deathbed, the sentimental old boy handed the cash over to him. Nicky didn't live to spend it, though. By that time, Fernie had cooked up her master plan – to kill Nicky and pin the blame on Joanna. We were lucky to catch up with her in time. I don't need to stress the point that by now the woman was totally insane, and obsessed with the idea that she could murder her way out of trouble.'

'But she's still at large.' Joanna hugged herself and seemed to shrink in her seat. 'Just knowing she's out there somewhere gives me the creeps. I don't think I shall sleep soundly again until she's put away.'

'It shouldn't take long,' Dabdoub said. 'And when they catch up with her, she'll go away for a long time. The cops have already got enough forensic evidence to convict her a dozen times over.'

Matt wasn't so sanguine. 'I don't know that catching her is going to be that easy. She can go a long way and last a long time with two thousand quid in her purse.'

But for once Matt got it completely wrong. The next day, the police got a tip-off that Fernie Brent was hiding out in a disused shed on some allotments near Alderley Edge. When they arrived they found her, not in the shed but walking round it in a dazed state, apparently hallucinating. Her clothes were torn, and she was wearing no shoes. She was clutching her handbag so tightly they had to prise it from her fingers. But there was no money in it at all. Not a penny.

CHAPTER 27

'I ought to go home,' Joanna said. She laid down the book she had been pretending to read, and looked out of the window. It was a nice enough view, though not spectacular: rough pasture, sloping down to a narrow stream fringed with straggly willows which had once been pollarded. She wondered idly what, if anything, Matt planned to do with all that land.

Matt was sitting at the kitchen table, making drawings and calculations in a large sketch-pad. 'When you're ready,' he said, without looking up. 'No need to rush things. Stay here as long as you like. I've had your house cleaned up, by the way. And there are new locks on the doors.'

'Thank you.' Having started the conversation, she felt no compulsion to continue it. In her mind's eye she was reshaping the landscape, sculpting the land, planting trees, creating shady walks ornamented with classical statuary. It was pleasant just to sit and day-dream.

Matt, as usual, took his duties as a host seriously. 'I'm sorry I haven't been around much, these last few days. I've had to spend a lot of time on the canal. I'm supposed to have a feasibility study prepared by the end of the month.'

'Don't apologize,' Joanna said lazily. 'Mrs Coolley's been spoiling me rotten. But I'm here under false pretences. I'm perfectly fit, and my life isn't in danger. I really ought to go home. The trouble is, I don't want to.'

'Then don't. Stay here. This old house really appreciates your company.' Matt still didn't look up, and his tone was elaborately casual.

Joanna smiled. 'You don't understand. I don't want to go back there ever.'

This time he did look up. 'Oh?'

'People have been ringing me up, telling me to put it behind me, pick up the pieces, forget it all. Atherton's desperate to have me back at work. Matt, I just can't face it. I think I'd rather die than walk into that school again. And as for living in Aldersgrove ... You know, I still can't believe how quickly my so-called friends fell over themselves to think the worst of me. Women I had sung with for years wanted me thrown out of the choral society because – what was their phrase? – because I had "always shown an unhealthy interest in young boys". How could I be civil, let alone friendly, with those people ever again?'

'So? What are your plans?'

'Sell the house. Move away. And I'm going to see if I can make it as a singer. The *Elijah* concert and Angela Bonneville's encouragement have given me the confidence I need. If I don't give it a try, I'll always wonder whether I might have made it.'

'I think that's a wonderful idea!' Matt's eyes were shining. 'Do what you really want to do.'

'It'll be a hard slog at first, but if I get downhearted, I'll think of what I'm missing – living among hypocrites and doing a thankless, low-paid job that nobody rates. I love singing. If I'm any good at it, I'll succeed. If I I'm not good enough – no, to hell with that. Of course I'm good enough.'

'I agree.' Matt pushed his work aside. 'I've been meaning to talk to you about your house.'

'Why? Do you want to buy it? It's for sale, as of this moment.'

'No, I would like your permission to examine it.'

'What on earth for?'

Matt looked uncharacteristically unconfident. 'Well, for one thing, I would like to know why your father soundproofed your drawing-room.'

'Did he? How do you know that?'

'I checked it when I was having your house cleaned. I had someone play my piano while I was in your drawing-room. The sound barely carried at all. Remember, you mentioned that the rooms in my house seemed bigger than yours? Well, you were right in one respect. My living-room is over a foot wider than yours. I believe your father put in a false wall, and packed it with soundproof material.'

'Are you sure my father did it? I mean, it might have been like that when he moved in.'

'It might have been, but I doubt it.' Having started this conversation, Matt was looking more and more uncomfortable with it. 'Look, I've been puzzling over this ever since I noticed there was something odd about that photograph on your sideboard. I just haven't been able to get it out of my mind.'

Joanna stared hard, but it seemed that Matt was quite serious. 'Every time you mention that photo you go all broody and mysterious. And now you're being even more broody and mysterious. What on earth has that picture to do with a soundproofed wall?'

Matt fidgeted nervously. 'It's a long story, and it's so far-fetched that you ll think I'm completely off my head.'

'You're being broody and mysterious again. Just tell me what's on your mind.'

'No, I can't. If I'm wrong, it would be …' Matt threw up his hands. 'I daren't risk it. You'd hate me for being such a fool.'

'That's infuriating. Why should I hate you for telling me some fairy-tale?'

'Please, bear with me for just a bit longer. You told me that your father mentioned that picture in a letter he wrote to you. May I see that letter?'

'I haven't got it with me. It's at my house.'

'OK. Tomorrow, let's go over to your place, and when I've read that letter I'll tell you what's been on my mind. Then, right or wrong, you'll understand why I've made such a mystery of it.'

After that he refused to be drawn any further that night. She had grown to like him a lot, but he could be infuriatingly obstinate when he put his mind to it.

'It's no good pretending I had any sleep last night,' Joanna said. 'I don't like mystery stories with no ending.'

They were in Matt's car, driving towards Aldersgrove. She had been nagging him all morning, but he had turned away all her questions with a smile and a shake of the head.

'Sorry,' he said. 'All will be revealed very soon, I promise.' He pressed on quickly, to distract her. 'You told me that your father became mentally confused towards the end of his life?'

'Confused, unhappy – and bitter. He had served his country, and he believed his country had betrayed him.'

'And you said he spent much of his fortune on your mother's medical bills?'

'That was one of the things that made him so bitter.'

'And his friend, Colonel Crawford-Webb: you said he died in '98. That was what, two years after your mother died?'

'Less than that, I think. I remember my father wept. But he didn't go to the funeral.'

Matt stopped talking for a few moments while he negotiated a tricky road junction. 'Would you say they loved each other?'

'I doubt that either of them would have put it that way. But they were old friends. As comrades in arms, I'm sure either of them would have laid down his life for the other. What made you ask?'

Matt didn't answer her directly. 'I remember reading Colonel Crawford-Webb's obituary in the papers. They were complimentary about his Army career, and about his work for various charities and sporting organizations, but the thing that attracted most comment was the fact that he had made no attempt to protect his estate from death duties. The taxman got nearly half a million pounds after the colonel died, and accountants were queuing up to explain how, with careful planning, he could have cut that bill by two thirds.'

'That wasn't his style. Uncle Peter believed that it was a privilege to be British, and that one ought to pay one's dues for that privilege.'

'But your father didn't share that opinion?'

'Not after my mother died, and the government cut his pension, no. Before that he was probably just as old fashioned and patriotic as his friend. But Mum's death embittered him. He genuinely held the whole NHS responsible for that wrong diagnosis, and he felt humiliated by the snub over his pension.' Joanna recognized that Matt had deflected her question. 'You still haven't told me why you're so interested in Dad's friendship with Uncle Peter?'

Matt was still hesitant, as if deliberating with himself whether to speak or not. Reluctantly, he took a bulky envelope from his pocket. 'I wasn't sure if you had ever seen this. Now, I'm absolutely positive that you haven't.'

'What is it?'

'It's a copy of Colonel Crawford-Webb's will.'

'What! How did you get hold of it?'

'I sent off for it. Cost me a fiver, but I felt it was worth it. The question was driving me crazy.'

'And now you're driving me crazy. What question are you talking about?'

'Just this: your father suffered a tragedy which left him impoverished. But his oldest and dearest friend was wealthy – his estate was valued at some three million pounds. So why didn't Colonel Crawford-Webb help his old friend out?'

'I expect Dad was too proud to ask for help. Anyway, it's not as if he was on the breadline.'

Matt saw it differently. 'Lifelong friends don't wait to be asked. I felt it was inconceivable that your father wouldn't be mentioned in his friend's will. Take a look for yourself. I've marked the relevant section.'

Joanna unfolded the paper and read the passage Matt had highlighted. '"I bequeath to my old friend Colonel Charles Godwin of the Old Rectory, Upper Holwood, Hampshire, my two shotguns and their cases; my medals and the miniatures; the red crayon drawing of a horse; my manuscript *Clausewitz Re-examined* and the turquoise-green tazza." What's a tazza?'

'It's a shallow bowl with a foot. Made of enamelled glass. I take it your father hadn't got anything like that when you moved in with him?'

'No. In fact, I don't remember seeing any of the things listed here.'

'Exactly. That's just another detail that's been driving me crazy.'

And that was all Matt was prepared to say until they reached Joanna's house, which, when she entered it, seemed like strange, foreign territory. It had obviously been dusted and vacuumed, but all the furniture was in subtly wrong places. She went upstairs and returned with a small square envelope. 'This is his letter. To be honest, just looking at it makes me want to cry ...'

Matt opened out the pages and studied the wandering, spidery handwriting.

'Are you sure this is the one? He seems to be wishing you a happy birthday.'

'Oh God, yes, that was really spooky. I know he meant it as a loving gesture, but it damn near broke my heart. It was like losing him all over again.'

'What happened?'

'Well, in his will, he said all the sweet things a daughter wants to hear from her father: how he loved me, how proud he was, and so on; and as you know, he left me everything he owned. But he also instructed his solicitor to forward that letter on my birthday. Read it, and try to imagine how I felt when I first saw it.'

Matt read slowly, hesitating over the barely legible script: '"*My dear, it seems most unlikely that I shall be around to celebrate your next birthday, so you won't be getting your usual cheque, alas. But the enclosed is meant as a special birthday present: I made the frame myself, from some hardwood I found in the attic.*"'

'His mind was wandering, poor old darling,' Joanna said. 'This place doesn't have an attic.'

Matt read on: '"*I know that you have that photograph of your mother that I used to keep in my study, but I felt sure that you would also like to have a memento of me with your godfather, who doted on you almost as much as your mother and I did.*"'

Joanna sighed. 'I told you, he was very confused. Dear old Peter was never my godfather. Dad was mixing him up with another of his Army buddies.'

'So, when did you get this letter?'

'I told you. On my birthday.'

'Which was?'

'Ten months after my father died. I was distraught. I know he meant well, but at the time it just seemed cruel. To get a letter from the grave was just too much to bear.'

Matt was thinking hard. 'Ten months later? You didn't tell me that.'

'Should I have? Is it important?'

But Matt wasn't yet ready to explain. 'Let me finish the letter.' He frowned over the straggling script. 'He goes on: "*I have some apologies to make. I now know that I was wrong to deny you the career you really wanted. I hope you can forgive me for that mistake. I just couldn't see what was clearly before my eyes. I know too, that over the past months you have suffered greatly, and it is a sadness to me that I have been too self-absorbed to give you the support and comfort you needed. I hope that by the time you read this you will have put the memory of that worthless man behind you, and are beginning to shape the kind of life you really want. Think of this birthday as a turning turning point.*" Well, apart from writing the word "turning" twice, there was nothing vague or disjointed about that bit,' Matt commented.

'I know. It's very sad and touching, but when he was alive he could never bring himself to say anything like that. He would have been far too embarrassed.'

Matt was still poring over the angular writing. 'This last bit is practically impossible to read. Can you make it out?'

'Not really. It begins "Dear Girl", and ends "all my love, Dad", but the bit in between is just loops and squiggles.'

'Yes. He either wrote this in a tearing hurry, or …' Matt turned the page from side to side.

'Or what?'

'Or he was deliberately making this sentence difficult to read. As if he meant it for your eyes only.' He ran his finger along the line. 'I can decipher some of it. That word I think is "photograph", and this one looks like "light", but I've no idea what this first word is. "Refer"?'

Joanna leaned closer. '"Refer the photograph in a light"? that doesn't make any sense to me. And this next sentence. Something about a reactor? It looks like "Dot hat reactor was down." Do you really think he wrote this for my eyes only? I can't make head nor tail of it.'

'I think he intended you to puzzle over it.' Matt's head came up. 'Puzzle!' he exclaimed. 'That's it!'

'That's what?'

Matt was getting excited. 'I bet your father was a crossword fanatic?'

'Oh yes. He and Mum did at least one every day. When they were overseas, they had *The Times* and the *Telegraph* sent out specially. What's your point?'

'Wait a moment.' He bent over the letter again. 'Got it! This first sentence reads: "*Regard the photograph as a light.*"'

'A *light*?' Joanna was beginning to catch on.

'It's an old-fashioned word for a crossword clue. He's telling you that the photo is some sort of clue. And I think the second sentence is part of the clue.'

Now that Matt had begun to make sense of it, Joanna concentrated hard on the meandering script. 'It's not "reactor", it's "the actor",' she announced. 'Something about what the actor wants to do.' A minute later she had deciphered it. '"*Do to it what the actor wants to do*." What does that mean?'

But she had worked it out before she finished speaking. 'Take a part!' she shouted. They both reached for the photograph at the same time. 'He's telling us to take the damn thing apart!'

But the frame was quite ingeniously made; and it took Matt some time to work out how to take the back off without breaking it. While he was puzzling over it he did his best to cope with Joanna's intense questioning. 'That letter was not the product of a disordered mind,' he said. 'It was very carefully constructed. Those obvious errors – the non-existent attic, the wrong godfather, the repetition of the word "turning" – were designed to alert you to the fact that the letter was not what it seemed to be. Even the timing of it was very carefully calculated.'

'The timing? What do you mean?'

'He calculated that by the time you got the letter and the photograph, probate would have been granted on his estate, and you would have inherited his property. He didn't want you to read the letter and solve the puzzle until that was safely out of the way.'

'That doesn't make sense. Why not?'

'Because he was going to leave you a fortune, and he was determined not to pay any death duties to a government he felt had betrayed him.' Matt saw that she was too bewildered to speak, and hurried on: 'As soon as I read Colonel Crawford-Webb's will I wondered whether the shotguns and the picture he mentioned were the same as the guns and the picture in the photograph. I was intrigued, because, as you can see, the decorative plate by the breech mechanism clearly shows the maker's name: Purdey and Sons.'

'What's so intriguing about that?'

'If those guns are a matched pair, and if their provenance is real, then we're looking at an auction value of about eighty thousand pounds. The picture on the wall in the photograph is a drawing of a horse. I'm no expert, but it looks to have quality. It could be valuable, too. What I'm saying is, that about two years before he died your father inherited some property. If those shotguns he inherited were indeed Purdeys, then the property was probably worth more than a hundred thousand pounds. But the probate value of your father's estate – which included your house and some shares – came in at barely a hundred and twenty thousand. So what happened to those guns, that picture, and the tazza?'

Joanna's mouth was dry. 'You're telling me Dad hid them behind a false wall in my drawing-room.'

'That's what I think.'

'Well ...' She was growing impatient, 'if that's what you think, why don't we just knock that wall down and find out?'

Matt was carefully removing thin strips of veneer from the back of the frame, exposing four tiny screws. 'Because,' he said absently, 'the will also mentioned a tazza.'

'Oh yes, the glass thing. Do you think it's valuable?'

'Depends. If it's fourteenth-century Venetian and perfect, probably tens of thousands of pounds. If it's chipped and ugly, zilch.'

'On reflection,' Joanna said carefully, 'I think it might be as well to approach that wall with caution. I also think that if there's nothing there, after all this build-up, I may approach you with extreme violence.'

'I guessed as much. That's why I've been so cagey all this time.' Matt carefully undid the four brass screws holding the back panel. There were three items under the panel, besides the photograph and its mount. Three pieces of paper, of different sizes. On the largest page was a series of rectangles and triangles drawn in ink, with measurements marked in feet and inches. The next largest, folded in four and heavily foxed with age, was a letter, its crabbed handwriting sloping sharply upward from left to right. The smallest was just the size of a postcard. On it was a small, neatly drawn picture of a hedgehog; and the inscription '*Be what you want to be! Love, Dad.*'

'You said something to that effect only yesterday!' Joanna gasped. 'It's an omen!'

Matt pointed to the sketch. 'I guess your father saw service in the East at some time?'

'Yes, he did. How did you know that?'

'The hedgehog is a symbol of wealth in some Eastern countries. Actually it refers to its reputation as a hoarder of food. It's a miser, therefore it's rich.'

Joanna furrowed her brow at that. 'Do you suppose he thought of himself as a miser?'

'Who knows? Perhaps it's just a good luck symbol. Let's look at the letter.'

Joanna spread it out on the table between them, so they could examine it together.

18, Stretton Place, York, 20th Nov. 1875

Dear Dr Crawford,
I have no words properly to express my gratitude for your conscientious and painstaking care of my husband during his long, last illness. I know he drew much comfort from your presence, and I believe that if anyone could have sav'd him it would have been you.

It was his wish, with which I haply concur, that you should have the drawing of a horse, which I know you have long admir'd. My man Abel will bring it to you tomorrow aft. I confess that I part haply with the picture, since the animal limn'd there is too boney for my taste!

The drawing has been in my husband's family for at least 4 generations. Walter's great-grandfather had it from Mr Bell the physician, who had it from a Mrs Spencer. The picture is not signed, but family tradition has it that it is either by Mr Seymour or Mr Stubbes snr.

I remain, etc.,
Alexandra Wootton (Mrs)

Joanna was the first to speak. 'I think,' she said carefully, 'that what this letter suggests is that Uncle Peter's picture is possibly by George Stubbs.'

'That's the way I read it, too.' Matt's mouth was dry. 'If it's true, I can't begin to imagine what it might be worth. Hundreds of thousands, probably.'

'You said you couldn't imagine, and then you made a guess,' Joanna said crossly. 'I'm beginning to suspect that this is all a cruel hoax.'

Matt picked up the final sheet of paper. 'Maybe this will settle it.' He studied the drawing, turning it this way and that. 'I think I get it,' he said at last. 'He built a framework – a kind of cage – and made secure compartments in it, separately, so that if one was damaged, the others might survive. The empty compartments he sound-proofed with egg-boxes. Then he covered the frame with thin plywood panels, topped with plasterboard. Finally, he plastered over the whole lot.'

'You can tell all that from this one bit of paper?'

'It's not all that complicated. He was an engineer, after all. Let's go and claim your inheritance.'

'So, we get to vandalize my house at last?'

'No need. This diagram tells me where all the screws are. I can take the panels off with hardly any mess at all.'

Panel by panel, Matt uncovered the treasures. He found the manuscript first, then the medals, wrapped in tissue paper in a leather case. Then the tazza, protected by polystyrene and wood and rubber; and, when it was unwrapped, so beautiful that Joanna cried aloud. Then the guns in their cases: handsome, lethal; works of art. Then the picture, in its own wooden cradle, wrapped and protected from any kind of attack from climate or creature. Finally, a bonus: a shabby casket, covered in blue leather.

'It's my mother's trinket-box!' Joanna cried. 'I thought her jewels had been sold to pay her hospital bills!' She opened the box and shed tears. 'And there's my grannie's things, too!'

'I reckon you're a rich lady,' Matt said, dusting plaster from his hands. 'Congratulations.'

A few weeks later Joanna put her house on the Causeway up for sale; to her surprise, the first person to show interest was Theresa Burgage.

'It's a lovely little place,' Burgage said. 'I envied you the first time I came round here. Though of course I was really sorry about the circumstances at the time.'

'Me too. But I always felt that you were more sympathetic than some of the other officers.'

'Well, I thought Nicky Tanner was such a horrible little shit. And now his stepfather has been arrested. Did you know that?'

'No. What has he done?'

'He's been pilfering stuff from the hospital. Not drugs – low-value stuff like cans of detergent, tubs of polish, bandages, packs of toilet paper. He'd stack the stuff in his van, and Fernie would drive it away and flog it to some street traders. He took one risk too many, though. The day before you were attacked, she persuaded him to nick a wheelchair and a flask of ether. That was a bit too much. The authorities might overlook the odd loo roll, but wheelchairs and ether were in a different league.'

'So that's how she got me from the Causeway to Oughton Lock! In a wheelchair!'

'Yes. Afterwards she pushed it into the canal, but of course the canal had been drained, so it wasn't much of a hiding-place.'

'I can't help feeling sorry for the mother – Mrs Steen,' Joanna said. 'She seems to have been the only decent one in the family.'

'She'll be OK.' Burgage grinned. 'One of the tabloids has offered her a fortune for her story.'

'Good for her.'

'Sorry – I didn't mean to stir up unhappy memories.'

'No matter.' Joanna shook her head. 'I'm just so relieved the nightmare is over. I thought that sergeant of yours was after my blood.'

'Constable, now,' Burgage told her cheerfully. 'He's got a job in the back office.'

'There seemed something very personal in his dislike of me.'

'He had very personal reasons for wanting you to be guilty. You're a woman. A talented, well-educated woman. That's a combination Benjamin Dewbury hates. And you were a teacher. Dewbury's wife ran off with a PT instructor.'

'He really frightened me. I hope there aren't too many policemen like him.'

Burgage shrugged. 'There'll always be a few. They don't usually last as long as he has, though. But he'll have to last an awfully long time to live down the reputation of being the cop who insisted on letting a serial killer go free.'

Joanna forced herself to ask the question. 'When is that – that woman being brought to trial?'

'Dunno. Probably next year. Meanwhile, she's in a very secure remand unit. She's in a raging temper because she says this guy Dudley grassed her up. Fed her LSD, took her money – two thousand quid, she says – and handed her over to the cops.'

'But you haven't caught Dudley yet?'

'No. We think he went to ground somewhere near the airport – there's a guy in that area who's a whizz at fixing fake passports. I personally think Dudley's out of the country by now. Tant piss, as Teddy would say.'

'Teddy?'

'The Super. He and I have been seeing a lot of each other lately.'

'That's nice. Let me show you around. Actually,' Joanna said artlessly as she led the way, 'this house is ideal for two. A young couple could be very comfortable here.'

'That's just what I was thinking,' Theresa Burgage said.

Later that day Joanna rehearsed the Hugo Wolf songs for the last time with Angela Bonneville. Angela was in boisterous and energetic mood and insisted that they work through all the songs in sequence, just as if it were a recital. It was a wonderful experience, but the thought that it was for the last time lowered Joanna's spirits. She managed a smile when it was all over, but she couldn't help but feel a little disappointed that Angela remained so resolutely cheerful.

'I think,' Angela was still thoughtfully regarding the last page of music, 'I think that was pretty good.'

'I enjoyed it,' Joanna said with feeling. 'But I'm sad to be saying goodbye.'

'Me too.' Angela looked up slyly. 'But I'm afraid I've been a bit sneaky. I recorded it all.'

'What! You might have told me!'

'I was afraid you might be self-conscious if you knew the mike was on. As it was you gave a fine, carefree performance. I'll give you a copy of it of course, but I'd like your permission to circulate some copies among a few interested parties.'

Joanna's throat felt constricted. 'I don't know what to say.'

'Then don't say anything. I've got champagne on ice downstairs. We have something else to celebrate.'

In the drawing-room, Angela had set out champagne flutes on an occasional table near the sofa. 'Sit there,' she commanded. 'We're going to watch the telly. You didn't see the lunch-time news, I take it?'

'No. I find the news a bit depressing, these days.'

'This'll be an exception,' Angela chuckled. 'I'll get the bubbles.'

But to Joanna the news bulletin seemed very much the usual mixture of horrific accidents, atrocities in foreign parts, and incredible promises from swivel-eyed politicians. She began to fidget, and Angela held up a warning hand.

'Wait.' Then, a few minutes later, she sat up. 'Here it comes!'

The newsreader stared solemnly at the camera, and looking only slightly disapproving, said: 'At the Charles de Gaulle airport in Paris today a British tourist, Mr Geoffrey Dudd, was arrested by the French police on a charge of uttering forged banknotes. Apparently the authorities were alerted when Mr Dudd attempted to buy an expensive wrist-watch on the plane with counterfeit three-hundred-euro notes. A police spokesman said that forged notes and fake bank securities amounting to nearly a million euros were found in the aptly named Mr Dudd's baggage. Mr Dudd declared to the Customs officials that he was the victim of a practical joke. French courts are particularly severe on currency fraud, and if convicted, Mr Dudd faces a lengthy custodial sentence. Scotland Yard has also expressed an interest in the case, with regard to an apparently unconnected offence.'

'How about that?' crowed Angela. 'The guy who said revenge is sweet didn't know the half of it.'

'Geoffrey Dudd?' Joanna was struggling to take it all in. 'Are you sure ...?'

'It's his real name. He changed it to Dudley because he thought it sounded posher.'

'But – those forged euros?'

'Made in this country. I got them dirt-cheap because the engraver wasn't happy with the quality. I understand his next batch was much better.'

'But it's all dreadfully illegal! Aren't you afraid of what Gerald will tell the police?'

'Well, first off he's got to admit to being a blackmailer. Then, his tale of getting the forged notes from me is thoroughly implausible, particularly if you and I are prepared to lie our socks off.'

'Which, of course, we are!' At last, Joanna had got the full picture.
'So, lady, rejoice, rejoice! As somebody once said. Come on, let's go listen to your lovely voice, finish this bottle and talk about your future.'

A week later, in the early evening, Matt called at Joanna's house on the Causeway.

'Are you OK?' was the first question he asked. 'I know you were a bit apprehensive about living here again.'

'It's not as bad as I feared,' Joanna said. 'Anyway, I have so much to do, I haven't time to mope. I'm selling this place to Theresa Burgage, by the way.'

'Yes, I heard. Have you talked to that art dealer yet?'

'My dear, he brought two experts up from London to look at my treasures. They were totally gob-smacked, and talked incessantly in telephone numbers. Translating their jargon, I understood that, discreetly and patiently handled, I should be able to exchange those goodies for about a hundred thousand a year for the next three years.'

Matt smiled. 'By which time you'll be a world-famous soprano.'

'Don't say that.' Joanna shivered. 'You'll bring me bad luck.'

'I didn't know you were superstitious.'

'I am now. I believe in luck, anyhow. I mean, look at us. Why did you walk into my life at the precise moment that I needed someone like you? Blind luck, that's all. Janice Pounder called you a "tidy-upperer", and she was right. Well, maybe half-right. You're a good deal more than that.'

'Now you're being over-generous,' Matt protested. 'I was just being neighbourly.'

Joanna was tempted to tease him, but stopped herself in time. She was already feeling awkward and a little guilty about what she had to tell him.

As if he was following her train of thought, he made things easy for her. 'Have you made any plans, yet? Apart from selling this place, I mean?'

'Well, actually,' Joanna was grateful that she hadn't had to raise the subject herself, 'Angela has invited me to stay with her in London until I can find a place of my own down there. She wants to introduce me to her friends. And of course, I shall have to find a teacher. As Angela says, I can go anywhere in the world, now.'

'That's good.' Matt looked genuinely pleased for her. 'Take your father's advice. Be what you want to be.'

For a while, they seemed to have run out of conversation. Matt was silent, still smiling, apparently content just to sit and look at her. Joanna's mind buzzed with things she wanted to say but had no adequate words for. Eventually, she blurted out the only thing that mattered.

'I shall miss you.'

'And I shall miss you. But we'll stay in touch. We have an office in London, so I might look you up from time to time. And I should be very surprised if you didn't come up to see Rose Kelsey every now and then.'

She wasn't sure that he had taken the point. 'What I'm trying to say, is that I've grown very fond of you.'

He frowned at that, and sat silent for a few moments. 'You know of course, that I am very fond of you,' he said at last.

She was beginning to find his calmness exasperating. 'We've been very close, these last few weeks.'

'That's true. I've taken much pleasure from it.' His smile came back.

'And yes, I know perfectly well that you've been attracted to me. Yet you've never made a pass at me.'

'You would have been offended if I had made a pass at you.'

'At first, yes. But there was a time when I wished you would.'

His smile faded and he looked away. 'It would have been a mistake.'

'Really? Would it have been so very bad?'

'It would have been a mistake,' he repeated.

'Ah. Because you're married?'

'That's part of it, certainly. But that problem will solve itself eventually. You and I have a much deeper problem.'

'Which is?'

Matt shrugged, and bit his lip. She thought he was going to refuse to answer, but then he began to speak, so quietly that she had to lean closer to hear him.

'The first time I saw you, I knew that your face would haunt me to the end of my days. I was frantic to get to know you, to become your friend.'

'Friend? Just a friend? Nothing more?'

He avoided her eyes. 'Friendship is worth a lot.'

Joanna felt her throat constrict. 'I'm sorry. I don't mean to tease you. It's just a nervous habit.'

His smile became wan. 'Then there was that concert – the *Elijah*. I'd never been to an oratorio before; I went because I knew you were in the choral society. And suddenly there you were – in evening dress, standing on a stage in front of an orchestra. I saw what every red-blooded man in the audience saw: a young, sexy, attractive woman. Then you began to sing. That moment transformed you. It was as if – I'm putting this clumsily, because I've no skill with words – it was as if the music sparked some inner radiance, exalted you, made you shine.'

Joanna swallowed hard. 'Now who's being over-generous? I think you were confusing the music with the musician.'

'I think not. I believe I recognized then that you were doing what you were born to do: singing. Singing fills you with a joy like no other joy in your life. You need it more than you need me or any other guy, right now. Tell me I'm wrong?'

'I suppose you're right. For now, anyway.' But Joanna found it somehow painful to hear it expressed so bluntly. 'You make it sound as if I'm some sort of freak.'

'You know I don't mean that. But face it, you're not ordinary, either. You can no more deny your talent than you can tell your heart to stop beating. Be what you want to be. Show off. Flaunt your talents. Be proud of your gifts. Make people happy.'

'But what about you? Will you be happy?'

'When you're gone, you mean? That's not really fair. I guess I'll just have to manage.'

'I expect you'll find some other mess to tidy up.'

'There's a lot of it about.' But Matt wasn't really in the mood to be flippant.

'Hell.' Joanna mopped her eyes. 'I wish I …' She lost track of what she was going to say. 'I hate goodbyes.'

'Then don't say it. You haven't asked me about my plans, yet.'

'That's because I'm a selfish bitch. Tell me about your plans.'

'I plan to be a part of your life for as long as you want me to be.'

'Is that it? That doesn't sound like much of an ambition to me. Anyway, I don't see how you can be a part of my life if I'm in London and you're up here.'

'I didn't say I'd necessarily be a big part of your life. But we can stay in touch. And I can see you quite often. London isn't the end of the world.'

'But what if I go to the end of the world? What if I wind up in Timbuctu?'

Matt thought about that very carefully. 'If your career winds up in Timbuctu, my love, I think I'd better be on hand. You'll need a tidy-upperer. And a new agent.'